The ANGEL
MAKERS

The ANGEL MAKERS

JESSICA GREGSON

Published by
Soho Press, Inc.
853 Broadway
New York, NY 10003

Library of Congress Cataloging-in-Publication Data

Gregson, Jessica
The angel makers / Jessica Gregson.
p. cm.
HC ISBN 978-1-56947-979-7
PB ISBN 978-1-61695-179-5
eISBN 978-1-56947-980-3
1. Women—Hungary—Fiction. 2. Self-realization in women—Fiction.
3. World War, 1914-1918—Hungary—Fiction.
4. Women murderers—Fiction. I. Title.
PR6107.R44493A84 2011
823'.92—dc23
2011024928

Printed in the United States of America

10 9 8 7 6 5 4 3 2 1

For my grandmother, Laurette, and in
memory of my grandfather, Clem

AUTHOR'S NOTE

Although this book is based on a true story, events have been heavily embellished by the author's imagination. Names and places have therefore been changed.

ACKNOWLEDGMENTS

Thank you to all my early readers (you know who you are), especially to Katy Anchânt, Rachel Coldbreath, and Germán Guillot, who provided much needed enthusiasm, encouragement and proofreading early on.

Thank you to all my friends, especially to Carlie Dawes, Jo Black, Kate Jones, Zavy Gabriel, Yogi Raste, Sophie McInnes, Angela Hughes, Sarah Cook, Leda Glyptis, Anne Pordes, Sarah Moore, Nich Underdown, Mary Macfarlane, Helen Finch, and Judith Logan.

Thank you to my family, especially to Richard and Julia.

Thank you, Mark.

Thank you, mum and dad.

PROLOGUE

She never answers, but still, I talk to her all the time. Listen, I tell her. I've made mistakes. When it first started, sometimes I would try to pretend that I was helpless in all of it, that I'd been buffeted by fate; that as surely as those eight women are twisting in the wind now, in my way, I've been twisting in the wind my whole life. It's not true, though; it's just a lie that I told myself when I wasn't feeling strong enough to face up to what I am, and what I've done. In truth, I've made my choices, and my hand is strong in all of this. Without me, none of this would have even started.

I'm twenty-eight, but I look older, and that doesn't even come close to how old I feel. That's not so unusual where I come from. In the city, I've heard that women are cosseted and coddled, treated like elaborate ornaments or playthings. Here, we carry our parents and our husbands and our children on our backs; we're the dumping ground for all of life's shit. Judit taught me that early on, and nothing I've gone through since has gone any way towards disproving it. They used to wonder why I was still alive; in the villages, people regularly kill themselves over less than I've endured.

When I was small, maybe eight or nine, Katalin Remény, aged sixteen, drowned herself because she was pregnant without a husband. She was hauled out of the river – at a time when bodies in the river were far rarer than they have been recently – and at her funeral her body was paraded through the streets, surrounded by howling mourners, but of course she had to be buried outside the churchyard because of her sins, and later, Judit and my father went to pour boiling water over her grave, to stop her from stalking the village in death, as suicides are said to do.

Judit came to speak to me a few days after Katalin was buried, and I remember she was hissing and spitting with fury: she told me that what Katalin had done was pointless and meaningless, that having a baby without a husband was only a sin in the eyes of those people who want to control women, and that, in any case, if a woman ever found herself with a baby that she didn't want, she could always come to Judit and Judit would take care of it – though, at that age, I only had a vague idea of what 'taking care of it' meant.

Like with most of Judit's rages, it was born out of a desire to protect me, and it worked. Katalin took up residence in my mind, a symbol of the opposite of everything I was going to be; a mindless, sacrificial lamb, caring more about the opinions of a few stupid villagers than her own life. I knew that I would never give up my own life if there were any alternative left to me in the world, and as it's happened, I could never be accused of failing to seek out as many alternatives as possible.

That's at the root of it all, I explain to her: my survival instinct, my will to live. That's behind all the choices I've made. I could have given myself up at any number of points, and I suppose it would have saved lives. But not *my* life, and not her life, and that's all I'm looking out for. I've learnt that it's too painful and dangerous to care about much else.

Is it odd that I feel like this, given the twenty-eight years

I've had? Maybe I should have accepted the bitter slice of life I got as something easy to surrender. But once I got it between my teeth, I was never going to let it go without the most violent struggle. What's good about life? Ask me that when you're watching a summer moon, bloated and white, floating over the plain. Ask me that when you're looking into my child's face. Of course, there are terrible things too, and sometimes – often – they outweigh the good. But you can't have beauty without a bit of terror.

1914

CHAPTER ONE

Sari is fourteen years old when they carry her father out, carry him through the village lanes, his face bare and blank to the wide sky, carry him through the summer wildflowers that bloom alongside the river, carry him to the cemetery. It is a public end for a private man, infused with the drama that makes village life bearable; a final chance to be the centre of attention, something that Jan Arany had never sought. Sari doesn't cry, because that isn't her way; instead, she wraps a cloak of silence around herself, and lets the other village women do the wailing for her. Her silence almost gives the impression of absence. It is misleading.

Her father had been a Wise Man, respected, a *táltos*, and they'd lived for all of Sari's life on the outskirts of the village, in a wooden house with steps that creaked, the grass in front of it worn thin by the feet of villagers in search of cures, help or salvation. Her father had been a big man, tall, broad-shouldered, light-haired – unusual in that place – a wide face like the sun, Sari thinks: warm, but remote. The villagers had loved him and feared him in equal measure. They just fear Sari.

As long as she can remember, she's been skirted by whispers wherever she goes. Her father had tried to explain it. 'It's because they loved your mother,' he said, but that's never made sense to Sari. She loves her mother too, a wraith-figure whom she's never met, only heard about, and woven her image out of stories and imagination; a young woman – barely older than Sari now – who had left her family, smiling, to marry Jan Arany. Still smiling, she'd swollen with Sari inside her, and then split open at Sari's birth, and died.

'I didn't want her to die,' Sari would say to her father, after someone or other had hissed *witch* behind her back.

'I know,' he said, 'But they just think it's unlucky, that's all.'

That's not all, though, and Sari knows it, though she's always appreciated her father's kindness to pretend other-wise. Sari understands that she is odd, that there's something in the way she holds herself, in the way she looks at people, in the things she says and the things she knows, that isn't what the rest of the village considers right and proper. She envies the girls she sees walking through the village, arm in arm with easy familiarity, but she can't see how to get from where she is to where they are, how to change her behaviour in order to be liked. The only concession that she makes these days is her silence. Keeping her mouth shut gives the villagers fewer new stories to tell about her, but as with most villages, many of them are all too happy to tell the same stories over and over again.

It happened the day her father died, too. It was morning, and Sari was at the door of the Mecs house in the noise-choked heart of the village, buying a bottle of *czerenznye* from Dorthya Mecs. As she reached out her hand to take it, she heard the voices – distinct, clear, dominated by Orsolya Kiss's high, nasal drawl. Hearing her name, Sari moved her eyes without turning her head, and saw Orsolya, one hefty buttock hoisted onto the edge of the Gersek porch, leaning and grinning, surrounded by three or four other women. Two, Sari saw, were Orsolya's best friends, Jakova Gersek and Matild Nagy, flanking her like bodyguards; one of them she didn't recognise, but the shape of her face recalled Orsolya's, and Sari remembered hearing that Orsolya's cousin from Város was visiting. Well-practiced at avoiding notice, Sari softened her body slightly, fitting herself easily into the swoops and shadows of the narrow, slanted lane.

'She's never quite been right,' Orsolya was saying, the mock sorrow in her voice unable to hide the underlying glee at being the bearer of a good story. 'A terrible trial for her father, who's a good man. And her mother—' Orsolya paused to raise her eyes piously to heaven, the other three following suit, '– Monika was a good woman. Her death was tragic, so young, but, forgive me, sometimes I thank God that she never had to live to see what her daughter is.'

'What does she do?' Orsolya's cousin whispered, in the hushed, excited tones of the consummate gossip.

The exchange was wearyingly familiar to Sari, a ritual song of call and response. She realised she was frozen, one hand holding the bottle of alcohol, as she met the eyes of Dorthya, who raised her eyebrows and gave a slight sympathetic shrug. Sari withdrew her arm, but remained rooted to the spot, listening, still. *Which one will it be, Orsolya?* she asked silently. *The one where I drive the dog mad because it won't stop shitting in front of our house? The one where I put the curse on Éva Orczy's baby because I think she looks at me oddly? The one about me having a birthmark in the shape of an inverted cross on my back? Or maybe something new that you've dreamt up? Come on, Orsolya,* Sari challenged. *Surprise me.*

'Well, I saw this one with my own eyes,' Orsolya said,

and Sari relaxed slightly. She'd heard this one, and it was almost comforting to hear it repeated; it had taken on the soothing quality of a fairy tale. 'She must have been four or five,' Orsolya continued comfortably. 'It was Sunday, and we were in church. It was summer, maybe late July, or August, and you know what the flies are like then – anyway, there was a big old *dongó* buzzing around Sari, and she was swiping and swatting at it, like children do, but it wouldn't leave her alone. So finally, she sat up straight, and just *stared* at it – this fly – and that was it. It fell onto the floor, dead.'

The breathless silence following Orsolya's declaration cleverly conjured the dull *plop* of the fly dropping to the ground. In another life, Orsolya could have been a performer, but here, her repertoire is limited, and Sari knew this particular piece off by heart. It was that silence that she had been waiting for. Whatever she did, they were going to believe what they wanted to believe, and so she was allowed a little fun, surely? She paid Dorthya, her hands perfectly steady, and turned to face the group of women. Deliberately, she took a deep breath, pulled herself up as if the top of her head was anchored to the sky and, with a gesture loaded with intent, flicked her hair back and hit first Orsolya, then her cousin, then her vapid, giggling friends with the stare she knew had come to scare people. She watched, gratified, as the smug smiles slid from their faces (like shit off a shovel, she thought), then turned, hoisting the bottle in her arms, and walked home.

She'd only just arrived, and was peeling the potatoes for the midday meal when she heard it: a thick, heavy thump from upstairs (for a moment she thought instinctively of Orsolya's fictitious fly hitting the ground), and she knew straight away what had happened. Her face didn't change.

First, she finished peeling the potatoes. Then, she got to her feet, shaking the water off her hands, wiping them on her skirt, before slowly, slowly climbing the stairs. At the top, she entered her father's bedroom, and there he was, on the floor, slumped and crumpled like she'd known he would be. She moved over to him, knelt down beside him and smoothed her hand over his face, closing his eyes. Of course he was dead: there was something in the timbre of the sound he made when he fell that just couldn't belong to something living.

For five minutes she was motionless, kneeling by her father, not weeping, not speaking, not praying (though later, she thought, she might tell people she prayed), just feeling her heart banging inside her chest, her blood thrumming at her wrists, soaking in the impossibility that she could still be living while her father was dead. She stayed there until she became conscious of the absence in the room, until she could feel that the corpse on the floor had ceased being her father and become a thing. It was all right for her to leave him then.

Sari is best known in Falucska for her unnerving silence and stillness, and at the funeral she embraces this image, gathering it around her like a comfortable old blanket. She seems unmoved as the priest speaks of her father, unaffected by the weeping of the women surrounding her. All the village is there, and all eyes are on Sari. While many genuinely mourn Jan's death, there's no doubt that Sari's presence at the funeral is a supplementary attraction. If she were to do something even slightly shocking, like laughing during the eulogy, it would enliven the funeral enormously, and give the village something to talk about for days. It's not outright malice in most people, Sari realises: it's the crushing boredom of life in a small village becalmed in the middle of the plain. While they'd never admit it, there are some in the village who are grateful to Sari for shaking things up a little. If it weren't for her, they'd be discussing crops and pregnancies and the weather all the damn time.

Sari can feel them watching, and resolves not to give them the satisfaction of behaving in the way that they expect. *This is not my father*, she says calmly to herself, and promptly sends her mind away – the ability to detach from any given situation is one she's fostered for years. Only when the first clump of earth hits the coffin is she brought back to the present: she has a brief, horrifying image of her father, worm-ridden, covered in soil, and that's it. She flinches as violently as if she's been stung – and the villagers are on tenterhooks, placing internal bets about what she's going to do: *she's going to throw herself into the grave; she's going to start screaming; oh, she'll attack the priest, for sure.* But all she does is turn and walk away, back towards the clutter of houses; Father István continues his droning after only the briefest of pauses, and a great sense of anti-climax settles over the crowd.

A twitch of movement at the edge of the knot of people, and Ferenc Gazdag, nineteen and desperately earnest-looking, makes a move to follow Sari, but his mother's hand on his shoulder stops him.

'Leave her,' she hisses. Márta Gazdag is the sister of Sari's late mother, and although she has very little liking for Sari (because, honestly, how can you be fond of someone who is so odd?), there's something in the straightness of Sari's back, the pagan swatch of black hair, that sometimes reminds Márta of her sister. Her sister, whose grave is only a few feet away. The eyes are still on Sari, following her as she walks away, watching to see where she's going, although they suspect her destination already. Sure enough, at the crossroads she heads left, instead of right; she climbs the steps leading to the midwife's door and lets herself in.

'Aunt Judit?'

Sari's never been sure whether Aunt Judit really is her aunt. She's always referred to her as such, but then so does the rest of the village, even the few people who are older than Judit herself. It's the only thing that ties Judit to respectability; the adopted kinship is the only thing that stops small boys throwing stones at her windows when they pass by the house (and they still do, sometimes), and the kinship has been necessary to adopt, because the village needs her, no matter what they may feel about her. Judit's the only midwife in town, and, more, the only person within several miles with any medical knowledge at all. You may be high and mighty enough to take your son to Város for his regular check-ups, or to have your teeth looked at there, but woe betide you when you're up puking in the middle of the night, woe betide you if Aunt Judit isn't on your side, cause that's who you'll be shouting for.

But Judit's always been Sari's second favourite person in the world, after her father. And now, she thinks, probably her favourite person altogether: not only has Judit never minded Sari's oddness, but she seems actually to revel in it, perhaps because she's no stranger to being an outsider herself. Judit fits everybody's definition of a crone. Thin as a whip, white hair that she tries to tame in a bun but ends up rebelling and sticking out crazily from her head. Coal pits for eyes, a hooked nose, and a black hole of a mouth, missing all but a few teeth.

'Be careful with your teeth,' she always says to Sari. 'You never know how much you'll miss them.'

Sari can't guess how old she is, perhaps seventy or even eighty, but Judit's still so strong and able that it makes Sari want to revise her opinion downward. Judit says it's a hard life that makes her look so ancient, but always follows that comment up with a cackle of such sublime enjoyment that Sari can't tell if she's being serious or not. Judit has the sort of face that inspires fear in children and, if they're honest, in some adults too, and she seems to enjoy it; at any rate, she does not go out of her way to dispel any of the rumours about her that clog the lines of village gossip.

Now Judit comes striding out of her kitchen, glass in hand. 'Sari – aren't you supposed to be at the funeral?'

Sari grimaces, yanking her boots off. 'It's mostly over. I got sick of it, Judit, sick of the people and the words and the crying. It's all wrong.'

'I'm sorry I didn't go,' Judit says. She eases herself down onto the wooden floor so that she's on eye level with Sari, who's still tugging at her right boot. 'You know István and I don't see eye to eye. Maybe I should have been there, to keep you company.'

Sari shakes her head vehemently. 'Don't be stupid. It would have made you as hypocritical as the rest of them. Besides, I can look after myself.' Her voice breaks on the last word and abruptly, she claps her hands over her face. Judit puts a twisted hand on her shoulder but doesn't hug her, because that would seem contrived. Sari's shuddering violently, but Judit doubts that she's crying. In the fourteen years she's known the girl, she's never seen her cry, and she doubts that this'll be the first time. She thinks there's probably something wrong with the child's eyes that makes weeping impossible.

In time, Sari stops shaking and takes down her hands; for a moment she sits there in the unnatural stillness that makes people fear and distrust her, before she brushes a hand roughly across her face. 'Sorry,' she says stiffly.

'It's fine,' Judit replies. 'Wait.' She goes into her kitchen and comes out with a small glass full of clear liquid, which she hands to Sari. 'Drink this,' she says. 'It'll do you good.'

Sari gulps it down in a couple of mouthfuls, making a face. 'God, Judit, it's worse than the stuff you made last year. This is why my father always bought it from the Mecs, not from you.'

Judit shrugs. 'It's still good for you.'

Footsteps crunch on the road outside Judit's window. 'There, the funeral's over,' Sari says. Her voice is deliberately light, but Judit picks up her meaning.

'And so what's going to happen to you now?'

Because that's the question, really. The house where Sari grew up with her father – it's hers now, and all Sari wants is to go back there, move through the rooms that held her father's presence. But it's not done; girls don't live alone, nor do women, unless they're widows, and while Sari's used to telling herself she doesn't care what the village thinks, she hardly wants to make herself more of an outcast than she is already. And then . . .

'Well, there's Ferenc,' Sari says.

'Yes. Ferenc,' Judit says slowly. 'He seems like a good boy.'

'He is,' Sari replies. She feels a general, unlocated fondness for her probable future husband. The idea of marriage still repels her slightly, but she understands her father's thinking now. These past couple of days she's had a hard, cold nugget of fear lodged somewhere between her lungs, and oddly, it's been the thought of Ferenc that has made her feel slightly better. At least there's one person who *has* to be nice to her, who *has* to take care of her (although, she adds swiftly, she can take care of herself).

'It seems like the obvious next step—' Judit starts, but Sari shakes her head violently.

'No, not yet. Not until I'm eighteen. I promised. I can look after myself until then.'

'All right, all right!' Judit raises her hands in surrender. 'But at least tell me how you intend to provide for yourself until then?'

Sari flushes. It's not that she's shy, but she is proud, and supremely unused to having to ask for things and so it's hard to get the words out, even though she suspects that Judit knows what she's going to say.

'I was thinking,' she says slowly, 'I was thinking that maybe I could work with you. I could help you, and start learning about what you do. If you'll let me.'

CHAPTER TWO

Ferenc still feels hot from where Sari's eyes landed on him at the funeral. The feeling is almost painful, and unbearably exciting. He is sad about Jan's death – his putative uncle, after all – but now he is wracked by a wild hope about what this will mean for him, whether he'll have a chance of Sari sooner rather than later.

Until six months ago, he had barely thought of her, and on the rare occasions that he did, it was with the same mixture of pity and derision that most of the village men did. He had torn through his adolescence with his mind filled with images of blondes, luscious curves, succulent pink and cream skin, and if someone had told him that a scrawny black-haired child would sneak into his subconscious like Sari has, he would have laughed.

And then . . .

He remembers the exact moment that it happened. Six months ago, spring: mosquitoes rising off the river like fog; flowers bursting out of the trees and the ground; heat hanging like a hint of smoke on the midday air. He'd gone with his father to see Jan Arany – for what? For some minor misfortune or mishap, probably – and they'd been sitting at the old, lined kitchen table, Jan dispensing advice as best he could.

Ferenc had been only vaguely aware of Sari's busy, mercurial presence behind Jan, until Jan had asked her for something and she turned around, raised her head and her eyes – those eyes! – seemed to physically hit Ferenc across the table. He couldn't have described the rest of her face if he'd tried; it melted into the background compared with those eyes. Pale, icy blue, surrounded by thick dark lashes, but it wasn't the beauty of the eyes that was astonishing; it was their knowing, searching, piercing quality. They weren't the eyes of a fourteen-year-old, and Ferenc felt laid bare, as if he'd never been seen before.

And that was it, that glance. She climbed into his head through that glance, and there she stayed, sometimes lurking uncomfortably just below his daily thoughts, and sometimes breaking the surface – mainly, predictably enough, when he was masturbating. He used to do it to the memory of a twenty-year-old Austrian blonde he'd seen bathing at Lake Balaton, but now his fantasies were invaded by Sari. The Austrian beauty, who used to gaze at him adoringly in his ardent dreams now stared at him with Sari's severe glare, or, at the crucial moment, her face would split apart and be replaced with Sari's visage. It was troubling, and unsettling. Ferenc did everything he could to rid himself of this dream-Sari. After a humiliating muttered conversation with Father István he tried fasting, and prayer, and cold baths, but to no avail. He was not an intellectually sophisticated man, but the irony of the situation did not escape him – the one person who could have rid him of the dreams was the one person who must not know about them, on account of their subject being his daughter.

But in the end, it was Jan who settled the matter. Ferenc would like to believe that it was just one of life's odd but fortuitous coincidences, but fundamentally he knows that Jan didn't deal in coincidence, particularly where his daughter was concerned. Six months ago, Ferenc was blinded by Sari's eyes; five months ago his father asked him to take something over to Jan's. Ferenc agreed, reluctant because he had come to dread seeing Sari, avoidance being the only tactic that had even the slightest effect on the dreams.

As it happened, either by luck or judgement, she wasn't there.

'She's at Judit Fekete's,' Jan explained, in response to the question Ferenc refused to ask. 'Sit down,' Jan added, gesturing to the empty chair opposite him, and as Ferenc handed over the couple of coins his father owed Jan, Jan opened a bottle of wine, sloshing a few inches of thick, blood-red liquid into a glass, pushing it towards Ferenc. 'Have a drink.'

Uncertainly, Ferenc sat and took the wine. To his surprise, it was good – not up to the standard that Ferenc was used to at home, of course, but still full-bodied and tasty. He realised two things then: that Jan knew his wine; and that he was deliberately setting out to please or impress. Both these realisations startled him. Jan was not someone who tended to try to impress, doing so naturally or not at all. Ferenc sipped silently at his wine, unnerved.

'So,' Jan said suddenly. Ferenc waited for the rest of the sentence, and when it didn't come:

'So,' he responded helpfully.

'My daughter,' Jan said.

Oh. Ferenc felt every inch of his body tensing, as if Jan was staring into the heart of his most shameful masturbatory fantasies. He cleared his throat awkwardly, staring at the table.

'You like her,' Jan continued.

Ferenc gulped. 'Well, yes,' he stammered.

Jan smiled. 'That's good.'

Further disquieted, Ferenc sat silent. He felt like a dog being teased by a cat, large and lumbering with Jan swiping at this foot and then that foot, turning him around and about.

'Have you given any thought to marriage?' Jan asked finally.

So that was it. Part of Ferenc wanted to laugh: it was absurd, surely, the idea that *he* could marry Sari? Sex was one thing, yes, and he couldn't deny that he wanted that, but marriage? Ferenc's no *grof*, but he's no peasant, either; his father's family had worked their way up to a position of wealth and importance by herding for the local aristocracy over the past couple of hundred years, and the land that they own, the places they go, the people and things they know – they might as well inhabit a different world from the rest of the village.

'I haven't thought about it,' Ferenc replied.

He had thought about it, though; he could hardly have reached the age of eighteen without the idea of marriage having occurred to him. It had always been assumed that he would never marry anyone from the village, that he'd have to look elsewhere for someone who would be his equal, and it was with a shock of something that could have been trepidation, as much as excitement, that he realised that if he were to marry anyone from Falucska, Sari, whose mother was his aunt, would seem to be the leading candidate.

'I was hoping that you might consider my daughter.'

A memory floated to the surface of Ferenc's thoughts. He'd met a girl a few years back, in Budapest, while on holiday with his parents. She'd been small and mousy, with glossy brown hair and a frightened expression, but his parents had introduced them with great joviality; it had obviously been important and desirable that they get on with one another. He had tried, but every story he had told her, of swimming in the river in the village, of climbing trees and catching frogs and romping with dogs had caused her to shrink back with barely disguised fear and revulsion. Afterwards, he had spoken of her to his parents in disparaging tones, only to be rebuked by his father, who had told him that she was from a good family, well brought up, the sort of girl likely to grow into a marriageable woman. It was the first clue Ferenc had ever had of how much things were likely to change once he was neatly married off to some carefully socialised woman. *Sari*, he thought, *she wouldn't be like that at all.*

'I think—' Ferenc began, utterly unsure of what he was thinking, but Jan held up a hand to halt him.

'I don't expect you to decide right away, of course. The two of you hardly know each other. But I'm not well.' Jan's voice became heavy. 'Sari doesn't know – or maybe she does; it's hard to tell what she does and doesn't know – but I'm not going to be around much longer. I know what the village thinks of Sari, and I'm worried about what will happen to her after I'm dead, who will protect her. I know you're a good boy, Ferenc, and I'm sure you'll be a good man. I've seen the way you look at Sari, and with your background, you're less superstitious than the rest of the people here – you can see what little truth there is behind the things that people say about my daughter. Also, her mother was from your family, so I feel your family would be more likely to accept her.'

Ferenc nodded. This was all very strange, but it was possible, perhaps, wasn't it?

'Her age is an issue, of course,' Jan went on. 'She's only fourteen – too young for marriage. You know, her mother – your aunt – she was married to me at just under sixteen, and it was too young. She was happy, I think, but certainly not ready to be a mother. I have my suspicions that it may have had something to do with her death – her age, I mean. Aside from that, though, Sari is different. She's not some feather-headed little girl who wants nothing more than to be a wife and a mother. She's clever, and outspoken, and difficult. She needs to learn to trust you, and she needs to become her own person before she becomes your wife. I'm talking to you about this now because of the state of my health, but the last thing I want is for her to marry now. I would want you to wait until she's eighteen.'

Four years? That gave Ferenc pause. Jan seemed to expect him to decide, if not immediately, then soon, but how was he supposed to know now what Sari was going to be like in four years? She could grow ugly in that time; he'd seen it happen. But Jan was looking at him with such implacable expectation of agreement that there seemed nothing else for it.

'That sounds – very sensible,' he replied at last. Jan smiled slightly, knowingly.

'I have talked to Sari about this,' Jan said, 'and I must tell you she's not overly keen on the idea. But that's to do with the idea of marriage, rather than with you, and she's agreed in principle.' He smiled more broadly. 'She did grudgingly admit that you seem nice.'

'Well. Good.' It was a start, after all.

'Yes. I should talk to your family about this, obviously, but I wanted to mention it to you first. You don't have to decide to anything straight away, but come back tomorrow, and you can start getting to know Sari. Make sure you're making an informed decision.' Jan heaved himself out of his chair, and gave Ferenc a clumsy, yet awkwardly affectionate clap on the shoulder – under the force of which Ferenc swayed slightly. 'You're a good boy,' he said, in a tone of dismissal, which Ferenc took as the hint to leave that it was.

So it began.

Ferenc had tried hard over the summer. After his talk with Jan he went straight home and spoke to his father, recounting his conversation with Jan and Jan's proposal. On hearing it, Ferenc's father laughed, a short amazed bark, which faded as soon as he saw the gravity in his son's eyes. 'You're not seriously . . .' he began.

'I am. I told Jan I'd consider it.'

After that, Ferenc's father was silent for a long time. He spoke briefly to his wife, who was also silent for a long time. Ferenc felt disapproval wafting off them like steam, especially from his father; his mother, he knew, felt a certain degree of familial obligation towards Sari, and while she didn't want to bid goodbye to pleasant fantasies of a smiling, pretty, pliant daughter-in-law (or, even better, a daughter-in-law with *money*), she grudgingly admitted that it seemed somewhat fitting to think about bringing Sari into the family. She capitulated first, and worked to bring her husband round – meanwhile, Ferenc found reserves of patience and persistence he never knew he had, and started to woo Sari.

Their first official meeting since the decision had been made was not comfortable. With Jan playing the role of chap - erone, the three of them sat awkwardly around the table, drinking thick, black Turkish coffee and saying little. Jan would pass some obvious remark, about the weather, or a piece of village gossip; Ferenc would reply by smiling manfully and attempting a witty riposte, and Sari sat almost entirely silent, drumming her fingers on the table at intervals, her eyes sliding around the room – window, chair, table, ceiling – never settling on Ferenc's face. After twenty minutes or so of this purgatory, there was a tentative knock on the door; Jan heaved himself grumpily to his feet, and an unhappy Ferenc rocked back in his chair, feeling that this must be his cue to leave, although he'd got nowhere. He hadn't realised until that moment how much he'd wanted this to work out, how reluctant he was to contemplate marriage to some insipid urbanite after he'd considered Sari. Jan's muffled voice came from the hallway, and then the sound of a door opening and closing, as someone from the village was led into what served as his consulting room.

'Well,' said Ferenc, nervously, and then she did it, hit him with those bright, fierce eyes, and asked:

'Do you like to read?'

'Oh, well, I—' he faltered, and then asked, 'Do *you* read?'

She nodded, slightly contemptuous. 'Of course. Magyar and German. My father taught me.' She got up and picked a book off the shelf, thrusting it at him. 'Here,' she said. He turned it over in his hands; a fat, blue volume, pages furring slightly at the edges from overuse. He opened the cover, and there, in German: *Jane Eyre*, von Charlotte Brontë. Looking up at Sari, he found her staring at him intently. 'Have you read it?' she asked.

He shook his head apologetically. 'No. I don't really get much time for reading, with, you know, the farm, and – and things—' He shrugged, trying to indicate a weight of important, manly tasks sitting on his shoulders, precluding all leisure activities.

'Oh,' she said, her voice flat. It was obvious that she was disappointed, and Ferenc felt an almost tangible gust of her frustration and stark intelligence.

'You could tell me about it,' he suggested diffidently, and she looked up sharply, scrutinising his face for possible mockery.

'Yes,' she said, after a brief pause. 'Yes, I suppose I could.'

It got easier through the summer. Ferenc came to see her the day after their initial conversation, and after making sure she could spare an hour or so, he took her for a walk down by the river, behind the backs of the houses, curtain after curtain twitching as they passed. As they walked, he talked about the news of the village, who'd been talking to whom, who'd bought what at the market, the minutiae of village life. She was silent at first, and he noticed her frown at certain names, Orsolya Kiss's most of all.

'Do you know what else I saw today?' he said, that day by the river, deliberately casual.

'What?' Sari asked, guarded.

'I was walking past the square, and there was Orsolya Kiss.' He saw her stiffen, but went on regardless. 'She'd bought some potatoes from the Gyulai family. She bought so many, I had to keep watching her, because I couldn't see how she was going to carry them all.' She was watching him now, trying not to be obvious about it, but shooting him furtive little glances under her eyelashes. 'Anyway. She came out of the house – and Tomas Gersek had just passed with his big dog, you know?' She nodded. 'And the dog had done its business there, by the square. And there was Orsolya, all puffing and struggling with this enormous mound of potatoes, and not looking where she put her feet – and she trod right in it, and slipped, and fell, and those potatoes went every-where—' and he'd done it! She was laughing. 'That was my reaction, too,' Ferenc confided. 'I had to hide in the alley so she wouldn't see me.'

She looked at him then, and smiled, the first genuine smile he'd seen her give, and such a feeling of happiness and triumph washed over him that he wanted to crow, to scoop her up in his arms and run off into the forest with her.

Instead, he just smiled back.

The next time they walked, Sari talked, too. They went along by the river and Sari paused every few paces to yank some herb or other out of the ground.

'Anise,' she would explain, customarily taciturn. 'Good for coughing.' Or 'Chamomile – for digestion.'

'Careful,' he attempted a joke. 'Don't tell me too much, or I'll do your dad out of a job.'

She laughed at that. 'Oh, I'm hardly telling you anything! You have to learn how to prepare them, what to mix them with, which amounts you should use before you can be of any help. There's other things, too,' she added vaguely, her face closing up. 'Things you have to do, to make sure they work.'

'You've learnt a lot from your father,' Ferenc said, slightly uneasily. While a *táltos* was respected more than feared, for a *boszorkány*, the female equivalent, the reverse was true. Sari shrugged, unconcerned.

'A lot from him, and some from Judit, too.' Seeing Ferenc's slight recoil, she snapped, with the swift change of mood he was coming to expect of her, 'Oh, don't tell me you're like the rest of them? There's nothing Judit does that's worse than what my father does – in fact some people go to Judit, rather than my father, when they're ill. Why do people respect my father but not Judit? Because she's a woman?' She let out a harsh sigh, and Ferenc reflected that this was perhaps the greatest number of words she'd spoken together in his presence. To his surprise, he found himself agreeing with her. He doubted he would ever feel entirely comfortable in Judit's presence; she had that disturbing way of *looking*, but:

'You're right,' he said thoughtfully. 'It's not fair.'

On their third walk, she told him about *Jane Eyre*, in short, straightforward sentences. It didn't sound like the sort of book that Ferenc would like to read – if he read at all, he would want stories with fighting, and adventure, and maybe pirates – but he was becoming so interested in Sari that he listened attentively, and a glimmer of understanding grew. A woman not the norm, a woman educated . . . there was bound to be a strong appeal for Sari in a heroine of this type.

'But this Mister Rock – Roch—' his tongue tripped over the English name.

'Rochester,' Sari supplied.

'Yes, him. I don't understand – why does Jane love him? He's so old, and not handsome, with his daughter, and his wife.'

Sari lifted one shoulder. 'I think he interests her,' she said slowly. 'In some lives, it doesn't take very much.'

On walk number four, he kissed her. He'd tensed himself for a slap, or a kick, or even a rake of her nails down his cheek, but she'd been swarming through his dreams like never before, and he found that he couldn't not touch her any more. And to his surprise and delight, after a couple of seconds where she stood rigid, she started to kiss him back. He'd kissed other girls, of course – furtive gropes on summer holidays – but this was palpably different. Sari couldn't have had any experience of this, he knew; how would she have got the chance in Falucska? He couldn't think of any local boys who would have dared to try, but she was somehow a natural; the way she shifted her body to accommodate his, the slight tilt of her head, and when he raised his hand to touch her cheek he found it shockingly hot. It didn't last for long, and when they broke apart his head and heart was pounding; he could practically feel the violent push of blood through his body. She looked maddeningly cool, eyes cast down, a faint colour on her bone pale cheeks the only indication that something unusual had occurred.

'Sari,' he said throatily, just to taste her name, not that he had anything to say to her.

She looked up at him and grinned. 'I have to go,' she said.

Walk number five was to have been the day after Jan died, so was cancelled.

It is several days after Jan's funeral before Ferenc's able to speak to Sari. He's desperate to talk to her, to find out if she's all right, and more, to find out what she's planning to do. Without him noticing, over the summer, the idea of marriage to her has gone from something that he was considering to something that he's taking for granted will come to pass. Sari's only fourteen, it's true – but she'll be fifteen in November, and that's young, but not too young to marry. When Jan was alive, that was one thing, Ferenc could have waited then, but he's decided that he wants her, now, wants nothing so much, and he's ready for marriage, he knows. And what's she going to do, otherwise? Live alone in her father's house on the edge of the village, and take care of herself? Instead, she could move into the Gazdag household, and be taken care of, absorbed into a family that she is almost a part of already, living the sort of life that no one else in the village could aspire to. And maybe, maybe it would normalise her somewhat, smooth off a few of those rough edges; by eighteen it might be too late. He loves her as she is, of course – or if it isn't quite love yet, it's something rather like it – but it wouldn't really hurt, he thinks, if she were just a little more like everyone else.

He's wanted to speak to her since the funeral but she's been with Judit Fekete so much of the time – and despite what Ferenc said to Sari about Judit, she still scares him a little. She's so small that it seems ridiculous that she could intimidate him, until he remembers her fierce, malevolent black eyes. But after four days of watching Sari from afar, he sees her leave Judit's house one morning – alone! – and head off, skirting the village, towards her father's house where it stands, crouching low by the edge of the woods. He follows her at a slightly shameful distance, loitering at the point where her path becomes grass as he watches her mount the steps, testing each one carefully with her foot for rot or damp. He finds himself unaccountably afraid of approaching her and he dithers, stepping forward and back, until the door opens again and Sari stands on the step, shading her eyes.

'Ferenc,' she calls, and his feet start to move, almost independently of his will, elated but at the same time irritated by his immediate obedience.

By the time he's in the house she's no longer waiting at the door, and he finds her on her knees in the kitchen, scrubbing the floor violently.

'This house,' she pants. 'The dust – it gets dirty so quickly.'

Ferenc doesn't know what to say, shifting his weight from one foot to another. 'I'm sorry,' he blurts at last, delving in his trouser pockets. 'Look – Sari – I brought you this.'

He holds his hand out to her, the book he is gripping shaking slightly. She rears back on her knees and looks at him silently for a moment before wiping her damp hand thoughtlessly on her skirt and taking it.

'I don't know if you've read it,' he blunders on, 'but I thought you might—'

She turns the book over. '*Wuthering Heights*,' she says to herself.

'It – it's by the same person who wrote—'

'No, it's not, it's her sister,' she interrupts, then smiles faintly at his crestfallen face. 'I haven't read it,' she says, her voice unusually gentle, 'but I've heard about it. Thank you. Where did you—'

'Oh, Mama had it round the house,' he spouts his prepared line, not wishing to let her know of the over-eager journey to Város the other day to buy it.

'Won't she miss it?'

'She doesn't read much.'

Sari gets up then, places the book carefully on the table, and sits down. 'Sit,' she waves at the chair opposite.

The silence is fathomless.

'How are you?' Ferenc asks at last.

'Oh, fine. Sad. But fine. I'd been expecting it.'

'You must be worried about what you're going to do,' he ventures, and she raises an eyebrow at him.

'Must I?'

'Well, you're on your own, and you must – you can't live on your own here, and I – I mean, I haven't spoken to my parents about it yet, but I'm sure . . . and I know Jan said we shouldn't until . . . but it seems to make sense now.' He trails into silence, having cunningly said nothing concrete, but framed his intentions clearly in unfinished sentences.

'Ah,' she says. 'I thought you might be thinking about that.'

'So . . .?'

'No.'

He feels as if the breath has been knocked out of him, as she sighs a little, suddenly seeming a lot older.

'Ferenc, I like you. I'm surprised at how much I like you. And I'm happy to marry you when I turn eighteen, if you're happy. But not yet. I promised my father, not yet.'

'But what will you—? I mean, you *can't*—' He can't bear the idea of her living alone in this old house; it's bound to only exacerbate her strangeness, both in the eyes of the village and in reality.

'I'm not going to stay here all the time. Judit says I can live with her, and I'll become her apprentice.'

'*Judit!*' he exclaims. He is hot, angry and humiliated, but

31

he can't quite say why. He just *wants* her, that's all, and he thought he was going to *have* her, and now she's going back out of reach, and how on *earth* could she prefer the idea –

She puts her hand on his.

'I'm sorry, Ferenc. I can see that this disappoints you. But you must just be patient, that's all. I don't want to break a promise that I made to my father. And I just – I'm not—' she falters, which is rare, Ferenc thinks. Normally her short, unelaborate sentences drop out of her mouth fully formed, seeming to reflect a complete certainty of opinion.

'I'm not ready,' she says at last. 'And I feel that this is a bad time.'

'A bad time for what? For whom?'

'I don't know. I just feel that it would be wrong to do it now.'

Ferenc feels suddenly, frighteningly, that he is going to weep with frustration, and for a moment he hates her. Whenever he's around Sari, it's as if he's unravelling: he's less and less what he thinks of as himself, and though he has no particularly exalted opinion of himself, reliability, steadiness, predictability – these are qualities that he usually feels secure in possessing. Over the past few months he's been like a horse maddened by a horsefly, wallowing in disproportionate bliss when the irritation is taken away. Sari has amazed him by making him feel more intense excitement than he thought existed, but, he realises, sometimes he doesn't like himself much around her. Twice since getting to know her he'd been woken from eerie dreams of the *szépasszony*, the fair ladies – and while he knows that Sari's nothing but a girl, he sometimes finds himself wary of her.

'You should go,' she says suddenly, and he looks down in surprise to see his hands gripping the edge of the table in a vicious, rictus-like grip. Later, he will find long, ridged bruises on the palms of his hands. He's vaguely conscious that, as far as marriage proposals go, this one has been far from an unqualified success.

'Yes,' he says, unmoving. She gets up instead, and moves towards the door, opening it for him.

'Goodbye, Ferenc,' she says quietly. 'Come and see me when you're feeling better.'

He leaves.

CHAPTER THREE

The summer gives no sign of ending, until one day, suddenly, the earth coughs and all the yellowed leaves fall off the trees to lie on the ground like shells. Sari feels like she's waiting for something elusive and indefinable. Fond as she is of Judit, living with her is odd. Judit hasn't lived with anyone for many, many years – village lore holds that she had a husband, years ago, in her youth, but Sari can't quite believe this; it seems preposterous that Judit hasn't always been as she is – and when she bumps into her early in the morning, Judit always seems surprised and a little put out. Sari's quite aware of the need to adapt, to smooth herself around Judit's angles and edges, but it's not always clear how to do so.

Still, Sari thinks that things could hardly be better. She misses her father, of course, both for who he was, and for how he treated her. As far back as she can remember, he treated her as if she was intelligent, involving her in every aspect of his work, and the older she grew, the luckier she realised herself to be, and the more at odds with the other women she knew. When he died, she feared that all that was over, that she would be crammed inexorably into the prefabricated mould out of which most village women seemed to step. Who would teach her things now? Who would care that she could read, let alone that she was at ease in both Magyar and German?

Judit cares, and for that Sari is passionately thankful. Judit embraces her quick mind and is happy to fill it with knowledge, day after day, and Judit welcomes the knowledge that Sari has brought from her father and listens, head cocked, as Sari explains alternative properties of a herb that they're using, or a more efficient way to prepare it. And Judit trusts Sari, letting her mix medicines and pick herbs, and, she says, Éva Orczy is due any day now, and when the time comes, Sari can accompany Judit to the birth.

Much as she loved her father, Sari always realised that he taught her things in spite of her sex; she's excited to find that there's no such sentiment in Judit, but quite the opposite.

'There's power,' Judit says, 'in here' – indicating her flaccid breasts – 'and here' – waving a hand over her midriff and the darkness enclosed – 'and especially here!' She points crudely at her cunt, elaborating with a salacious wink. Sari has dimly sensed the power of these things with Ferenc, but under Judit's tutelage she begins to get an inkling of what this power can do. Perhaps, she thinks, there are arenas where being female is an asset, not a hindrance.

She knows that Judit doesn't tell her everything, however. Judit sets far more stock in incantations and mystery than Sari's father ever did, and there are some parts of her work that she's seemed reluctant to explain to Sari. Once, only a week or two after Sari had moved in, she'd woken, thirsty, in the middle of the night; stumbling through the unfamiliar house on the way to the jug of water that stood in the kitchen, Sari had been taken aback to find Judit sat at the dining table, lit only by a dim oil lamp, in deep conversation with a pale, tight-faced woman whom Sari didn't recognise.

When Judit looked up she'd frowned. 'I'd forgotten about

you,' she said, sounding annoyed, and Sari had hurried to fetch her water and leave as quick as she could.

In the morning, the woman was gone, and Judit had responded to Sari's queries in even shorter sentences than usual. 'She's from the next village,' she'd said, 'Nothing you need to worry about.'

Since then, there have been a couple of occasions when Judit has left the house, with a terse shake of her head at Sari if she makes a move to follow, and Sari soon gives up trying to prise information out of Judit's shut-fast mouth; she'll tell her when she was good and ready, and not before. Still, sometimes when Sari is lying in bed, hearing Judit moving in the kitchen, speaking low-voiced to herself, Sari wonders quite how much she really wants to know.

And then there's Ferenc: that's perhaps the one area where Sari feels most confused. After she refused to marry him immediately, she didn't see him for days, and this made her unaccountably sad. She's always surprised to find that she likes him. He's steady, and she likes that; she sometimes feels as rootless and flexible as the long grasses that flap in the wind on the plain, and she feels that Ferenc may be able to anchor her. And the light of respectability in which he could cast her shouldn't be underestimated. Sari cannot remember ever being treated better than with mild disdain, or fleeting fear, or faintly patronising pity, and much as she tells herself she doesn't care, she sometimes feels a wistful longing to be liked. She imagines, maybe, walking through the village with Ferenc, and not having people slide their eyes to look at her, or raise their hands to hide their whispers.

After those few days, Ferenc started to visit again, and she was relieved. But something had changed. While his conversation was as light and friendly as ever, he would now sometimes fall silent, and the cast of his face as he looked at Sari unsettled her. She misses his simplicity, now, which has somehow been shed, but she doesn't know how to get it back. He doesn't try to kiss her any more, and she's not even sure whether they're properly engaged, as they've not performed the traditional ceremony, both drinking from the same cup. But perhaps Ferenc, with his wealthy family, and his frequent trips to Budapest, is beyond that sort of nonsense? In her spare moments, she's embroidering a handkerchief for him, the sort that engaged men wear, but she's not sure whether she has the courage to give it to him – not just because of the clumsy unevenness of her stitches, but because she's not sure what it will mean to him.

She's still certain that she made the right decision not to rush the marriage, though. Ferenc has something to do first, she knows, and whatever it is, it scares her. She's had dreams from which she's woken up, her mouth full of her blanket or her hair, to stop herself from screaming. She can never remember the dreams (her father used to burn herbs to help her remember, and then talk her through them, but she's too shy to ask this of Judit), only a sense of relentless movement, of darkness, of sinking into something and getting stuck. She thinks she is Ferenc in these dreams, and they only strengthen her resolve.

It's September when she sees the *délibáb*.

Éva Orczy has just had her baby, attended by Judit and Sari. Judit tells her it was a straightforward birth, and this horrifies Sari. She's white and stunned, her mind endlessly replaying Éva's groans as she sees, over and over again, the way that Éva seemed to cleft in two, the dark, brackish ooze that seemed to flood from her. 'A beautiful boy,' Judit had cooed (as best she could), but Sari hadn't seen it as such. It was stringy and wrinkled, an unnatural shade of pinky-red, and covered in what seemed to be white scales.

When they left the room, Sari expected a knowing wink from Judit, equal parts pity and glee, an intimation that all was not as it should be with the baby. None came.

'The baby—' Sari hints at last.

Judit sighs, unpredictably sentimental. 'Yes, yes. Lovely boy.'

'But didn't you notice—' Sari stops.

'Notice what?'

'Surely he looked a bit—' Lost for words, Sari grimaces slightly.

'What, the Orczy nose? Yes, poor kid, but that was bound to happen.'

Sari is frustrated. 'Not the nose! The – the *skin*, and the *colour!*' She breaks off in embarrassment because Judit has stopped dead, cackling.

'Sari! You're not serious? That was a perfectly normal baby boy. That's just what they look like when they come out!' She stops laughing and wheezes slightly, getting her breath. 'Surely you've seen – but no, why should you have? I assure you, Sari,' she says seriously, 'you couldn't hope for a better baby than that one. Count yourself lucky that he didn't have a rat's feet and ears, like an *üszögösgyermek* – or a wolf's head; they must have got him around Christmas Eve.'

Automatically, she makes the sign to avert the evil eye. Sari feels slightly sick. She's never wanted children particularly, but having seen the grim reality, she's horrified. *Never*, she says to herself, *no matter how much Ferenc* – and then Judit catches her arm, and points.

They're on the edge of the village, by the river, walking back from the Orczy house, right where the plain fades off into the smudged horizon, and Judit's pointing at the *délibáb*, the mirage that's sometimes seen on the plain. Usually it's of water, or houses, something absent but longed for, but this time –

'*Oh*,' Sari says, quietly but heavily. 'Oh, oh, oh.' She is breathless, and Judit turns to her in irritated alarm.

'Sari, what? It's only the *délibáb*; you've seen it before.'

'No,' Sari's voice is light and detached, half-dreaming. 'Not like this. Not like this!' and Judit, half panicked, waves her hands in front of Sari's face. In an instant, her eyes clear and her face relaxes; she turns to Judit, shivering.

'Quick, let's go home,' she says.

'What did you see?' Judit asks a few minutes later, when they're back home. Sari frowns.

'It's hard to describe. It was like . . . I've been having these dreams. They feel like movement, having to keep moving forward, towards something bad, and through mud, or something clinging—' She shudders. 'What I saw was like that. Men, a line of men, moving forward. They were afraid. They didn't want to move forward, but they had to. I thought Ferenc would be there, though,' she adds, puzzled, 'but I couldn't see him. I thought that the dreams were about Ferenc.'

'So?' Judit asks.

'I think something bad is coming.'

Three weeks later then, when there is a clamour of horses from the north, and a group of officious-looking strangers arriving in Falucska, neither Sari nor Judit are surprised. They hear them at eleven o'clock, as they are preparing the herbs that they'd gathered the day before. Sari gets up to look out of the window and sees the horsemen surging across the plain, the hooves sending up gouts of mud, and when they're out of sight, she comes and sits wordlessly by Judit at the table, and together they wait.

At half past eleven, the church bell begins to toll, persistent and insistent. Doors creak and slam all over the village, and a steady stream of people start to flow past Judit's door towards the church. Sari stands up. She is burning with energy and curiosity, she feels (knows) that something momentous is happening.

'Are we going?' she asks Judit, peremptorily.

Judit shrugs. 'Go ahead. You know how I feel about churches.'

'But – aren't you curious?' Sari bursts out, frustrated. 'This is important! This is something big!'

'You think it's something to do with your dreams and the *délibáb*, don't you?'

'You *know* it is.'

Judit relents. 'Fine. I'll walk with you. But I'll stay on the porch; I'm not setting foot inside.'

As they near the church, electricity seems to whip and crackle through the air. The church is always crowded, built for the village when its population – and its people – were smaller, but today Sari notices people there whom she normally doesn't see on a Sunday; older relatives of some families, who are generally thought to be too ill to attend, have somehow hauled themselves (or been hauled) out of their beds, and are watching the pulpit with anxious, over-bright eyes and silent, working mouths.

Judit halts, muttering to herself, on the porch, while Sari squeezes through the door, pressed back against the white-washed walls. She sees Ferenc out of the corner of her eye, on the opposite side of the room, catches his eye and gives him a discreet wave, fluttering her fingers; he smiles (a grim, tight smile) back. Everyone is tense and quiet, exchanging glances but few words. A light mist of fear and anticipation is clouding up the room.

The priest is a small man, twisted and wizened, an obscenely bulbous nose and a fringe of hair so black that it draws in all the surrounding light. The older people in the village who have known him since he arrived in the village as a young man, twenty years ago, joke amongst themselves that his vocation sprang from the simple awareness that he would never find a woman to marry him, but like most rumours, it's only part of the truth. Father István has a Voice – a splendid, powerful, rolling voice, which can thunder like a god, or purr silkily like a big cat; that voice is his pride and his vocation, for what better than to use his vanity to praise God?

'We are at war,' he booms now, his words dropping like boulders.

Yes, Sari thinks, *of course*. In the stillness she's able to slip to the door and stick her head out; she mouths to Judit, *did you hear?* and Judit nods impatiently.

Father István gestures to three men standing at the front of the church, military men, gleaming with wealth and privilege and barely disguised disdain.

'They're looking for strong, brave men,' Father István explains.

41

That afternoon, the market square is filled with men. Watching, Sari doesn't know quite what she feels, but it's mainly puzzlement and sadness. These men and boys are people she's known since childhood; they're moving towards danger, and despite her uneasy relations with much of the village, she doesn't wish harm on any of them. At the same time, she's amazed at their compliance – and she's sure it *is* compliance, rather than bravery in most cases. She knows that *she* certainly wouldn't be leaping into the breach so eagerly, should she be asked to risk her life for some nebulous idea of a homeland. Mátyás Szabo, whom she knows to be only a year older than she, is puffing up his chest and adopting a studiously mature expression; she knows Ferenc is milling around in the group somewhere. She knows there's nothing she can do.

Ferenc catches her arm as she's walking out of the church; his eyes are aflame with some strong emotion, but she can't tell what it is; his face is white and his mouth dry, and he licks his lips before speaking.

'Are you really a witch?' he whispers. She jerks back involuntarily at his words, but says nothing as he continues to stare at her.

'You knew this was coming. You knew.'

She is frozen for a moment, before her strength returns in a flood.

'I'm not going to talk to you now,' she says gently and calmly, removing his hand from her arm, and she walks away.

The recruiters are not discerning. They take every man who is willing, able being a less pressing requirement. They overlook the doubtful claims of age, and take all that they're offered. Tomorrow, the men start their march to Város, get the train for Budapest, and from there, no one is quite sure.

That night, Sari goes to her father's house to wait for Ferenc, knowing he won't come to Judit's. Sure enough, scant moments after she sits down at the table, there's a tread on the steps and a knock on the door and there he is. He is pale and obviously agitated, but Sari is glad to see that he's less wild-eyed than he was outside the church.

'I'm sorry about earlier,' he says stiffly.

'That's all right.'

They sit quietly. Night is falling, and the darkness in the room heaves and swells. Ferenc's face is gloomily shadowed.

'I'm going tomorrow,' he offers, finally.

'I thought you would.'

'I just wanted to say goodbye. And to apologise. I understand now why you wouldn't – you know. It's good that we didn't. It makes sense.'

'I'm glad you think so.'

'Yes.' He swallows hard. 'Sari, is it going to be all right?'

She's taken aback at his question. 'What do you mean?'

'You know – the war. Us. Me. Is it . . . will it . . .?' He stops, seeing her shaking her head.

'Ferenc, I don't know any more than anyone else. I can't just summon up the answers for you.'

For a moment she thinks he's going to get angry again, but he doesn't. Instead, he asks, half pleadingly, 'After this is over, will we —'

He needs something to hang on to, Sari realises, something

43

he can take with him. She nods decisively. 'I made a promise to you, and to my father. I'm not going to go back on that.'

'All right.' His relief is palpable. They sit in silence for a few moments longer before he stands to leave.

'Well, then. This . . . I mean, I—' he looks down, discomfited. Impulsively, Sari gets to her feet, slips her arms around his neck, and kisses his cheek.

'Goodbye, Ferenc,' she says, and then adds quietly, 'I think it will be all right. I mean, I think *you* will be all right.' She doesn't know if she's telling the truth, but he deserves a little reassurance. It's the only farewell gift she can give him.

He doesn't speak when she releases him. Instead, he gives a curt nod, and doesn't look at her as he leaves.

Judit and Sari watch them leave from the door of Judit's house. As they disappear into the stillness of the plain, Mátyás Szabo's mother bursts from her house and flops to the ground, like a dead crow, like a fallen cloud. The sound of her keening thickens the air, and Judit turns away. 'Well,' she says.

That night, the wind is strong. Sari is wide-eyed in the darkness.

1916

CHAPTER FOUR

Rounding the corner, Sari hefts the dishevelled pile of material in her arms and sees that a hint of spring has cracked the ice on the river, the first day of the year that the women haven't had to do it themselves. She is glad: the winter this year has been harsh and unforgiving, and food has been scarce.

Picking her way delicately through the mud and snow and rocks down to the river, Anna Csillag appears beside her, arms also full, jostling her with a friendly shoulder. 'Morning, Sari.'

'Morning, Anna.'

A slow smile creeps across Sari's face. This is what has kept her buoyant through the winter, the reason that she can shrug off so easily the recent hardships. War and its deprivations have brought about an outbreak of camaraderie in the village: feuds dissolving, frostiness melting due to the simple fact that people need each other more than ever before – and for the first time in her life, Sari has found herself with friends, found herself able to walk through town without her specially-prepared face of slightly pitying disdain, ready to deflect insults, because now no one – or almost no one – is shouting, or whispering, or trying to trip her up. It feels like she can breathe more easily, after years of not even knowing that her breathing was restricted.

Anna has been a revelation. She is twenty-two, tall and broad-shouldered, with wide cheekbones and a dark riot of hair, and Sari feels like she's only just met her, although she's lived in the same village all her life. She knows that this is due to the fact that Anna's husband, Károly, is gone. When she tries, she can remember Anna's old incarnation, but it's hard to connect that silent, cowed woman who skulked around the village trying to hide her bruises, with the expansive, explosive Anna who's appeared: humorous, lewd, good-spirited in the face of anything.

Lujza's down by the river, and Lilike, and they greet Anna and Sari with grim cheerfulness. 'How's the water?' Anna asks, grinning, and laughs as Lujza holds up red, chapped hands with a grimace.

'Goddamned freezing, like always.'

They hunker down together. Sari doesn't say much herself, but these days the women's conversation hums around her rather than stopping dead, which is good enough for her. There's little gossip these days – what gossip can there be without men? Lujza sniffs dismissively – so the conversation is banal, but friendly. Talk turns inevitably to sex, and Anna laughs to herself as Lujza describes in vivid detail quite how much she's been missing it. Lujza was married barely six months when Péter went away, and the way she tells it, they'd been fucking like rabbits all that time – 'And now,' she says heavily, 'nothing. Nothing for nearly a year and a half.' She shudders theatrically. 'The way I feel,' she adds, grinning sharply at Sari, who's beside her, 'I'm going to start going after you lot, soon.'

Sari smiles, but can't help blushing, and she looks away.

She wishes sometimes that she could join in these sorts of frank discussions; sometimes, an image of Ferenc floats in her head, looking at her the last time they saw each other alone, and it had been as if she could see right inside him, into his heart and his groin, feel how badly he wanted her at that moment, to fuck her in defiance of the danger he was going into. Still, if she listens closely enough to the women's conversations, she might learn enough to make it good for him one day; he deserves that, at least, for when he comes home.

Lujza's stopped laughing now, and slaps wet cloth onto the wooden boards with vigorous distraction. 'I just wish—' she bursts out at last, then falters.

'Wish what?' Anna asks. 'Wish you could find someone to give you a good seeing to?'

Lujza doesn't laugh. 'I wish I knew how he was,' she says quietly. 'He can't write, and I can't read, so I get no letters. And he's too proud to get someone to write for him, the stupid bastard. All I know is he's alive, because I haven't heard he isn't. But I wish I had some idea of what it's like, where they are.'

'Don't look at me,' Anna replies, 'Károly doesn't write, either. I get letters from my cousin Lajos sometimes, but they're always the same – hope you're well, hope the family's well, I am well, the weather is good. Or sometimes he says the weather is bad; that's it. And Lilike's brother can't write, either, can he?' Lilike shakes her head, and Anna pauses for a moment. 'Sari, you must hear from Ferenc, though, don't you?'

Sari nods awkwardly. 'I do. But—' How can she explain? 'He doesn't say much, either.'

He doesn't need to. She dreams about him once a month

– but no, that's wrong. She dreams *inside* him; she smells the blood and the mud, and wakes up rocking to the beats of gunshots, tasting his acrid fear on the back of her tongue. She can't explain this to them, though.

'He must give you *some* idea, surely?' Lilike asks, but she's wrong, he doesn't. Ferenc's letters are long and wrought through with a desperate thread of need and longing, but he glosses over his present surroundings in a couple of anodyne sentences, leading to lengthy, discursive passages detailing the many ways in which he misses Falucska. His most recent letter, which Sari received the week before, followed his wandering imagination through the first twitches of spring in the plain, speculating which flowers would be blooming when, and when certain birds would start reappearing. These letters always make Sari ineffably sad, but she writes back, describing the minutiae of the village as lyrically as she can, because she senses that's what he wants more than anything.

Ferenc's head is full of death, and sometimes he longs to share it with Sari, to unburden himself by cataloguing the men he's seen with heads blown off, limbs blown off, limbs he's seen unattached to bodies, men he's seen dying in agony, raving in lunacy. He still cannot comprehend the ease with which someone can simply cease to exist, and maybe Sari, with all of her oddness, her familiarity with death, might have something to say about that. But Sari's become his talisman in this place; when things get bad he conjures her up, fixes her image so hard in his mind's eye that he can sometimes physically see her, shimmering above the battle-field in a bubble of light and silence. He has to keep her separate from this, keep her suspended above the mud and

*the shit and the corpses. His letters become memory trails;
Sari allows him to access the bright parts of his mind, and
guides him through them. He clutches the thought of her
convulsively.*

That afternoon, Sari is back at Judit's, making up a treatment
for Lujza's mother, who has been suffering from severe
headaches. Although Judit would never say so directly, she
believes that Sari coming to live with her when she did saved
her livelihood, if not her life. The war has taken away the
young men, and without young men, there's a distinct lack of
babies to deliver. But Sari's brought with her not only the pig
and the few geese she inherited from her father, but the arts
of a *táltos*, and they've been far more able to vary their
medical repertoire than Judit would otherwise have been.

Of course, they've got to be careful: there's a difficult line
to tread between being seen as effective and being labelled a
boszorkány. Over time, Judit has started to trust Sari a little
more with the spells and chants she uses in her work, but
Sari has always had to swear to keep all she learns secret.

There's a knock on the door so violent that Sari drops
what she's holding and curses. From the kitchen Judit yells
'For God's sake! Calm down!' and Sari goes to answer,
expecting someone laid low with stomach pains, or with a
face pinched with toothache. Instead, it's Anna.

'Sari, you have to come and look!'

Sari is already pulling on her boots. This happens semi-
regularly, as Sari's known for being hawk-eyed, extremely
far sighted, able to discern a face on what to everyone else
just looks like a shapeless lump in the distance. 'What is it?'

'I don't know. People, on the plain to the south of the

village by the Gazdag house, and they're . . . doing something. Bringing something, or building, but we can't tell. Oh, come on!'

A tangle of about ten people is clustered by the river, the village clinging to the bank behind them, all peering out into the middle distance, where the plain sweeps away to the north. Anna, clearly feeling somewhat self-important, shoulders her way through the crowd with Sari, and points to a series of dots, maybe a mile away. 'There. Do you see?'

Sari shades her eyes against the sun, squinting slightly, and they pop into focus, one by one.

'It's a group of men,' she says to Anna, and the news spreads out through the group.

'Men!'

'But all the men are away fighting, surely?'

'Is it anyone familiar?' someone calls out from the back of the group.

Sari shakes her head. 'No. There's – there's some in uniforms. The rest – they look like foreigners, actually.'

'Foreign men! But why would they come here?'

Sari sighs slightly, an exasperated hiss of expelled breath. *Honestly*, she thinks.

'Perhaps,' she says quietly, in the tone she generally reserves for children, 'they haven't *chosen* to come here.'

'Prisoners?' Anna asks. Anxiety and excitement fight for precedence on her face, and Sari can understand how she feels. Although she's glad, as most of the women are glad, that they're not having to kill and be killed for a set of amorphous ideals, it's rather frustrating at times to know that something so incomprehensibly enormous is going on, while Falucska is oblivious to it.

'They might be,' Sari replies.

Silenced by this, the small knot by the river turns its eyes
to the distant shapes on the plain, bobbing back and forth,
as industrious as ants. Sari shades her eyes again, and leans
forward, intrigued.

'What?' Anna asks.

'Look. You see the men?' Anna nods. 'Look at the one on
the right. See what he's standing next to?' Anna squints, but
shakes her head. She can't make it out, though she sees it's
far greater in size than any of the men.

'What is it?'

'It's a cart, and I think it's full of – it looks like wood.
They're building something.'

Sari starts slightly as there's a movement on the very edge
of her vision. 'And there's another one!' she says, barely able
to keep the excitement out of her voice. 'Another two – three
carts, and more men. Whatever they're doing, it's something
big.'

By nightfall, the flush of activity has died down, but the lazy,
circular movement of a guard proves Sari right: prisoners.

The Gazdag property has been empty since the start of the
war. When Ferenc, his father and brother went away to fight,
the herds went to Ferenc's uncle, who has some land not far
away, as well as a lame leg and a water-tight excuse not to
join the army, and Márta, once it became clear that the war
was to be more protracted than the brief skirmish predicted,
had gone to stay with her sister in Budapest. The property
had been empty for nearly a year and a half; some of the
more daring boys (too young to fight, so desperate to prove
their worth in other ways) had broken in after a few months,
to see if there was anything left there that could be of use to

the rest of the village, but they found next to nothing in the vast, empty rooms and no one had bothered going near the house since.

And then the prisoners arrived, and now Ferenc's family house is a hub of activity, the epicentre out of which gossip now swirls. There is initial speculation that the army has appropriated the property without permission, and a clutch of villagers stalk off in high dudgeon to talk to the officers in charge, only to slink back in embarrassment, having had a contract, clearly signed by the Gazdag family, brandished at them like an amulet by a boy barely old enough to grow a beard. It's clear, then, that Ferenc's mother is not planning to come back to the village for some time, if ever, and Sari wonders whether Ferenc knows. His attachment to the village is so strong and visceral that it seems strange that his family can forsake it so easily.

It's nearly a week by the time word starts moving from house to house that they should get to the church because there's going to be an official announcement of what's been going on. Sari catches Lujza's eye on the way there, and Lujza yawns theatrically, obviously expecting no surprises. Still, she looks bright-eyed and excitable: the fact that the change is being acknowledged makes it all the more real.

The war has taken its toll on Father István; he's much thinner and sallower than he was before, and nobody's quite sure why. In reality, Father István's decline has little to do with physical hardship. He had assumed that when the war started and the men of the village left, those women who were left behind would need him all the more. For the first few months, he was right; people flocked to the church, including many of those who had excused themselves from regular worship on the grounds of age or illness. Father István had delivered what he knew to be magnificent and moving sermons and more than once he'd been triumphant to hear hollow sobbing from some corner of the church. However, after some time his words seemed to fall on stoney ground, and the faces before him moved from rapt attention to blankness, to rank unconcern. By January his flock was back to pre-war proportions. They would rather go to Judit Fekete with their problems, subjecting themselves to any manner of pagan practices that send a shiver down his spine. Disappointment sits bitterly in Father István's stomach: what seemed like his big chance, his one opportunity to break through the casual crudity and dismissiveness of his flock, has come to nought.

He hasn't told anyone yet, but he's decided – his sister is in Vienna with her husband, and when the weather is better he'll join her there. He stopped loving the village when it stopped loving him, and feels little when he looks down from the pulpit. Already he's wallowing in pleasant fantasies of providing consolation and spiritual solace to the war wounded, who, he hears, are besieging Vienna these days.

The official statement comes from one of the scrubbed, clean-looking, shiny-buttoned soldiers they've all been spying on from afar, and of course it comes as no surprise at all to everyone assembled: the Gazdag family have generously offered their property to be used to house enemy prisoners for the duration of the war, and a volley of knowing glances shoots around the church.

Adrián Jokai is the first on his feet after the official stops speaking, which is to be expected. Adrián is fourteen, and his two older brothers as well as his father are away, fighting. Adrián stammers and always has, despite the remedies that

Judit and, latterly, Sari have made up for him, but this time he manages not to tangle his words around his tongue. He asks the obvious questions – how many, and who, and what about the security – and the answers are comforting: the prisoners are largely Italian officers.

Lujza manages to catch Sari's eye, and winks.

They will be allowed a little more freedom than ordinary soldiers, but they certainly won't be permitted to wander around unsupervised; while they won't be kept in confinement all the time, their walks will be limited to areas of countryside away from the village, and they'll be accompanied by guards all the time. The women of the village have nothing to fear.

Judit waits on the porch throughout the announcements and subsequent buzz of questions, but grabs Sari's arm as soon as it's over, her face twisted into its slightly ferocious grin. Sari can't help grinning back, though she senses a tinge of connivance in Judit's expression.

'Why are you looking so cheerful? Did you hear all of that?'

'Of course I did, fool. There's nothing the matter with my ears.'

'What do you think, then?'

They are surrounded by a crowd of people, and Judit shakes her head abruptly.

'Not now. Wait until we get home.'

'This is going to be very interesting, Sari. Very interesting,' Judit says, as soon as they are safe inside the kitchen.

'Really?' Sari is casual, and Judit responds by growing snappish.

'Think about it, idiot child. This is the first time – as long as I've been alive, at least – that so many new people have come here. New men, too, and when so many of our men are away. What do you think's going to happen?'

Sari shrugs. 'You heard what they said. They won't be coming anywhere near the village. What difference is it going to make that they're here, if we're not going to see them?'

'Oh, Sari,' Judit laughs. 'You can't put people so close together without things starting to happen. Maybe they'll relax their system after a while, and the men will start coming closer to the village. Or maybe the women will start going up there – after all, they'll need things, washing, and cooking, and,' she grins suggestively, 'and maybe medical care. They can't live in isolation, you know. Well, maybe they could closer to the town, but all the way out here – they're going to need us.'

'Maybe, maybe not. I still don't understand why you find it all so funny, though.'

Judit raises a ragged eyebrow. 'When you've been alive as long as me, you know that nothing's going to happen to you anymore, so you become more interested in what happens to other people. And when you've been alive as long as I have, you realise how pointless everything is, how little any of this matters. So you start either laughing at nothing, or laughing at everything. And it's a lot more agreeable to laugh at everything.'

CHAPTER FIVE

Irritating as Judit often is, with her tendency to present herself as grand provider of wisdom, Sari has to admit that she's got a habit of getting things right. Within a week, when Sari meets Anna and Lujza down by the church, and Anna says, good-humoured, 'God, Sari, you should hear what this one's been up to,' Sari is remarkably unsurprised when Lujza gives a conspiratorial smile, and says:

'I went down to the Gazdag house yesterday.'

Anna laughs, and Sari can't help but roll her eyes. Lujza looks slightly put out.

'What are you looking like that for?'

'Nothing, really. Just that – Judit was saying just the other day how she thinks that, no matter what the officers said about keeping the officers apart from the village, something was bound to happen. I should have known that you—' She breaks off because Anna is laughing again, and so, rather reluctantly, is Lujza.

'Well, I'm glad not to disappoint you. Now, do you want to hear what happened or not?'

Sari grins and shrugs; Lujza's obviously going to tell her story, no matter whether anyone else is listening or not. Anna's calling over Lilike to listen as well; for a split second, over Anna's beckoning arm, Sari catches the eye of Orsolya Kiss, and quickly looks away.

'I was thinking about the prisoners,' says Lujza, 'and I thought about all the things that they would need in that camp. They need to wash their sheets and clothes, and they need food – maybe not every meal, but at least bread, and things like that. I heard that at the big camp near Város they have enough staff to take care of those things, but all the way out here, I thought they might be having problems. And so I thought well, times are hard, we all need a bit more of everything at the moment, so what would it hurt to ask whether they had any use for me?' Lujza pauses, frowning slightly, as Anna and Lilike guffaw, and Sari smiles. 'Not that kind of use, you filthy women! I mean, mending, or washing, or cooking. I spoke to that man, you know, the one who came to talk in the church, and he seemed very pleased that I had come—'

'I'm sure,' Lilike murmurs, as Lujza ploughs on regardless.

'– and he said that they were hoping that some of the women from the village would want to come and help with those sorts of things, and in exchange they could offer us food, and fuel, wood and coal, and material, things like that – or, if we were prepared to accept it, some of the men could come and do some work for us – the officers don't *have* to work, he said, not like the ordinary soldiers in the other camps, but it must be boring for them, stuck in there, and so they might be able to give us a hand with, you know, the sort of jobs that men do . . .'

Anna snorts at this, and Lujza stops, looking genuinely disgruntled. 'What? Look, I know you all think that I'm just interested in picking up some sort of – I don't know, some sort of *playmate* – but I'm not. This is *work*, this is a chance to get something better than the shit that we've got to deal with at the moment; this isn't about fucking foreigners. In case you'd forgotten, I'm married, and what's more, I actually *like* my husband.'

She shoots a pointed glance at Anna as she says this, who flushes slightly; Sari feels for her. 'Anyway. Gunther – the one who was talking in church, you know – he said I should tell my friends about the offer, and if anyone's interested – in *work*, not *men* – we should come along tomorrow morning and meet him outside the stables. He'll be able to tell us how many of us he needs, and what we can do, and what we can get in return. I've already told my mother; she's going to be coming along, and so will some of the other older women, and so we'll be quite safe.'

Recovering quickly, Anna raises an arch eyebrow. 'But will the men be safe from you?' she asks.

Lujza sighs deeply. 'Fine. If none of you are interested, I'm off to find someone who is.' Lujza stalks off, eyes scanning for someone else to tell. Behind her, Anna puts on a stage whisper:

'I give it a month at most before she's fucking one of them.'

Judit cackles when Sari gives her the news later.

'You see? See? This is how it starts. And how typical of Lujza to start it!' Judit has a soft spot for Lujza; with her crude talk and open humour, she's sufficiently unlike the conventional woman to please Judit's eccentric ways.

'So are you going to go along?' Judit asks.

Sari sighs. 'I – I don't know, Judit. I mean, we're doing all right, aren't we? We're doing better than a lot of other people here. Some people – like the Orczy family – they're really desperate. Maybe I should leave the work for people who really need it.'

Judit grunts derisively. 'Nice words, Sari; very public-spirited. What's the real reason you don't want to go?'

'I don't not want to go, necessarily. I might. It just feels – it just feels odd, that's all.'

'Sometimes,' Judit says craftily, 'sometimes I wonder whether you really should have become engaged to Ferenc. He's a nice boy and all, but you – oh, you had so many options, and now you're tied to the village.'

Sometimes, Sari wonders whether Judit can read minds. 'Ferenc's not tied to the village,' she snaps back. 'Look at his mother – off to Budapest as soon as the war started, and she hasn't even been back to look at their property. And now they're letting *prisoners* live in it. I don't think they're ever planning to come back. Ferenc and I might go and live in Budapest.' A fierce hope blossoms as she says this, a hope she had only vaguely thought she had, even as Judit's shaking her head.

'Ah, no. Ferenc's different from his parents. They've spent so much of their lives away, but he's always lived here, and he loves this place – the devil knows why. He'd never leave.'

Sari sets her mouth. 'Well, and that's all right, too. This is my home; of course I'd be happy to stay here. 'There's no point in thinking about other things that I could have done, or other things out there. This is my life, here, and that's all right.'

She's not going to the camp, Sari decides, definitely not. She doesn't need the work, she probably doesn't have time for the work, and so there's no point wasting time on something that's pointless. And she'd only really be going to gawp, anyway, which is horrible – she, of all people, should know what it's like to be stared at like some sort of performing animal, and she doesn't want to do that to the prisoners: they might well be the enemy, but they're still people. No, she'll leave it to the others, and instead, she'll set out early to go into the woods and gather some wild chicory – which they need; they've nearly used up their supply – so that even if Anna or Lilike or Lujza come to try and drag her down there, she won't be here to be dragged. She's not going, definitely, certainly not.

She oversleeps.

Lujza and Anna are banging on the door as Sari is frantically pulling on her boots and eyeing up escape out of the kitchen window. If Anna's decided to go, she knows that she'll be no match for their combined persuasive skills, and it's with grim resignation (smothering a bright bubble of anticipation) that she trudges down the road on the way to what used to be Ferenc's family house. Women are converging from all over the village, not just the young ones but the older ones too, married and respectable, and Sari finds that comforting; it means that it really is about work, rather than ogling men. It's just before eight when they assemble outside the stable doors, and the sky is exploding with glorious spring light, about twenty women in all, murmuring in knots of two or three, some looking apprehensive, some eager, some – Éva Orczy among them, Sari sees – looking on the verge of desperation.

The doors open. The official who spoke at the church is

there, along with another two similarly dressed men. The crowd seems to draw back en masse, as if suddenly nervous, but Lujza steps forward. She's never been what Sari would describe as pretty; her face is too narrow and her eyes too small, but suddenly her attractiveness is shown by her straight back and her bold stare.

'I brought some people who want to work, like you told me,' she says.

The official runs a practiced eye over the rabble. His face is expressionless, and for a moment he is silent, as if displeased. Then he steps back, and motions them into the stable.

Inside, they have set up a long wooden table, behind which the other officers take seats. Gunther himself sits down in the centre.

'Thank you all for coming,' he says in the slightly husky, accented voice that Sari remembers from the church – he is obviously Austrian, and his command of Magyar is shaky. 'Today, we just need to take your names, and what work you are interested in doing. Then we will organise different groups for different tasks, and if you come back tomorrow, you can start working. Payment will be in food – potatoes and bread mainly, but sometimes meat when we can get it. We need women who are willing to cook, and to clean.'

As Sari takes her place in the queue that's formed at the table, women start asking one another what tasks they prefer. Éva Orczy is in front of her, talking to Anna.

'I want to clean,' she says, 'I'm happy to clean sheets or clothes, but I don't want to do anything that means that I would have to be in there, with them.'

Anna disagrees. 'Who wants to spend more time down at the river than we already do? I'll cook, or peel potatoes, or do whatever they want me to do, as long as it's inside and warm.'

'But it's nearly summer; you'll be boiling in the kitchens over the summer.'

'I don't care.' Anna is obstinate, and holds out her hands, which are badly chapped and bleeding in places. 'This is what washing does to me. Give me a kitchen any day, even if it is as hot as hell.'

Éva and Anna reach the front of the queue, and they bend down to give the officials their names. These officials are clearly struggling even more with Magyar than Gunther was, and Sari notices that the one writing down Anna's name misspells it disastrously. She refrains from pointing it out. The same official has to ask Anna to repeat her choice of job three times; when he finally makes sense of what she's saying and scribbles it down in his crabbed hand, Anna tosses her head back, and says in a loud, disgusted tone: 'You would have thought that they could get some *Magyar* officials to deal with this.' A small shiver of laughter runs through the room.

It is Sari's turn, and she can't seem to help spelling her last name for the official, as if she's being helpful, whereas she knows she's really doing it to make him feel small. Her reward is his contemptuous expression when he looks up at her and asks her what type of work she would like to do. 'Cooking or cleaning,' she replies. She has no real preference, and is not even sure that she will be coming back the next day. He writes it down, and on impulse, she adds: 'I could nurse, too, if you want.'

The word 'nurse' is clearly beyond his meagre knowledge

of Magyar, and from the look he shoots her, she realises that she's making no friends here.

'What?'

'Nurse,' she repeats, slowly, and then, deliberately goading him, '*Krankenschwester.*'

He glares at her with undiluted loathing. 'We don't need them,' he says in angry, faltering Magyar. 'We have a doctor.'

Sari shrugs, her mouth quirking slightly, and moves on, finding Anna leaning up against one of the stable walls.

'Idiots, aren't they?' Anna says dismissively.

'They must wonder what they're doing here,' Sari replies. She feels a stab of unwanted compassion for the officials: what do they know of the wide sweep of the plain, and the people who live there? It must be frightening for them.

Lujza's just given her details to the men behind the desk, and as she turns to find Anna and Sari, they see her mouth open slightly, and her eyes go round. Her step quickens.

'What?' Sari asks, and instead of answering, Lujza takes their shoulders and swings them around, so that the three of them are staring out the window of the stable, into the courtyard beyond.

Men.

A great bolt of excitement shoots through Sari, and she feels riveted to the floor, a voice in her head chanting exultantly, *strangers, strangers!*, even as she notices they don't look too different from the men she's always known. There are two of them. One is tall and dark; his back is to them, but they can see the cigarette that's held awkwardly in his left hand, and the tuft of bandage that sticks up over his right shoulder, the white flag of his injury. He's gesturing with the cigarette, seemingly in conversation with the other man, who lounges against the wall, a cigarette at the corner of his mouth. He's smaller than the other man, slimmer, with a sharply angled face under a swatch of fair hair. Despite his relaxed demeanour, he gives an impression of carefully banked energy and watchfulness.

And then the taller man turns without warning. Lujza swears sharply, and she and Anna duck down below the windowsill to avoid being seen. Sari doesn't – can't – move, and suddenly she's locking eyes with this big foreign man. He smiles slightly, and calls out to his companion in a language that sounds like bubbles blown underwater. As Anna and Lujza cautiously raise their heads, he raises his hand to wave.

There's a moment of stillness, and then Lujza is grinning and waving back, and then all three of them are waving for all they're worth. The tall man is laughing, and his companion, still leaning against the wall, looks wryly amused. Abruptly, there is the sound of a door opening, and a voice barks something indistinct in German; both men's heads turn toward the sound, and reluctantly, they start to saunter inside. Just before they drop out of view, however, the taller man turns back to the window, smiles broadly, and blows a kiss; his companion slaps his shoulder chidingly, and, raising his eyebrows, sweeps into an elaborate and deeply ironic bow. As he straightens up, Sari sees a flash of fierce intelligence in his dark eyes, and then they're both gone.

Anna, Lujza and Sari turn to one another. Lujza is shaking with silent laughter and can't get any words out, but Anna is grinning broadly.

'This,' she proclaims, 'is going to be the best fun we've had in ages.'

Sari feels unable to say anything at all.

By eight o'clock the next morning Sari's mind is made up. When Anna thumps on the door, she opens it, looking apologetic.

'I can't come, Anna, sorry. Judit wants me to do some stuff for her this morning.'

Anna raises her eyebrows. 'Well, come along later then. I'm sure they won't mind.'

'No, Anna, sorry, but I just don't think I'll have time for it with everything else going on. We've had three people in the past week with terrible sore throats, and Judit's worried that it'll spread, and so . . .' Her voice runs down, hands gesturing ineffectually. She knows she sounds unconvincing, and Anna looks duly sceptical.

'If you're sure . . .'

'I am, Anna. Could you tell them that, please? That I won't be able to come back?'

'I will. And I'll be back here later, to tell you all about it!'

The door slams, and Judit shuffles out of the kitchen, looking curious.

'What is it that I want you to do for me, Sari?'

Sari flushes. There certainly *isn't* anything wrong with Judit's ears.

'Nothing, Judit. But we really do need some more wild chicory, and I thought that I should . . .'

Judit sits down, sighs heavily, and looks at Sari with mock sorrow.

'Ah, Sari, Sari. I never would have taken you for a coward.'

'I'm not!' Sari is outraged. Cowardice is the one accusation that infuriates Sari more than anything else, after a childhood where her father constantly praised her for her bravery and recklessness.

'Don't try and fool me, Sari. What is it that you're so afraid of?'

'I'm not afraid of anything! We have enough to do with – with people getting sick from hunger, and the people from outside the village coming to us – and we don't need the extra work – and if you're so enthusiastic about the idea, why don't *you* go down there?'

Judit, infuriatingly enough, is laughing at Sari's distress.

'Sari, it's not as if Anna and the rest of them are going down there to act as whores for the prisoners,' she says. 'It's just a bit of cooking and cleaning; where's the harm?'

'If it's just a bit of cooking and cleaning, then why are you so keen for me to go?'

'I think it would be good for you to spend time with people who are not from here. I think that you want to learn about other places, about the rest of the world, and that this would be a good place to start. I don't like to see you cutting yourself off from things. What happened there, anyway, that's got you so upset?'

'Nothing, really. We just – we just saw a couple of the men.' Sari swiftly describes the two prisoners, their appearance and their behaviour. 'They obviously had *ideas* about us, and Anna and Lujza just laughed, and so I think that they had . . . the same sorts of ideas.'

'And what's so wrong with that? If it's all right for the two of them, why isn't it all right for you?'

Sari's had enough. Arguing with Judit is like arguing with herself, that rebellious part of her brain that never stops questioning all her actions. Deliberately, she shuts off from Judit, making her face expressionless.

'We really do need some more chicory,' she says. 'I'm going to the woods for a couple of hours.'

Somehow, fate conspires to prove Sari right, and over the next few days she and Judit are busier than they've been in months. Jozsua, Éva Orczy's baby is ill, and Éva is panicking. Sari, who has a slightly baffled fondness for the boy, as the first birth she attended, spends her time running back and forth between the Orczy house and Judit's house, as remedy after remedy fails to bring down Jozsua's fever, and so it's not until three days later that Sari meets Anna in town. Anna is looking enormously cheerful; it's eleven o'clock and Sari is exhausted, on her way home from the Orczy house where at last an infusion of angelica has broken Jozsua's fever and sent him into a sweat-drenched sleep.

'Morning, Sari!' The perky tone of her voice makes the back of Sari's head prickle.

'Morning, Anna.'

'How's Jozsua Orczy?'

'Better, I think. He should be all right.'

'Thank God,' Anna says absently. Her eyes are sparkling in a way that strikes Sari as slightly child-like, and she is suddenly touched, remembering Anna's life before the war. Surely Anna deserves a bit of excitement, if anyone does.

Relenting, she asks, 'So how's it going, down there?' She motions in the direction of the Gazdag place.

'Oh, it's all right.' Anna's face belies her noncommittal

tone. 'I'm on my way down there now. I got on the cooking rota in the end, so I'm off to peel potatoes for their lunch; what fun.' Anna rolls her eyes, but the cynical pose doesn't suit her in the least.

'Have you met any of the prisoners yet?'

'Well . . . a few. They come into the kitchen sometimes when we're working – they have jobs to do down there, too, so they always have an excuse to hang around the kitchens, but you can tell they're only doing it to get a look at us.'

'And have you spoken to them?'

Anna shakes her head, regretful. 'Well, what language would we speak? Some of them speak a little German, but my German's shaky enough – and of course none of them speak Magyar, and none of us speak Italian.' Anna pauses, smiling slightly to herself. 'We still manage to communicate, though. A little.'

'I'm not surprised.' Sometimes Sari hears words coming out of her mouth that sound like they could have come from a woman twenty years older. She doesn't like it much.

'You know,' Anna continues, dreamily, 'smiling, waving, hand movements . . .' she trails off. Sari suddenly has an overly vivid mental image of the possible hand movements involved.

'God, Anna, you can't have fallen for one of them already, surely?'

Anna looks affronted. 'Of course not! And anyway, I'm a married woman!' Sari waits patiently, and after a few moments, Anna relents, her voice confidentially lowered, 'There is one man though. Jan.'

'*Jan?*'

'Well, I can't get my mouth around his real name, can I? Something Italian that just goes on and on – but apparently it's the same as Jan, which is far easier to say. But anyway, he seems to like me, and – oh, for God's sake, Sari, he's just so different from Károly, they all are – it's just nice to feel—'

Anna stops abruptly, and following her gaze, Sari sees Orsolya Kiss passing by; Anna is reluctant to have her private affairs splashed over the village by evening. Once she's gone, Anna's tone is much lower.

'Sari – are you sure that you don't want to come and help out? Lots of the men have been wounded, and some of them are sick – they could really use someone like you down there.'

Sari sighs. Suddenly, she really wants to confide in Anna, whose open face is looking at her with interest and concern, seeming eminently trustworthy. 'I just can't, Anna.'

'If you're worried about what people will say—' Anna starts, her face angry, and Sari has a brief, treacherous thought that Anna wouldn't be so brave if Károly were here. She shakes her head.

'It's partly that, but mainly . . . I don't feel like I can trust myself. Don't tell anyone I said that,' she adds hurriedly, and feels her face turning red, wishing vehemently that she'd kept her mouth shut. But Anna's just smiling.

'God, Sari, don't you think I feel the same way myself sometimes? If Jan miraculously decided to offer me a whole new life in Italy, I'd definitely be tempted. Very tempted.'

For a moment, they look at each other silently. Sari is remembering the thin, cowed, silent Anna of two years before, and she feels certain that Anna is seeing within her the bitter, strange, lonely girl that she'd been herself.

'It's strange, isn't it . . .' Anna starts, and Sari nods.

'You won't mind hearing about it, though?' Anna asks.

'Of course not. I need to keep abreast of the gossip, or Judit'll be furious.'

'I should really . . .' Anna moves to leave.

'Go on,' Sari says. 'I'll see you later.'

CHAPTER SIX

I

'His name is Umberto,' Lilike says. She keeps her head down, scrubbing the sheet that she is holding with uncommon precision and concentration.

His name is Umberto, and he kissed Lilike for the first time at the end of May. They can all tell straight away that something has happened; Lilike's smile has changed into something silken and secretive. Lilike has never had a proper lover before.

They started letting the men out a few weeks after they first arrived. At first they weren't allowed past the gates of the camp, but Sari sometimes caught sight of them playing games in the yard, calling to one another in that intoxicating language, syllables running together like bead necklaces. The girls working in the kitchen always cluster by the window when the men are out there, pushing their sweaty hair out of their faces with their forearms. 'When they get too hot,' Anna confides to Sari, 'they play with their shirts off.'

The men know that the girls are watching, and the girls know that the men know; elaborate acrobatic and sporting feats just happen to occur by the kitchen windows. The girls initially tried to avoid being seen, but after a while they stopped caring, and the men stopped pretending that they didn't know that the girls were watching, waving lazily up at the windows when they catch sight of a flash of blonde or dark hair.

Lilike has always been quiet but determined, and from the time that the prisoners appeared in town, she promised herself that she would have as much fun with them as possible. She works in the kitchens with Anna, and while they all flirt, Anna's flirting has a slight edge of desperation.

Lilike's, on the other hand, is cool and controlled. Umberto was not the first to show interest – Lilike is sleek and blonde, the sort of girl to inspire interest in most places – but he's the first that Lilike chose to encourage; there's something about his silly, curly hair and his overtly cheeky manner that appeals to her – he's somehow carefree, in a manner that none of the village men were ever able to be. It's been a challenge to make any progress without being able to speak, but after a few days of Umberto grinning and winking and gesticulating whenever she passes, she decided to smuggle in a peach, which she wrapped in a handkerchief and pressed into his hand as she passed him on the way to the kitchens.

The following evening when Lilike was on her way home, she'd just reached the gates with Anna and Lujza when she heard someone shouting behind her. All three of them turned, to see Umberto, haring across the lawn, clutching a small, ragged bouquet of daisies and dandelions. He squashed them into her hand, eyes flashing, and she gave a small smile, an even smaller curtsey, and slipped the bouquet deliberately in the top of her bodice.

Anna reported all of this back to Sari as soon as it

happened, and so Sari is not surprised by Lilike's blushes that day in May when they're next washing clothes at the river, in response to a flippantly crude remark from Lujza.

Seeing Lilike's reaction, Anna rounds on her abruptly. 'So?' she challenges. 'Has anything else happened?'

'Yesterday,' Lilike continues, regaining her composure, 'He was out walking with some of the others. He saw me washing clothes in the river and . . .' She flushes and looks down. 'He kissed me,' she mumbles.

'And what was it like?' Anna asks breathlessly. None of them are making any pretence at washing any more, and the sheets lie discarded, half in and half out of the river, flapping like ghosts.

Lilike pauses, considering. 'It was nice,' she says at last. 'He was – I think he is well practiced at kissing.'

Lujza gives a short bark of laughter. 'So?' she asks. 'What next?'

'We're meeting tomorrow. Same time, same place.' That was about as much as they'd been able to communicate without a common language.

'Will you fuck him? You know that's what he wants, don't you?'

Lujza's voice is slightly harsh, but Lilike doesn't flinch. 'Of course I will,' she says to Lujza, her voice cool. 'What's the point, otherwise?'

II

Every night, Anna dreams, and she dreams that Károly is dead. Every morning she wakes up and her stomach swoops

75

in disappointment, and as she dresses she prays for forgiveness, prays for God to make her a more dutiful and grateful wife.

She's been failing dismally on that score lately.

She never wanted to marry him. She'd barely given marriage any thought at all, and on the occasions when she had, the hulking, loutish son of her neighbours had never crossed her mind – she would have laughed if anyone had suggested it. But when he raped her, she was sixteen – she had been walking in the woods; he had been following her for days, waiting for his chance – and all choice was taken away from her, for she'd conceived a child, and no other man would want her after that. She wonders, sometimes, what would have happened if she'd taken Judit up on her offer to get rid of the child, but although she felt nothing but indifference for the small life curled inside her, she couldn't bear to even consider Judit's vague suggestion, which was certainly some sort of wickedness. By the time she miscarried, the wedding was two weeks in the past, and her destiny seemed to have been decided.

The funny thing, she thinks, is that she's not like Lujza, and she's not like Sari – both of whom she loves, both of whom scare her sometimes. Anna doesn't wish for a life outside the village, and had Károly not taken matters into his own hands, she would have been perfectly happy to marry and bear children and live in Falucska forever, living the life of her mother and grandmothers. She knows that she's not brilliant, and she's not beautiful, and she's not talented, but she's kind, and nice enough looking, and has enough common sense to be a good wife and mother. Since her miscarriage she's never conceived again, and she's never been sure whether she's unable to, or if she just doesn't want to. Although she has no plans to leave Károly – how could she? – she knows that a child would bind her irrevocably to him, and that's a thought too horrible to entertain.

Anna's a good, religious woman and so she's racked with guilt. Although her prayers are respectful, and standard, asking God to look after her husband and end the war, her heart is rebellious, and along with dreams of Károly's death comes a defiant sense of gratitude for the war, for taking him away and putting him in danger, and for giving her her life back – or lending her her life; she's not stupid enough to think that this will be permanent. And now there's something else that she stubbornly refuses to mention in her prayers, but which she rejoices in all day, and that's the arrival of the prisoners.

She watched Lilike eyeing them all up, choosing which one she wanted, but it was never like that with her; from the start, she'd always watched Jan – Giovanni – the closest. It's his smile that she likes – it's not cheeky, like Umberto's, or insinuating, or condescending, like so many of the others' – it's just open, and friendly, and warm. That smile tells Anna all she needs to know about Jan: that he's a good, honest, kind man. She's not looking for excitement, or a bit of fun; she'd never admit it if anyone asked her, but she's looking for someone to take her away. If Károly comes back from the war, she wants more than anything not to be waiting for him.

Anna's not like Lilike; she's in no rush, and feels no need to take charge, because she feels certain that it's going to happen. While Lilike has been choosing and planning and making gifts of fruit to her intended, Anna and Jan have been communicating with each other through nothing but smiles; huge, dazzling beams whenever they catch sight of one another, and those smiles seem to heat her from the inside. While Lilike is making assignations, Anna is content to wait. It'll happen.

In the meantime, she decides to speak to Sari in private, and see if she can get something that will make sure she doesn't get pregnant. After all, there's no harm in being prepared.

CHAPTER SEVEN

By July, Falucska is suffocating under a blanket of heat and hormones, and Sari feels like she can never quite clear her head. This has always been her favourite time of the year – the village, which can look stark and desolate in winter, is at its best when the crude wooden buildings are smothered in greenery; everything always runs far more slowly at this time of year, and this year is worse than normal.

'Well, of course it is,' Judit says, when Sari mentions it. 'It's bound to be, with all the distractions around.'

Sari had laid a bet with herself that it would be Lilike, and so was surprised when the first person to approach her, blushing with every inch of her exposed skin, with the whispered request for something to stop her from falling pregnant, was Anna. Lilike was not far behind her, however, followed closely by Fransziska Imanci, much to Sari's amazement: Franzsiska is half a generation older, married for as long as Sari can remember; she never would have imagined that she'd be the sort of woman to take a lover.

Since then, there has been a steady stream, maybe one or two each week, wanting to make sure that the new freedoms of the prisoners weren't going to leave any lasting reminders in the village. Every woman who comes to see Sari and Judit holds her head slightly higher than the last; spirits in the village seems to be bubbling irrepressibly upwards, and despite the cynical pose Sari's come to adopt, she admits that she likes the changes that have been wrought on the village. She likes the pervasive sense of rather frantic excitement; she likes the way that tongues have got looser, and jokes cruder; most of all, she likes the jocular, collusive looks that the women have started to throw each other, as if they're all part of a secret club. Most of the other women seem to feel the same way, happy to seize an excuse to push the war to the back of their minds. Sari finds that where she used to be asked every couple of days whether there was news of Ferenc, enquiries have slowed almost to a complete stop, and when Lazslo Mecs is sent back from the front, missing half his right arm, jumping and jerking as if he's still being shot at, he's met with more embarrassment than admiration.

By midday, Sari has to get out of the house. Judit is unbearably bad tempered due to the heat (she sometimes claims that she's only happy for about a week in spring and a week in autumn, and Sari's not convinced that it's a joke), so Sari invents some flimsy pretext, and five minutes later she's sliding down the river bank, dipping her feet in the water, and scanning the plain for activity. It's a slow day, though, too hot for many people to be about, and she's considering giving up and going for a walk in the woods instead, when there's a noise behind her, a pounding, like running feet.

Sari gathers up her skirt and tenses, prepared to make a dash for it if necessary, but when she turns she sees that it's only Lilike, and relaxes again. Only Lilike's not looking as calm and smug as she normally does these days: her hair is crazily untidy, she's soaked in sweat, and her eyes are wild.

'Sari!'

Sari thinks that no one has ever looked so glad to see her. She scrambles up the bank to meet Lilike.

'What is it? What's wrong?'

Lilike is panting. 'I've been looking for you – went to Judit's house, but she – said you might be—'

'What's wrong?' Sari asks again, surreptitiously looking Lilike over for signs of illness or injury. It must be something medical, as she knows that Lilike wouldn't come to her in emotional distress.

'It's Umberto. He's ill.'

Sari feels herself going very still; she's suddenly extremely conscious of Lilike's darting eyes and laboured breathing beside her.

'What's wrong with him?'

'It's his stomach. He has terrible pains, and he's vomiting.'

'But they've got a doctor down at the camp, haven't they?'

Lilike shakes her head impatiently. 'Doctor, yes, but he doesn't know what's wrong, he's tried different things, but nothing works and this afternoon he's busy at the other camp near Város, anyway. I think – I think it might be something he ate, something poisonous, and so you might know something that can help.'

Sari notices that Lilike's crying now, though she's not sure that Lilike's aware of it herself; the tears are leaking from the corners of her eyes and she's not bothering to brush them away. Sari is horribly excited, thrillingly frightened.

'What about Judit? Can't she go?'

'She said that you're better and she's right. She's great with anything to do with pregnancy and birth and babies, but when it comes to everything else – you really know what you're doing, Sari. Everyone knows that.'

Sari knows Lilike's right – it's the legacy of growing up with her father – but is honestly surprised that anyone else has noticed. Of course, every now and again people express a preference to see her rather than Judit, but she never thought that was anything more than reluctance to have Judit's wizened face staring down at them when they were already sick or in pain. It's that – the feeling of being trusted and respected – that decides her, more even than the thought of an iron-clad excuse to go down to the camp.

'Wait here,' she says to Lilike abruptly. 'I just need to get a few things. I'll be back in a second.'

Ten minutes later, she's being ushered by a shaking Lilike through the gates to the camp. Gunther comes out to meet them – Sari hasn't seen him up close since that morning in spring, and she's shocked at the change the past few months have brought about in him. He's like an old man gone to seed, spreading around the midriff, his eyes pouchy. Lujza has muttered darkly about how much Gunther and the other guards have started to drink – her own father has been selling them his *szilva* – and it shows, both in his physical appearance and his lazily swaggering manner.

'This is Sari,' Lilike says eagerly. Sari wonders whether Gunther can understand Magyar spoken so fast, but his eyebrows raise.

'She's a child,' he says flatly. Defiant, Sari lifts her eyes to meet his, and he recoils ever so slightly from her direct gaze.

'I'm sixteen,' she says in slow, clear German, 'I've been dealing with the sick people in this village for two years, and I helped my father for years before that. But if you don't think I am suitable to treat your prisoners, well . . .' she turns, but Lilike catches her arm and grips it tightly. Her back to Lilike and Gunther, she hears Lilike say in a low, fervent voice: 'Please . . . please . . .' Lilike has always been persuasive, and Gunther sighs, as Sari knew he would, and says 'Very well.'

The prisoners are housed in what used to be outbuildings and servants quarters. Sari has never been to this part of the Gazdag house before, and from the looks of it, neither has Lilike. No matter how lax discipline has become here over the last few months, Gunther has evidently not relaxed so much as to allow women into the men's living quarters. It's not as unpleasant as she would have thought, the beds in neat rows like a ploughed field, and despite the unorthodox surroundings, it's clean and tidy and reasonably comfortable looking.

Gunther gestures towards the end of the long room, where a group of men are clustered around one of the beds. Sari gathers together as much dignity and gravitas as she can muster, and, with Lilike gripping her hand, approaches.

Umberto doesn't look at all well. His face is unnaturally pale, which makes his olive expression look drawn and sallow. His skin has a sheen of sweat, and his eyes are unnaturally bright and feverish. Sari's never seen him up close before, but certainly, in his present condition, he fails to live up to Lilike's exalted descriptions of him. She pushes through the crowd and drops down next to the bed. Ignoring the murmuring behind her, she attempts a nervous smile to put Umberto at ease, but when it ends up looking more like a grimace she's glad that he's too distracted by pain to notice.

She touches his stomach and he moans slightly: it is hot and rigid. 'You said you thought he'd eaten something?' Sari calls over her shoulder to Lilike.

'I – I don't know. He still – we can't talk much to each other, but I know that before, when we've been out walking, he's picked berries and eaten them – always things I knew were safe,' she adds, hurriedly, at Sari's thunderous expression. 'But he was out alone this morning, while I was at the market, and so I think that maybe—' she stutters to a close.

Sari looks back at Umberto, eyes slightly wild. 'Lilike – how's your Italian? I need to ask him some questions.'

Lilike reddens. 'I know a few words, but I don't think they'll be of any use to you . . .'

'What about Gunther, or one of the others?'

Lilike shakes their head. 'None of them speak more than a few phrases.'

'Right,' Sari says to herself, 'Right,' and, raising her voice, she addresses herself to the surrounding throng: 'Do any of you speak Magyar?'

There's a subdued muttering but all the eyes staring at her are uncomprehending.

'All right,' she says, switching languages. 'Does anyone speak German, then?'

For a moment she thinks she's out of luck, that she'll just have to try a variety of potions on Umberto and hope for the best that she doesn't poison him. But then there's movement to the left of her and a man steps out of the crowd. He looks familiar, and Sari realises that he is the man who was leaning against the wall in the courtyard that day back in spring.

'I speak a little,' he says, and despite his slightly haughty appearance his voice is diffident and stumbling.

'Fine,' she says briskly, and turns back to Umberto. 'You'll do.'

Looking down at Umberto sweating and shaking on the bed, all her nervousness and insecurity starts to ebb away. 'Right, then,' she says, decisive. She *knows* this, this is her area; this is what she does. Her mind stills and her hands become steady, and when she speaks, she is surprised at how firm and confident her voice sounds.

'What's your name?' she asks the man who's now squatting down beside her.

'Marco.'

'Right, Marco. Can you get everyone else out of here, please?' Marco turns and speaks to the other men, who start to move away from the bed slowly, obviously reluctant – Sari's not sure about whether it's out of concern for Umberto, or a scavenger-like appreciation for any bit of drama in their dull and sedentary lives.

Marco squats beside her again and gazes at her with intense curiosity. 'Who are you?' he enquires in slow, halting German.

'My name's Sari.'

'No, I mean—' He waves his hand eloquently, encompassing Umberto on the bed, and the small pile of bottles and bags that Sari has brought with her. 'What do you do?'

She doesn't know the German word for *midwife*, so she tells him that she's a nurse; it's close enough. 'Marco, I need you to ask him some questions. I think he's eaten something that he shouldn't have, but I need to find out exactly what it is before I can treat him. Do you understand?'

His eyes narrow with concentration as she's talking, then he nods with comprehension.

'Ask him if he ate anything in the forest.'

Marco turns back to Umberto and starts to speak. After a pause, Umberto responds, clearly in the affirmative.

'He says that he did, but nothing he hasn't eaten before, when the girl – Lilia? – was with him.'

Sari sighs. 'Some of the plants are easy to confuse. Can you ask him what he ate? Was it berries? Or mushrooms?'

Over the next few minutes they manage to establish that he ate some berries, and that they were small, and round, and red, and came from a bush with dark green glossy leaves. Sari is relieved.

'It's not serious,' she says to Marco, who looks relieved in his turn and translates the news to Umberto, who looks in far too much discomfort to be relieved about anything. 'I'll go down to the kitchens and prepare some medicine for him to take now. Lilike can help me prepare what he'll need. Tell Umberto I'll be back in half an hour or so.'

Umberto's still looking distinctly miserable and slightly frantic by the time they reappear with a collection of vials and bottles. He says something in agitated tones to Marco, who smiles slightly and asks, 'He wants to know what took you so long.'

Ignoring Marco's comment Sari explains how to take the medicines, which are in three bottles.

'It's important that you get this right,' she says to Marco, 'so you should write the directions down.'

She hands Umberto the bottles and waits while Marco translates, scrawling cryptic notes on a piece of paper as he does so. Clearly sceptical, Umberto sniffs at the murky liquid before taking a tentative gulp, and then grimaces, letting fly a torrent of rather harsh sounding words in Marco's direction. Marco suppresses a laugh, looking a little embarrassed.

'He says—'

'I don't care what he says,' Sari replies coolly. 'It's his taste for sweet things that got him in this mess in the first place.'

There's a pause, wherein Marco's eyes move and settle deliberately on Lilike, his mouth quirking upwards. Sari struggles with a sudden, wild desire to laugh, uncommonly pleased that her intended double meaning has survived her imperfect German and Marco's imperfect understanding. Lilike, standing at the end of the bed, picking at the loose threads in her skirt, is oblivious. Umberto mumbles something and Sari looks questioningly at Marco. 'He says he's sorry,' Marco says, 'and thank you for coming.'

'That's quite all right.' Now that she's no longer needed she feels self-conscious, and it's making her prim. 'So – I should go.'

Lilike has sat down on the edge of Umberto's bed, and is stroking his hair in what's supposed to be a comforting manner, though Umberto looks far more interested in the clear view he has of her cleavage. When Sari moves to leave, Lilike shoots a pleading look at Gunther, who is slouched in the corner.

He looks bored, and gives a defeated shrug. 'Do what you like,' he mutters.

Lilike looks pleased. 'I'll stay then,' she says to Sari.

Sari and Marco walk out of the room in silence. She is suddenly conscious of a need to get out of there, and heads swiftly for the stairs but before she gets there he catches her arm. 'Wait,' he says.

'What?'

'How do you know all those things? Who taught you?'

Sari sighs. How can one explain these things to a foreigner? 'My father—' she struggles for a way to phrase it – 'he was like a doctor. I learnt a lot from him. And now, I work as a – a nurse for babies and—' She doesn't know the word for 'pregnant', so she mimes it, hand curving sinuously over her belly. He nods as if he understands.

'How old are you?'

'Sixteen. You thought I was younger, didn't you?'

He shakes his head. 'No. You have – you have old eyes.' He pauses in thought. 'I've seen you before, haven't I?'

'I came here on the first day, when all the women came looking for jobs. I think I saw you, out there.' She points at the courtyard, and a look of recognition spreads over his face.

'Of course! You were with two of the other girls who work in the kitchens now. But you've never been back. Why not?'

'I'm busy. People are always getting sick, so we always have enough work to get by.' A shriek of laughter rings out from the room behind them, and they both jump; evidently Umberto is feeling better already. 'And also,' Sari continues, her face pink, 'I'm not like *that*.' She jerks her head in Lilike's direction.

'Are you married?' Marco asks, frowning.

'No, but I—' She doesn't know how to say 'engaged'. 'I will get married when my – my man comes back from the war.'

'I see.' There is a silence, and then Marco says, abruptly, 'But you will come back now, won't you? You can see that we could use someone like you here.'

He's looking at her intently, and, furious with herself, she feels herself blushing again.

'I – I'm not sure that I—'

88

'I get these headaches, myself. From an injury. The doctor here, he's too busy with the camp for ordinary soldiers, and when he's here he just gives morphia, nothing else. I hate it. Perhaps you could—'

She should just walk away, she knows she should, but part of her mind's already ticking, working out how she could put together some sort of potion for Marco that would best relieve pain.

'No one else would take me seriously. You saw the way they looked at me when I arrived today.'

He shrugs. 'Perhaps. But I would take you seriously. So would Umberto. And perhaps the others . . .'

'Where did you learn German?' she blurts out in desperation, playing for time. He looks taken aback at her sudden change of subject, but he answers. 'I'm from the north of Italy, near the border with Austria. There are a lot of people who speak German there. I never learnt it properly; I just picked it up.'

'That's obvious,' she says, almost without thinking, but he laughs.

'I know.'

'And what did you do – before all this?'

'Before the war? I was a teacher at a university. I taught history.'

Just like that, her decision is made. Her head buzzing slightly, she says swiftly, 'I will come back tomorrow, with something for your head,' and before he can answer, she flees down the steps and into the sunshine.

Sari returns home to find a letter from Ferenc. When she opens it, she finds him rhapsodising about the glorious

Falucska summer that he's living through in his head. She's aghast to find that his lush descriptions bring tears to her eyes, when she hasn't cried in years.

Three in the morning, and Sari can't sleep. Ignoring Judit's indistinct muttering, she slips out of bed and out of the house. Last night, she managed to evade Judit's questions and fled to her father's old house, a sanctuary still, which she visits once or twice a week to make sure that rats or spiders aren't taking over. Judit's house is in the centre of the village, the sounds of footsteps and conversation are always just outside, but hardly anyone ever comes near Sari's father's house, set back as it is from the main knot of houses by the bend in the river. Last night, Sari went there for privacy, and there she scrawled a ten-page missive to Ferenc, bright and shot through with minute details of village life; she hopes that he won't notice its slightly frenzied tone, or its redemptive nature. She told herself that she must think of Ferenc, she must hold him in her mind's eye, but as soon as she got back to Judit's house, she found herself getting out the herbs needed for a pain-killing draught, and muttering the incantory words meant to ward off harm. That's not the sort of thing she does for just *anyone*.

She's gone over it all in her head so many times that she feels she's worn a groove in her brain, and so she rises at three, walks out of the village and onto the plain, as if the wide sweep of land and sky could clear her head. The village is dark from where she sits, the ground still warm from the day's heat – not a light burning. She tries not to look, but the camp is in darkness, too.

It's not about Marco. Well, it is, but it's not, not like it is with Anna and Giovanni (Sari can't bring herself to call him Jan, even mentally, and Anna's finally getting the hang of his real name), or with Lilike and Umberto, or with any of the other couples that have sprouted in the newly permissive attitude of the village. It's different because she doesn't feel about Marco the way that Anna feels about Giovanni, or the way that Lilike feels about Umberto. Anna keeps talking about weak knees and beating hearts, while Lilike's area is more bruised lips and scratched backs and lovebitten breasts, but all Sari feels about Marco is a fierce, crackling interest, nothing to do with either falling in love, or fucking in a forest. She knows that she has been astonishingly lucky to end up with Ferenc, that it would be ungrateful for her to want anything else, given that she now has more than she ever would have thought possible for someone like her.

But the thrill of the camp is still with her, as if a fresh breeze has blown through the village and through her and into her mind, tickling her there. The questions she's been avoiding all summer are now jostling for precedence. What are the men like? What do they know? What can they teach her? What happened the day before was like a gift. Anyone who hears of how she dealt with Umberto cannot accuse her of inventing spurious excuses to go to the camp. She wonders, sometimes, why she still sets such stock on what little reputation she has, when other women in the village seem to be flinging theirs to the wind – but that's it; her reputation is scant, and so she must hoard it carefully, for fear of jeopardising the status she has.

All her letters to Ferenc have skirted around the existence of the camp. He must know that it exists, as it's his family who has offered their land for it, but as long as she doesn't mention it, she thinks he can believe that it's having minimal impact on village life. Ferenc's a conservative man, at heart, and Sari knows that he would be shocked at the behaviour of some of the women. There's the worry, then, that any involvement with the camp, however innocent, would taint her, in Ferenc's mind, with the same sort of behaviour that's infected so many of the other women.

And yet she knows that she's going to go back. If she'd had less success with Umberto, if Marco hadn't treated her with respect and interest, if he had been anything else but a history teacher from a university, she might have been able to resist. But much as she tries to sit on it, squash it, bite it back, curiosity always has been the strongest motivator in her life, and the chance to learn, to know something outside her own limited sphere is intoxicating.

She doesn't want to fuck Marco, she knows that she doesn't, of *course* she doesn't, but she wants to talk to him, and get to know him, and so it's imperative to set some ground rules. When she goes back to the camp, she decides, she will go to him, and she will ask him to teach her what he knows. That way, there can be no doubt about their relationship, not from the point of view of any of the villagers, nor on his part, nor on hers.

Marco doesn't sleep well at the best of times, but since he's been in the camp he seems to have nearly stopped altogether. It seems odd that he should sleep less well here, where the only nighttime noises come from the birds and animals of the plain and his own sleeping comrades, than when he was lulled by gunshots and shrieking explosions and cries of pain and misery, but it's the truth. Perhaps it's the case that external silence just amplifies internal noise. Perhaps it's at least partly due to the headaches that claw ferociously on the inside of his skull when they come, leaving him limp and panting in their wake. Whatever it is, though, he now goes for days without anything more than a light doze to sustain him, before being abruptly engulfed by exhaustion, the strength of which makes it a challenge to get to his bed before passing out. Twelve or fourteen hours of deep sleep (during which his friends cover for him, making sure that he's not disturbed), and then the cycle begins again.

So it is not unusual that he lies awake that night, that at two in the morning he climbs out of bed – the comfortable grunts and snuffles of the men beside him getting too much to bear – and walks quietly out of the dormitory. In another life, in his previous life, he would have gone walking; every nerve in his body remembers the cloaking feel of night air on his skin, and the lush, deep silence. But no matter how relaxed (or negligent) the guards have become, he knows that an attempt to leave the building at this time of night could very easily result in a bullet in the back of his head. Instead, he sits on the wide sill of the landing window, a window that looks out across the plain, now blanketed in indigo darkness. Someone has mercifully left the window open. None of them are used to still, dull heat like this, and without a breeze it feels suffocating.

On a good day, he's able to see the humour in his current situation, in the utter impossibility of imagining, this time three years ago, that by summer 1916 he would be living on the outskirts of a dead-end village on the Hungarian plain. On a bad day, the sheer level of his rage astounds him, as does the fact that it hasn't dissipated over time; he's constantly struck anew by the furious, frustrated awareness that *this wasn't what was meant to happen.*

Marco never meant to be a soldier, *was* never meant to be a soldier, but is in possession of a particular, perverse type of ego that means he has to do everything he does as well as humanly possible, and as a result he was a damn good soldier. In retrospect, he thinks, that makes the whole experience far more obscene, that he killed people, risked lives (his and those of others) not because of patriotism or martial fervour, but out of pride, and a desire that he could be as good at war as he was at everything else he had ever tried. And all that brought him nowhere but here.

He thinks of his wife, sometimes – not with the desperate urgency that some of the others do (tinged in many cases by guilt, because there's hardly a marital vow able to withstand the distance of time and space and experience that now separates husbands and wives), but with a sharp, tangy sorrow. Benigna is his converse, soft curves where he is hard edges. She's intelligent, of course – he could never have married a stupid woman – but her intelligence is a gentle, gradual throb, while his is a clutching, grasping thing; she has a kernel of contentment at the heart of her, while he is driven. Their house is full of books but pride of place is Benigna's piano; she would play for hours, while he would pretend to read, but a stiffness or a stillness in his posture always told her that he was listening, and she would always alter her repertoire accordingly, playing the music he liked the best. He misses her, but with a kind of melancholy resignation; he hates himself for it, but more than missing her, he misses the effect she had on him, a kind of cooling and comforting. He has no buffers any more.

He'd known it was a bad idea at the time – worse than a bad idea, sheer idiocy; their fourth attempt to cross that damn river and reach those mountains and with every failed attempt the Austro-Hungarians had dug in deeper until they were virtually impervious. Winter by now, bitter, driving wind and constant sleet, and not enough artillery on their side, a helpless feeling of being mown down with ease. And then he'd been hit, a flash, a blast and then nothing, a hiatus; then consciousness again, pain, and an unforgettable memory of the fact that, moments before a shell had pockmarked the ground next to him and decorated his skull with shrapnel, Aldo Damasco, who Marco had known since they were children, had exploded in a shower of blood and mud in front of him. Marco was not conscious of much but that, that and the pain, had not cared whether he was living or dead, not cared whether he was with the enemy or with his own men. He did not recognise anyone around him, and their speech was incomprehensible, but he was sensible enough to know that could be a factor of the injury that he'd sustained. Pain, memory and then nothing as he passed into fog again.

The next time he woke he realised that he was with the enemy, and this time he did care. His memory is still shaky on that part of his recent past; it's more a mélange of emotions and pain than anything else, overlaid by the constant presence of people whose language he didn't understand and who seemed to care very little for his well-being. As he got better, he tried to tune his ear more and more to the language, and eventually memories came back to him of the German he heard while growing up in Como. It was that which sped his recovery more than anything – in the absence of books and companionship, the chance to flex his brain, to coach it through its first tottering steps to recovery made him grip onto life more than any sort of physical improvement.

And then, when he was well enough to march, he joined the group of Italian officers en route to Falucska.

His memory is still slippery, still shaky on the events of his own life. His wedding, yes, that's clear, and the few days after it, but then his mind stutters into blankness, and that's it, until another memory of Benigna weeping, he thinks because another month had gone past without her becoming pregnant – but when was that: weeks, months or years after the wedding? He doesn't know, and the thought makes his fists clench. He knows, rationally speaking, that he's lucky, that there are plenty of men who sustained injuries like his, who now have minds like still, dark water, not only lacking any memories from the past, but any new input is like dropping a stone into that water; ungraspable, it seems to float on the meniscus for a moment, then drops, leaving first ripples, and then nothing. And even *they* are lucky compared to some of the others, the ones who have become like babies, who cannot talk or eat or even shit like adults. But Marco has built his life and his career around knowledge and learning, and it's as if his brain, the organ that he's always subjected to extreme discipline and control, has betrayed him utterly.

He looks out onto the darkened plain, and sees that the bowl of the night sky has been lifted an inch or two, the sun glimmering on the horizon. Above him, the stars must be fading, but he can't see them due to the angle of the window. This makes him unaccountably sad; he imagines that the stars out here must blaze. He's starting to engage with the landscape, which is not beautiful in any way that he can understand, but its vastness is somehow awe-inspiring, and the featureless expanse naturally directs one's attention to the sky. Brought up with mountains and graceful, elegant towns as his idea of beauty, Marco's never given the sky much thought, other than as a gap between peaks or buildings, but now its vagaries have started to fascinate him, and when he is allowed outside he watches it almost obsessively. It's a wide, ever-changing landscape; clouds roll and break like waves. He wishes that he could see it properly at night, wishes it so fervently that sometimes when he's lying sleepless in bed, staring at the ceiling, it seems to shimmer slightly and become translucent, letting in the dusty, smoky light of the moon.

CHAPTER EIGHT

Sari is back at the camp by midday, her head roaring with nervousness, her hands shaking so slightly that no one but she would notice. Head up, shoulders squared, she walks past a group of men playing football in the garden, past Gunther (who seems to remember her from yesterday and simply raises a lazy hand,) and finds Marco sitting, legs stretched out, in the shade of a cherry tree near the main house. He gets to his feet when he sees her approaching, his movements oddly precise; she waves at him to sit back down, and sits down next to him.

'I brought you this,' she says, in careful German, handing him the bottle she had brought. 'For the headaches. I'm not sure what morphia does, or how this will compare to the things that the doctor here can give you, but it will be good for the pain, and it shouldn't make you feel ill afterwards.'

'How often should I use it?'

'Take two spoonfuls when the headache starts, and then after that no more until at least four hours later, even if it doesn't work. It can be dangerous to take too much.'

'Well, thank you.' He feels awkward. 'I wish I could pay you, or —'

Sari shakes her head hurriedly. 'Oh, no. That's not important. But, just—' Now she is the one to look uncomfortable. 'You said that you were a teacher, back in Italy. History.'

'That's right.'

'Well, I was wondering if maybe you could . . . teach me things. I've never been able to speak to someone who's not from around here,' she goes on swiftly, trying to get the words out before embarrassment takes hold and she changes her mind, 'and I want to – to know more about the world, not just about the things that you taught at the university, but about where you're from, and the language you speak, and – things like that.' She trails off.

'So, you want to become a learned woman?' The irony in his voice is unmistakeable. She flushes, suddenly hot, and jumps to her feet.

'Forget it. It doesn't matter.'

Marco curses inwardly. He wishes he knew where the mocking streak inside him comes from, why he finds it so difficult to respond to a simple request without sarcasm.

'No, please – sit back down.'

Sari looks sceptical, and he sighs. 'I'm sorry. I didn't mean to insult you. Please.' He gestures for her to sit down, and she sinks to her knees, still looking somewhat mistrustful, legs tucked under her in case she needs to spring to her feet again.

'Look,' Marco says, and beckons her closer. He pushes up his hair on the left hand side of his skull, exposing his scalp, and she leans forward, intrigued, despite herself, by the ornate-looking scar that scrawls its way across his head.

'I was hit there,' he explains, 'by some metal. I was ill for a long time.'

'And now you get headaches?'

He nods. 'Yes, and—' God, why should he feel humiliated

divulging this to an uneducated sixteen-year-old? Yet he does, as humiliated as he would feel telling one of his former colleagues. 'And now I forget things, sometimes. Not everything; I – I think I remember most things, but there are spaces. There are things missing.' He spreads his hands apologetically, and says, for once without a trace of mockery, 'I don't think I would make a good teacher, these days.'

She's silent for a moment, her eyes still on his face, and then she shrugs. 'Is there anyone else here better educated than you?'

He shakes his head, smiling slightly. 'A couple of the men are qualified engineers, but for the sort of thing you're looking for . . .'

She shrugs again. 'Well, then. Looks like you're still the best option that I've got.'

'But—'

'You wanted me to come back, didn't you?' She decides to risk it. 'You wanted me to come back, and not just for this.' She picks up the little bottle cradled in the grass and shakes it illustratively. 'You asked me all those questions yesterday – you want to learn, too, don't you? About all of this.' She waves an expansive arm, looking intently into his face.

For the past day, Marco has been refusing to think about how much he was hoping that Sari would come back to the camp, and in a few short sentences she's laid him bare. He's intrigued by her sharp, swift mind, her directness, her stern, proud face, all of which seems so different to the other women in the village, so out of place.

'You interest me,' he says. It's the best he can come up with, hamstrung as he is by language, and he's never been much good with sweet words even in his native tongue.

'And you interest me,' she says calmly.

'You aren't like the others.'

'Neither are you. So we have something in common.'

Silence settles between them. Sari's still not much good at talking to people, she knows – something in the way her words come out makes them spiky, liable to disconcert or offend – but remembering Marco's reflexive sarcasm, she feels an unexpected kinship, and a bright thread of relief runs through her. Two people less likely to fall in love, she thinks, would be hard to find: both awkward and rough-edged and far too little concerned with propriety and the way things should be done.

Marco gets to his feet.

'Let's walk,' he says, 'You can tell me the sorts of things you want to know.'

The camp becomes part of Sari's routine. She starts getting up earlier than usual, to get her chores and duties out of the way, and she walks to the camp at mid-morning. Each visit is longer than the one before. A grateful Umberto spread the word of her medical abilities, and gradually other men have started to approach her with maladies of their own that the camp doctor and his morphia cannot fix.

Marco acts as her translator and they approach her like supplicants; she doesn't know what they think of her, whether they believe she's curing them with some sort of pagan magic, and sometimes, when she's feeling boisterous, she plays up to this image, adopting a set of inexplicable mannerisms, or chanting ominously while preparing a potion. She likes the way that this amuses Marco, the way that he has to choke back laughter when she performs ever more outlandish routines. Sari has never been much good at making people laugh – not intentionally, at least – and she finds this new power is fun to wield, even as she's a little ashamed to be making fun of the work that she and Judit do; she's always careful that her joking chants are as different as possible from the incantations she makes in private, and she knows she would be obscurely embarrassed if Marco ever guessed that there is more to her work than just crushing up a few leaves and flowers.

Every afternoon, she walks with Marco. She is transforming his perception of the plain through her acute awareness of every plant, every weed, grass and flower, and he has tried to persuade her to show him the forest where, he knows, even more interesting plants grow, but she always refuses. She insists that they only walk in places that are in broad view of the village and the camp, to avoid arousing suspicion – something that Sari feels she is doing admirably. Her friends tease, of course, now that she's going down to the camp, but an affair with a prisoner has now become so acceptable that nobody needs to lie about it any more, and so Sari's simple denial of any improper activity tends to be accepted at face value. Besides, her reputation as a nurse and healer is spreading and she is gaining more respect in the village: it is one thing to treat local people for the familiar round of ailments to which they succumb, and another entirely to manage to cure foreigners – for all anyone knows, their bodies may be constituted completely differently, and prone to a different variety of illnesses.

She calls them lessons, but they are more open discussions with Marco. He tells her stories from which she gleans a cluttered comprehension of Italian history, geography, politics and society; he, in turn, learns about the more pragmatic aspects of the art of healing ('I can tell you this,' she says, 'because you'll never have the chance to use it and put me out of business'), about the patterns of the plain, invisible to anyone who has not lived with it their entire life, about superstitions and about her way of life. The discussions are far from orthodox, punctuated as they are by Marco pounding the ground in frustration when he reaches a dead end in his memory, or one or the other of them sketching something in the dirt with a stick when language fails them.

Marco's German is not good, and Sari's is far from perfect (a fact that she would never willingly admit), and so it is not long before they decide that they need another language in which to communicate. Sari tries to teach Marco Magyar, but he finds himself defeated by the knotted vowels and the tussles of consonants. Instead, Sari starts to learn Italian, which sounds to her like smooth, round pebbles dropping into still water. She is intoxicated by it, by the new shapes her mouth learns to make, and the liquidity of the words, and often in the evenings, after a day spent with Marco, she finds herself speaking to herself – nothing sensible, it is too early for anything like that, but noun after noun, repeated like a prayer, like an incantation.

Sari often repeats Marco's stories to Judit in the evening. It's mainly to help her remember them better, but Judit is fascinated.

'It's wonderful,' she says, 'It's like a gift, to learn something new,' and it occurs to Sari, almost for the first time, that while she may be bored in the village sometimes, that is nothing compared to how Judit must feel, surrounded by the same houses, the same families, and the same miserable pieces of earth for years upon years upon years.

'Tell me about your wife,' Sari says to Marco one afternoon, her tone lazy but her eyes watchful.

'How do you know I'm married?' Marco counters.

'I don't. But a man of your age' – Marco is thirty-two – 'and you're not a professional soldier, so I would expect you to have a wife.'

'You're right, for once.' Marco pulls something out of his pocket and hands it to Sari. 'That's Benigna.'

The woman in the picture takes Sari a little by surprise; she is smiling, head tilted slightly, looking half-shy. Fair hair floods over her shoulders in springy curls and waves; her face is heart-shaped and kind-looking, and what Sari can see of her body is smooth and rounded. She is about as different from Sari as she could possibly be.

Just a few weeks ago, the realisation that she and Marco were totally incompatible made her shiver slightly with relief. Now, she feels a small, but traitorous pang of disappointment. She bites it back viciously, and resolves not to think about it. 'What's she like?' she asks, hoping her voice won't give her away.

'She's very quiet. Gentle, and kind. She likes to read, and to play piano, which she does very well. She is the sister of one of my colleagues at the University: that's how we met.'

'She's a good mother?' Sari hazards, her heart thumping.

Marco is silent for a moment. 'No,' he says shortly, 'We don't have children. We would like to, but it hasn't happened yet.'

'I'm sorry.' Is she? She isn't sure.

They walk on in silence for a moment, and then Marco says, 'I used to worry that we had children, or a child, but I'd forgotten them. I don't think that's possible, though, is it? To fail to remember something like that?'

His voice has a slight pleading edge; Sari has spent enough time with Marco lately to learn how much of a constant torment his memory gaps cause him.

'No,' she says carefully. 'You would remember, I'm sure. You remember marrying Benigna, don't you?' He nods. 'Well, then, that shows that you remember major events. You would remember a child.'

He nods again, seeming to take comfort from her certainty. 'You know, you've never told me about your fiancé, either,' he says, his tone light. They are still speaking German, but she knows enough Italian by now that, when he slips in an Italian word because he doesn't know the German one, more often than not she will understand.

Of course, she thinks, she's avoided mentioning Ferenc to him, but she realises now that this in itself could be seen as suspicious. Surely it is reasonable for two friends – for they are friends now, despite the often combative nature of their friendship – to discuss their spouses and fiancés; surely it is odder if they don't.

'Well, you may know a little about him yourself,' she says. 'You're living in his house, you see.'

Marco cannot hide his start of surprise that she is engaged to someone who is from by far the wealthiest family in the village. He tries to cover his shock, but she is already looking at him, half-smiling, eyebrows raised.

'I can tell you, it was just as much of a shock to me.'

'I'm sorry, I just didn't expect—'

Sari gives a short laugh. 'Neither did I. It was my father who arranged it, really. He was respected enough to be able to do so. I think he knew that he was – that he was dying, and he wanted to be sure about what would happen to me afterwards. I doubt Ferenc's family were too happy about it, but—' She shrugs. 'They couldn't really do anything. It's one thing to stop a daughter from marrying someone inappropriate, and another thing entirely to stop a son. Our mothers were sisters, so it wasn't really a problem of blood. More a problem of me being – well, me.'

'And that wasn't a problem for Ferenc?'

She looks up at him sharply, but he is smiling.

'I mean – was he in love with you?'

Sari feels herself going red. She finds this sort of thing terribly embarrassing to talk about, but knows that to admit so would be childish.

'Yes, I suppose so. He certainly – he wanted to please me very much, and sometimes he would act strangely around me. From what I have heard, that's what people do when they're in love. Isn't that right?'

Marco gives a bark of laughter. 'Maybe. People are all different when it comes to these sorts of things. And were you – are you – in love with him?'

Oh God. This is a question that Sari has asked herself over and over again, and has never been able to come to any sort of conclusion – not one that she's happy with, in any case.

'He is a good man. He risked a great deal – his reputation, and his parents' opinions – for me. I am very fond of him.'

'Come on, Sari. Being grateful to someone isn't the same as being in love with them. Young as you are, I would have thought that you were smart enough to know the difference.'

They've stopped walking now, Sari staring at Marco balefully: what right does he have to pry into her feelings in this way? Seeing that he's upset her, he holds out his hands, palms upwards, and frowns slightly.

'I didn't mean anything by it, all right? I doubt that most people are in love with the people that they marry, but that doesn't make the marriage any worse. I was just wondering whether you felt the same way for Ferenc as the way he seems to feel for you.'

A breath. A beat. The implacable rush of the river.

'No, I don't think so. I think I love him – or I think I *can* love him, over time. I think he will be kind to me. That's enough.'

Marco nods. 'You're right, you know. That is enough.'

She's silent for a moment, amazed and horrified at what she's just said. 'And you?' she asks, attack being the best form of defence. 'Are you in love with your wife?'

He is irritatingly unruffled by her question, though she supposes that he must have realised that a counterattack was inevitable, given his military background.

'I love my wife. We live very well together. She gives me what I need – calm, and stability – though I don't know what I give to her. But no, I'm not in love with her.'

They look at each other for a moment, still, appraising.

'It doesn't matter,' Sari says.

'No, it doesn't,' Marco agrees.

Sari thinks, these days, that she's probably happier than she's ever been. It's not very fair either to Ferenc or her father for her to be so happy without them, she thinks guiltily, but she has friends, and she's learning so many new things, and she can't help revelling in the luxury of it all.

Judit is always one for spoiling a good mood, though, and the third time she comes across Sari humming cheerfully in the kitchen, she draws a laboured sigh. 'Don't get too comfortable, Sari,' she says. 'You should never get too comfortable.'

Sari grins and scoffs and the words are out of her head within moments, but then one afternoon in August, Anna has nothing much to do and asks to accompany Sari on one of her walks into the forest to look for burdock leaves.

As they go, Sari talks quietly about the latest things that Marco has been telling her – he's been scraping his memory for Roman myths, and they've captured her imagination like nothing before. The shade of the forest is like balm to their skins, and before long they give up the search for burdock – 'It wasn't urgent, anyway,' Sari says – and settle together under a tree and talk about Giovanni. He and Anna have made great strides in communication, thanks in part to Marco's Italian lessons which Sari has been passing on, but it's mainly down to the fact that when two people want nothing more than to speak to one another, they will find reserves of time and patience that they never would have thought they possessed.

Giovanni, it turns out, is a country boy from the south of Italy. 'He has a farm,' Anna confides, 'With sheep and cattle.' Sari can tell that already in her mind's eye Anna is seeing herself there, in some Italian farmhouse in the country, cooking for a brace of children and a smiling Giovanni, but of course there is another part of her mind that can't help imagining the end of the war, Giovanni leaving for the west, and Károly returning. Anna is determined to fight the return of her old life every step of the way.

'Is there news of Károly?' Sari asks after a while.

Anna shrugs bitterly. 'I had a letter from Lajos a few weeks ago. Says Károly's fine, as usual. He – I—' she stumbles into silence again.

'Sari?'

'What?'

'Can I ask you something?'

'Of course.' Sari is puzzled. Anna is direct, and normally she comes straight out with what she wants to say; even when asking for something to stop her from getting pregnant she didn't hesitate and prevaricate like this.

'I was wondering,' Anna says haltingly, 'whether there is anything you can do to – to stop Károly coming back from the war.'

There is a silence as loud as the clashing of cymbals. Sari, used to having nothing to say, has never found herself literally speechless before. It's as if she's dropped back two years into the past, hearing the whispers of *witch* from ill-meaning villagers.

'What do you think I am, Anna?' she asks quietly.

'I—' Anna refuses to look at her; she's digging the earth violently with her fingertips.

Sari's heart is racing, and she can't seem to pull enough breath in to her lungs to speak. Finally, she says, 'Never say anything like this to me again.'

'I'm sorry.' Anna's voice is shaking now, and Sari sighs.

'I know that you wouldn't have said it if you hadn't been desperate. It's all right. But I am serious: never say anything like this to me again.'

'I won't,' Anna whispers.

A bird calls, its cry harsh and too-loud within the suddenly smothering forest; Sari will not look at Anna afraid that she will see some sort of fear or awe in Anna's eyes. *Judit's right*, she thinks. *You should never get too comfortable. Things don't change; people just get better at hiding them, that's all.*

CHAPTER NINE

It's August 18th, 10 in the morning, and Lujza is at the door, holding what looks to be a telegram.

Sari's mood has been buoyant for the past few weeks, and she's only properly able to appreciate how happy she has been when she feels it all drain out of her at the sight of the telegram. She looks from it, to Lujza's face, and then back again. Lujza is white, even her lips are pale, but her eyes are dark and burning.

'Lujza – come in.'

Lujza doesn't move. 'I can't read, you know,' she says, and her tone is almost conversational. 'So I need you to tell me what this says.'

She presses the telegram into Sari's hands, and just the touch of it makes Sari feel nauseous. The village has been lucky with deaths so far, and the few that they've had news of haven't made too large an impact: mainly husbands from loveless marriages; younger sons from large families. It's been easy to pretend that the war's not real, that something happening so far away can't touch the village; in the middle of a long, lazy, beautiful summer, and in a climate of unprecedented freedom, it's easy to choose to forget why that freedom has come about.

'Lujza—'

'Sari. Just tell me.'

She knows, of course they both know, but Sari forces herself to look down at the paper she's holding, and she's right, they're both right, *Dear Mrs Tabori, it is my unfortunate duty to inform you that your husband, Péter Tabori* . . .

'He's dead, isn't he,' Lujza states; it's far from being a question.

Sari nods, and with that the strength seems to go out of Lujza's legs. She doesn't faint, but sits down heavily on the rough wooden steps, and Sari sits down beside her, not knowing what to do. If Lujza were crying it might be easier, but she's not. Her eyes are blank and tearless, but her breath is coming in ragged bursts, and she's rocking slightly, arms crossed in front of her, hands clutching convulsively at her elbows.

'Sari?' To Sari's enormous relief, Judit appears on the porch behind them, and seems to take in the scene at once – the telegram, Sari's white face, Lujza's tense, shuddering back. She looks at Sari searchingly.

'Is it Péter?'

'Yes.'

Judit brings *szilva*, which Sari has often derisively remarked to be her answer for everything, but she's never been more grateful to Judit's plum brandy than she is now. Judit sits down on the other side of Lujza, old knees cracking, and puts the cup to her lips, uncommonly gentle.

'Drink this,' she says, and uncommonly pliant, Lujza obeys, coughing sharply as the taste hits the back of her throat.

Sari closes her eyes, feeling sick. She tries to imagine what it would be like losing Ferenc, and then wishes she hadn't: the thought provokes no more than mild regret, while Lujza's bitter grief is so sharp that she can almost taste it. Time passes, and all Sari is conscious of is the warmth of the sun on her face, and the tightly-wound tension wafting off Lujza next to her. She wonders vaguely whether they should do something more for Lujza, take her home, or fetch her family, but perhaps silent company is all she wants right now. There's a shadow of a movement beside her, and Sari opens her eyes, almost afraid to look at Lujza, but a faint tinge of colour has returned to her cheeks, and something has come back into her eyes, some sense of life.

'All right,' Lujza says quietly. 'All right,' she repeats, louder this time, and Judit and Sari look at each other, concerned.

Lujza's eyes are far from blank now, but there's something lit in them that Sari doesn't like at all. She's come to like Lujza a lot over the past couple of years, but she's never come to trust her, and this is why: she's always had a sense that Lujza, with her recklessness and her violent unpredictability, is just a couple of twists away from insanity, and right now there is no sense, no rationality in Lujza's face, just a bleak, desperate sort of zeal.

Lujza gets to her feet, and the brandy cup falls to the ground, sending up a disconsolate puff of dust. Sari and Judit stand up beside her.

'Why don't you come inside?' Judit entreats. Her voice is cajoling in a way that Sari's never heard before, not even when talking to mothers in the throes of labour, which just serves to make Sari more anxious. 'Have a sit down, something to eat maybe – Sari can go and get your mother, if you want . . .'

But Lujza doesn't seem to hear, and takes a couple of unsteady steps away from the house.

'Lujza, where are you going?' Sari goes to take her shoulder, but Lujza shakes her off. The unsteadiness vanishes from her steps, which become strides heading unmistakeably downhill, in the direction of the camp. Sari shoots a desperate glance back over her shoulder towards Judit.

'Go with her, foolish child!' Judit shouts, and so Sari does, half-jogging to keep up, some vague, superstitious inkling warning her not to try and touch Lujza again. She only pauses when they reach Anna's house, banging hard on the door, grabbing Anna's arm when she appears, tousle-haired, dragging her along with them.

'Sari – what's happening?'

'It's Lujza. Péter's dead.'

By the time they reach the gates to the camp, Lujza is a stride ahead of Anna and Sari. One of the younger guards, Werner, slouches by the entrance, looking bored as usual, but something in Lujza's frightening, pale face seems to alert his interest and he gets up out of his chair as Lujza pushes through the gates.

'Wait – hold on – what do you—'

Without even turning her head to look at him, Lujza's right arm flashes out and punches him hard in the gut, and he crumples with a short yelp of surprise as much as of pain and fear. Lujza walks on into the yard, where the men are sitting, talking or reading or writing, and they're swamped by silence, every eye on the white faced woman who is familiar to many of them yet, at that moment, utterly unfamiliar.

Anna moves to go after her, but Sari grabs her arm and points to the vicious-looking scissors that Lujza is clutching in her right hand. A man she doesn't know seems to notice the scissors at the same time and shouts a panicked-sounding warning in Italian. A couple of the men who have started to get up and move towards Lujza freeze where they are, in positions that would be comical under any other circumstances. Heads swivel in unison to where Werner is still slumped on the ground, blood like a scarlet blossom on his shirt.

That's when Lujza starts to scream.

At first it's just a litany of meaningless invective, as if Lujza's purging herself of every horrible word and phrase that she can think of. Sari hears Anna sob beside her, and it brings her partially back to her senses.

'Run and get her mother,' she hisses, and Anna goes, but even as she leaves Sari is wondering why she sent Anna rather than going herself. She can't do anything here; this is far beyond her knowledge or control.

Almost reflexively, she starts towards Lujza, who chooses that moment to take the scissors and use them to tear open her bodice. Some of the watching men shrink back in response to the suddenness of Lujza's movement, and one man grabs Sari's arm and pulls her back, halting her steps. She doesn't bother to fight, not knowing what she would do even if she could reach Lujza, whose screaming has changed. Barebreasted, Lujza seems to have become conscious of the men around her, and is turning on them one by one: 'Do you want to fuck me now? Do you? Do you want to fuck me?' Her voice is hoarse and half-lunatic, and the men can't understand Magyar anyway, but they recognise the tone of her voice, and their horrified incomprehension starts to take on an air of pity, which intensifies as Lujza seems to lose her grip on words again, and screaming incoherently, drags the nails of her left hand across her face, drawing blood.

Someone moves.

It is Marco.

The man standing next to him, who Sari recognises as Marco's friend, Bruno, the man who was with him in the courtyard that first day, tries to stop him, but Marco shakes off the restraining hand impatiently. Walking with a gentle but certain grace that is almost animal, he approaches Lujza straight on. Her eyes are screwed shut and she is oblivious. He stops when he is about a yard in front of her and catches Sari's eye, raising his eyebrows in a silent question.

She understands. 'Lujza,' she mouths.

'Lujza,' he says firmly. He looks completely unafraid. Her eyes open, and he extends a hand, his movements slow and smooth. 'Give them to me.' He speaks in Italian, but his meaning is clear. She falls suddenly silent, her eyes on his outstretched palm. 'Give them to me, Lujza,' he says again, his voice gentler this time.

There is an agonising pause, during with no one seems to breathe, all eyes fixed on the tableau in the centre of the yard. Then, tortuously slowly, Lujza raises her shaking right arm, and drops the scissors in Marco's hand. He swiftly throws them to one side where they land, harmless, in a patch of dry grass, and just in time, because Lujza gives a broken, painful sob that chills the entrails of everyone who hears it. Her knees buckle, and it's only Marco slipping his left arm under her shoulders, his right hand holding her bodice closed, that stops her from falling. All heads turn again in response to a shouting and a pounding of feet which halt by the gate, and *thank God*, Lujza's mother and brother-in-law arrive, both weeping, and gather her up.

When she is out of his hands, Marco approaches Sari, his face grave. Around her, people are starting to move again, and a buzz of noise is starting up. 'Her husband?' he asks.

'Yes,' she whispers, not trusting her voice to remain steady with any more volume. He nods, his expression sad and thoughtful, before looking at her, suddenly businesslike.

'Come on,' he says, and leads her over to where Werner is still lying by the gate, seemingly forgotten by everyone else. Sari kneels down beside him, swiftly unbuttoning his shirt, and finds to her enormous relief that the wound is just a shallow, glancing cut, tracing the edge of his abdomen, and that Werner's silence and stillness is just down to shock, rather than anything more sinister.

'He's fine,' she says to Marco.

'Good,' he replies, before turning to Werner. 'Listen to me,' Marco says, this time in German, and Werner's head turns. 'She pushed you. You fell. You cut yourself on a stone. Do you understand?'

Werner looks blank, and Marco shakes him slightly. 'Do you understand? You fell. You cut yourself. Do you understand?'

Werner nods his head: yes.

'Good,' Marco says again, and turns back to Sari. 'Patch him up.'

Sari binds Werner's wound with agrimony to stop the bleeding, and with the help of some of Judit's brandy, he's soon back to a quiet and chastened approximation of normal. As a gesture of goodwill, to thank him for keeping quiet about how he really got his injury, Sari and Anna offer to wash and mend his shirt that is torn and bloodstained after Lujza's attack.

Although it's only really a one-person job, both of them go down to the river to do it. Sari doesn't feel much like being alone, and Anna doesn't seem to either; she's uncharacteristically quiet, but Sari can imagine what she's thinking – that if she could swap Péter's death for Károly's, she would do it in a heartbeat.

'I knew she was a bit odd, you know,' Anna says tentatively, plunging Werner's shirt into the water, 'but I never would have thought she'd be violent like that.'

'She didn't mean to hurt anyone,' Sari says.

'Why do you say that? She *stabbed* Werner!'

'Yes, but – think about it. If she'd gone down to the camp meaning to hurt someone, she could have taken something far more effective than a pair of scissors. She's got a whole kitchen full of knives. The scissors – I think they were probably just in her pocket, and she pulled them out when she thought she needed them.'

'Maybe.' Anna is unconvinced, and Sari changes the subject.

'Did you know Péter well?' she asks.

Anna gives a one-armed shrug.

'Not really. He wasn't originally from the village – I think his family moved back here when his father died, because his mother was from here. She's my mother's cousin, or something like that. He always seemed nice, though.'

'Yes, I suppose so.' She doesn't really remember Péter much; he was always somewhat overshadowed by the force of Lujza's personality.

'Do you think Lujza will be all right?' Anna asks. She's still slightly pale from the shocks of the morning.

'Physically, I think so. Otherwise – she's always been – she's a bit – you know.' Sari can't quite think of the words she needs without sounding uncharitable, but Anna has no such qualms.

'A bit of a loon,' she supplies, and Sari gives a half-hearted laugh.

'Yes. I don't know how this will affect her in that way.'

They slip into silence again, and for a few minutes there's nothing but the repetitive slop of cloth on water.

'Marco did well today,' Anna says with feigned casualness, watching Sari out of the corner of her eye.

'I suppose,' Sari says. She hardly wants to admit, even to herself, quite how impressed she was at the ease with which Marco took control of the situation.

'Why do you think she listened to him?'

'I don't know. Maybe it was just that he was the only one to approach her. Maybe she would have been the same with anyone. Or maybe—' and suddenly she finds that she wants to talk about him – 'have you noticed he has this – this kind of stillness? Not quite calm – he's too intense to be calm – but there's something that, I suppose, draws attention? And also,' she adds, not quite knowing what she's going to say until it's out of her mouth, 'he was the one person there who wasn't afraid of her. He's never afraid.'

She stops. Anna is staring at her, unabashed, and Sari feels her cheeks flushing; she's terribly conscious that she's probably never said so many words about Marco to anyone since she met him.

'Well!' says Anna, with the irritating air of someone who has just made a fascinating discovery. 'Well, well, well. How interesting.'

'Oh, shut up, Anna.'

Anna clearly has no intention of doing any such thing. She

pulls the shirt out of the water – now showing only a faint hint of a stain where Werner's waistline would be – and sits back on her heels, surveying Sari in a maternal way that is profoundly annoying. 'You know, you just about had me convinced, before. All those innocent excuses: *oh, no, of course we're not interested in each other like that; I just want to learn from him!* Yes, I really was starting to believe you.'

'Anna. Shut up.'

'You've been very discreet, I must say. So, how long have you been . . .?' Anna wiggles her eyebrows suggestively. *Oh God.*

'We're not! Nothing's happened, all right?'

Anna looks downcast for a moment, but then brightens. 'All right, maybe nothing's happened yet . . . but you admit that you want it to?'

'*God*, Anna! No!'

'Liar!'

They pause, staring at one another. Sari is grinning now, a brittle sort of hilarity running through her, a powerful surge of exhilaration that although something bad has happened, it hasn't happened to *her.*

'Just because *you're* a fallen woman doesn't mean that everyone else is going to go the same way!'

Anna gasps at that, mock-shocked. 'I don't know *what* you mean, Sari. I am a dutiful married woman.'

'Really?'

'Of course.'

'Hmmm,' is all that Sari says, her tone disbelieving. She waits until Anna's guard is down, and then pounces.

'Sari! What do you think you're—?'

Sari yanks down Anna's bodice as far as the top of her

breasts, and there they are, a series of five elegant little love bites, just below the line of her clothing. Anna blushes a deep red, but doesn't look displeased.

'Not so much of a dutiful married woman *now*, are you?' Sari asks, smirking.

'Mosquito bites,' Anna says, straight-faced.

'Oh, *now* who's the liar?'

There's a tussle then, the sort of silly, fun fight that neither of them have had since they were children, with pushing, and playful, open handed slaps, and a bit of gentle hair-tugging – all of which is fine until Sari pulls the ribbon out of Anna's hair and drops it in the mud, to which Anna retaliates by grabbing Werner's shirt off the bush where it has been drying, and flinging it into the river.

'That's Werner's shirt! You can't just throw it in the river!'

Sari kicks off her shoes. Two minutes later, Anna is wheezing with laughter, as Sari, dressed only in her chemise and petticoat, steps gingerly into the water. It's warmer than she expected; the current is not strong, there, and the sun's been heating the water all day. The bottom is uneven though, and Sari curses to herself when she stubs her toe on a smooth, hidden stone and lurches sideways, only to be engulfed suddenly in water up to her waist.

The shirt has caught on a rock, about two arms' lengths away from where she is, and she boldly wades out further, the water tickling the bottom of her ribcage, then lapping up over her breasts. Arms rearing up out of the water to grab the shirt, she's nearly there when Anna cries out 'Sari!' in a voice that's both shocked and amused.

'What?' Sari says, irritated, turning in Anna's direction,

but Anna's looking past Sari, up the bank on the other side of the river. She's looking at Marco.

Well, of course, Sari thinks crazily, before shooting a horrified glance down at her front, to find that, yes, it's as she suspected, the cream cloth covering her breasts has become almost entirely transparent. She bends her knees sharply, plunging below the water so that only her head is visible, and calls out, in a shrill, shaky voice that sounds utterly unlike hers, 'What are you doing here?'

Marco is not even bothering to suppress his grin at Sari's scandalised expression. 'I was looking for you,' he says, and behind Sari, Anna, who evidently understands a bit more German than she lets on, says, dryly, 'Well, you found her.'

Sari starts to splash for shore. 'Don't look!' she shouts at Marco, voice slightly wild. Obedient, he turns his back, and she stumbles through the shallows, holding out her hands as Anna, who is still giggling to herself, passes her clothes. 'He's not looking, is he?' Sari hisses. Anna shakes her head, as Sari drags on her skirt and bodice over her wet underclothes.

'All right,' she calls to Marco, 'you can turn around now!'

For a moment, no one says anything; the two girls simply gaze at Marco from the opposite side of the river. Then Anna seems to come to her senses. 'Right, then!' she says, business-like. 'I've got to go and do some . . . things. So, I'll see you later, Sari!' and she scrambles up the bank, back towards the village, still emitting occasional spurts of laughter.

'Meet you at the bridge?' Sari calls to Marco.

Werner's shirt, forgotten, drifts elegantly downstream.

They walk across the plain, not talking about anything very much, and yet Sari is uncomfortable. Despite the heat of the sun, wearing sodden undergarments with heavy clothing on top is not a pleasant experience. But she's also uncomfortable because she knows what she must look like, mud-smeared and bedraggled, and that makes her even more uncomfortable, because she's never bothered about how she looks in front of Marco before.

Marco keeps up a stream of respectful questions about Lujza, how she is, who's looking after her, and whether she will be all right, but eventually even he seems exhausted by meaningless small talk. They have nearly reached the edge of the woods, the village squatting, dark and low, on the horizon.

'Why did you approach her?' Sari asks the question that's been on her mind all day. Much to her annoyance, her heart is hammering, and it feels like her stomach is frosting over. *So this is what Anna's been going on about*, she thinks.

'She wasn't going to hurt anyone. If she'd meant to do any damage, she wouldn't have drawn so much attention to herself, and she would have armed herself with something more effective than a pair of scissors. She was just – sad.'

Sari nods. He's not helping matters, echoing her own thoughts like that. She can't think of anything else to say, looking fixedly at the ground, until he raises a hand and plucks a damp, slimy twig from her hair, and then she doesn't know where to look, and so she looks at him.

Marco swallows. 'Sari,' he says, his voice dry and scratchy. She stays silent. 'You're too young,' Marco says.

'I'll be seventeen this year.' (*What is she saying?*)

'I don't want to – to mess things up for you.'

'I know what I'm doing.' (*No, she doesn't!*)

This is it, Sari thinks. She can't shift her eyes from his face, feeling a slightly painful mix of elation and reluctance. He puts a hand under her chin, and raises it.

'I'm only human,' he says, as if to himself, sounding almost angry about the fact. She doesn't answer, because by then he is kissing her.

CHAPTER TEN

'Of course, this means nothing,' Marco says. 'You know it means nothing.'

Sari rolls her eyes and expels a hissing sigh. It is the third time that he has said those words in the past two hours, and the repetition is becoming tedious. 'I know,' she says, pauses a little, and then adds, slyly, 'And I know why you keep going on about it, too.'

'Oh, really? Why is that?'

'After the war, you'll go home, back to your job and your wife, and the last thing that you want is some Magyar peasant girl turning up on your doorstep. Am I right?'

He has the good grace to look slightly chastened.

'I don't want you to leave your wife,' Sari continues. 'This is just . . . a holiday.'

It is October, and the leaves are beginning to curl and bronze. They are in Sari's father's old bed, a fact that disturbs her less than it otherwise might. She has a faint suspicion that he might be grudgingly pleased about her latest course of action. He always wanted her to be safe, yes, but that desire always battled with his pleasure in her curiosity, and her stubborn refusal to bend to fit the shape she is supposed to occupy.

They are naked, but they haven't had sex, and Sari doesn't intend for them to. She knows how conservative Ferenc is, knows that he will know whether or not she is a virgin when they marry, and so it is far too big a risk to take. Marco allowed himself some token grumbling about her intransigence, but generally he seems to understand. They don't talk about love, haven't mentioned it, but Sari doesn't mind; not yet, anyway. She's still preoccupied by how much she's learning. While she's understood the basic biological facts behind sex for a long time – they're rather hard to avoid in her line of work – its subtleties and pleasures have come as a delicious series of surprises.

Marco rolls over onto his side, and in doing so, winces.

'What?'

He pulls the blanket down to his thighs; two months ago she would have blushed furiously, embarrassed but too proud to turn her face away, but now, she notices with some satisfaction, she can look at even the oddest parts of Marco's anatomy without minding.

'Look at this,' he says, his voice slightly irritable. He's indicating a large, plummy bruise that's risen on his left thigh. 'From climbing in that bloody window.'

The location of the house, on the edge of the village, near the woods, has allowed them to keep their relationship a secret for far longer than would otherwise have been possible, so long as Marco is prepared to wander casually into the woods, as if he is doing nothing more than having a stroll to take the air, circle round to the back of the house, and allow himself to be inelegantly hauled in by Sari through the kitchen window, which is sheltered by trees.

'I don't see why we have to keep this up,' Marco says now, gloomily regarding his purpling leg. 'What does it matter if people know? We're not doing anything that half of them aren't doing, too.'

'It's not a question of whether people *know* or not. It's a question of not flaunting it. Not being obvious,' she replies.

'But other people are. Look at Umberto, and Luigi, and Paolo. None of them have to be smuggled in through windows.'

'Well, none of their . . .' It's always hard for Sari to choose a word for this. 'None of their *girlfriends* are engaged to the son of the most respected family in the village. And none of them are in a position as . . . as delicate, socially, as me.'

He sits up and looks at her searchingly. 'Yes, you keep mentioning this, but you never explain it to me. What do you mean, "socially delicate"?'

Part of her is glad that he asked, as it shows that he's been paying attention, but all the same, part of her has been dreading the question, and so she sidesteps.

'It's hard to explain to a foreigner.'

'Yes, and so are a lot of the things that I've told you about where I'm from. I can tell you're different, Sari, but I don't know why, really, or how, or why it matters so much.'

Sari sighs. 'Well – you know what I said about my father? About how he was like a doctor?' Marco nods. 'Well, that's not exactly right. He treated people's illnesses, yes, but also he treated their – their other problems. He was what we call a *táltos*, a Wise Man. Do you understand?'

'I think so. You mean that your father had – or that people believed he had – certain skills, abilities to – to make things happen. Is that right?'

'Yes, I suppose that's a way to explain it. So – here, men who have these abilities, they are respected, but for women it's different. We call them *boszorkány* – I don't know how to say it in German, but it's like an evil woman, a woman who has special abilities to do bad things to people.'

'*Strega*. I understand. So people thought that because of your father, you might be one of these – a *strega*.'

'Partly. Also, my mother died when she was giving birth to me, which is bad luck – and it was worse because my mother was part of Ferenc's family, and the village respected her a lot. I expect that if I had been pretty, and loveable, and like everyone else, people wouldn't have thought the things about me that they did, but I'm not like them, I don't know why, but I'm not, and so it's easier for people to say bad things about me.'

'But it's not like that now, is it? Or not so much. So what changed?'

'It helped when I started working with Judit. People don't really *trust* Judit, she's a bit scary . . .'

'Can I meet her?'

'Maybe,' Sari says warily. She would have loved to have been able to keep her relationship with Marco a secret from Judit, but Judit has a way of gleaning an enormous amount of information from just a glance and she has been making increasingly unsubtle jibes ever since Sari came home that day in August.

'Anyway,' Sari goes on, 'No matter how people feel about Judit, they need her, and now that I work with her, they need me, too. It's also partly to do with Ferenc – people don't feel they can treat me so badly any more, because they don't want Ferenc to find out. And it's also partly to do with the war – everyone needs everyone a lot more, now that the men aren't here. It sounds horrible, but the war really has made things a lot better for me.'

It's coming into late afternoon now – the shadows in the

woods are stretching, and Marco gives a slight shiver. There's something eerie about those woods, he thinks, and gets up out of bed to close the curtains. Sari, supine, admires the gentle wedge shape of his body from behind – she's never seen a grown man totally naked before and wasn't expecting the elegance of Marco's muscled back and curved buttocks. She knows that she probably should get back to Judit, and he should certainly get back to camp before too much longer, but she is terribly reluctant to leave. The constant reiterations of *this means nothing* mean little to her; while she knows that what they have is never going to last beyond the war, it doesn't make it any less real now.

'Do you really think things have changed that much?' Marco asks.

'What do you mean?'

'I mean, the way people think of you. Do you really think that the war has changed things that much that when it's over, and people don't need each other so much any more—'

'But I'll be married to Ferenc by then.'

'And you're happy for people just to tolerate you because of the person you've married?' He sounds exasperated. 'I would have expected more of you. It doesn't bother you that people will be nice to you because of Ferenc, and then go home and think the same things about you that they've always thought?'

Sari starts to protest, but then she remembers. 'Sometimes I believe that people have really changed the way they think about me,' she says, slowly, her thoughts formulating as she speaks, 'But sometimes I think – do you know what Anna asked me a few months ago? Before Péter died?'

'No, what?'

'She asked whether I could stop Károly – her husband – from coming back from the war. I never would have thought that Anna would believe that I could do something like that.'

Marco looks intrigued. '*Do* you know how to do things like that? I mean, it's not that I believe in it, but – *do* you?'

Sari doesn't like talking about this sort of thing very much; she's never quite sure where her own beliefs lie – less superstitious than much of the rest of the village, she knows that she's far more so than someone like Marco. 'I know some curses,' she says shortly. 'I learnt some from Judit, and some from my father. They would never use them – well, I don't know so much about Judit, but not my father. He didn't believe in them, and neither do I, but I would never want to take the risk.' She's silent for a moment, and then bursts out: 'I just wish that I wasn't so different from everyone else.'

To her annoyance, Marco reacts to this melodramatic statement by bursting out laughing. She swats him half-heartedly with a pillow.

'You know the problem with you, Sari?' he says, dodging easily. 'You take yourself far too seriously.'

1918

CHAPTER ELEVEN

'What's he saying?' Judit asks irritably. Although she's been surrounded by spoken Italian for two years now, she's never got much further than a few words of random vocabulary and a full repertoire of swear words.

'He says,' Sari replies, 'that it's all going to be over soon. The war.'

'How does he know?'

'They hear things, down at the camp. From the guards down there, and from the new prisoners, the ones who are just back from the front.'

Marco looks impatient throughout this exchange. Two years has done little to improve *his* understanding of Magyar, and standing half-naked in the middle of a kitchen while the woman who is supposed to be fixing his shirt is babbling in that twisting, incomprehensible language can be rather trying.

Nobody is really looking forward to the end of the war. To an outside observer, the village looks perhaps like any other, men and women going about their daily business, but anything more than a cursory glance shows that while the women are Magyar, the men are Italian and still don't sleep in the village, and there are no children to be seen. Everything has slipped sideways into an approximation of normal life, and unlike a life that has been turned entirely upside down, it has become very hard to remember what things were like before, or to imagine that it could have been much better than the present state of affairs. The few Magyar men who have returned from the front have been easily assimilated, simply because they have been sick, or wounded, or mad, and as such hardly in the position to challenge the new world order that's sprung up in their absence. But when the great bulk of them return, the ones who aren't so easily quelled . . . The thought makes Sari feel uneasy.

'Well, the Italians will be gone by then, won't they?' Lilike said airily when discussing this a few days ago, and although no one said anything at the time – no one really likes to discuss it – they all know that Lilike wouldn't talk like that if she were married or engaged. After all, her life isn't going to change as radically when the men come home.

Sari and Marco have slipped into an easy, leisurely familiarity in the past year or two, and Sari can't quite imagine life without him in it any more; he's the bright spark at the centre of everything she does these days. They still don't speak of love, and Sari has pleasantly surprised herself that she still refrains from entertaining fantasies about living happily ever after in Italy with him. But although Marco insists that he would not and will not leave his wife, to Sari's irritation, as she has never asked it of him, his concern for Sari's future seems to grow day by day, the closer things are to being all over.

Shirt duly mended, they walk together through the village back towards the camp. The March wind roars past their ears, almost a physical presence; their feet slip and scrabble on the rutted, icy slush, and Marco shivers theatrically.

'Well it sounds like you won't have to put up with this climate for too much longer, will you?'

Sari knows she shouldn't have said that; a look that she has come to recognise immediately appears on his face, and she groans inwardly.

'I worry about you, Sari,' he begins, and she cuts him off.

'I know what you think.'

'Well, will you consider it?'

He wants her to leave the village when the war is over. She does not even consider the idea, because it is patently absurd. She can't understand why he wants her to leave when he has specifically said that he has no intention of leaving Benigna, and she doesn't trust his motives in offering to lend her – give her – money, to set her up somewhere new, but each time she refuses, he looks so sad that she can hardly bear it. 'Oh, Sari,' he always says, 'What you could be, somewhere else.'

These are thoughts she can't afford to entertain. Ferenc is a good man and she will have a good life with him, and anyway, she can't possibly leave Judit – and, what on earth could she do outside the village? There's no point even thinking about it.

'He thinks it will be over soon, then?' Judit asks that evening, while Sari is writing to Ferenc and trying very hard not to think about anything at all. She shrugs.

'That's what he says – but how many times have people been saying that since the whole thing started? I don't know how they can tell whether it's true this time or not.'

She's had dreams, though. Ferenc slid out of her dreams two years before, around the same time as she met Marco and he started to fuel her subconscious with Roman myths and stories of the ocean – but in the past month or so Ferenc has made a startling reappearance in nightmares that leave her gasping and sweating. She wasn't initially sure that it was him, because he looked so different, ten years older rather than four, but as soon as he opened his mouth it was clear it was.

Nothing much happens in the dreams, certainly nothing that would justify the extreme reaction Sari has to them: she is standing on the plain, and around her is nothing but silence, silence so full and intense that she feels that she could touch it. The first snow of the year has settled, and the wide whiteness tugs her breath into gasps. Someone is walking towards her from very far away, and she watches the figure in the distance, hunched, tiny as an insect, looking at it with no more than faint curiosity, but as the figure approaches the curiosity changes into dread as the face she has come to recognise as Ferenc's swims into focus and he says, 'Sari', just that, just her name, just 'Sari' but that is enough to blast her so far out of sleep that it is driven away for the rest of the night.

She still gets letters regularly, though they have changed their tone slightly – more of the war has seeped into them. Before, the letters could have been written from anywhere – a business trip to Paris or London; a holiday on Lake Balaton – but now, with a mixture of bitterness and elation, Ferenc has started to write about his surroundings. Nothing specific, of course, that wouldn't be allowed, but he talks of failure, of being driven back, and through the words, ringing with anger that a man as proud as Ferenc is bound to feel when encountering failure, burns a bright, blazing hope: that it will be over soon, and that he will come home. She's almost touched at how clear is his assumption that when he comes home everything will be the same, that the past four years will be easily excised from both of their memories.

Sari and Marco still meet at Sari's father's house, but she lets him in through the front door now. She had not known what she was waiting for, but she realised as soon as Orsolya Kiss had a lover from the camp (a fact that Sari and Anna laughed about together: you knew that something had become ordinary and expected when even *Orsolya* was able to attract someone to fuck her) that she was safe to be more open about Marco. Orsolya was not going to tell Ferenc about Marco, for fear of Sari telling her husband about her own indiscretions. They don't flaunt their relationship, still, unlike some of the women who parade their Italian lovers like they're the latest fashion from Vienna, but Sari has stopped going to such extreme lengths to hide it. Anyway, everyone's so caught up in their own little intrigues these days that she would be surprised if they'd attract much attention going at it on the porch of the church.

March is still freezing, the ground singing like iron when struck, and Marco insists on piling the bed high with embroidered eiderdowns, sheets, even tablecloths – everything that they can find. He's almost entirely obscured by the massive pile of material, so Sari can pretend to be talking to herself when she says: 'Do you really think it'll be over soon?'

'It looks like it,' he mumbles.

'I had a letter from Ferenc. He seems to think the same.'

'Mm.' Marco turns his head into the pillow and opens his eyes into the muffled darkness; sighing, his own hot breath heats his face.

'Maybe I don't want to go home.'

He doesn't know that he's going to say it until it's out of his mouth.

Sari's small, cold hand lands on the back of his neck. 'Well,' she says, trying to force some common sense into her voice, 'We both know that if – *when* – it's all over, you'll go back to your lovely house in Milan, and your beautiful wife, and having your books and things will help you fill the gaps in your memory, so you can go back to your old job. And maybe you'll have children – maybe two, a girl and a boy.' With a quiver of laughter in her voice, she adds: 'You can call the girl Sari.'

He snorts. 'Sara.'

'Is that what it is in Italian?'

'And what about you?'

'After the war? Well, Ferenc will come home, and we'll get married – oh God, I hope he won't want anything too fancy, but knowing his family he probably will. And then once all you lot are out of the way, we'll move back into his house. His parents will stay in Budapest – his father was blinded in the war, did I tell you that? – and he'll take care of the land and the herds, and I'll – I suppose I'll keep doing what I'm doing now.'

'What about children?'

'Maybe,' Sari says doubtfully. She's eighteen now, a perfectly respectable age to be a mother – her own mother had been fifteen, though the fact that she'd died in childbirth isn't much of a testament to early motherhood – but thought of a whole miniature human to care for is more frightening than almost anything else she can think of.

'I expect you'll be able to afford nurses to look after them,' Marco says, reading her thoughts.

'Probably.'

For a moment, they are both silent, locked in their own future worlds. Then Marco says, his voice tentative: 'So, we both know *that's* what's going to happen. But just for a moment, imagine I didn't go home.'

'All right.' Sari smiles. Marco's never spoken like this before and it's nice to know that she's not the only one to entertain the occasional flight of fancy. 'So what happens? Do we set up house together here?'

'Don't be ridiculous! What would we do about Ferenc?'

'Well, I suppose you could be waiting for him with a revolver . . .'

Marco shifts onto his side, facing her, and shakes his head impatiently. 'No, no, no – I don't want to shoot Ferenc. Anyway, this is a *fantasy* – we can do whatever we want, which certainly isn't going to involve living here.'

'Fine, fine. So where?'

'We would need to go to a city, where we'd have no trouble finding jobs, and where it would be hard to find us. Not Budapest – it's too cold, and anyway, my Magyar isn't good enough—'

Sari interrupts: 'Your Magyar is non-existent!'

'All right, all right. And my German's not up to much either. Maybe Rome.'

'No, that's not fair – if I have to leave my country, you should have to, too.'

'But Rome – ah, there's no point arguing about it. How about Paris?'

'Do you speak French?'

'Enough that I could get a job there. And you could learn – now that your Italian is good, you'd find it easy. Maybe you could train to be a proper doctor. Would you like that?'

'I think,' Sari says, 'maybe I'd like to study for a while – history, and books, and things like that.'

'Well, you're the right age for it. I could teach history and Italian; we could live in a little apartment on the left bank. You could wear terribly glamorous clothes, and have a small fluffy dog. We would eat in restaurants, and drink champagne.'

Sari laughs, delighted. 'I'm glad we've got that organised, then,' she says.

'Yes, it's a relief to have a plan, isn't it?' He draws an enormous sigh, and pulls himself out of bed. 'I must get back, Sari.'

She passes him his clothes and watches in silence as he dresses, then pulls on her skirt and bodice to see him to the door. 'Well,' he says, 'I'll see you tomorrow, then.'

'You will.'

He opens the door and the wind whips it so that it bangs against the side of the house; she leans a hand on the doorframe as he laces his boots.

'Ah, Sari,' he says, standing – he puts a hand on her cheek in an unusually tender gesture.

'What is it?'

'You always look so – so *resigned.*'

She doesn't know quite what to make of that, but her confusion is wiped out by his next words: 'I do love you, you know. Whatever happens, remember that.'

He leaves. His absence rings in her ears like thunder.

The letter arrives two weeks later, and Sari knows what it says before she reads it, sitting on the worn wooden steps of Judit's house, strikingly reminded of sitting here with Lujza almost two years ago. She reads it, and then reads it again before putting it down. She is still for a moment, not thinking, just breathing, and then gets up, goes back into the house.

'Ferenc is coming home,' she says. The words taste curious and bitter in her mouth.

Dearest Sari,

I am writing to let you know that I will be home soon. It is not over, but it looks like it is over for me, in any case. A week ago I was shot through the leg, and the doctors say that I will not be able to walk properly for two months or more, and I may always have a limp. I do not really mind. I can be of no further use here, so I am being discharged. I will go first to stay with my parents in Budapest for a week or two, but I do not want to be away from you, and from Falucska, for too long, and so I imagine I will be there in about six weeks. I know that my house is still being used for the war effort, so I will stay in your father's house.

I cannot tell you how much I am looking forward to seeing you, and the village.

Your loving
Ferenc

Half an hour later, she is translating the words into Italian for Marco, walking through the chilly grounds of the camp – *of Ferenc's house*, Sari thinks; she'll have to get used to associating this place with him again, rather than with Marco.

Marco is silent initially, biting his lip, hands thrust deeply into his pockets. 'Well,' he says at last, 'We knew that it was bound to happen sooner or later.'

'Yes,' says Sari, 'Only I was wishing that it could have been . . . a bit later.'

'He just assumes that it's all right for him to stay in your father's house?'

'We're engaged. Of course he can make that assumption.'

'Shit,' Marco says, sudden and vehement. 'Shit, shit, shit.'

'I know.' She wants to cry. No matter how prepared they have tried to be for this, no matter how resigned she has been, throughout the whole relationship, to its inevitable end, she still feels as if she has been kicked in the gut. Experimentally, she tells herself that she is lucky that Ferenc is still alive, that many women would give anything to be in her position, to be expecting their men to come home from the war, and finds, unsurprised, that it makes no difference at all.

'We have six weeks,' she says. It is something, after all.

CHAPTER TWELVE

Ferenc doesn't look like he did in her recurring dreams, but nor does he look like he did four years ago. He is thinner, he is bearded, and he looks – he looks old, yet not adult. Sari can't quite work out how this can be so, how he can look so broken, yet still seem childlike, lacking the assurance and maturity of someone like Marco (and God, she has to stop doing that, she has to stop comparing). He is standing by the table of her father's house; it is May, and the air, clogged with the scent of spring flowers, rings with the sound of birds. He looks like a man in a trance, though whether a pleasant one or otherwise she can't tell.

'It's all – it's unreal,' he says.

His voice is louder than she remembers it, and it takes her some time to realise that it's not her imagination, that he speaks louder now, to compensate for the hearing he has lost from four years of constant shelling and gunshots.

She can do nothing but stare at him, fighting back a rising tide of gut-deep panic. *I cannot marry this man*, she thinks. He hasn't tried to touch her yet, not even to shake her hand or kiss her cheek, and she only prays that she will not cringe when he does. It is not that he is repulsive in himself; he is just *not what she wants*. All the things that Marco has been saying for the past two years suddenly start battering about inside her skull: the fact of her life if she stays here, if she marries Ferenc, has abruptly become a reality.

He arrived that morning, putting his dirty, worn rucksack on Judit's front porch, waiting patiently until she came outside to speak to him. She took him straight to her father's house; she and Marco have been avoiding it for the past weeks, unsure of when Ferenc would arrive, not wanting to give him any reason to suspect anything. The rest of the village is being similarly circumspect. Ferenc and his family command enough respect that nobody wants to parade anything in front of him, and walking through the village that morning, every woman that they see gives the impression of servile respectability, welcoming Ferenc home; welcomes that he largely ignores.

Ferenc touches the soft, smooth wood of the kitchen table to ground himself. He's been away from the front for weeks now, but still he finds the silence frightening; it's as if his ears have been packed with mud. It wasn't silent in Budapest, except at night, and he found himself jerking awake again and again from dreams of the battlefield.

Sari has changed; that is beyond doubt. When he left, four years ago, she was hardly more than a little girl, and he had thought longingly of the woman that she would become. Now she is that woman, and he finds himself thinking longingly of the little girl, his mascot, his imaginary amulet that sustained him through the war. The woman he looks at now is still not beautiful, but there is something different about her, something perhaps better, or rarer – it's almost an elegance, although he feels ridiculous calling an eighteen-year-old peasant girl with snarled hair elegant. He only realises now that he's been used to feeling superior to her, but something is stopping him from doing that now. She has confidence, that's what it is; she's come to know her body, how to use it, and despite the awkwardness of the situation – and he doesn't blame her for feeling awkward; it's only to be expected – in some deeper, more fundamental way, she looks more comfortable than he's ever seen her, arms lightly crossed, weight on one hip, head cocked to one side. She has always looked at people directly, but he notices the defensiveness that used to barb her gaze has gone. She's still thinner than he would like, but there is swelling, a roundness under her clothes that wasn't there when he left, and feels a sudden throb of desire, which does a lot to dispel his panic. At least he still has that. Although, at the moment, he can't imagine what to do with it.

They look at each other for a long time, and Sari is the one who speaks first.

'Welcome home, Ferenc,' she says, relieved to find that her voice sounds passably sincere and, steeling herself, steps forward and gives him a kiss on the cheek. It's not the trial that she expected it to be; *that's a start*, she thinks, *and after all, we have time to get things right.*

'I missed you, Sari,' he says, huskily. 'I missed you so much.'

'You must be exhausted,' she replies. 'I've made up the bed upstairs. You should sleep.'

'Will you stay?'

'I – I can't. I have work to do – I've been doing some nursing down at the prison camp.' She thinks it's best to tell him this straight away, but he doesn't react.

'Please, Sari. I won't do anything, I promise. Only . . . just stay until I fall asleep, will you?'

She feels a surge of contempt at his display of weakness, and instantly hates herself for it. 'All right,' she says. 'I'll stay until you fall asleep, but after that I really do have work to do. And this evening I'll cook at Judit's house. You should come around six.'

He looks disappointed. 'Can't we eat here?' he asks, but she shakes her head.

'You know that wouldn't be right,' she says, taking unusual refuge in propriety. 'Now, go upstairs to bed. I'll be down here if you need anything, and I'll check on you before I leave.'

It's like walking through water. Sari makes her way to Judit's house with an almost total unawareness of her body; it seems stupid, on some level, to be so badly shocked and affected by something that she has always known to be inevitable, but nevertheless, nevertheless . . .

She's hardly got her foot on Judit's front step before Anna is at her shoulder. 'Sari,' she says, her voice low and breathless, 'I just heard that Ferenc is back. Are you – are you all right?'

'Oh, come inside,' Sari replies, weary. 'I don't want to tell you things and then have to repeat them straight away for that gossip-fiend in there.'

She's expected a barrage of questions, and so is surprised that, once inside, both Judit and Anna just sit, silent and expectant, waiting for her to speak. She realises gradually that this is not down to any sort of reticence on their part (Judit and Anna reticent? The very idea is absurd), but due to their complete uncertainty as to her mood. Her confusion and distress about Ferenc's homecoming has been roaring so loudly inside her that it seems incredible that it isn't obvious to everyone around her, but her natural reserve, her constant mouthing of dutiful words about how lucky and grateful she is to be engaged to Ferenc, and that he's coming back from the war, these things have *fooled* people, she realises. It's astonishing, but Judit and Anna are genuinely unsure as to whether she is happy or sad, rejoicing or despairing.

'How – how is he?' Anna asks, tentative.

'I can't really tell, to be honest. He seems . . . all right, I suppose. His leg is healing quite well, but he's shocked, I think, to be back here, after four years of fighting. I don't think he quite knows what to do with himself. I feel – I feel sorry for him, more than anything else.' She pauses for a moment, but concludes that there's no easy or pleasant way to say it. 'I don't remember, but – was he always so *ordinary?*'

Anna and Judit exchange glances, but don't answer – who can comment on the ordinariness, or otherwise, of someone's fiancé? And Sari knows that any answer would be meaningless; she's already condemned him in her own heart. She shrugs, self-deprecating.

'I knew that I should never have gone down to that camp,' she says. 'It was always going to end like this, with me being dissatisfied with things here. I knew that. I just thought – oh, this just couldn't be worse, could it? I thought that the war would be over, and Marco and all of the others would go home, and I would have time to adapt, to get used to the idea of Ferenc, without Marco in the way, before he came home. And now – God, I just saw Marco yesterday.'

She doesn't say it, but Anna and Judit exchange glances

again, and Sari knows that they understand Ferenc's inadequacy, at least from Sari's point of view, in comparison to Marco.

'So what are you going to do?' Anna asks.

Sari laughs, a dry, brittle sound. 'What can I do? I am engaged. Marco is married. From what I hear, the war will be over soon. Marco will be going home to his wife, and I will be left here with Ferenc. I have to make the best of things. Ferenc is a good man, and he will be a good husband. I just need to get used to the idea again.'

'Where is he now?'

'Sleeping. He looked tired. I'll go back to see him when I get back from the camp.'

Anna's eyebrows shoot up so high that they are nearly lost in her hair. 'You're going to the camp?' she asks, shrilly.

Sari is impatient. 'Well, yes. Not to see Marco, but, you know, Paolo still has that fever, and Umberto that rash, and I'm not going to stop going down there just because Ferenc's come back. I'm not doing anything improper.'

Judit gives a disbelieving laugh, and Sari turns on her.

'I'm *not*! It would be far too risky. It's over. I don't have any choice.'

True to her word, Sari is back from the camp in an hour, having briskly doled out medicines and advice, and chopping potatoes for dinner, having warned Judit that she must be on her best behaviour tonight because of Ferenc's presence. She knows that Ferenc already fears her slightly, and she doesn't want to run the risk of Judit alarming him so much that he refuses to let them work together any more. That would be unbearable.

'So, did you see him today?' Judit asks.

For a perverse moment, Sari considers asking Judit who she's talking about, but then capitulates. 'No. He was out by the time I'd arrived. I think he was avoiding me, but I don't know whether it's because he doesn't want to see me, or because he doesn't want to put me in an awkward position.'

Judit doesn't say anything more for a moment, just stumps around the kitchen, looking thoughtful. Then: 'What you said before, Sari.'

'*What*, what I said before?'

'About not having a choice. It's not true. You do have a choice. You always do.'

Sari sighs, irritated. 'It's all very well to say that, Judit, but—'

Judit holds up a hand, cutting her off. Her face is stern, and Sari understands that this is not a question of good-natured teasing, or needling Sari just for the sake of the challenge: this time, Judit means business.

'Don't tell me I don't understand. Maybe I don't know what it's like to be you, right now, but credit me with a little knowledge of human nature. There is *always* a choice, Sari, always. If you fool yourself into believing there's not, you've got no one to blame but yourself. Sometimes all your options look pretty nasty, but remember they're there.'

Sari swallows. 'Judit—' but Judit is shaking her head.

'I'm not going to talk about it any more, and I'm not going to question the choice you make. I just wanted to be sure that you know that you're making one.'

He's been home for a week now, and in that time he's been out of Sari's father's house once, the first night he was home, to Judit's house for dinner. It was intolerable. Every step he took, everywhere he looked, the differences slapped him in the face. The way Judit's face has aged over four years; the degree to which Sari is at home in Judit's house, in her role as domestic and professional assistant; the way the village looks, stripped of its men (and those strange looking men, one or two, that he'd glimpsed skulking in doorways – he cannot bear to think about them, the enemy, the marks of their feet on his village, the touch of their hands in his house); the changes, each as sharp as a gunshot, as wounding as a bayonet blow, and a personal affront, directed at Ferenc alone. It is *intolerable*.

From Sari's father's house, all he can see is the woods, and the woods haven't changed. They are a comfort. The house hasn't changed, either, except for the absence of Jan and child-Sari, and it is easy to conjure up their memories. *Too* easy, perhaps; he has found that when adult-Sari comes in through the door, there's often a moment of vertigo, as if he's looking forward in time. He has to remind himself that this is the present.

Sari. She didn't say anything, but she must have noticed his reaction, that first night he was home, and so she no longer asks him to have dinner at Judit's house. Instead, she cooks there, and after she and Judit have eaten, she brings him a panful of whatever she has made, sitting with him while he eats it. She is often silent, but that doesn't disturb him; she was always like that, and now, he is often silent himself.

She will not stay the night.

He knows that it's proper for her to refuse, but that doesn't stop him from wanting her, a soul-deep longing that is painful and bitter. There's no answering longing in her eyes, however much he tries to deceive himself, and that hurts, but brings about a steely certainty. It doesn't matter; her desire will come, and even if it doesn't, it still doesn't matter. They are engaged, they will marry, and then she will be his. She will be just the tonic that he needs, to build up his strength, to make him brave enough to leave the house, to reclaim his life again. It's different, everything is different now, but she's still his. She is still his.

Sari is just waiting for the day that she gets used to things. So far, it hasn't come. She sees Ferenc every day, brings him food, does his washing, and tends his wound. During the day she feels nothing but pity and slight repulsion for him, with his collection of nervous ticks, his paranoid rituals, and his intermittent illness – a fever, he says, picked up on the battlefield that has never quite disappeared; but Sari interprets things differently and sees the stomach pains that he complains of, as a sign of a troubled heart and mind. At night, however, when he is not there and so unable to inspire sympathy, thoughts of him frighten her, and he seems somehow emotionally vast and uncontrollable. This is no way for a woman to think of her fiancé, but she can't seem to stop herself.

He talks of marriage after the war is over – he expects it to be soon, soon enough that he is prepared to wait, for marriage while the war is still going on would be an affront to decency, he thinks. It gives her a little respite, a little time to accustom herself to the idea. She makes herself imagine living with him, and that is bearable; cooking for him, cleaning, these things she does already. Sleeping with him, though . . . she forces herself to think of it because she knows she must, but she still cannot see how she's going to make herself go through with it. She knows he wants to fuck her – she's learnt that from being in close company with men for the past couple of years. He hasn't asked yet, he's too shy and too jumpy to build up the necessary confidence, but every day that she sees him, he seems to relax further in her presence, and she knows that it's just a matter of time. She could refuse, of course; he would find that acceptable, even admirable, though frustrating, behaviour; but refusal will only get her as far as the wedding, and after that she will have no power to refuse. There's nothing to be afraid of, nothing to worry about, she tells herself, and waiting until they are married will just give her more time to build up reserves of dread. She decides that she had better sleep with him as soon as he musters the courage to ask.

What is it that she finds so horrifying about this idea, she wonders? She realises that the problem is not just that Ferenc isn't Marco, but something inherent to Ferenc himself. His wounded leg doesn't help, but Sari's never been squeamish, and if everything else were in place that would fail to put her off. She doesn't care for the pale pink of his skin, or the insipid blue eyes and fair hair, equating them with childish-ness; she doesn't like his slow, lumbering mind, or his deliberate and ponderous way of speaking – but it's not these things that bring out a cold sheen of sweat on her skin when she thinks about being naked in front of him. It's the way he looks at her, hungry and desperate. She remembers this from before she went away, and she had always found it obscurely flattering that she could see how much he wanted her. Now, it's just alarming. Whether the war has added an edge to him, or whether she's just learnt more about love, the fact remains that there is nothing tender in those eyes, he does not look at her with pleasure or pride or fondness, but with gaping need, and a desire to possess.

CHAPTER THIRTEEN

Later, Sari wonders, sometimes, where exactly the line was. It's an irrelevant question. The point is that the line was crossed, and that had consequences, and whether or not those consequences were appropriate is also irrelevant. But it's funny, really, that sometimes so much happens, so quickly, that when you react, it's impossible to tell what you're reacting to, and Sari wonders whether, if things had just been a tiny bit different, if things had been bad but *not that bad*, she would have swallowed her doubts and got on with things. It isn't a nice thought, but then, the reality isn't nice either.

Ferenc is always quiet these days, but Sari is perceptive enough to be able to tell when the timbre of his silence changes. When she brings him his dinner that night – three, four weeks after he has come home? – the atmosphere in her father's house is like a blow to the face, and she feels the atavistic heart of herself respond, hairs rising on the nape of her neck; *something is wrong here.*

He's sitting at the table in the dark – again, there's nothing unusual in this; it's as if stimulus hurts him, which is why he has to hide from it, even in that house – and there's

153

something in the tense line of his shoulders that makes Sari think, *this is not good*. Part of her wants to simply leave the food on the table and slip away – surely it's not beyond him to heat it up? – but she ignores that impulse. This is the man she's going to marry, and so she's not going to run away from his every mood, because soon, she won't have anywhere to run.

She sets the pan on the table, lights the lamp, and begins to prepare his food. She doesn't speak, and for a long while, neither does he. It is only when she puts the plate of paprika chicken in front of him that he says, in a voice hoarse through disuse, not looking up from the table, 'I saw something interesting today.'

Oh, God. 'Did you?' Sari asks, her voice deliberately light.

He nods, but says nothing, and starts to eat. Sari is still, but some part deep inside her is trembling. She looks down at the table, too, watching him from underneath her lashes, counting every spoonful of food that goes into his mouth, willing the meal to be over so that she can escape.

'Do you want to know what it was that I saw?'

Go carefully here, Sari tells herself. He's trying to provoke a response and she will not give it to him. 'What was it?' She is suddenly thankful that she is not a good conversationalist at the best of times; her voice sounds stilted to her, but it's not far from normal.

'I saw your friend Anna, Anna Csillag, Károly's wife, Anna. She was going into the woods with a man that I didn't recognise. He looked like he was one of the men from the camp. They were laughing.' There's a pause, tight, crackling. 'What do you think they might have been doing, Sari?'

Feigning ignorance would be transparent, she realises.

Instead, she sighs. 'I don't think that's any of our business, Ferenc.'

'Do you know what I think?'

She doesn't answer; it doesn't seem like he's expecting her to.

'I think that Anna's been playing the whore. Your good friend Anna. What do *you* think, Sari?'

Again, she doesn't answer. He's staring at her now, and it's just about killing her pride not to look him in the eyes, but she has an idea that it would just enrage him.

'And I think maybe Anna's not the only one playing the whore, Sari. When we were going to Judit's the other night, I saw some men in the village, some men who shouldn't have been there at all. I don't know what's going on down at that prison camp, but I think I'm getting an idea of what's going on in this village. Do you want to tell me about it, Sari?'

She can't stay silent forever. 'All right, yes, some of the women here have been going with the men down at the camp—'

'While their husbands have been fighting and dying for them?' He speaks loudly, but more than anger, hurt vibrates through every word. Sari feels a lurch of pity, though not of guilt; *things happen*, is what she thinks, *and people hurt other people, and what's done is done.* She feels sorry for Ferenc, though; deep, crushing sorrow that he feels that he and the others have been heroes, and that they're not getting the treatment that they deserve.

'And what about you, Sari?' he asks then, his voice lowered now, but intense. 'What have you been doing while I've been away?'

'What? Nothing!' Mingled guilt and fear hit her like a slap in the face, stunning her momentarily.

'You've been going down there—'

'To nurse! To help them with problems that the doctor can't deal with! Nothing more!' She suddenly feels flooded with outrage, and she clings to it gratefully; for a moment she's almost convinced that she really has been doing nothing wrong, and she knows that she must believe it, if she's to convince him.

'Why should I believe you?' he asks.

She doesn't know what he wants to hear, and the silence stretches between them, until, with staggering suddenness he seizes the plate in front of him, and throws it against the wall, where it shatters. '*Why should I believe you?*' he yells.

She has never lost her temper before, not since she was a small child, but there's something about the tantrum that he is throwing, the wanton destruction, the fact that he is suspecting her infidelity out of pure paranoia rather than anything solid that stirs her to action and before she has the chance to judge whether she is being wise or not, she is on her feet, eyes blazing, head thrown back.

'I cook for you, I clean for you, I look after your injuries, I wrote to you every week while you were away. What reason have I given you to doubt me? I live with Judit and I spend my time taking care of sick people. When would I have had time to have this affair that you've imagined for me? Why would I do something like this? *What reason have I given you to doubt me?*'

She doesn't shout, but it's as if she has; the silence when she stops speaking is ringing. She's still for a moment, then turns, takes a cloth, and starts to clean up the mess that he has made.

When she hears his footsteps behind her, she tenses, not knowing whether to expect a kick in the ribs or a reconciliation. A series of bangs and thumps and he crouches down behind her – not an easy task with his injured leg – and puts his hand on her shoulder. 'I'm sorry,' he says, quietly.

'It's all right.' It isn't. Of course it isn't.

'You're right, you've never given me reason to doubt.'

She puts the cloth down and turns to him, realising that he had been testing her, rather than accusing her, that the last thing that he wants to believe is in her infidelity – such an affront to his honour would be disastrous to him, as well as to her – and so he will clutch at any straw to avoid it.

Not knowing what to say, she says again, 'It's all right.'

Ferenc shakes his head. 'No, it's not all right. *Nothing* is all right. Nothing.'

He rocks backwards so that he is sitting on the floor and puts his head in his hands, and with utter horror, Sari realises that he is crying. She tries to think how she should behave in this situation. No matter how she feels about their engagement, leaving him weeping on the floor surrounded by scraps of food and broken plate seems callous. Awkwardly, she reaches out to grip his shoulder, and he lurches forward, wrapping his arms around her waist, and burying his head in her breasts. Immobile for a moment, she thinks *like a child*, and strangely, it's a comforting thought; children, she can deal with. Tentatively she puts her arms around him and kisses his hair, and when, after a few minutes he raises his head and kisses her, pushes her down onto her back and lifts up her skirts, she feels the weight of inevitability on top of her and does nothing to stop him.

As they have sex on the kitchen floor she steps outside of herself, able to watch the proceedings with a sort of remote interest. It's no worse than she thought it would be, at least, but although she longed for this with Marco, with Ferenc it seems like such a bizarre thing to be doing. It doesn't last long – a quick, sharp pain, a minute or so of breathlessness and then he slumps, face beatific, as if he's travelled far into another dimension, while she's remained here on the kitchen floor.

After a while, he sits up, and that's when they notice the blood.

'I'm sorry,' he says again, and sounds genuinely regretful. 'I didn't mean to hurt you.'

'It didn't really hurt,' she says, absently; inside, she realises that she has just proven her fidelity as much as it could ever be proven in his eyes.

'I love you, Sari.' It's the first time he's said it in so many words. She recognises the lie behind the words, but recognises also that it's a lie that he believes.

'I know you do,' she replies. He seems content with that.

When she goes back to Judit's that night, Judit knows, straight away, and Sari is taken aback by her reaction.

'Did he hurt you?' Judit asks, with a steeliness in her tone that Sari hasn't heard before, and it takes Sari a moment to realise that Judit's asking whether Ferenc raped her. She shakes her head, and Judit relaxes, but it disconcerts Sari that rape was Judit's first assumption.

'Why did you ask that?'

'I'm sorry. I'm just worried for you.'

'He wouldn't do something like that,' Sari says, uncertain. The Ferenc that she knew four years ago wouldn't have done something like that. The Ferenc that she knew four years ago also wouldn't stay shut up in a house for weeks on end, and he certainly wouldn't throw plates and food. This new Ferenc is a worrying proposition, and Sari is both heartened and depressed that she is not the only person to think so.

She needs to think.

'Anna, would you do something for me?'

Next morning, and the sun is low and bright. Anna's face is beautifully open and uncomplicated.

'Of course. What do you want me to do?'

'Will you let me use your house for a couple of hours this afternoon? Just, I don't know, go for a walk, or something, but let me borrow your house. Please.'

Sari does not look at Anna when she says this, but she can imagine Anna's face, full of consternation.

'This is for Marco, isn't it?' Anna says. 'You want somewhere to go together?'

Sari nods. Anna's house is perfect – set a little way out from the main part of Falucska, with a side door that can be easily accessed without being seen by the village. Anna has never met Giovanni there; she's able to ignore her betrayal of Károly when she's not in such familiar surroundings, but Sari is hoping that's not going to stop her from letting her and Marco use it.

When Anna doesn't answer, she raises her head. '*Please*, Anna,' she begs.

'I don't know, Sari. I mean, when Ferenc was away, it was all very well, but now . . .'

'*Please*.'

Sari can read the disapproval on Anna's face, and has a good idea of what she is thinking. She's never said as much, but it is clear that Anna has justified her own infidelity by Károly's vicious behaviour, that Anna has created a moral universe in which betraying a bad man is acceptable, but betraying a decent one is not – a fact that can be overlooked when the decent man in question is far away, but not when he is there. In Anna's mind, Ferenc is a decent man, and Sari doesn't have the heart to dispute that, nor is she sure enough herself of who or what Ferenc is any more.

But Anna capitulates, as Sari knew she would. She's going down to the camp later to see Giovanni, and Sari gives her a note to pass to Marco. She's never written in Italian before, but urgency has overcome shyness, though she still blushes at the thought of the terrible mistakes she must have made. And then she waits.

She's in Anna's house early that afternoon and time seems to stretch like honey. He's not coming; of course he's not coming, and he's sensible not to come. Anna was right, it was a stupid plan, stupid and wrong, stupid and wrong and *dangerous*, and Sari should just give up and go home; she has work to do, after all. She stands up and sits back down, half hoping, then stands again, and has taken one tentative step towards the front door when she hears the light tap on the side door.

It's only been a few weeks since she saw him last, but Marco looks older than she remembered, and more worried. He comes into the house quickly and shuts the door behind him.

'Did anyone see you come?'

'Of course not.'

For a long, tense minute, they seem to have nothing to say to each other, and simply stand gazing at one another; Sari feels oddly combative, almost expecting him to strike at any moment, to accuse her of recklessness and stupidity. *You didn't have to come*; she's already responding mentally to his anticipated attack. Then he smiles, swiftly and suddenly, and her bones melt.

'I missed you,' he says.

Inhibitions loosened, she crosses to where he is standing, lifts herself up on tiptoe and kisses him, deceptively chastely, on the lips.

'What are . . .' he begins, but she hushes him.

'Don't talk. We shouldn't be here, and we shouldn't be doing this. We won't get another chance, but I . . .' She stops, suddenly shy. 'I wanted to give you something.'

Five minutes later, Marco is lying on his back on pile of eiderdowns on the floor – Sari is too protective of Anna's feelings to use the bed – with Sari rearing up above him, and it occurs to him, briefly, hazily, as she slowly, slowly lowers herself onto him, how few pleasures in life are really complete, how he's dreamt and hoped for this moment for nearly two years, yet now that it's happening, he can't quite let go of the knowledge that the only reason it's happening is because Sari has been possessed by another man. That is his last coherent thought before the heady spiralling down into sensation begins. Then there is nothing, nothing but Sari, her body, an arc, a bow, hushed breaths lapping against the silence.

Afterwards, he asks her – diffident as a schoolboy – how it was for her, and, being Sari, she refrains from glib pleasantries, but instead bites her lip, thinking.

'It wasn't as nice as some of the other things that we've done,' she says after a while, 'But it was good in a different way. More . . . more *real*. More about us.'

'Did Ferenc—' he starts, but she shakes her head violently, eyes screwed shut, forehead pressed against his shoulder.

'Don't talk about him,' she says.

They lie there in silence, then, until Marco starts to shiver. 'It's cold.'

'I should go,' Sari says, and Marco curses his feeble, warm-blooded body. If he'd just been able to lie there, still, for a little longer . . .

'You were serious, weren't you, when you said that this was the last time? This won't happen again.'

'No,' she says. 'Perhaps we were silly to do this; perhaps it's just going to make things worse – but it all seemed so unfinished, before.'

He nods. 'You'll still be coming down to the camp, though, won't you?'

'I think so, for the time being.' The unstated implication being *unless Ferenc decides to stop me*. 'There's no reason to avoid me when I come, though. We were friends before any of this started, and so maybe . . .' she shrugs.

'Maybe,' he echoes. He looks at her, watches her make the deliberate mental shift between being with Marco to being with Ferenc, and he can't stop himself.

'I'm sorry, I know you don't want to talk about him with me, but I have to ask. Is he treating you well? Tell me at least that much.'

She's torn between the desire not to lie to him, and the desire not to worry him, because what good would that do, after all? As a compromise, she says, 'He's treating me as well as he knows how.' As soon as she's said the words she can taste their inadequacy, knowing that all she's done is imply vague problems, without giving Marco any information at all.

He seems satisfied with her answer, though, perhaps having expected nothing more from her. She is dressed now, tucking her hair behind her ears with impatience; he tugs on his trousers, and within a couple of minutes he is ready.

'Thank Anna for me,' he says, as they scout from the back door, checking that no one will see him leave.

Sari laughs.

'I think she's horrified at my behaviour, though she didn't say anything. She's a good friend, Anna.' She glances quickly from left to right, and nods. 'No one's here. You should go now—' but he can't quite bring himself to leave; he takes her face between his palms, and leans in until their foreheads are touching.

'Goodbye, Sari.'

She tries to laugh: 'Don't be so dramatic! You'll see me,' but he shakes his head.

'Not like this. Remember this, Sari – will you promise me that? No matter how hard it gets.'

His words are garbled, but she reaches for the meaning behind them, and grasps something, at least.

'I will. I promise.'

And he leaves, bounding down the back steps, running across the grass, slowing to a walk when he gets to a safe distance. She watches his every step. He doesn't turn around.

CHAPTER FOURTEEN

That should have been the end of it, and for a week or so, it seems like it is.

Ferenc is chastened and quiet for the first few days after his accusation of infidelity, and Sari is not quite sure whether he should be coaxed out of the self-castigating mood he's clearly fallen into, or left to it. She decides on the latter. Although they're not yet married, Sari realises that how she behaves towards him now can serve as a template for how she behaves towards him for the rest of her life, and she's seen enough marriages in which the wife caters to the husbands every whim, humouring his foul moods, to know that's not the sort of marriage that she wants, nor the sort of marriage she could possibly sustain, as her prickly nature is bound to sabotage it sooner or later.

Sure enough, Ferenc gradually begins to emerge from his slump, and Sari is just beginning to congratulate herself on how well she has dealt with him when he hits her.

Afterwards, she can never quite remember how it came about. It is evening, he has just finished eating his dinner, and she is washing his plate. They are talking, unusually, just casual conversation about Sari's work, the people who are ill at the moment, and what Sari has done for them. And then he says something – what? Later, she can never quite remember – something that strikes her as silly, and so she laughs a little and says something back – what, again? – something that implies that he's said something wrong, and that she knows more than he does on this particular subject. The next thing she knows, her cheek is hot and smarting, and she can taste blood against her teeth, and it takes a moment for her to understand that the reason for the pain and the blood is that he's struck her a swift back-hander.

Hand to her face, she just looks at him, astounded, and he stands, staring back, breathing harshly and heavily.

'Don't be cheeky,' he says at last, as if drawing the reason from somewhere deep inside him, and then goes upstairs. Sari winces slightly with every loud step, hating herself for her instinctive fear.

She finishes washing the plate before she does anything else, checking it carefully for marks, drying it and putting it away. She leaves then, shutting the door carefully behind her, and steps out into the dark. Her face burns and pounds, and her mind is working furiously. No one has ever hit her before, not even her father, and the assault on her pride and dignity is intense. She's angry, yes, but she's more astonished than anything else, and it's that sense of shock that dispels her initial intention to sneak into the house and hide from Judit. Instead, she walks straight up the steps, opens the door, and announces to the kitchen at large:

'He hit me.'

Judit stares at her for a moment, as if preparing to shout or scream, then shakes her head. 'Sit down,' she says.

Sari does, falling heavily into a chair by the table. Judit brings a cloth and water, and cleans her up as best she can. The side of her mouth is split and bleeding, one entire side of her face is blooming with bruises, but when Judit instructs her to run her tongue along her teeth she's pleased to find that they're all still sound.

'That's something, then,' Judit says, her tone grim. Sari is waiting for the lecture she knows to be inevitable, but Judit stays silent until she's finished tending Sari's cuts and bruises, and then sits down opposite her.

'What happened?' she asks.

Sari feels panicky, drawn by a thousand contradictory impulses – to protect her pride, to rail against Ferenc's behaviour, to protect Ferenc (surprisingly), to break down and wail. She lifts her shoulders with a desperate hitching motion.

'I don't know. We were talking – I thought everything was fine. He's been depressed this week, quiet, and today he seemed much better, he was talking and everything – and I said something, I don't really remember what – and he hit me.'

She pauses, and then looks at Judit with genuine bewilderment. 'He said I was being cheeky.'

A man hitting a woman, a husband hitting a wife – that's nothing new and unusual, they both know that; Sari has stark memories of Anna, ashamed, trying to hide her injuries before Károly went away, and Judit's long experience has included several evenings tending women who have been punched and kicked and otherwise abused; she's learnt what men will do, and the few things that women can do to stop them. But Sari – this wasn't supposed to happen to Sari, they both know that, too.

'Break the engagement,' Judit says abruptly. It's what Sari is thinking herself. Breaking the engagement could be social disaster; her chances of marrying someone else in the village are slim, slimmer still now that she's no longer a virgin, and for a woman for whom marriage and children were of utmost importance, it would be unthinkable. But those things have never been desperately important to Sari, other than a vague assumption that they would be part of her future; financially, she is as close to being an independent woman as is possible in that place, and she knows that as long as Judit is alive, she can go on working with her. And after that – well, she could take on Judit's role, or, if life in the village after having jilted the son of the most important family there proved unbearable, she could always leave.

But then there's Ferenc. The war has wrought terrible changes in him but perhaps the real Ferenc, happy and clear-eyed and hopeful as he had been four years ago, is still there somewhere. Sari remembers how determined he was to marry her and to take care of her, despite the risk to his reputation and standing in the village, and the thought of giving up on him now gives her a lurch of shame. It's not as if he's changed without reason, and beyond recognition – four years of suffering can break a person, but that doesn't mean that they can't be fixed.

'I'm not going to tell you what to do,' Judit says, breaking Sari's freewheeling thoughts, 'But I will tell you one thing that I know, from seeing this happen to women over and over again. A man will never do this just once. The first time, women always say *oh, he's never done it before, it's not like him, it won't happen again* – but it always happens again. Always.'

Sari nods. She cannot – *will* not – live like that, sneaking around the village hiding her bruises as if she's the one doing something wrong. Not for anyone will she embrace that life and yet she wants to give Ferenc a chance.

'I'll go and see him tomorrow, and tell him that I won't marry him if he ever does it again,' Sari says.

Judit frowns, looking dubious. 'Sari—'

'No, it's all right, I promise – because I really will break the engagement if it happens again; I'm not scared of the consequences. I just want to give him a chance. You know, a week ago, when we had sex – before that, he shouted at me and broke a plate, and then for the next few days he was very quiet and sad, very apologetic. I think he'll be like that again tomorrow. I think he'll listen to me.'

The next morning, the bruising isn't as bad as Sari feared; certainly not very noticeable as long as she keeps her head down and nobody looks at her too closely. She considers going over to speak to Ferenc straight away, but decides to give him a little longer to cool down, and instead gathers together some supplies of arnica for Luigi's ankle, and heads down to the camp.

Luigi greets her cheerfully; the swelling seems to have gone down a little, and she rebandages it and gives him something for the pain. He doesn't comment on the marks on her face, and Sari mentally thanks Judit for her swift work last night – the last thing that she could bear would be people looking at her with concern and pity. Just as she's about to leave, she's approached by Umberto, who is concerned about some insect bites on his arm; she reassures him as best she can that it's nothing to be worried about, and is halfway down the stairs on the way out before she sees Marco.

He starts to smile when he sees her, and then suddenly his smile falls away; Sari feels her heart drop into the pit of her stomach. She goes to push past him but he grabs her shoulder and turns her around to face him. One hand gripping her to stop her bolting, he pushes her hair back from her face, and lifts her chin, staring at her hard. She should have known, she thinks miserably, if anyone was going to look at her intently it was going to be Marco.

'Did he hit you?' he asks. His voice is low but shaking; Marco is quick tempered but she has never seen him angry like this, cold and controlled.

'Marco—'

'Sari. *Did he hit you?*'

Think, she tells herself. She considers and discards all sorts of implausible excuses – she walked into a door, she fell down and hit her head on the table, she opened a window too vigorously – it would do Marco no good to have him know the truth. But the pause she has left is already a fraction too long, and she sees his eyes change as her silence confirms his suspicions. His lips draw back from his teeth in an unconscious snarl, and in a low hiss he expels a string of vicious curses. All she can do now is try to limit the damage.

'Marco, listen to me,' she says, but he is still cursing. She takes his shoulder and gives him a little shake. '*Listen.*'

He looks at her again, eyes narrowed.

'He hit me last night for the first time. I won't stand for it. I'm going to speak to him today, and tell him that if he ever does it again that I will break the engagement.'

He's already shaking his head. 'No. No, no, no. You must leave him now. He won't listen to you.'

'I think he will. He was a good man before the war, Marco, and he deserves another chance.'

Marco gives a harsh, bitter bark of laughter. 'He deserves *nothing*.'

At that, Sari feels her temper snap. The last thing she needs at this moment is to be pampering another man's thwarted, frustrated ego.

'You listen to me,' she says coldly. 'You have no right to talk to me about my life here, no right to tell me what to do – *none*. You have made it clear from the start that at the end of the war you will go back to your beautiful, virtuous wife, and so you've renounced any right to make judgements on what I do here. I have to make a life for myself without you as a consideration, and I'm doing that.'

She takes a deep breath; Marco looks so astonished at her outburst that she softens her tone somewhat in sympathy. 'It's kind of you to be concerned, and thank you for that. But this is the way that it's always been between us, just a holiday from real life. I don't tell you what you and Benigna should do when you get home, and you need to trust me to make the right choices in my own life. You know me, and you know that I'm not the sort of person who will stand to be treated like this by Ferenc. But you don't know Ferenc, and I do, so you have to leave me to handle this in my own way.'

He lets go of her and drops his head, rubbing his face in despair and weariness. 'I love you, Sari,' he says helplessly. 'I never meant for this to happen.'

She doesn't know quite what he means by that, but it doesn't matter; she takes his hand in one of hers and kisses it. 'I know,' she says. 'We'll be all right.'

Marco thought the war was bad, he thought his injury was bad, and the long months after that, with the pain and the memory-loss and the confusion, but he was wrong, he would laugh at that now. He didn't know what *bad* meant. This is the worst, he thought; this impotence, sitting uselessly on the edge of his bed, clenching and unclenching his hands, unable to think about anything but Sari, Sari and Ferenc, whether right now he is hitting her again, beating her perhaps, beating her and raping her. An image of her face is constantly before him, as if it's been burnt onto his eyes – her expression, angry and humiliated and defiant all at once, and he buries the heels of his hands in his eyes to try and drive it away.

Sari is right: Ferenc's in a pliable, repentant mood when she visits him that afternoon. He looks at her with sad, watery eyes, and when, her voice stern, she says: 'I have to talk to you,' he dissolves, head in his hands, sobbing piteously, promising that he will never hurt her again.

'You mustn't,' she says, 'because if you do, I will not marry you. And if you hurt me after we're married, I will leave you.'

He raises his head and gazes at her with amazement, tears forgotten (very quickly forgotten) on his cheeks. 'You can't do that.'

'I can, and I will.'

'But—'

'I don't need you, Ferenc. I don't need your status and I don't need your money. If I wasn't fond of you, and if I didn't feel that you weren't yourself when you hit me last night, I would break the engagement now. But I know that things are very difficult for you now, and that the war caused a lot of damage, and I know that you are a good man. So you deserve another chance.'

He frowns, as if unsure whether he should be affronted or grateful; he plumps for the latter.

'Thank you, Sari. And I am so sorry. I will never lay a hand on you again.'

Does she believe him? She's not sure, but she believes in herself enough to know that she will keep her word, and that she's strong enough to leave him if he breaks his promise. That's enough for now.

CHAPTER FIFTEEN

Evening is racing in across the plain, and Sari is standing at the stove in her father's house, heating up Ferenc's dinner, when everything starts crashing down. She doesn't really heed the footsteps at first, pounding on the path outside – someone running home for supper, perhaps – but the steps don't go past the house. Instead, they seem to be approaching, and as Sari carefully puts down the pan she is holding she just knows – not exactly what is going to happen, but she knows that it's going to be bad. She turns to Ferenc, who is rising from the table, looking alarmed.

'Who—?'

'I'll go and check,' she says. She's surprised at how calm she is. Perhaps it's just Judit, perhaps someone's fallen ill, perhaps everything is going to be all right after all.

It's Marco.

He's standing on the front steps with a wild look in his eyes, and for a moment Sari is paralysed, she can't move, because surely this is too nightmarish a scenario to be true.

'Go!' she hisses, her voice sounding unfamiliar with panic.

Marco's face doesn't change, and he doesn't turn around. Instead, he grabs her wrist.

'I've changed my mind,' he says. He's not shouting but still Sari recoils from the volume of his voice, with Ferenc just inside. 'I can't leave you here. Come with me. I won't be missed for another two hours, we can get far enough away in that time to be safe—'

'Marco, are you insane?'

'I don't know. I don't care. I won't leave you here. You know the plain, we can hide out for a couple of days, and then head for Budapest—'

'But Ferenc—'

And Ferenc speaks, from just behind Sari's shoulder. 'Sari, who is it?' and then drops into silence as he looks out the front door and sees a tall, furious-looking Italian officer gripping the wrist of his fiancée, staring at her ardently.

Ferenc's brain does not move quickly, and just as he is beginning to process this information and draw the obvious conclusions, Marco springs. He has a couple of inches on Ferenc, and the element of surprise; moreover, he's both fit and furious and then Ferenc is on the floor with an almighty crash, Marco crouching over him, pounding his face again and again with a sound like rotten fruit falling from a tree.

Sari watches, blank, her life dissolving before her eyes until she notices Marco's raised fist is slick with blood and that wakes her up. She screams for Marco to stop it, unsure whether she's speaking in Magyar or Italian or neither, she bounds across the room and grabs Marco's hand, which is just starting its next inexorable downward swing. The force of movement nearly wrenches her arm out of its socket but she hangs on, and Marco turns to look at her, his face frighteningly white and vacant.

Taking a deep breath, Sari says in clear, careful Italian: 'Get up. Get off him.'

For a moment, it looks as if Marco hasn't heard or understood what she's said, but slowly some animation returns to his face, and without taking his eyes off Sari he rises to his feet, stepping back from Ferenc's prone body. With a twitching, hitching movement, Ferenc turns over and clambers to his knees. Blood is pouring from his nose, and his face is already rising in a collection of plum-coloured bruises. Lifting his hand, he opens his mouth and spits out two teeth. Then, silent and expressionless, he turns around and thumps up the stairs.

'You have to go,' Sari says, turning to Marco. He is looking down at his bruised and bleeding hands with what seems like incomprehension. 'You have to go,' she says again, louder this time, urgent. Things have been shattered, and she doesn't know what she can do to fix them, but she knows that she can't do anything with Marco here. And his crazy talk about them leaving together – oh, she's touched, there's a warm fluttering in the pit of her stomach despite the awfulness of the evening's events, but it's impossible, and he must see that it's impossible.

She hears Ferenc moving about upstairs, and gives Marco a gentle shove towards the door. 'Please go. For both of our sakes.'

'I can't,' he says simply.

What happens next happens very quickly. There is a sound like thunder – Ferenc running down the stairs. Sari feels him move behind her, very close, and then pain pours through her head as he grabs her by the hair, winding it roughly around his fist, pulling so tightly that her chin is raised, her neck aching. She sees Marco's expression change from wariness to horror, and that's when she becomes aware of the cold, round barrel pressing into her left temple.

'Let's go,' Ferenc says through clenched teeth. Sari feels the puff of his breath on her cheek, and of course Marco doesn't understand, but when Ferenc roars 'Move!' his meaning becomes clearer. An awkward, four-legged beast, Sari and Ferenc shuffle towards the door, Marco ahead of them, casting desperate glances back in Sari's direction. They stumble down the stairs and over the silvery grass, wet with dew, towards the forest.

This is it, Sari thinks. She's surprised to find that she's not afraid. She wonders where Ferenc got the gun. She wonders whether death will be painful, and whether Ferenc will kill her or Marco first. She looks up at the moon, bobbing white and serene over the treetops, and is comforted by the thought that other people are looking at that moon, other people who are oblivious to the sordid little drama being played out in Sari's corner of the world.

'Stop,' Ferenc commands, and they lurch to a halt. They're not so deep in the woods that Sari can't see the faint glimmer of lights from the village through the trees, but they're far enough away that they won't be disturbed, she's sure of that. She knows every inch of these woods, every gnarled stump and skein of bracken, and the familiarity is steadying – but whenever she looks at Marco, it's as if she's seeing the woods through his eyes, the inexplicable tangles of blackness, the tilted unevenness of the ground, the eerie noises that surround them. *Oh, Marco*, she thinks, *what a frightening and alien place to die.*

Ferenc unwinds her hair a couple of times so that he's still holding her, but she's not pressed so tightly against him, and as she moves away she catches sight of his face – bone white in the moonlight and still swimming with blood. His eyes look as flat and expressionless as pieces of silver, and his mouth is twisted into a strange expression as if he's forgotten to remove an earlier smile. She realises then how stupid she was to think that it was possible to reason with him, to believe any promise that he made; she realises that the essential Ferenc has gone, the disintegration starting during the war and ending in these last, deceptively calm few weeks. Yet, despite the circumstances she feels a brief flare of pity for him.

'You've been fucking my fiancée,' Ferenc says to Marco. His tone is mild and almost friendly. Marco looks quickly between Sari and Ferenc, frowning in incomprehension, and Sari fights back the temptation to translate for him; what good would it do, anyhow? The moon glints off the barrel as Ferenc moves the gun until it's pointing at Marco. His hand is steady.

'Run,' he says to Marco. Marco doesn't understand, and looks imploringly at Sari. Ferenc tugs roughly on her hair. 'Tell him,' he orders.

'He wants you to run,' Sari says to Marco in Italian. Her voice is barely above a whisper and her lips feel numb. Marco's brow creases; it's as if, even now, he can't quite believe the ridiculousness of the situation. Nothing in his ordered, civilised background has prepared him for the rough and ready way that things work out here. Spreading his hands, head on one side, he takes a step towards Ferenc, like this is just a misunderstanding over a game of cards that can be easily worked out with a bit of sensible discussion.

Ferenc shrugs. 'Suit yourself,' he says, and smiles, black gaps glaring from his bloodstained mouth.

Sari sees Marco fall. For a split second she thinks he must have tripped, and then she hears the shot – a dry crack, like someone stepping on a twig, only louder – and notices the dark smear in the centre of Marco's forehead. She feels nothing, dimly realises that she must be in shock, and is thankful for it. Thankful still when Ferenc pushes her roughly down into the sodden leaves on the ground, pushes her skirt up, and fucks her, hard, unyieldingly, and yet she's only faintly aware of the pain, the burning, the wet smell of the leaves, the slimy feel of them on her back and he slaps her once, twice, turning her face from side to side and then he is spent, panting like a dog on top of her as she stares at an unrecognisable shape she only later realises is Marco's lifeless legs.

She's suddenly cold as Ferenc lifts himself off her but she doesn't move.

'Get up,' he says, but she still doesn't move. 'Get up,' he says again, accompanied this time by a kick to her ribs.

She gets up. She feels nothing, though a dozen emotions occur to her (anger? grief? humiliation?) – she just can't be bothered to deal with any of them right now.

'Come on,' Ferenc says. He's let go of her hair now, and is gripping her wrist instead. They move away from Marco's body and the shadows close in on it behind them, but Sari is unconcerned; whatever it is that made Marco is gone, and what's left is just a husk. She wonders half-heartedly where Ferenc is taking her, and why he doesn't just kill her there, with Marco, but then realises that he is leading her out of the woods – not back towards the village, no, nor towards her father's house, but in a wide, sweeping arc across the plain. They are heading for the camp, for his old house.

Gunther is on guard, standing at the gates, and he scarcely looks up when they approach. 'Excuse me,' Ferenc says in German – his German is very good, better than Sari's though she's loath to admit it – and Gunther raises his head, his bored expression vanishing as he takes in the blood, the manic glint in Ferenc's eyes, Sari's white, strained face. His hand moves for his gun, but Ferenc reaches out and seizes his wrist, stopping him.

'Ah, no,' he says, indulgently, as if he is talking to a child, 'You won't need that. My name is Ferenc Gazdag, and my family owns this property.'

Gunther's eyes widen. It's hard to believe that this blood-stained, half-mad looking wretch can be from the richest family in the village, but his precise, accentless German, and his easy, urbane manner support his claim.

'I just thought I should let you know,' Ferenc continues, in the same easy, friendly manner, 'that one of your prisoners is dead in the woods over there. He has been fucking my fiancée, you see. You should probably go and collect the body. If anyone asks what happened to him, you should tell them that he was shot while trying to escape.'

Gunther's mouth falls open, closes, and opens again. 'What? But—'

Ferenc shakes his head, smiling slightly. 'No arguments, please. My family has allowed our property to be used in good faith. I doubt that my parents – or your superiors – would be happy to hear how things have been run around here, how enemy prisoners have been allowed to walk around the village and take advantage of our women. I don't think they'd like that at all, do you?'

Gunther is silent for a moment, looking stunned. Slowly, he shakes his head.

'So you'll stick to my story, then? Good. I am a proud man, you see, and I don't want people to know what this little bitch—' his composure slips slightly as he shakes Sari by the shoulder – 'what Sari has been up to.'

By the time they get back to the house – walking the long way again so that they won't be seen – lights are bobbing in the woods; Gunther has despatched some of his men to find Marco's body. Ferenc has not said a word since they left the camp, but nor has he let go of Sari's shoulder, and she knows that she will have bruises in the pattern of his fingers later.

Ferenc shuts the door quietly behind them, and on some level Sari knows that she should find his façade of calm frightening, but she just cannot summon the energy. It's as if all the vital, vibrant parts of her have flickered out, leaving an insipid, disinterested shell behind. He turns from the door, again with that unsettling smile, and walks towards her, pulls back his arm, and punches her in the face. All his weight is behind that punch. She falls. The beating goes on for a long time, and then there is space, and silence. It's as if she's still falling.

When she comes to, she is lying in bed and Ferenc is sitting beside her, dabbing at her swollen face with a damp cloth. He's cleaned himself up and changed clothes, and looks deceptively normal. His hands on Sari's face are gentle, and when she opens her eyes he doesn't stop what he's doing, cleaning the blood from the corner of her mouth.

When he is finished, he looks at her and gives a friendly grin. 'Quite a set of bruises you've got here, Sari! You're going to be a sight for the next few days, silly girl.' He pushes her hair back from her face, and she winces slightly as he grazes a cut on her scalp. 'How are you feeling?'

How is she feeling? There are no words. 'All right,' she says.

'Good girl.' He smiles again, looking into her face. 'We need to have a bit of a talk, Sari. Things are going to change a lot for you, and I'm sorry about that, but you do see that you've brought it on yourself, don't you?'

She doesn't answer, but he doesn't seem to expect her to.

'Now, you're going to be living here from now on. I already spoke to Judit about it, and she didn't seem too happy, but that's her problem, the dried up old cunt. You're not to go out without my permission, and I should tell you now that I'll only give you permission to go out to the market, or to do washing. No more work for you, Sari. I'm sorry if that sounds harsh, but you see, it's how all this trouble started in the first place, isn't it?'

Again, she says nothing.

'And if you have any thoughts about running away, Sari, you should forget them right now. My family knows people in all the villages around here, and if you leave, they will help me find you. And I will find you, Sari, I will not give up until I find you, and then I will kill you. Do you understand me?'

She nods gingerly, and he smiles, obviously pleased.

'Good girl. That's what I like to see. I'm sorry to have to be so strict, but you must see that I can't tolerate this sort of behaviour, can't you? A lot of men wouldn't be so forgiving, but I love you, Sari, and so if you're good, I'm still prepared to marry you, even though you're spoiled goods. Not many men would be so generous, you know. Really, you should thank me.' His face hardens suddenly. 'Thank me, Sari.'

'Thank you,' she whispers. He voice is cracked and painful.

'Say my name.'

'Thank you, Ferenc.'

He claps his hands, looking delighted again. 'Very good!

You're welcome, Sari. And now—' he yawns theatrically. 'Well, it's been a busy day, so it's about time for bed, don't you think?'

Without waiting for an answer, he gets to his feet and strips off his shirt and trousers. Sari notices that his body bears the marks of where Marco hit him – it seems like a hundred years ago. She shuts her eyes. The bed dips as he climbs in beside her, and there's a whisper as he blows out the lamp.

'Goodnight, Sari.'

Within minutes, he's snoring beside her. She stares at the ceiling, wondering if this is what it feels like to be dead. She's not so far from Marco after all.

Sari finds that she gets used to being beaten surprisingly quickly. At the end of every day, she mentally tallies what she has done to provoke Ferenc – burnt the dinner, spoken out of turn, footsteps too loud – yet no matter how careful she is, every day she seems to find a new way to offend him, which requires discipline and punishment. He doesn't *want* to do it, of course he doesn't, he insists; he loves her, so why would he want to hurt her? But he has to; it's for her own good.

Sari doesn't believe this, but she doesn't not believe it, either. Nothing really penetrates her brain any more, nothing touches her. She's shut off all the dangerous, painful parts of herself, as deliberately as someone snuffing out a candle; she's sent the important parts of herself away somewhere, leaving behind only enough to be functional. She doesn't think of the future any more, and she's forgotten the past, living in an eternal present. Sometimes she wonders why

Ferenc didn't kill her along with Marco that night, and then she realises that he basically did.

She sees Judit once by the river, and that's bad. Ferenc is usually quite good about not hitting her face on days before she is going to have to go out and be seen, but he'd given her a nosebleed the night before, and she'd managed to get blood all over the good sheets, and they need washing. Her hair is down in a way that best hides her bruises – a rather impressive black eye, in this case – and she's managed to wash the sheets without making eye contact with anyone, which is good. She's just about to leave when somebody says her name, and Judit's claw-like hand fastens on her wrist.

She never used to be this jumpy, but she drops the bundle of cloth on the ground, thereby preventing a swift escape. She doesn't look at Judit but drops straight to her knees and starts gathering them up, and much to her consternation, Judit drops to her knees beside her, puts a finger under Sari's chin, and turns her face. Sari keeps her eyes resolutely down, but feels herself flushing, knowing that Judit is taking in the new, shiny bruise, the dark smudges of old bruises, the cuts and scratches.

'Oh, Sari,' she says.

'I'm fine,' Sari says quickly, snatching the rest of the sheets from Judit and springing to her feet. Judit's face is almost more than she can bear; she's never seen her looking so upset before, and very faintly, at the back of her mind, Sari feels something, some emotion that she can't afford to let in.

'If you need me, you know where I am,' Judit says gruffly, but Sari has already turned her back on her, and is striding resolutely towards home.

CHAPTER SIXTEEN

The first time Sari is sick, she doesn't think anything of it. Ferenc kicked her hard in the stomach the day before, and when she finds herself retching over a bowl the next morning, she assumes that it's simply the aftermath, and that it will pass.

The next time she is sick, it is harder to ignore. Already the knowledge is tickling at the edge of her consciousness, but she pushes it back; impossible to think about that now. She hides it as best she can, making sure she is never ill in front of Ferenc, staying away from foods that make her feel queasy. When her time comes, she binds herself up with rags as usual, and Ferenc doesn't question anything – after all, he's not the one to do the washing, so he's not to know that the rags are clean rather than bloody by the end of the day. It is just the stress, she tells herself. Plenty of women skip their period when they are worried, or if they haven't been eating enough, both of which definitely apply to her. Things should be back to normal soon.

A few nights later, they are in bed. Ferenc has just fucked her, and she is naked, unusually – often he is happy just to push her skirts above her waist to gain access – and as he eases himself off her, she notices that he is looking at her strangely.

'You look different,' he says, eyes narrowed, slightly accusatory.

'Different how?' she asks, and he puts a hand on her breast.

'Different *here*.'

She pushes herself up onto her elbows and looks down at herself. Her breasts are bigger, undeniably, and her nipples stand out, pinker and larger than they did before. Of course she hasn't forgotten everything she learnt during her four years with Judit, and again there is a subtle click in the back of her mind, a shift in knowledge, but she is not ready to accept it.

'I suppose I'm growing up at last,' she says. He looks at her suspiciously, but says nothing more. It is two more weeks before he confronts her with it, when she is standing at mirror, brushing her hair before bed, and he comes up beside her, places a hand on her stomach, slightly swollen below the waist of her skirt.

'You're pregnant,' he says.

Click.

'Yes,' she replies. She puts down the brush and turns to him; he is biting his bottom lip, his hands curled into light fists.

'Is it mine?' he asks.

She knows she should lie. She knows that she should just tell him what he wants to hear, that his knowledge of women's bodies is such that he would believe her if she said that she has some arcane way of knowing who the father of her baby is, because he wants to believe it. Instead, she is honest.

'I don't know.'

She's prepared for the slap, and the punch that follows it

and knocks her to the floor. She's prepared for the kick in the ribs, and the kick in the stomach.

She's not prepared for the bitter, violent rage that fills her with that kick. It rushes through her with a speed that is dizzying. She hasn't felt a real emotion in weeks, and she probably should have weaned herself back onto them with something light and bearable – concern, perhaps, or sympathy. In her condition, this murderous fury has a similar effect on her that a full, rich meal would have on a starving man; she's almost maddened with it. Ghost-Sari is gone, and real, flesh-and-blood Sari is back, together with a primeval urge to protect the tiny life coiled inside her, the life that Ferenc is setting out to destroy. As he pulls back his leg to kick her again, she rolls backward, out of his range, and he flails, comically, as his foot connects with empty air. It gives her the time that she needs to get to her feet. As he staggers backwards, trying to regain his balance, she casts around for a weapon, anything that will stop him from coming at her again. She is between him and the mirror, and swiftly, instinctively, she drives her elbow into it. It shatters. She seizes a dagger-shaped shard, oblivious to it cutting into her fingers, and holds it in front of her.

'If you come closer, I will kill you,' she says. Her tone is matter-of-fact. 'You can hurt me all you want, but you will not hurt this child.'

He looks from her face to the shard and back again. She knows that he could probably overpower her. Her main weapon against him is surprise, and she doesn't know how long that will last. She takes a step towards him, and he moves back sharply, sitting down on the bed.

'Get out,' he says hoarsely. 'Get out.'

She goes.

As she runs, she feels as if the last weeks are catching up with her – emotions that she avoided at the time battering against her body in quick succession. Grief for Marco – poor, heroic, naïve, idiotic Marco – and pain and humiliation and anger for herself. How can she have let this happen? It is unthinkable. She, who has always castigated herself for a surfeit of pride, rather than a lack of it – how could she have let someone treat her like this? It's as if her real self has been on holiday for a few weeks, and is horrified to see the destruction wrought in her absence. *It's all right*, she says to her sad little shadow-self that has been holding the fort, *I'm back now. It's going to be all right.*

Despite the hour, Judit answers the doors surprisingly swiftly – perhaps it's from her habit of dealing with medical emergencies, or perhaps she's been expecting this knock on her door since she saw Sari by the river that day. Either way, she shows no surprise to see Sari standing there, but simply steps back from the door, letting Sari past. Sari looks around the familiar room, soft, worn wood, and comfortably tatty furniture, and is hit by the contrast between when she was last standing there – worried, certainly, but strong, intelligent, independent – and the way she must seem now, in her torn, tattered night dress, bare feet bloody, hair tangled, face bruised, clutching a shard of mirror in bleeding fingers.

Wordlessly, Judit extends a hand and places it on Sari's convex belly – oh, of course she knows, you can't have dealt with as many pregnant women as Judit has without knowing something like this – and a shiver of ice pours through Sari, as she notices for the first time a damp feeling on the inside of her thighs, and a red, ominous stain on the front of her night dress.

'He kicked me in the stomach,' she says. Her voice is very small. 'He was trying to kill it.'

She starts to cry. She can't remember the last time she wept, and it's a painful, wrenching experience, as she puts her face into her hands and weeps for Marco, for her baby, for herself, even a little for the man Ferenc had been. Judit holds her with an unexpected lack of awkwardness, but it doesn't last long – she's so unused to this that her tears dry up in minutes, leaving her with a bone-deep sadness and a brittle, burning rage.

When she lifts her head, Judit leads her into the bedroom, and automatically Sari climbs up onto the bed, lifting her night dress and spreading her legs. She's watched Judit do this so many times before, but still she's taken aback by Judit's gentleness as she examines Sari.

After a few anxious moments, Judit withdraws her hand. 'I think it will be all right,' she says. 'It was a hard kick that he gave you, but you're tough, and you're still pregnant.'

'But the blood . . .'

'Pregnant women sometimes bleed, you know that, and often it means nothing. You'll need to be careful over the next couple of days, but I think it will be all right.'

Sari nods, coasting on a flood of relief. She's amazed at how much she wants this baby, and how quickly that desire has seized her. The baby only became a reality when Ferenc's foot connected with her abdomen, only – what? Half an hour ago? But it's already wielding a disproportionate influence over her choices, as it seems to have taken over as the most important thing in her life.

'Do you know whose it is?' Judit asks.

'No.'

'Do you care?'

Again, Sari shakes her head, surprised to find that she is being honest. She feels no less fiercely protective of this child when imagining Ferenc to be the father than when imagining it is Marco's. It's hers – that's all that matters.

'And Ferenc?' Judit asks. Sari's not sure quite what the question is, but she answers the one in her own head.

'I'm going to kill him. I'll do it whether or not you help me, but if you help me I'll have less chance of getting caught.'

For a moment Judit says nothing, and then she gives a curt nod.

'Of course I'll help you, as much as I can. But first, you need to sleep. We can talk about things in the morning.'

'If you think that I'm just saying this because I'm tired and upset, if you think that I'll change my mind after a bit of sleep, you're wrong.' Sari's voice is sharp and cold.

Judit shakes her head. 'I don't think that at all. But if you're going to do this properly, you need to pay very careful attention to me, and I don't think you're in a state to do that, do you?'

Sari agrees, but is still reluctant. 'I won't sleep. I feel wide awake.'

'Try it, at least. If you're not asleep in half an hour tell me, and I'll give you something to help you relax.' Sari still looks dubious, and Judit adds: 'The baby needs you to rest, you know.'

That decides it. Sari lies down, wriggling under the blankets, and Judit turns down the lamp. There's a shadow of light patterning the walls, but nothing more. Sari closes her eyes, still certain that she's too overwrought to sleep, but within minutes, wave after wave of tiredness breaks over her and she slips eagerly into darkness.

When she wakes it's very early. The night is not quite properly over, but there's a hint of pink at the window. She can't have slept for long, but she feels refreshed and full of energy. In a way, she has been sleeping for the past few weeks, so it's no wonder that just a few hours are enough for her now.

There's no forgetfulness when she wakes, no period of blankness in which she doesn't remember the events of the night before: she wakes into perfect awareness, and a comforting clarity of purpose. As she swings her legs out of bed, she checks herself quickly and is relieved to find that there's no more blood on her thighs; moreover, she feels an early twinge of nausea that makes her uncommonly cheerful. She still *feels* pregnant, at least.

Judit is sitting at the table, still dressed as she was the previous night. She hasn't been to bed, and is looking exhausted. Sari feels a spasm of guilt – at Judit's age she doesn't need this sort of excitement, fleeing women and attempted murder – but despite the tired lines on her face, Judit's grin is as animated as ever.

'How are you feeling?'

'Better,' Sari says, sitting down gingerly. 'The bleeding's stopped, and I think everything is still all right – in that department, anyway. Thank you.'

'Fine, fine,' Judit says dismissively. 'No bother, you know

that. As for the other thing, though – do you remember what you said?'

Sari nods. 'I still mean it. But it's unfair of me to ask you to help me. I would understand if you refused.'

Judit shrugs. 'You were right, though. You have a better chance of getting away with it if I help you. And I'm happy to do that. You know,' she adds, contemplative, 'it's a funny thing about getting old – you start to care less and less about things that used to matter, things like morals and ethics.' She gives her characteristic cackle. 'Or maybe that's just me, I don't know. I've always been rather lacking in concern for my immortal soul, and that's certainly not changed, the older I've got.'

Judit gets to her feet, and picks up a small bowl that's sitting on the counter behind her, setting it on the table in front of Sari. When Sari looks inside, she sees that it contains a neat little rounded pyramid of powder.

'What is that?'

Judit holds up a hand. 'Before we go any further, I want to be sure that this is what you want to do.'

'It's the *only* thing I can do,' replies Sari fervently, but Judit shakes her head.

'You know I don't believe that. Remember what I told you about choices? It might be that this is the best choice, but I need to be sure that you've at least considered the others. Have you thought about leaving?'

'He said, the night that Marco – you do know that he killed Marco, don't you?'

'I knew he'd died. They're telling some story down at the camp, but I guessed what had happened. I'm sorry.'

'He said that night that if I tried to leave, his family know enough people around here that I would be found, that he wouldn't give up until he found me, and when he found me he would kill me.' Judit just looks at her. 'I believe him, Judit. If it hadn't been for the baby, I might have given it a try, but now . . . I'm not going to risk it. I can't.'

Judit shrugs. 'All right. And you wouldn't even be talking to me now if you still thought that staying with him is an option, am I right?'

'He'll kill the baby,' Sari says flatly. 'I can't let him do that.'

'Fine,' Judit says. 'So that leaves us here.' She taps the side of the bowl lightly in illustration.

'So, what—'

'Arsenic,' Judit says. 'Fairly easy to get hold of. You just boil off a few of those—' she waves her hands at a couple of tattered old flypapers, flapping, dejected, at the windows – 'and there it is. Very effective. Or so I gather. I prepared this a couple of weeks ago – had an idea that I might be needing it.'

Sari can't help but laugh. 'I was expecting something a little bit more . . . subtle, Judit.'

Judit grins, unperturbed. 'I didn't get where I am by being subtle, Sari. Anyway, we're trying to kill a man, not give him a touch of nausea. This will do the trick.' She snorts. 'Surely you weren't hoping I could provide a nice, simple curse so that you could keep your hands clean?'

Sari flushes, not wanting to admit that part of her had been hoping for just that, but Judit, as usual, sees straight through her.

'Sari! You've worked with me for four years now; I thought you knew better. You're not some naïve housewife from the plain . . .'

And her words trip something in Sari's memory. Suddenly

she's taken back to a night four years ago, soon after she'd moved in with Judit, when a strained-looking woman sat with Judit in the half-light, and she knows, suddenly, as surely as she's ever known anything, that Judit has done this sort of thing before.

They look at one another for a long moment. Sari's heart is hammering, but Judit looks as cool as ever eyes bright and watchful, before Sari takes a shallow breath:

'You—'

'Sari,' Judit says, and her voice is gentle. 'Don't ask me if you don't want me to tell you the truth.'

There is a silence as long as a heartbeat, and then: 'All right,' Sari says, looking down at the unassuming bowl of powder.

Part of her feels relieved – she's not naturally squeamish by nature, but the idea of killing someone discomfits her, and bar any quick and clean curses that Judit obviously doesn't know, poison is far preferable than any number of unpleasantly real and *fleshy* methods of murder that she'd dreaded Judit suggesting; she'd had all sorts of horrible visions of having to hack Ferenc to pieces and bury him in the woods, or push him down the stairs. But with poison – just a little bit slipped in his food – and he'll get ill and die; the only blood on her hands will be metaphorical. Easy.

'So how do I do it?' she asks.

'You don't want to kill him outright. It needs to look like a natural death, the result of an illness. No, no—' as Sari starts to protest – 'you said that you want to get away with this, and this is how you're going to do it. I know you're worried about him doing more damage, causing more problems if you don't finish him off right away, but I promise you, Sari, I know men and illness. Just a touch of pain and discomfort and he'll take to his bed, desperate to be mothered by you. All you need to do is just be a bit nice to him and I guarantee that he won't lay a hand on you.

'Now, you're in luck. I remember you mentioning, when Ferenc first came home, that he was having some sort of stomach trouble – maybe the result of tension, or maybe some fever he picked up on the battlefield. Do you remember telling me that?'

Sari frowns. When . . .? 'Oh yes!' she exclaims. She gets a sudden, vivid image of the conversation in question, standing in this Judit's kitchen. She'd been trying to keep her voice down, not wanting to embarrass Ferenc, but Matild Nagy had been sitting at the table, waiting for a headache treatment, and just as Sari was leaving, had said in unctuous tones: 'Do give my best to Ferenc – I hope he feels better soon.'

'You remember?' Judit presses, and Sari nods again. 'Good. That's going to be a helpful way of deflecting suspicion. It's also useful that Ferenc's been seen so little around the village since he's been back. We can let people believe that it's because he's been ill. And you've been seen out so little because you've been nursing him.'

She shrugs. 'Whether people will believe that or not I don't know. Rumours have been flying about since Marco was killed – you know what this place is like – but the point is that they are just rumours, nobody really knows what's been going on, and if your story is plausible enough, well, people may not necessarily believe it, but they can't disprove it, and that's all that matters.'

'It all sounds very risky,' Sari says.

'Well, of course it is! You're killing a man; there's no safe way to be doing that. You can't do it without taking a few

risks. But with a little bit of care, and a little bit of organis-
ation, we can minimise the risks. There are some other things
on your side, as well, you know. You have to remember how
your average woman around here thinks.'

'What do you mean?'

'For one thing, you're pregnant, and it's going to start
showing soon. What woman in her right mind would kill her
fiancé when she's pregnant? You'd have to bring up the child
alone, and no other man is going to want you if you've got
somebody else's child, especially if you weren't married in
the first place. It doesn't reflect very well on your morals,
Sari,' Judit adds, slyly.

'And of course the other thing is the money. Ferenc's a
wealthy man – or his family is wealthy, at least – but you're
not married to him yet, and so you have no claim on any of
that money if he dies. Any woman in her right mind – with
a little murderous intent – would just wait a few months
longer and kill him once you're married, so that you can get
your hands on his cash. You see, in the eyes of anyone in the
village, you're going to be in a pretty bad state after Ferenc
dies – pregnant, penniless, soiled goods. That can all work in
your favour.'

Sari thinks it over, and what Judit says makes sense. There
are plenty of holes in the plan, of course, but there's no way
to block all of them. This can work; it will take a bit of luck,
and a bit of manipulation, but it can work.

'Fine. So what do I do?'

'A little bit of it in his food at every meal, and he'll start
falling ill with stomach problems. You need to start coming
to me more often – preferably at times when other people
are here – and telling me that his illness is getting worse. I'll
give you some possible treatments. They won't work, of

course, but it will get people talking. You'll probably need to write to his parents – has he been in touch with them since he's been here?'

'Not often. They write to him quite a lot – I think they want him to come back to Budapest and help his father – but he doesn't write much to them. I saw one of his letters once, and it said nothing, just news about the weather, things like that.'

'All right. Well, you will have to write to them and tell them that he is ill, and that you've been trying to help him, but it's getting worse.'

Sari looks thoughtful. 'You know what they'll do, though? They'll try and make him go to the doctor in Város. Or they'll try and get the doctor to come and see him. They can do that, I think – they have enough money and influence.'

'Then it's all a question of timing. You have to be sure when you write the letter that, by the time they have received it in Budapest, and have thought about what to do about it, they won't have time to act. He will have to be dead before the doctor in Város can see him.'

Sari shudders slightly. Judit has a way of talking about this that makes it seem terribly real. She has an idea that Judit is doing it on purpose, forcing her to face up to the reality of what she is proposing to do.

'It's always possible,' Judit says, ruminatively 'that his parents will call for an investigation, that they won't be satisfied with me filing the report of the cause of death as usual. I'm not sure what we can do about that. I'm sure that if a doctor was to cut him open after he was dead, he could work out the real cause of death. All we can do is to try and ensure that they have no reason to be suspicious. No matter what they think of you, it would be quite a stretch for them to imagine you a murderer. The facts point away from you – you've got no motive. Now, let me put this stuff in a bottle for you. Do you have a good place to hide it?'

'I'll bury it in the forest. There's no way that anyone would find it there.'

'Good idea. Just try not to lose it. I can always make you some more, of course, but I don't like to think of any of this stuff out there and unaccounted for. And now,' Judit looks out of the window at the sky that has shimmered into gold, 'you should get home. If you leave now, you'll be back before Ferenc gets up.' Her smile is unsettling. 'You can have a nice hot breakfast waiting for him.'

CHAPTER SEVENTEEN

Sari lets herself back into the house quietly; Ferenc is a heavy sleeper in general, but she doesn't want to risk waking him. She needs some time to think.

Like Judit, Sari's never given a great deal of thought to her immortal soul. Brought up by her father, he instilled in her a sort of distant respect for the church, more for its power over other people than for any intrinsic value that it might hold, and the subsequent four years with Judit did nothing to further endear the church to her, as Judit has an excoriating disrespect for it and all of its rules.

'I have no respect for anything,' Judit has said on many occasions, 'that only wants to stop people from doing things. Out here, we need as many possibilities as possible.'

Sari is inclined to agree, and as a result she cares little for the doctrines of the church – she's not even sure if she believes in God. She's even less sure if she believes in hell, which always seems too convenient a concept to explain the unfairnesses of life. Religion is an irrelevance for her.

Still, Sari works to bring life into the world, and to sustain life; the idea of taking it has always been anathema to her. But she realises now that the only people whose welfare she can truly be responsible for are herself and her unborn child, that it is not her job to protect Ferenc from herself, but to protect herself from him. He's bigger than her, and stronger, but she has resources, too. It's a fair fight, and one that she's prepared to lose, but she'll be losing by default if she doesn't even try. Sari has heard about the fierce protective impulses that assail women when they become mothers; she'd never believed them until now, but it's more than just that. One never knows how strong one is, or how selfish, until pushed.

Ferenc's tread on the stairs comes an hour later, while she is preparing breakfast for him. She's already added a touch of what she's taken to calling, with grim humour, 'special seasoning'. A small amount of it is wrapped in a handkerchief and stored for safekeeping in the toe of her boot. The rest is buried in the roots of a tree a few paces away from the house; she carved a mark on the trunk to remind her where it is, for when she needs to replenish her supplies.

'So you're back,' Ferenc says behind her, voice gruff and croaky from sleep. She's thought carefully about how she needs to behave around him. She needs to give no indication that she has changed from the cowed, conquered woman she has been in the past few weeks. Her behaviour the night before is going to be difficult to explain or excuse, but throwing herself on his mercy can't hurt, and may just flatter him into forgiving her.

'Ferenc, I am so sorry for the way that I behaved last night,' she says, in a low mutter that feels alien on her tongue now. 'I don't know what came over me. I promise that nothing like that will ever happen again.'

He stares at her, obviously wary, asking himself whether she needs some more discipline to bring her properly in line. She thinks fast, and goes on,

'You were right to be angry with me. I don't know why I behaved like I did, but sometimes women – in, in that state – act like that, act irrationally. That is the only reason that I can think of.'

There's a worrying pause, and then his face cracks in a smile. Sari is relieved. She should have known that playing the stupid, irrational female with him would work.

'I forgive you,' he says expansively. 'Did you go to Judit's last night?'

Sari nods. 'I wanted her to check that I was all right.'

'And are you all right?'

'Well, *I* am,' she says. She wants for him to believe that the baby is dead – with any luck (and she has stopped shivering at thoughts like these) he'll be in the ground by the time it becomes obvious that she's still pregnant.

'Ah,' he says, looking concerned, picking up on her hint. 'I'm sorry if you're upset about this, Sari, but I'm sure you see my point. We will have children ourselves, I do want us to, but *this* child,' his face twists with distaste, 'I could not have this child in my house. And,' he goes on, forcing his tone back to lightness, 'we're not even married yet! There's plenty of time in the future for children.'

She struggles to smile back and manages it, knowing that she has to for her own survival, but she loathes him with all her being. She finds it odd that he can say anything he wants about her, hurt her as much as he likes, but it's only when he tries to hurt or insult her child that she feels that she could rip his throat out with her bare hands.

Oblivious, he sits down at the table, and she places a plate in front of him. 'There you go,' she says in what she hopes pass for fond tones. 'Breakfast!'

It's four o'clock and Ferenc is still walking around, strong as an ox and Sari is growing concerned. Judit hadn't been able to give much advice on levels of dosage ('It's not as if I make a habit of this sort of behaviour,' she'd said, though Sari's not convinced that she's as inexperienced as she would have Sari believe), but suggested that she start off small and work up from there. Sari chides herself now for being overly cautious that morning, and when she is preparing the evening meal she is more generous with her seasoning. Ferenc washes down the *tésztakása* with a bottle of rough red wine, and is in bed and snoring by eleven o'clock. Disturbed by the depth and comfort of his sleep, but still hoping for the best, Sari joins him at midnight.

She wakes in shock. Something is wrong, someone needs her help and it takes her a moment to realise that what she is hearing is not the sounds of things going wrong, but things going right. Ferenc is twisting and moaning on the mattress beside her.

'Ferenc? What is it?' she asks. He gives a shuddering groan, and she gropes for the matches on the table by the bed, lighting the lamp. In its dim glow he looks sweaty and greenish, not well at all but, she is pleased to notice, no different to anyone else with stomach problems. She'd had a vague, irrational idea that somehow the fact that he'd been poisoned would be obvious, written on his forehead, and she's happy that's not the case.

'My stomach,' he moans. 'It's come back – thought I'd got rid of it.'

Play the nurse, says Judit's voice in Sari's head. She leans over him and places a hand on his cool brow, composing her face into a simulacrum of sympathy. 'Oh, you've got a fever,' she lies smoothly. 'It must be that sickness you picked up at the front come back. Let me get you something for the pain.'

She runs out of the room and down the stairs, and by the time she's in the kitchen she's bent over herself but not in pain; instead, she's biting hard on her knuckle to stifle a hysterical giggle. It's working! It's horrible and wonderful all at once, and she has to be so, so careful from now on. A million unconsidered concerns flap at her. What if he decides that he wants to see the doctor in Város himself? She hadn't even thought of that. It would be unlike his recent reclusive demeanour, but it's possible, isn't it, that the pain could drive him to it? There's not much that she can do about that. The degree to which Ferenc has isolated himself from the rest of the world is on her side. She is in the unusually privileged position of being able to manage and manipulate the information that comes in and out of the house, and it's up to her to use it to her best advantage.

A thump from upstairs reminds her what she's there for, and she scrabbles in one of the cupboards for some medicine, before running back up to Ferenc. It turns out the thump was merely the sound of Ferenc knocking a cup off the bedside table, rather than anything more ominous. He's still in the bed, face contorted with pain, and she feels a swift twist of revulsion: so ready to give out pain, and so unable to take it. He's pushed the covers down and his stomach is exposed – it is distended, though whether it's the result of the poison, or the sheer size of the dinner he ate earlier she doesn't know. She sits down on the edge of the bed, and he opens his eyes.

'It hurts,' he says pathetically. Swallowing her exasperation, Sari puts on her most syrupy tones.

'I know,' she says, hoping that he doesn't notice how unlike her this sugary voice sounds, 'but I have some medicine for you which should help you feel better. Here.' she pours a liquid into a small glass and lifts it to his lips. A simple painkiller, laced with a sleeping draught, it's next to useless but she needs to court his trust, make him believe that she is helping him. He swallows it down as obediently as a child, and Sari remembers what Judit said about men and illness, marvelling at how right she was.

'It'll take a few minutes to work,' she says, but already his moans are decreasing in anticipation of feeling better. She places a hand on his swollen gut and strokes it gently. He gives a little whimper, but she can tell from his face that it's one of relief, rather than pain. 'Your stomach's been weak since you came home,' she says. 'It's partly my fault – I should have known not to cook a rich dinner like that last night; it was bound to upset your stomach. I'll stick to lighter foods from now on, shall I?'

He nods, eyes closed. She takes her hand off his stomach, thinking to get back into bed herself, but he says 'Don't stop,' and so she doesn't, shivering slightly in the chilly night air, rubbing soothingly until he falls back into a fitful sleep.

Sari soon discovers that it doesn't take strength to kill a person, only persistence and cunning. By the next morning, Ferenc claims to be feeling a great deal better. The pain is gone, at least, but he seems vague and disorientated, complaining of a headache, and Sari brews him up some chamomile tea to settle his stomach, while he blames the headache on a surfeit of red wine the night before. To her relief, he seems unsuspicious about the origins of his stomach pain, but she decides to engage in a little acting herself, occasionally holding her stomach with a grimace of pain on her face. It takes him a while to notice.

'Are you all right?' he asks eventually that evening, and she shrugs.

'I feel a little unwell. Judit said that there's some illness going around the village, people are complaining of stomach pains and vomiting . . .'

'Maybe you picked it up when you were at Judit's?'

'Maybe. Maybe that's what was wrong with you last night.'

'Maybe.' He doesn't look particularly convinced, but at least he doesn't look disbelieving. If she can just get him to believe that the symptoms that he is experiencing are normal, it will make things so much easier. Then, by the time it's clear that they're not normal, she hopes that things will have progressed far enough that he won't be able to do anything about it.

As she cooks dinner that night she feels resolved; now that she's sure that the stuff Judit gave her works, she can afford to be a little more sparing with it over the next little while.

Day four, morning. Ferenc has passed another painful night, but as ever, the next morning he doesn't seem too worried by it. Tucking into a large breakfast, he comments casually that this latest illness that's been going around is rather nasty, and he hopes it passes soon.

He seems sleepy that day but that is understandable, the pain kept him up for a couple of hours the night before and Sari encourages him to nap that afternoon. He takes her suggestion well. He has definitely softened towards her over the past few days. Judit was right: men are naturally chastened by illness, inclined to cling to people, and this is to Sari's advantage. After lunch he is tucked up in bed. When she brings him some water, he pats her hand fondly and she notices something odd – strange marks on his fingernails that she's sure weren't there before. She doesn't comment on them, not wanting him to notice, but once she is sure that he is safely asleep, she takes the opportunity to slip away and visit Judit.

Judit is on her own. Sari knows that in some ways it would have been better if someone had been with her, so that they could start rumours flying about Ferenc's progressing illness and her corresponding concern, but she also wants to be able to speak honestly.

'He's asleep,' she says, as soon as Judit opens the door. 'I don't have long.'

Judit invites her in and gives her a cup of coffee before asking: 'So? How is it going?'

Sari feels a surge of exultation and dread. She's constantly surprised at how mixed her feelings are about what she's doing, part of her horrified at the very idea that she is hastening someone's departure from the world and part of her – always the bigger part, though not by much – certain that it's the right thing for her to do, for herself and for the child.

'It's working,' she says. 'I'm giving him a bigger dose in the evenings, and he usually has quite a lot of pain during the night, but I spun a story about some stomach illness that's spreading through the village, and he seems convinced by that.'

'Is he having any other symptoms?'

'Headaches, sometimes, and he seems quite tired, but I don't know whether that's because he's so often ill during the night. Also, just this afternoon I noticed that his finger-nails have changed – there are marks on them. Do you know anything about that?'

Judit frowns. 'No idea, I'm afraid. What are you doing for him?'

'I'm giving him wild chicory for the pain. It seems to work quite well, and it's helping me look' – she struggles for the word – 'convincing, I suppose. I don't think he's at all suspicious. And you were right, he's been so much nicer to me since he's been ill.'

'Ha!' Judit snorts. 'Of course. He needs you now, doesn't he?'

'He always needed me. I'm the one who does all the cooking, all the cleaning, going to the market—'

'Yes, but you're the woman, and you're supposed to do that. This is different. Men are children at heart, looking for a mother's tit to suck on. Never is it more obvious than when they're ill.' She looks hard into Sari's face. 'And how are you feeling about it all?'

There's a long silence, as Sari tries to sum up what she's thinking and feeling. 'I'm having nightmares,' she says at last, speaking slowly. 'I know that this is . . . it's not right. But I think I've stopped caring about things like that. I've stopped caring about anything much outside of this.' She motions with her arms, an arc around her body, containing herself and the baby tucked inside her. 'I think when it comes down to survival, everything else stops mattering.'

Judit nods. 'Let me know what's going on, if you can,' she says.

Day ten, midday. Ferenc has been getting incrementally more and more ill, but Sari's not sure whether he's noticed it himself. She's seen it with other people when they're suffering, when pain becomes a constant and it's hard to judge whether things are getting worse or better. She asked him once, while dosing him with wild chicory tea in the small hours of the morning, whether perhaps she shouldn't fetch Judit, and see if she could do anything about it, but much to her relief he refused; not that Judit would cause any problems, but she knows that his reluctance to see anyone other than herself while he is so ill is likely to extend to the doctor in Város, too, which is going to make things a great deal easier.

But that day Sari's downstairs, mending one of Ferenc's shirts, when she hears a noise from upstairs, a bang. The bang is followed by a series of quieter bangs and thumps, almost a drumming, which is strange enough to impel Sari to venture upstairs and investigate.

She finds Ferenc on the floor by the bed and is shockingly thrust back four years (a lifetime) to the day when she found her father in much the same position. But there the similarity ends, for when her father was lying there he was still and dead, while Ferenc is twitching violently, and Sari realises that he is having a fit.

She doesn't know what to do, torn between duelling impulses. Should she try to help? Is this it, the end? In which case she shouldn't try to help, but let things progress as naturally as she can. But what if it's not the end, and he comes to and finds her standing idly by? She dithers for a moment, steps towards him, then jumps back again as his arm jerks towards her. She's never seen anything like this before. His eyes are half open and his tongue is protruding; he must have bitten it, as a trickle of blood runs down his chin – she's both repulsed and perversely pitying.

His chest hitches and he vomits and she can't leave it any longer, can't just leave him to choke to death on his own vomit on the bedroom floor, so she kneels down beside him and lifts his bucking head and shoulders into her lap, turning his head to one side, scooping the vomit out of his mouth with her fingers. He won't suffocate, but what now? The fit seems to go on for a long time, but gradually the jerking movements still, and she looks down at him. Is his chest rising and falling, is he still breathing? Yes, and his eyes are opening, rolling around the room before they settle on her face, upside down from his prone position.

He coughs once, and spits weakly. 'What happened?'

'You – you were having a fit. I think I should fetch Judit.'

He blinks hard, trying to clear his mind, and then shakes his head. 'Don't need her.'

'*Please*, Ferenc. I don't know what this means, I don't know how to treat it. Please let me get Judit to have a look at you.' She puts on her most imploring expression, and is quietly impressed at how her acting skills are developing – she finds that there are real tears standing in her eyes.

He seems to be moved by her pleading, and finally he nods in curt agreement. 'All right. If you can get her to come here, I'll see her.'

Even as she walks, she wonders why she's insisted on summoning Judit. Of course, it's more convincing from Ferenc's

point of view to do so, but what does that matter? Ferenc is
unlikely to leave the house or speak to another person again
before he dies, and so what difference does it make whether
he spends his final few days (or weeks – though God forbid
that should be the case) suspicious and paranoid, or as
trusting as he seems to be right now?

But she's in luck; as she rounds the curve in the path and
Judit's house comes into view, she sees the unmistakeable
broad arse of Jakova Gersek disappearing through the doorway. A perfect chance to spread gossip of Ferenc's illness,
and thereby ensure that her own name stays as clear as
possible! But yet she hesitates. It was one thing to plan the
discussion of a theoretical illness in front of others; it's
another to contemplate Jakova hearing of the reality of
Ferenc's plight, if not the causes. It seems like an unpleasant
invasion of Ferenc's privacy. But this, she tells herself, is not
the time to worry about propriety and Ferenc's delicate
sensibilities. She reminds herself of the far greater sin that
she is in the process of committing, and this has a surprisingly motivational effect that serves to carry her down the
road and up to Judit's door.

She enters without knocking, and feigns surprise when she
sees Jakova sitting at the kitchen table, clearly suffering from
toothache, her cheek puffy and her mouth amusingly twisted.
She's clasping a poultice of Judit's to the side of her face, and
regards Sari out of ill-tempered eyes.

'I – I'm sorry,' Sari stammers in Jakova's direction. 'I need
to see Judit.'

'Of course,' Jakova replies, with a half-hearted effort at
good humour. 'How is Ferenc, by the way?'

'Oh, quite well,' Sari lies airily. It's for the best to do so,
she decides, so that it can't be claimed that she's deliberately

spreading word of Ferenc's illness. Jakova is the type to prick up her ears in response to lowered voices. Word will get out easily enough as it is.

'Hello, Sari,' Judit pokes her head out from the kitchen. 'Everything all right?' She raises her eyebrows meaningfully.

'Um,' Sari replies. 'Could I have a quick word with you?'

Judit beckons her into the kitchen, and as soon as she's out of Jakova's line of sight, Sari jerks her thumb towards where she is sitting, winking, to which Judit nods in response.

'It's Ferenc,' Sari says, in a stentorian whisper. 'You know he hasn't been well recently? He hasn't been too good since he came back from the front, but he's been worse in the past couple of weeks.'

'I'm sorry to hear that,' Judit hisses back, grinning broadly, clearly enjoying the play-acting.

'He hasn't wanted to see you, or anyone else, but this afternoon I went upstairs and found him having a fit. I don't know how to treat it, so he agreed that he would see you, if you came to the house . . .'

She lapses into silence for a moment, before adding, 'So, can you help?'

There's a pause, while Judit weighs up what the right response is. 'Is it true?' she mouths silently at last, and when Sari nods in response, she says out loud, 'Very well. Just let me finish with Jakova, and I'll come up to the house. You run back now, make sure he's all right. I should be there in about a quarter of an hour.'

When Sari lets herself back into the house, everything is silent. She climbs the stairs as quietly as she can, not sure what she's afraid of disturbing – Ferenc in the act of dying, perhaps? – and when she gets to the door of the bedroom she's reluctant to look inside. But it hasn't happened yet; Ferenc is asleep, or unconscious, perhaps, but certainly alive. She can see the bedclothes pitching and tossing with the rise and fall of his chest. He seems quite peaceful, so she leaves him there and goes back downstairs to wait for Judit, who arrives twenty minutes later. As soon as she pokes her head around the door, Sari puts a finger to her lips. 'He's asleep upstairs,' she whispers. 'If you keep quiet, we can talk down here before you go up and see him.'

Judit comes inside and sits down; she seems to be tightly coiled, almost humming with excitement.

'If you'd planned it, that couldn't have been better,' she says, with hushed exultation. 'As soon as you'd gone, there was Jakova, fake concern plastered all over that squashed face of hers, saying that she *just couldn't help overhearing* – Judit affects a falsetto whine in imitation – 'and wondering what was wrong with Ferenc. Didn't tell her much, of course, only that he hasn't been well since he came home, and that's why he hasn't been out a lot, but I'm sure he'll be fine given time.' She smirks, rolling her eyes. 'It'll be all around the village by nightfall.'

'Thank God for gossips,' Sari says, only half joking.

'So, what's going on?'

'It's as I told you – he had a fit this afternoon, and then he vomited. The vomiting is nothing new. He's been doing that since all this started; he still thinks he's got some sort of stomach illness that's been going round the village, and that it's affecting him particularly badly because of that fever that he got when he was away at war. But a fit . . . I didn't know what to do about it.'

'Well, you're not supposed to do *anything* about it,' Judit says, looking at Sari searchingly.

'I know, I know. It's just . . . it's hard. Since he's been ill, he's been acting so differently, it's sometimes hard to remember why I started doing this in the first place.'

'Are you planning on stopping?'

'No! No. I don't think so.'

'Because you could, you know. Let him believe he had some sort of nasty bug, but now he's better. That's one of the advantages of this plan, and one of its pitfalls – you can stop any time before the end.'

Sari laces her fingers together, fixing her eyes on the intricate patterns that they make. She doesn't really know if she's thinking of backing out. It hadn't occurred to her until Judit suggested it. Adding the powder to Ferenc's food has become second nature to her, a habitual culinary ritual. An image of his face suddenly swims before her, the trusting way that he looked at her when she suggested she go and fetch Judit after his fit, and for a moment she thinks about letting him off. Perhaps this illness will have wrung all the violence out of him; perhaps they can find a modicum of happiness together. Perhaps.

'He would never let the child live,' she says to Judit, her voice flat. 'My duty is not to him. It's to my child, and to myself.'

'Good girl.' Judit nods in approval, as if she's been presented with a series of perfectly executed sums, rather than the agreement to continue murdering a man. 'Now, shall I go up and take a look at him?'

Sari lets herself into the bedroom and wakes Ferenc, who is disoriented but calm. She explains to him that Judit's here to see him, and he doesn't seem clear on why she is here, but accepts it without question. It's that trust again, Sari thinks, with a spasm of self-loathing. *Forget it*, she tells herself harshly. *If he were well, he'd hurt you without a second thought, kick and punch that child out of your womb. Have no pity for him.*

She leaves Judit alone with him, and is waiting downstairs when she reappears a few minutes later.

'I gave him some Spanish garlic,' Judit says. 'Won't do anything, of course, though he'll maybe think that it's working.'

'All right. Judit . . . ?'

'Finish him off, Sari,' Judit replies harshly, without waiting to hear Sari's question. 'Write to his parents tonight, and finish him off over the next few days. You can start giving him double the dosage you've been giving him. He's confused now, and if you bring it to an end now, you can make sure that he's never properly himself again before the end. That's for the best, Sari. If you're going to do it, that's how you should proceed.'

Judit leaves, and for a few moments Sari stands stock still in the middle of the room. *This is it*, she says to herself. *This is it.* She waits for the enormity of it to hit her, but it doesn't, and after a minute Sari realises that she's mentally planning this evening's meal; she's not even thinking about Ferenc and his demise any more. How far she has fallen, morally! She waits for the guilt of that to hit her: again, nothing. For the best, really. She goes to the drawer and takes out some paper, then sits down at the table to write to Ferenc's parents and tell them of his illness.

Day fourteen. Midnight. This is it, Sari thinks. It has to be. She's done as Judit suggested, doubling the dose of powder in all the food and drink she gives to Ferenc, and it's had the effect that Judit said that it would. He is constantly disoriented and confused now and his occasional flashes of lucidity are becoming rarer and rarer.

Judit has come by every day since the day of Ferenc's fit, to keep up appearances – it wouldn't do to have him die without having been properly attended in the days leading up to it, and Ferenc has been obediently swallowing the potions that Sari and Judit have been pressing upon him. They do no more good than unpleasant tasting water, but he doesn't seem to have noticed. He's unconscious much of the time, and those times that he is conscious he seems to be in terrible pain, so it's always a relief when he lapses into insensibility again.

Sari has stopped thinking about it as much as she can, going about her daily rituals much as she would if he weren't ill. She is often struck by the absurdity of it, when she finds herself assiduously mending his old socks or torn shirts; she can't seem to stop herself, but every time she leaves the room, she hopes that he will be dead the next time she returns. It never happens. She considered starting to sleep downstairs, to give him more room and comfort in the bed (and, in theory, to give her a good night's sleep, although she knows that she would jerk awake every five minutes and scurry up the stairs to check on him), but he still turns to her for comfort – a blind, infantile kind of comfort that is not linked to her, but to any nearby warm body – and she can't quite bear to leave him whimpering alone. Instead, she sits up for much of the night, often on the edge of the bed next to him – she can't bring herself to get under the blankets with him, no matter how pathetic he seems – and sometimes at the kitchen table downstairs, where she drinks cup after cup of coffee and stares at the black panes of the windows, her nightgown a dim white smudge in the gloom.

Night fourteen. The room is heavy with the feel of death, and Sari's sure that this is it. He seems worse than he has ever been, talking nonsense between groans of pain. He vomits regularly, and shits himself more regularly still, and Sari deals with this with the stoicism of a nurse, but she can't help shuddering slightly at the indignity of death. Something else distresses her more than all the foul-smelling unpleasantness, and that's the fact that his hair is coming out in handfuls. Every time he moves his head on the sweat-sodden pillow, he leaves behind a dark smear of sticky hair. On some parts of his head, the white scalp is already shining through. She cleans him and changes the sheets as often as she needs to, and puts cold cloths on his head and prays for him to die, begs the God that she doesn't believe in just to intercede and take him now. She wants this, she's asked for it, of course – but the process is so hard. She cannot bring herself to weep; the closest she gets is when she realises that one of the cloths she is using to wipe his brow is the old handkerchief that she had started to embroider for him before he'd gone to war, unfinished and untouched for four years.

At about 3 am, he lapses into silence, and Sari tenses with apprehension. Is *this* it? He's become terribly still, but no, he's still breathing. Soon, though, surely? Gently, disturbing the bed as little as possible, she leans down to look into his face. It's white and clammy, his lips have become shockingly pale, but his eyes are still twitching beneath the veined lids.

She wants to sob with exhaustion, tears pricking behind her eyes – she just wants it to be over. A sudden pain in her palms makes her look down, and she realises that she's balled her hands into such tights fists that her fingernails have cut into her. She takes a couple of deep breaths and forces herself to relax. Soon, soon. This can't go on forever. But what if it does? The letter is already on its way to his parents; supposing he lingers like this for weeks? There would be time enough for them to take action; to come to Falucska perhaps, to demand that the doctor in Város comes to visit him. And what then? Would he know what she's been doing? It is unbearable – *unbearable.*

Two hours later she jerks awake. She had managed to fall into a doze, despite her racing mind, and some evil, threatening dream has woken her. Immediately she looks towards Ferenc – still, he hasn't moved, but his chest is still rising and falling, though erratically. It takes a moment for her to notice what has changed: his eyes are open.

'Ferenc?' she asks softly. His head does not move, but his eyes swivel towards her.

'Sari,' he whispers, and then something else, but the words seem to stick on his dry lips. She leans closer in order to hear him. His mouth moves convulsively in a pattern that she almost recognises, but it seems as if his breath has left him; he is soundless.

'What do you need, Ferenc? Can I get you water? Anything?'

His head moves minutely from right to left: no. His lips are still moving, and she leans still closer, her ear only inches from his mouth. At first, nothing, and then on an exhaled breath: '. . . who art in heaven . . .'

He is praying.

She's not religious, has never been religious, but what can she do? She may be a murderess but she's not unnecessarily cruel, and she has no desire to withhold from Ferenc one of the last comforts that is within her power to give. She grips his hand, which is so cold it chills her, between two of hers, and says in a voice that she keeps deliberately quiet and steady: 'Our Father, who art in Heaven, hallowed be Thy name . . .'

Is she imagining it, or does a flicker of animation pass over his face? He is still inaudible, but the patterns made by his soundless lips change to fit in with the words coming from hers. He closes his eyes, and she prays on, repeating the only words that she knows. She wishes she knew more prayers, anything else that would give him solace, that would enable him to let go of life with comfort and let it end – but he breathes on. The window by the bed starts to glow dull yellow: dawn is breaking, another day, and Sari's heart sinks. Not another! Let it end!

His lips are still moving, his chest still dipping every so often. She keeps reciting the words and they soon become meaningless, like clods of earth falling from her lips, an inarticulate string of sounds. Her voice becomes rough – unused to speaking this much, after speaking to no one but Judit and Ferenc for weeks. Still he breathes. Still.

The window is almost entirely light when he gives a violent jerk and cries out, his face creasing with pain. She is badly shocked after his long silence. Heart hammering, she leans closer to him again, and his eyes shimmer open. They are no longer focused and they roam around the room, but then fasten on her face.

'Sari,' he croaks, 'Please. Please.'

What is he asking? For her to make him better? Imposs-ible, of course, and even he must know that by now. Is it meaningless pleading, brought on by suffering? Or could he be asking for something else, for release? Hardly believing what she is doing, she extends her arm, so that her palm is over his face. His eyes do not move from her face. She puts her hand gently on his face, and still his eyes do not waver. She starts again: 'Our Father . . .' and he closes his eyes. Her palm covers his mouth, forming a tight seal, and with her thumb and index finger she pinches his nose shut. Still he does not struggle; his chest stops moving. Sari looks towards the window, the rays of light stealing over the sill, and she prays, sending empty words out to an empty universe, while Ferenc dies under her hand. He twitches once before the end, but his eyes do not open, and she takes it as a subconscious rejection of death, nothing more. The morning is beautiful, the sky multicoloured, and the light turning the grass into a vivid, glowing green. He's gone, she feels it, but it's a long time before she takes her hand away. When she does, it's as if her soul takes flight as well as his. She feels light, not with relief, but simply with hollowness. It is over. It is done. Her child is safe.

CHAPTER EIGHTEEN

November is always the grimmest month, in Sari's opinion, but this year it isn't affecting her as badly as usual; she's mainly just relieved that the summer is over. The heat never bothered her much before, but it's a different matter now, simmering and sweltering through July and August as a pregnant woman. *Next time*, she thinks, *I will plan things better*, and then she smiles to herself at the preposterous idea that there could be a next time. It's not a bitter smile, nor even one of resignation, just simple certainty that this baby is, for her, the first and last.

It will be a January baby, and how she is looking forward to her birth. Yes, it's a girl – she knew, and Judit confirmed it. Girls sit in the womb differently to boys, anyone who's dealt with as many pregnant women as Judit has can tell that. It's been a difficult pregnancy, and Sari can't wait for it to be over. She's nearly lost the baby twice already, once from Ferenc's kick, and once since, from illness, and she is looking forward to it being safely out of her, where she feels she'll be able to look after it better, dependent more on her brain than her treacherous body.

Judit is always telling her that she needs to rest, that she's risking bringing the birth on early, but she can't sit still. Judit tries to give her gentle tasks to keep her busy – mending, embroidery, or preparing medicines – but more often than not she will come back from visiting someone to find the house empty, and Sari off tending to some poor unfortunate.

'They can wait!' she scolds Sari, after the second time that it's happened. 'They can always wait until I come back! After all we've done for this baby, surely you don't want to risk its life unnecessarily, just because you're bored?'

To this, Sari just shrugs and smiles self-deprecatingly. She can't explain to Judit that she knows that this baby will be born, but she does – she feels that she's carried it this far by will alone, and sheer determination is all that's needed to keep it alive a little longer.

It's only in the past couple of months that she's really started to believe that she's safe, that she's got away with it, that she's not going to be awoken in the middle of the night by an army of policemen at her door denouncing her as a murderess and dragging her away to the hangman's noose. For the couple of months after Ferenc died, she would regularly wake, sweating and shuddering, from nightmares along these lines, and then lie awake for hours afterwards in morbid contemplation. If she were to be charged with murder and sentenced to death, what would become of her baby? Surely it wouldn't be condemned also, just because of the acts of its mother? But what would they do? Would she give birth in prison, her newborn whisked away to an orphanage just as swiftly as she would be whisked to the gallows? Or would they – God forbid – would they cut it out of her, to excuse them hanging a pregnant woman? But the knock on the door never came, and Sari has finally understood that they have made it. Things are going to be all right.

It was surprisingly easy, all things considered. The morning that Ferenc died she walked to Judit's to tell her the news

220

– the village was just starting to wake up and move about, but nobody spoke to her and nobody approached her, and she only realised once Judit opened the door to her and stared hard at her that she was weeping steadily, tears coursing down her face. When she thinks of that now, she laughs a little – the only two times that she can remember crying in her adult life, and both for the sake of men! There'll be no more of that, absolutely not.

As news spread through the village that day, Sari braced herself for the whispering, and maybe outright accusations to begin, but there was nothing, and to her amazement, still nothing over the next few days. She stayed with Judit during that time, and Judit tried to reassure her: Sari had been convinced that it was only a matter of time before fingers started to be pointed at her, but Judit insisted that there was no reason for suspicion. Some malicious minds might wish to spread rumours, yes, but in Judit's view Sari had done herself an enormous favour by weeping that morning: it had softened the hearts of everyone who saw her, and made them less inclined to listen to vicious whispers.

'It couldn't have been better,' Judit had said gleefully, 'if you'd done it on purpose.'

The village taken care of – for the time being, at least – Sari's main worry remained Ferenc's parents. She telegraphed them the morning of his death, and heard nothing back from them until they appeared in the village a few days later in time for the funeral. They looked lost and baffled when the unknown priest, brought in from the next village for the occasion, mouthed impersonal platitudes, and Sari couldn't help her heart aching a little for them. To lose an oldest son is a tragedy, even more so when the younger one, now the heir, was still away fighting, his safety uncertain. Sari had expected to be met with caution or coldness or even down-right hostility, but what actually happened was almost worse. Months later, Sari still blanches at the way that Ferenc's mother flung her arms around her neck, sobbing into her shoulder, telling Sari again and again how fond Ferenc had been of her, and how unbearable it was that he was gone, and gradually, Sari had begun to realise that, far from being suspicious of her, they were grateful to her for nursing him through the throes of his final illness. She had to fight back a hysterical burst of laughter. *The poor bastards,* she thought.

But their potential suspicion was only the first hurdle, the second being the issue of the baby. Sari had decided that by no means must they know about her pregnancy. If they found out, they would assume that the baby was Ferenc's, and Sari couldn't bear the thought of them taking an interest in it, trying to control the way that she brought it up, or – worst of all, but a definite possibility – insisting that Sari, as a single woman in a poor and isolated village, was unable to give the baby the upbringing befitting it, and instead they should take it back with them to Budapest.

The obvious solution would be simply to tell them that the baby was not Ferenc's, but that would risk their extreme displeasure, and also lay open a motive for his murder – also an impossible course of action. So Sari decided that the best option was to hide it – they hadn't seen her in four years, after all, and so they could believe that the barely perceptible swell in the centre of her body was down to her growing up, rather than anything else. The whole time that they were in the village, Sari was terrified of giving herself away and having the baby taken from her, but the Gazdags' eyes were so misted over with grief that they were not inclined to look at her too closely.

She'd managed it all so well that she could barely believe it, and then fate, or stress, or whatever it was intervened and helped her a little more, in a rather backhanded way. As soon as the funeral was over, and the Gazdags had left the village, Sari started feeling very peculiar, light headed and nauseous, in a deeper, more wrenching way than she had felt throughout her pregnancy. By the next day she was delirious with fever and Judit was frantic, sponging her sweating forehead and forcing medicines and potions down her that seemed to have progressively less and less effect.

'We didn't work so damn hard so that you could die on me now,' Sari remembers Judit saying, teeth clenched, grim-faced, as another hour passed without Sari's fever breaking, but she remembers little else from that time, other than her own voice, every time Judit held a cup to her lips, insisting, 'Nothing that will harm the baby – *please*, Judit.'

'You'll be no good to that damn baby if you're dead.' Judit would retort, and now that she's herself again Sari knows that the fever that she ran for four days in the end was probably more risk to the baby's health than any of the foul-tasting liquids that Judit forced down her throat. Nothing she can do about it now, though, and she takes comfort from the fact that the baby is one of the most active that she's ever heard of – kicking and squirming non-stop, to the extent that Sari is sometimes exhausted and fractious, but simultaneously pleased: at least the child is full of energy. At least she's alive.

When Sari first ventured out of doors after her illness, pale and shaky still, she was overwhelmed by the response of almost everyone she met. People seemed to go out of their way to offer her a few kind words, and she realised that her illness had served the useful purpose of making Ferenc's death even more convincing. She's still not sure, when she looks people in the eyes, that they don't have an inkling that some sort of foul play was involved, but even so, the general consensus seems to be that Sari has suffered enough for now.

That was when she finally started to relax, when the spectre of prison and execution stopped haunting her nightmares. It doesn't matter whether they believe her or not, deep down – they believe her enough to keep her safe. Neither she nor Judit knows what caused the illness, but Sari suspects that it was some sort of purging. She's not naturally superstitious, no more so than anyone else in the village, at least, but the fact that the illness struck her after she'd just committed great evil seemed to be a little more than a coincidence.

She feels lighter after her illness, at times almost too light, as if she's barely anchored to the earth any more, and she feels no more grief for Ferenc, other than a removed sort of regret. He could have been a good man, she thinks sometimes. He could have been so much more than he was. Marco, she tries not to think about at all, and most of the time it's not that difficult to shut him out of her mind; already, when she thinks of him, it seems like scenes from someone else's life, and in a way that's what it was. In the weak days after her illness, she allowed herself a brief fantasy of what it would have been like if she had fled with Marco that night, managing to evade Ferenc and cross the plain, but she's practical enough to know that it would never have worked between them; anywhere else, her naïveté would have irritated him, and she would have found his learnedness unremarkable. She has a clear, sharp image of them sitting together in an anonymous city somewhere, bored with one another, nothing at all to say.

There's a knock on the door. It's probably Anna, she thinks, though it's a little early for her. Since she's come out of her Ferenc-imposed exile, Sari has re-established some friendships, and since Sari is largely housebound in the latest stages of her pregnancy, Anna comes around to visit every day. Sometimes Lilike comes too, but Lujza rarely leaves the house these days, and Sari is resigned to not seeing her until after she's given birth.

Sari's never sure quite how much any of them know. Anna's never said anything out of line, never dared to suggest that Ferenc's death might have been anything less or more than the result of a tragic illness – but sometimes she looks at Sari in such a way that makes Sari wonder. She doesn't want Anna to suspect, but it seems possible that those few people who know the extent of her relationship with Marco might suspect something, and she trusts that Anna would never do anything to give her away.

There's also the fact of the delicate scar that laces the outside of Sari's eye, the result of a well-placed blow from Ferenc, a scar that no one else has commented on, but Anna asked about it the first time she saw Sari after Ferenc died. Sari made up some glib excuse at the time – opening a window into her own face, ha ha, how silly of her to be so clumsy – but she noticed something flickering in Anna's face at that. She thinks perhaps that women who have been treated badly by their husbands or sweethearts have an unspoken understanding, some sort of code that enables them to slice through the lies that convince others.

Sari moves towards the door, thinking fondly of the days

when she could do this lightly, easily, not like the lumbering beast of burden that she has become. She's not resentful of the way that her baby has commandeered her body, but she misses having a body that is easy and enjoyable to control. It *is* Anna at the door, but as soon as she sees her face, Sari's prepared smile shrinks and shrivels. Anna is bone white and gasping.

'Come in,' Sari urges, and Anna pushes past her, collapsing on one of the rickety wooden chairs by the table. Sari eases herself down opposite her, while Anna regards her with an expectant eye.

'Well?' asks Sari, hearing an echo of Judit in her slightly impatient tone. 'What's going on?'

'It's over,' Anna says.

For a moment, Sari can't quite figure out what she means. '*Over?*' she repeats.

'The war,' Anna says, a hitching sob in her voice. 'It's over.'

'Who—?' Sari knows that this is a stupid question; they have been hearing reports of their imminent defeat for months, but nevertheless . . .

'We lost,' Anna says, as if this is a side issue, something that matters little in the great scheme of things – and for her, it's true. Sari feels a tiny stab of regret that Marco can't be here to see the end of it, his side victorious, and that Ferenc is missing it too; not that he would be gracious in defeat, but she has a sense that the war was enough of a nightmare that part of him would always celebrate its end, regardless of the outcome.

'So they're going,' Anna says, evidently tired of waiting for Sari to catch on. 'The prisoners. They're going back to Italy. And our men are coming home. What I mean is,

Giovanni is going back to Italy, and Károly is coming back here.' With that, she puts her head on her folded arms and sobs.

Sari puts her arm around her. It's an odd thing, she realises, but pregnancy has made her better able to deal with physical affection. She's achieved the ultimate intimacy, a human being residing inside her, and next to that everything is easy. She waits patiently until Anna quietens. It doesn't take long – Anna's never been one for public displays of emotion – and within a couple of minutes she is upright again, face hectically flushed and damp, but dabbing her eyes with great dignity.

'Sorry,' she says to Sari, shamefaced.

'Don't be,' Sari replies. She is feeling a little emotional herself. She's a step removed from the immediacy of the situation, but she still cares, in an abstract way – cares about the Italian men who are leaving, many of whom she has dealt with intimately as a nurse, and cares about the men of the village who will be returning, many of them maimed and distressed, to a village that has stopped having much use for them.

'Have you spoken to Giovanni yet?' Sari asks, and Anna shakes her head.

'Not yet. I know what he wants – we've spoken about it, and he wants me to come back to Italy with him. You know that he has no wife, and he wants to marry me.' Despite her distress, Anna can't help swelling a little with pride as she says this – a man, a foreign man, wanting to marry *her*! 'But of course I can't go back with him now, the army will deal with that. I would have to make my own way, and you know,' she shrugs helplessly, 'I have no money. I have *nothing* that isn't Károly's. All our valuables have been with his cousin in Város since he's been away, that's how much he trusts me.'

'And when—?'

'Nobody knows. We just have to wait until people get orders from the army. It's not as if we're important,' she adds, with ill-fitting sarcasm. 'Not as if we're people who need to know anything.'

The camp disbands amid much confusion, mixed joy and regret. In general, the prisoners who have been there the least time are the most excited about going back to Italy, whereas the long term residents regard the notion of home with emotions ranging between trepidation and outright reluctance. They don't know home any more, they don't know how it may have changed in their absence, and in the meantime they have adapted to a routine that is familiar enough and comfortable enough to be pleasant. The more thoughtful of the men are anxious for other reasons – they have seen the way that the war has affected some of the women in the village, and who's to say that their own wives and sweethearts might not be similarly affected? Will they go home to find cuckoos in their nests, the stains of other men in their beds? Perhaps it's best not to wonder, and not to find out.

There's barely a man who hasn't formed an attachment to one or more of the villagers, and so the camp, in its final days, is surrounded by weeping women. Some are genuinely distraught – Anna, for one, who is dreading the return of Károly, and being enveloped back into her old life, but doesn't know what she can do about it, in the absence of funds – while others are simply nostalgic, appreciating the past two years as a pleasant diversion from normality, but not denouncing its return.

Sari is neither, though she goes down to the camp with the other woman to say goodbye. She is genuinely fond of some of the men, particularly Bruno, who had been a good friend of Marco's, and Umberto, despite, or perhaps because of his buoyant idiocy. She feels pleasantly removed from the emotion surrounding her – she's had her turn, and she's done what she has to do. But she understands now Judit's voyeuristic interest in the affairs of others and she can't deny that she'll be interested to see what comes next.

Things change so quickly. It's as if the Italians leave overnight and the village contracts to cover their absence. The Gazdag house stands empty and its emptiness seems to change its entire character. It now squats malignantly on the outskirts of the village, and Sari finds that she can't bear to look at it at night, as its black windows remind her of the still eyes of corpses. *Too many ghosts*, she thinks, and it's true that the two ghosts most likely to haunt her both have connections with the place. She has no desire to bump into the insubstantial forms of either Ferenc or Marco.

She's sure by now that the Gazdags are never going to come back to the village, crammed as it is with memories of Ferenc, and she wonders what they will do instead – sell the house, or install a caretaker? She hopes for the former, for while she could always stay out of the caretaker's way, she would far prefer that the Gazdag family sever all ties with the village, to leave her and her baby in peace.

The village seems quiet and brittle, almost at a loss without the Italians. Even those few people who never formed personal attachments with any of the prisoners realised the village was enlivened by their presence, and there's nothing to do now but wait until their own soldiers come home.

And then they come. At first in a trickle and then in a gush, the men come home. Sari and Judit watch it happening, Judit with prurient glee, and Sari with detached curiosity and a modicum of sympathy. The village breathes out as it expands to receive the returning men, and the visual change is immediate and startling. They seem to be everywhere, and the first market day after their return Sari is struck by it.

She hasn't been to the market for a while, as Judit has insisted that she stay home rather than risk the baby, but Judit relents and lets Sari accompany her this time, to satisfy her curiosity. The change is immediately noticeable, more as a taste in the air than anything more tangible and Sari instantly feels uncomfortable. Looking down, she realises that she and the other women of the village have become used to dressing in a rather more casual way since the men have been gone, and now she feels embarrassed and exposed.

There aren't many men around, as the market is traditionally the women's domain, but every now and then she catches sight of a man on a porch, or a glimpse through a window. The main change is in the behaviour of the women. There's little laughter about, none of the bawdy jokes that have become common currency in the past few years. Everyone is acting like children on their best behaviour. There's a sense of unsettlement, as if everyone is watching everyone else to see how they are dealing with the change, as if no one is quite sure how this is going to work out yet.

Then Sari catches sight of Anna out of the corner of her eye, and feels suddenly sick. Anna is sporting a series of livid purple bruises down one side of her face, but horrible as that is, it's not what shocks Sari the most: it's the change in every other aspect of Anna. Last time Sari saw her, she was tall and straight-backed, and now she seems to have lost inches in height as a result of a frightened hunch, as if her friend is denying her own existence, trying to disappear into herself, swallow herself up. Her hair swings loose and untidy over her face, and her clothing, while neat, is ugly, a dull, old-fashioned dress that Anna hasn't worn at all since Károly has been away. The eyes of all the other women slide away from her, the way they used to do with Sari. Sari can't bear to be a part of it.

'Stay here,' she says to Judit and approaches Anna, putting a gentle hand on her shoulder.

Anna jumps in a way that's a painful reflection of Sari's own behaviour at the start of the year, but to Sari's surprise she doesn't keep her head down or try to scurry away. Instead, she slowly raises her face until she's looking straight at Sari. The extent of her injuries are revealed – her left eye is bloodshot and swollen mainly shut, her lip is split and when her mouth opens in a joyless smile, Sari notices a gap in her teeth that she's sure wasn't there before.

'Hello, Sari,' Anna says, her voice rasps slightly and an image springs into Sari's mind, unpleasantly vivid, of a shadowy Károly gripping Anna around the throat.

'You've hurt yourself, Anna,' Sari says gently.

Anna nods, wincing slightly.

'Walked into a door,' she says, each word unnaturally distinct as she manoeuvres her tongue around her swollen lip.

As Sari raises her eyebrows in disbelief, Anna's mouth quirks upwards in a supremely sarcastic smile. 'Should be getting home,' she says.

'Wait! Do you want to come around to Judit's? I could have a look at your face, give you something—'

'More trouble than it's worth, Sari,' Anna replies. The travesty of a smile drops from her face so quickly that it's as if it were never there. 'I don't know what to do. I thought that maybe the war would have made him better, but he's worse than ever. Won't leave me alone.'

'Anna—'

'Why couldn't he have been killed? I've stopped believing in God, you know. Can't believe in him, because I don't want to believe in something that would let Lujza's husband be killed, while bringing Károly back safe.'

'Anna, please—'

'I've got to go,' Anna says abruptly. She swivels on her heels and walks away and Sari watches her go, thinking that if she didn't know that it was Anna, she would never have recognised her from that cowed, nervous walk. Sari realises that she is shaking, and turns back to where Judit is standing, leaning on one hip, clearly having watched the entire encounter.

'I'm going home,' Sari says. She feels as if her legs won't hold her up any longer.

For the next few nights, Anna haunts her dreams – Anna dead, Anna being beaten by Károly, Anna being beaten by Ferenc – so when, three days later, Károly arrives at Judit's door, she's disoriented. She hasn't seen him in the flesh for four years, but he's been so lifelike in her head at night that she feels that she could draw him blindfolded, every crease, every mark on that stupid, craven little face.

'What do you want?' she asks. She knows she should be

polite, that it's only going to hurt Anna in the long run if she can't be civil to this man's face, but she feels as if she's filled with rancid, boiling bile, and she can't possibly keep it all in.

'Where's Judit?' he asks.

'She's out. Looking after Zsofia Gyulai. Can I help?' If it were anyone else, she would stand aside and let him into the house, but she can't bear to do that with this man, not just because she loathes him, though that is part of it, but also because she doesn't trust the way that he will behave alone in a house with her.

'Can't I come in?'

'No.'

He looks discomfited, glancing around to see if there's anyone watching him, and Sari hopes that he'll get spooked and leave. Let him come back when Judit's there to deal with him, she thinks. But he doesn't, and instead lifts his right arm.

'It's my hand. I hurt it, and it's not healing properly.'

His knuckles are bloody and scabbed, and the surrounding skin is flushed red with infection.

'Wait there,' Sari says, and without hearing his reply she slams the door and leans on it heavily. She must behave, she *must*, for Anna's sake if nothing else, but Károly turning up at Judit's house expecting treatment for a wound resulting from beating Anna, while she is covered in bruises and won't dare to get help. She wants to spit in his face, slap him, rake her nails down his cheek, kick him where it hurts most.

Moments later, when she opens the door again, she half-expects him to be gone, but he's still there, a dumb, mulish expression on his face.

'Here,' she says, thrusting a bottle at him containing pounded, boiled anemone root. 'Clean it with this. It should help.' She pauses for a moment, wondering whether she dares. 'You might want to offer some to Anna, too,' she says at last, and is gratified when a flicker of uncertainty passes over his face.

CHAPTER NINETEEN

Late in her pregnancy, Sari has taken to napping in the afternoon. She hates the way her previously energetic nature has been eroded, but she can't fight the exhaustion that overwhelms her sometimes, and it's yet another reason to look forward to the birth of the baby. So she's sleeping when Anna comes to see her, and she's woken by Judit gently shaking her shoulder.

'What is it?'

'Anna's here. She says she wants to see you, and it's urgent.'

Sari is so comfortable; her feet have been hurting badly lately, and the thought of standing up again is far from pleasant. She groans.

'Can't you deal with it?'

Judit shakes her head. 'Sorry, love, but she says that I won't do, that she has to see you – in private, too. Not sure what it's all about. She looks rather battered about, but then, she always does these days.' The scowl that crosses Judit's face at these words makes Sari think that perhaps Judit wouldn't have had the same compunction about not spitting in Károly's face a few days before.

Five minutes later, Sari's heaved herself to her feet, and made a few token efforts to make herself presentable. Still grumpy about being woken up, she tells herself to behave as pleasantly as possible. After all, Anna's having a tough time at the moment, and Sari's sure that she wouldn't have come to visit without genuine need, not after her words at the market the other day hinted that Károly wouldn't want her coming there, so it wouldn't do to be unfriendly.

'Sorry to wake you, Sari,' Anna says from where she is sitting at the table. Sari runs an eye over her as quickly and unobtrusively as possible. The bruises she'd had when Sari last saw her have faded to a liverish yellow, but she has a new bruise on her right cheek, some ugly-looking marks on her throat that make Sari suppress a shudder, and she seems to be carrying her left arm in an odd way, as if her shoulder has been wrenched. She looks bad, but no worse than she did the other day, so there are no obvious clues as to why she's seeking Sari's help now. Perhaps it's something unseen, some sexual violation that Anna's too ashamed to share with Judit?

'Well, then,' Judit says, with false heartiness. 'I'll just . . . go and see to the geese, or something.' She shrugs a little, lost for words, and heads out the back door, towards the little herb garden.

'Do you want a drink of anything?' Sari asks Anna. Anna has an oddly set expression on her face, as if she is trying to build up the confidence to say what's on her mind, and Sari senses that some coaxing might be needed.

'Coffee would be good. You sit down, I'll do it.'

Sari doesn't protest, and eases herself down at the table, biting back a groan. That's another thing she hates about pregnancy, these unwarranted groans and moans and whimpers that spring all too readily to her lips!

Anna sets down a cup of coffee in front of Sari, and circles around the table to sit down herself. Sari notices that she's walking with a slight limp, holding herself very carefully erect, and that she winces slightly as she sits down.

'I can't stay for long,' she says. 'Károly has gone to visit Zsigmond Kiss, but I have to be home before he is.'

'All right,' Sari says. 'So, what's he done to you this time?'

Anna gives a humourless laugh. 'Oh, the usual. He's worse than he ever was before, now. He drinks all the time. I think the war made him depressed, and he drinks to try and forget it, and maybe he does forget it the next day, but at the time, it just makes him worse, sad, and then angry. He's just – just unbearable.'

'Your arm – what happened?'

'He was – he was holding me down. He had my arm twisted behind my back, and he was holding it so that he could – you know.' Anna blushes, and Sari remembers how open she was when talking about sex with Giovanni; this embarrassment and coyness is new to her and linked, Sari supposes, to the humiliation inherent in sex with Károly. 'I think he likes it better – enjoys it more – when he is hurting me at the same time.'

'Bastard.'

Anna nods, with a wry smile. Does she just want to talk? Sari wonders. She doesn't mind. She recalls how isolated she felt when she was living with Ferenc and feeling that she was the only person who had ever gone through what she was going through. She wishes she could tell Anna that she understands, but just then Anna lifts her head, looks straight at Sari for the first time, and says: 'I need you to help me, Sari.'

Sari is nonplussed. 'Well, of course I'll help you, Anna!

What's the problem? What do you need? I've got plenty of stuff that will help with the bruises, and—'

Anna is shaking her head. 'No. You don't understand. I need you to help me deal with Károly. In the same way that you dealt with Ferenc.'

Sari's vision goes black, and for a petrifying moment she is sure that she is going to faint. And then it clears, and she hopes desperately that she misheard what Anna said, that there's been some mistake, that she's misinterpreted and that Anna means something silly and simple and utterly different to what Sari thinks she means. But when her eyes settle on Anna again, she's still staring at her with that fixed and desperate and determined expression, and Sari knows that she knows, and, God, there's an ocean, a world, a *universe* of difference between the idea of Anna suspecting, and the certainty that she knows for sure.

'What do you mean?' she asks weakly, playing for time.

'You don't have to lie to me, Sari. I don't blame you. No one blames you.'

'What do you—? Who—? *Does everyone know?*'

Anna looks surprised at the strength of Sari's reaction. 'No, no, not everyone, of course not. A lot of people believe that he just got ill and died. But some of us – we don't blame you, Sari; the only reason we guessed is because we know how he was treating you, and what he did to Marco. Anyone would do the same under those circumstances, *anyone.*'

'How do you—?'

'I can tell, Sari. When it's happened to you, you can tell when it's happening to someone else. That story about Marco being killed trying to escape – well, a lot of people believed that. You were pretty discreet, and I think some people never even knew that you two were lovers, but I always thought that was suspicious. And for it to happen at exactly the same time as you moving in with Ferenc, and never being seen in public any more – that just made it even more suspicious. And on the few occasions that you did come out of that house . . . You hid it well – I'll give you that, but when you know what to look for, like I do, it was easy to work out that he was beating you. It was hard to believe at first. I always used to like him, and respect him; I thought that a man like him wouldn't behave like that. But I suppose the war can change people.'

Sari struggles not to put her head in her hands, forces herself to keep looking at Anna, who keeps talking. Now that she's started it's as if she can't halt the rush of words.

'And when I heard he was ill again, I'm sure a lot of people believed it, because I almost did, too, but I couldn't quite. Because I knew you had a motive, you see, and because I know,' her voice becomes bitter, now, 'I know that for women like us, God, or fate, or whatever it is doesn't intervene so neatly. So when he died, I knew that you had to have done something to cause it.'

Sari's mouth is bone dry, and she takes a large gulp of her coffee, nearly scalding herself. 'Oh God,' she says, her voice shaking. 'Shit.' Inside her belly, her baby jerks suddenly, as if sharing Sari's terror.

Anna's hand darts across the table to grasp hers.

'Don't you understand? You don't have to worry. I'm on your side. I understand why you had to do what you did, and I'm not going to tell anyone. I promise.' Anna forces a laugh. 'It's not so unusual, what you did – women have been dealing with things in that way for centuries. Ask Judit; she'd tell you.'

'Who knows?' Sari whispers.

'Not many of us. Me, Lujza, Lilike, I think – a few of the other girls who used to work down at the camp. Just people who know you, Sari, and like you. You can trust us. You can trust *me*. No one's going to say anything.'

'All right,' Sari says, 'All right.' She takes a deep breath. It's not that bad, she thinks. It could be worse. Anna's not going to run to the police, and neither are the other girls. It's not as bad as it could be.

'So will you help me?' Anna asks. Sari remembers – Oh, yes, it *is* very bad, after all.

'Anna,' she says pleadingly, 'It's not like it was for me. You're not pregnant. Ferenc's family know people in all the villages around here. You could run, but if I'd run, he would have found me and killed me. He would have killed my baby.'

Anna leans across the table. 'You think Károly hasn't said the exact same thing to me?' she asks. 'That if I ever left, he wouldn't rest until he found me and killed me? Oh, of course, he probably wouldn't do it. He's not as intelligent as Ferenc was, and he doesn't have the connections that Ferenc did. So maybe I could run. But with what money? Károly may not have the resources that Ferenc had, but neither do I have the resources that *you* have. I have nothing of my own, nothing, and I don't have the knowledge of the countryside that you have, all those things about plants and animals and how to hide, things that you learnt from your father and from Judit. I wouldn't last a day out there, on my own; I'd die, or be killed, or be found by the police, and that would be the end of me.'

She pauses for a moment, collecting herself. 'Listen. When Giovanni left, he told me that I should come to him. I know where he lives, and if I had money, I could get there. He can't afford to send me money, not as much as I would need, and the only way I'm going to get hold of as much money as I need is if Károly's dead. I have jewellery that my grandmother left me, but Károly has it locked up, and he keeps the key with him at all times. I'll never get it off him while he's alive.'

'If you're so keen to kill him,' Sari says slowly, 'I don't see why you necessarily need me. Especially if you're going to kill him and run.'

'Sari, the way you did it with Ferenc, you made it look like he just got ill and died. Yes, maybe some of us were suspicious, but there was no proof. As satisfying as it would be to bury the fire axe in Károly's head, if I did that and ran, people would think I was a madwoman, and they'd be swarming over the countryside looking for me. If I did it your way – well, everyone around here knows what Károly's like. I used to hate that, but now I realise it can work in my favour. If it were anyone else, perhaps people would be suspicious, but with me, if Károly got ill and died, who would blame me for taking what I could and leaving as soon as possible? Everyone knows he's been a bad husband to me, and it's not as if he has family left to make a big fuss about his death. I've *thought* about it, Sari. I can do this. It's possible. But I need you.'

Sari listens to Anna, and she's almost convinced. Almost. Poor Anna, she's in the same situation Sari was in a few months back, and what would Sari have done if Judit hadn't been there to help her? But no. It's impossible. She can't possibly do it.

'I've already got two deaths on my conscience, Anna. I can't add a third. I'm sorry.'

Anna bites her lip, looking as if the last thing she wants to say is what she's about to. 'You'll have three deaths on your conscience, either way. If you don't help me, if I stay with him, he'll kill me before long, or I'll kill myself. You know it happens, Sari. I can't stay with him.'

'That's not fair. It's not fair of you to say that.'

'*Nothing* is fair. Damn it, Sari, I'm just trying to survive. That's all.'

Silence falls. Anna seems to realise that she's pushed her persuasive powers to the limit, and that if that hasn't persuaded Sari then nothing will. Sari, meanwhile – she's smarting, she's shocked and horrified and sick, but *what would you have done if Judit hadn't helped you?* she thinks. *What would you have done?* And she finds that she can't get that thought out of her head.

'I didn't curse him, if that's what you're thinking,' she says abruptly. 'Nothing that easy. I poisoned him. You'd have to do it yourself, put stuff in his food. It's not quite as bad as – I don't know, as hacking him to death with a hatchet – but you're still doing it. It's not fun to watch. You'd have to be sure you could do that.'

'Sari,' Anna looks up at her, eyes shining with an uncomfortable mixture of fanaticism and exultation, 'it would be a pleasure. Every step of the way.'

'I haven't decided,' Sari adds quickly. 'I'm not definitely going to help you. But – just come back tomorrow. Same time, if you can. I need to think about it.'

Anna just looks at Sari for a moment, as if trying to decide whether to say anything further, but then nods and stands up. 'All right,' she says. 'I'll try to come back tomorrow. But I'd better get home now.'

'Forgive me,' Sari says, indicating her swollen belly, 'if I don't see you out. This makes it rather difficult for me to get up, you know.'

Anna grins – the first genuine smile Sari's seen from her in a long while. 'Of course.' She walks to the door, and then stops, one hand on the latch. 'I just want you to know,' she says, turning back to Sari, 'that I'm not blackmailing you. If you don't help me, I'm not going to be happy, but I won't tell anyone about Ferenc. I don't want you to think I'd do that to you, or to your baby.'

'Thank you,' Sari says, and means it. Anna's kindness is the strongest weapon in her arsenal; it makes sense that she should have saved it for last.

CHAPTER TWENTY

It's curious, Sari thinks, how easy it is to become a murderer. Of course she's going to help Anna. Despite her doubts, it was inevitable from the moment that Anna asked her, but this is different from the way it was with Ferenc. Károly, despicable as Sari knows him to be, has never harmed her personally, and she can't possibly claim that she's fighting for her own survival in the way that she was with Ferenc. It's a sort of remote type of murder, as she's not the one directly doing the killing, and she's not the one who has directly been wronged, and in her mind she likens it to a war, where it becomes acceptable to kill people you've never met, because they mean harm to your country and your loved ones. In this war, Sari and Anna are definitely on the same side.

She talks it over with Judit once Anna is safely gone, and Judit's response is predictably dispassionate.

'You know I couldn't care less about morality,' she says, 'and even if I did, I'd probably make an exception for that bastard Károly, who certainly doesn't deserve to live. If you want to help Anna, you should go ahead – and she's right, you know, this sort of thing has been going on for years. It's nothing new. The only thing that concerns me is the possibility of you coming to harm through this. One mysterious illness in a village can be explained away, but another, particularly if it's the husband of someone as closely connected with you as Anna, is liable to arouse suspicion. I don't care about me – I've lived more than long enough; I could die tomorrow with no regrets. But I don't want this all to come crashing down on you.'

Sari doesn't want that either. She knows it's a risk, but the more she thinks about it, the more she feels that she can't possibly abandon Anna to her fate. Besides, killing Károly is not as much of a risk as it could be: Anna is right, he is hardly the best-liked person in the village. People are generally fond of Anna, and aware of the way that Károly treats her, and he has no close family to love him despite his considerable flaws. In a lot of ways, it's a far safer bet than Ferenc was, and that turned out all right . . .

'I'm going to help her,' Sari says to Judit, who grins and shrugs in return.

'I thought you would. Well, let's get to it.'

'I've still got some of that stuff left, from Ferenc . . .'

'Can't hurt to make some more, though. Who knows who might be needing it yet? This could turn into quite a little business, Sari!'

Although Judit is joking (or at least Sari thinks she is), Sari can't help thinking about those words. She keeps crossing lines. With killing Ferenc, she crossed a line that most people refuse to cross, and since then, any lingering belief she may have once had in salvation has gone, making it so much easier to cross the next line. Would she keep going with this? She doesn't think so, but there's a part of herself that asks why it actually matters any more.

Anna doesn't come back the next day. She's at the whim of Károly's plans, Sari knows. She wouldn't be able to come without either a watertight excuse, or without his knowledge, but still, she can't help worrying that Károly may have somehow got wind of their conversation yesterday, and preempted things. It's entertaining that possibility that eliminates any last doubts that she may have had. If she has to have another death on her conscience, she would infinitely rather it be Károly's than Anna's.

She's there the next morning, though, grimacing as she walks through the door.

'Sorry about yesterday, he wouldn't—'

'It's all right. You're here now.'

Sari shoots a significant glance over towards Judit, who draws a long-suffering sigh and hauls herself to her feet, heading for the garden. Sari's sure that Anna knows that Judit's probably in on whatever's going on, but Anna's never been totally comfortable around Judit – few people are, given her acerbic nature – and so Anna is likely to feel more comfortable discussing matters as delicate as murdering one's husband with Sari alone.

Sari can't quite help imitating Judit when she places the bowl of powder in front of Anna. She's alarmed to find that she gets a strange sort of excitement from helping Anna do this; delicately prodding her conscience, she finds that guilt is nowhere to be found. No point worrying about that now; if there is a hell, she's already hell-bound, after all, and she imagines being unrepentant for two murders is not much worse than being unrepentant for one.

She explains to Anna how the innocuous looking powder works, and all the while, Anna is silent, wide-eyed, as if only now getting to grips with the reality of what she is planning. When she's reached the end of a word-for-word recital of the instructions that Judit gave her, she sits back and eyes Anna critically. Anna doesn't look back, as she is still gazing, transfixed, at the blunt pyramid of powder.

'You want my advice, Anna?' Sari asks, and Anna nods, wordlessly.

'Give him a lot straight away. He's not like Ferenc – Ferenc was trusting, not naturally suspicious, but Károly is. You need to knock him out straight away, so that he can't do anything, can't hurt you, or tell anyone that he thinks you've done something. All right?'

'So why don't I just – you know, give him enough to kill him straight off?'

'Come on, Anna. You've said it before, and you're right, no one here's got much fondness for Károly, and no one's going to look into his death as long as you don't invite it. But killing him suddenly would be inviting it – not a lot less suspicious than a hatchet in his skull. Do you understand?'

'I think so.' Anna looks down at the powder again, and for a moment Sari wonders whether she's going to back out and change her mind, she looks so nervous and uncertain. But instead she looks up at Sari, with an unexpectedly animated grin.

'Right, then. I should go home and get started.'

Sari smiles back, but feels oddly melancholy. Anna has always struck her as such a profoundly good person, and the thought that Sari is helping her to do this, to besmirch her eternal soul – something Anna certainly believes in, even if Sari does not – makes Sari sad.

'Before you go – tell me what you're going to do, again.'

And Anna recites, like a child repeating her lessons: 'Knock him out tonight. Come here tomorrow, say that he's ill, and I don't know what's wrong. You or Judit will come and see him. Finish him off after a couple of days – and then

I'm going,' she adds defiantly. Sari has tried to persuade her to stay around at least until the funeral, just to deflect suspicion, but Anna refuses point blank, and Sari's given up trying to persuade her. It probably won't make much of a difference, either way.

'Good. Just – just be careful, Anna. And I suppose I'll see you tomorrow.'

Like clockwork, Anna is banging on the door at half past ten the next morning, and Sari smiles, because the timing could hardly be better. The day is getting underway, and the streets are thronged with people, plenty of witnesses to see Anna bringing Sari and Judit to look at her ailing husband. It's lucky that no one else is there, as Anna can hardly contain her excitement.

'It's working, Sari!' she says in a gleeful whisper. 'He's in agony, the bastard!'

Sari and Judit both accompany Anna back to her house. Sari has to elbow Anna repeatedly. She looks as if she's having the time of her life, rather than acting like an anxious wife.

When they get to the house, Anna drops all pretence, and as soon as the door's shut behind them, she says, in clarion tones, 'The bastard's in there. No point going in to see him; I'm going to finish him off in a couple of days, and I don't want you giving him anything for the pain. I want the son of a whore to *suffer*.' Sari's torn between horror and laughter, but Judit has no such confusion and gives her characteristic cackle.

'That's the spirit, girl. Well, you may as well put some

water on to boil – we'll have to stay here a while, make it look like we're taking care of him, so you can give us a cup of coffee while we're waiting.'

They stay nearly an hour, and the whole time Anna seems unable to sit still. Practically vibrating with nervous excitement, she gets up at intervals to peer at Károly from the door of the bedroom, but not once does she venture further. She's not even making a pretence of caring for him.

'I want him to know that I'm doing this,' she says to Sari, as she and Judit get up to leave. 'This is my last chance to show the bastard what I think of him.'

'We'll spread word around the village that he's ill,' Sari says, 'though anyone who saw us come here will be talking already. Give him another couple of days, and then finish it.'

Anna nods. 'I've already got the key off him – I've got all the jewellery and money I need. I'm almost tempted to go now, but I'll wait, I promise.'

'You must wait, Anna. You mustn't attract suspicion. You're still determined to leave as soon as he's dead?'

'Absolutely. I'll go the night that he dies.'

'All right. Just let me know, will you? Leave – oh, I don't know. Leave a twig from a cherry tree on the steps of the house. Then I'll know to come and check on him. I'll wait a day or so, to make sure you've got a good head start in case anyone wants to go after you.'

Anna looks close to tears. 'I can't thank you enough, Sari – and Judit, both of you.'

Sari leans forwards, and gives Anna a brisk, tight hug. She's still not quite used to casual physical contact, and the pressure of Anna's body against her is both unsettling and pleasant. 'Good luck, Anna. If there's any way that you can let me know that you've made it, that you're safe . . .'

'I promise.'

The door clicks shut behind them.

For the next two days, Sari thinks of nothing but Anna, with a mixture of sick anxiety and excitement. She is terribly worried about something going wrong, Anna ending up dead or in prison, but at the same time, if Anna manages to do this right, it will be the escape that she never quite dared to dream of. Sari's never been very good at waiting patiently and is desperately tempted to go round to Anna's and find out what's going on, and by the afternoon of the second day she's got as far as putting on her coat before Judit asks her where she's going.

'Round to Anna's,' Sari says defiantly.

Judit shakes her head. 'No, you're not. You can't help her more than you have already. You have to just leave her to it now. She's a bright girl; she should be able to manage this alone.'

'But won't it look suspicious if we don't call round? If Károly's ill enough to be on his deathbed, we should be there, trying to help him, shouldn't we?'

'Well, that's one way of looking at it. On one hand, you're the person who takes care of people when they're ill. On the other, you're a woman whose fiancé died suddenly not too long ago. Could be that you visiting that house just before Károly dies could cause suspicion, rather than avert it,' Judit says.

Sari hasn't thought of that, and she dithers, one arm half in and half out of the sleeve of her coat.

'Either way, you can't do anything by going around there. Just leave it. You can deal with your own curiosity for another couple of days, can't you?'

But Sari doesn't have to deal with it for that long. When she wakes up the next morning she can feel the difference in the air. Something's happened. And when she opens the front door, and finds a small, unobtrusive cherry twig sitting sedately on the front step, she's taken unawares by the sharp stab of grief she feels. Anna has gone – the one person in the village (Judit excepted) whose friendship Sari could be absolutely sure of. And underneath the grief is a persistent throb of jealousy. Until these past few days, she never would have dreamt that Anna would get away from the village while she, Sari, was left behind. For a moment, she curses the mud and the discomfort and the utter banality of the village before her, before stepping back into the house, twig in hand, and closing the door.

As soon as Judit sees what she's holding, her wizened face cracks open in a wide grin. 'Oh, good girl, good girl! She did it!'

They wait a day before going around to Anna's house, where Anna's absence is palpable. Károly's deathbed is not pretty; it's clear that Anna has done little in the way of nursing through his short, sharp illness, but Sari feels no pity. Nevertheless, she and Judit clean him up as much as possible, before Judit goes to spread the word of his death.

As predicted, no one much mourns Károly. Even the men he would have called his friends, the ones that he would drink and gamble with were not particularly fond of him; his vicious temper didn't end at Anna, and did nothing to endear him to anyone. He is buried with minimal fuss, Sari writes out the death certificate as usual for the authorities in Város, and nobody even suggests summoning the priest from the next village to conduct the funeral. Anna's disappearance is far more upsetting to everyone, as she was always well liked, more so than even Sari would have guessed, for even gossip is kind to her.

'Who can blame her for leaving as soon as he's dead?' Sari overhears Matild Nagy saying in the square, voice lowered to give a false impression of confidentiality. 'Everyone knew how he treated her. Good for her, I say. She deserves a better life.'

The tale of Károly's sudden death and Anna's subsequent vanishing act leaps around the village for a few days, and then dies down, leaving Sari with nothing but a feeling of sweet relief, mingled with an ache of loneliness. She thinks of Anna often, tries to follow her imagined steps in her mind – oh, she misses her, so much.

A week later. Anna could be in Budapest by now; Sari tries to imagine her there, her fantasy only slightly hampered by the fact that she has to imagine Budapest too. There's a knock on the door and Sari bids a hasty farewell to Anna-in-her-head; she starts to lever herself up from the chair where she's been sitting, sipping a cooling cup of tea, but before she can move too far, Judit shoots past her, moving unnaturally fast for a woman her age.

'Sit down!' she snaps, zooming past. 'Rest! I'll get it.'

It's Orsolya Kiss, flanked by Jakova Gersek and Matild Nagy. Judit takes half a step backwards in surprise. There's no love lost between any of the five women there, and normally Orsolya and her henchwomen would only come to see Judit and Sari when in the direst need, but a quick glance over the three of them doesn't reveal any obvious illnesses or injuries. Quite to the contrary, Orsolya looks uncommonly well, her pug-like face wreathed in smug smiles.

'Well, Orsolya, Jakova, Matild,' Judit says, recovering quickly. 'What a surprise to see you here. What can we help you with?'

'Ah,' says Orsolya, and her smile grows ever wider. 'It's rather a delicate matter. Perhaps best discussed over a cup of coffee. You don't mind putting some water on, do you, Sari?'

'I'll do it,' Judit says swiftly, and heads for the kitchen, while Orsolya and her friends sit down at the table, facing Sari, without waiting to be asked. Every inch of Sari's body is tensed: she doesn't trust these three, not in the slightest, and she thinks that she can smell trouble. The other two look slightly discomfited, nervous, and they keep fidgeting as if keen to leave, as if they'd rather be anywhere but here. Orsolya, on the other hand, sits at the table as if she owns it, the embodiment of calm, and turns her unctuous smile onto Sari.

'Sari. You're looking well, all things considered.'

Sari tries to smile back – it can't hurt to try and stay as much on Orsolya's good side as possible – but her mouth will not obey her and it's a struggle to get the words out. 'Thank you, Orsolya. You're looking very well yourself.'

Orsolya ignores the implicit second half of Sari's sentence: *so what are you doing here?*

'I *am* well, Sari. Very well.'

The conversation stops there, and by the time Judit returns, Sari is in an agony of awkwardness; Orsolya, on the other hand, looks as though she's never been more comfortable.

'So,' Judit says, as she sits down at the table, passing out cups of coffee. 'How can we help you?'

'Well,' Orsolya says, with another beatific smile, 'We were hoping that you could share some of your . . . *expertise* with us.'

Sari freezes. *This is it*, she thinks, but Judit appears not to have understood.

'Of course,' she says, frowning slightly in confusion. 'That's what you're here for, isn't it? So what's the problem?'

'Ah, no,' Orsolya says, sounding as if she is choosing every word with careful precision, 'You misunderstand me. We don't need your help *curing* anyone of anything. Quite the opposite, in fact.'

There's a short, punchy silence. Then Judit says stiffly, 'I don't know what you're talking about.'

Orsolya laughs, falsely coy, in response. 'Oh, come now! You don't have to hide these things from us. We don't blame Anna in the slightest for doing away with Károly, and we don't blame you for helping her, either. Quite why you saw fit to kill Ferenc, Sari, I can't quite imagine – he struck me as quite a nice boy, I always thought you did very well to catch him – but then, who am I to question?'

'What do you want?' Sari asks at last.

'Well, I rather thought we'd made that clear. You shouldn't be selfish, Sari, hogging these things to yourself, only sharing them with your best friends. Things have changed around here since the end of the war, since the men came back, and we don't really like it this way. We got used to the way things were during the war, and now . . . now there are a few things that we would like to get rid of, and I think that you can help us with that.'

'And if we don't?' Judit asks. She is remaining impressively calm, but her cheeks have turned a bright, violent red.

'Oh, I don't want you to think that I'm threatening you or anything like that. But I do have a cousin who's a police officer in Város, and I'm sure he'd be very interested to hear about a couple of suspicious deaths that have happened around here.'

'You have no proof,' Sari says, her heart hammering against her ribs. Her baby gives a sickening lurch inside her.

'Perhaps not. But that doesn't really matter, does it, if Ferenc's parents get wind of what really happened to him? I mean, I don't want to sound harsh, dear, but his family's got rather more standing than the two of you have. No one's likely to dispute any claims that they make, now, are they?'

'And if we help you?' Judit asks.

'Then it'll hardly be in our interests to tell anyone about what's been going on, will it?'

They agree – what else can they do? A series of brisk, tacit arrangements are made; Orsolya and her friends will come back in two days, to give Judit and Sari enough time to prepare what they're going to need. The words Judit spoke a week or so ago, about this becoming a business, clang through Sari's head. *We're in the murder business now*, she thinks to herself, and has to swallow a hysterical giggle.

As Orsolya takes her leave, Sari can't help but ask:

'How did you know? How could you be so sure?'

Orsolya laughs again, and puts a hand on Sari's arm. 'Oh, dear, no, I wasn't sure, not at all. But in a lot of ways it doesn't make any difference whether it's true or not – there are enough people around here who'll take my word over yours. I mean, what you seem to forget, Sari,' and she leans in closer, as if imparting an important secret, 'is that *you* don't really matter around here. Neither of you do. Not in the slightest.'

1920

CHAPTER TWENTY-ONE

Lilike hadn't really wanted to leave Falucska. She'd lived there all her life. Her world had been bounded by the flat expanse of the plain and the dizzying sky, and although she'd visited Város once in a while, she'd never really been able to conceive that it was as real as the village, that the streets that brimmed with horses and carts could exist in the same world that held the river and the woods and the marketplace she'd grown up with.

She's adapted well, though, if she does say so herself. When her mother told her, a year ago, that they were moving to Város to be with her aunt a year ago, Lilike had wept for days, but already she looks back at that sobbing girl with pity and condescension. She had been worried, at first, that her cousins, sophisticated town girls one and all, would shun her and her country ways, and she'd barely built up the courage to speak to them for the first few weeks. But since then, they'd become so kind. Her wardrobe is littered with their off-cast dresses, and when she slips a cool muslin gown over her head in the morning, she reflects that she barely misses the village at all, any more. She had worried, a little, that her time with Umberto would affect her chances of finding a husband in Város, but she's pleased to find that's not the case – her cousins, when she awkwardly admits what she's done, greet her story with congratulations rather than with censure; she understands that, since the war, that sort of thing is, if not acceptable, then at least understood.

She and her mother have never properly talked about why they left, but Lilike has a fair idea. She had tried to keep Umberto a secret from her mother at first, but before too long she had become more lax. After they'd got word that her brother was dead, her mother had barely done anything but arrange and rearrange his old clothes in the trunk at the foot of her bed. Lilike started to go out more and more, staying out later and later. On the occasions she spent time with her mother, she started to notice that her mother was starting to seem happier, but Lilike put that down to nothing more than time passing since her brother's death until one day, heading to the forest with Umberto, she came across her mother, entwined with an older Italian officer Lilike had seen from time to time.

Saucer-eyed, Lilike had tugged at Umberto's hand, pressed a finger to her lips, and they had tiptoed away. Later, Lilike was surprised to find that she was neither shocked nor disapproving. She remembered her mother, her hands red from washing, nursing her father through the throes of his final illness; she remembered hearing her, pacing and weeping in the next room as Lilike and her brother huddled together in bed, and decided that she did not begrudge her mother whatever happiness she could carve out for herself.

She should have known that it couldn't last, though. Lilike had adjusted fairly well to the departure of the Italians. She'd known that they had to leave sometime, and she and Umberto had had so little to say to one another when they weren't busy fucking that she had had no illusions about them sharing a long and happy life together. Her mother, however, had adjusted less well, and within weeks had gone back to her old clothing re-arranging ways. Lilike started to wake in the night to the sound of her mother crying out in her sleep, twisting in nightmares she can't describe when she wakes.

It's the death of Orsolya Kiss's husband that's the final straw. He had been a second cousin of Lilike's mother, and throughout his short, sharp illness (which had been broadcast all over the village), her mother had started to look more and more haunted. The very day that the news had gone around that he had died, Lilike's mother had started to pack, and they had left only days later. Whenever Lilike mentioned the village afterwards, her mother would change the subject and Lilike had soon stopped talking about it at all.

When they hear about the death of Tomas Gersek, then, Lilike expects her mother to succumb to another attack of nerves, but instead she straightens her back. The Gerseks had been neighbours of Lilike's family. Lilike remembers how, when her father had been ill, Jakova used to help her mother with her cooking, while Tomas would chop firewood and mend fences and do all the sorts of things that her father wasn't able to do any more.

'We should go back for the funeral,' Lilike's mother says, and Lilike feels a throb of excitement. She wonders which of her new dresses is likely to make the best impression back in the village.

But it's not like she thinks it's going to be. The journey across the plain in a rattling old cart seems beneath her dignity, and the village, cloaked in November mist, seems shrunken and silent, so different from the bustle of Város. The road to the cemetery is rutted and muddy, and even though Jakova has gone to the trouble to ask the priest from the next village to perform the funeral, it seems like a half-hearted, almost sinister affair.

Jakova, black-veiled, stands with her head bowed by the grave, oddly still; the priest can't seem to think of anything to say, and instead of staying silent, seems to decide that he will say all the words that he can think of, in the hopes of stumbling on the right ones. Lilike is chilled; she's wearing obligatory black, but the sharp, stylish cut of her dress and it's trimmings seem oddly obscene among the browns and greys of Falucska in autumn, and she feels as if her heart is swelling in her chest as, increasingly panicked, she looks around for a friendly face. She spots Lujza and her family in the crowd, but Lujza's eyes are blank and still, and she doesn't seem to see Lilike at all.

A swirl of colour on the edge of her vision makes her look around, and there is Sari, a child in her arms with the reddest hair that Lilike has seen. The girl was a baby when Lilike left for Város, and now she's a silent, self-possessed two-year-old, long-legged and thin, whom Sari hefts in her arms as easily as if she were a kitten. And Sari – Lilike catches Sari's eye, and Sari smiles, a smile that stops far short of her eyes, a smile that is little more than a perfunc-tory showing of teeth, and suddenly Lilike understands: Sari is afraid, Sari finds Lilike's presence frightening, and *some-thing is going on here*, something that Lilike had blindly guessed at, but only now really comprehends, feeling the weight of it on her chest.

It's all she can do to stay still and silent for the rest of the funeral. Her mother clutches her hand so tightly that Lilike is sure that she is feeling the same way. When the funeral is over, they put their heads down and walk back to the cart that they've hired as quickly as is decent. They do not talk to anyone. Lilike feels the ice in her chest dissolve as soon as the village is behind her, and knows that she will never go back.

1922

CHAPTER TWENTY-TWO

Keled Imanci is hungry. It's been three days now, and as he sits in his chair, he can hear the gurgling and growling of his stomach trying to digest itself. He's not sure how much longer he can hold out, although he remembers someone from the front who had been a doctor in his previous life, saying that, as long as you've got plenty of fluids, it's possible to last indefinitely without food. *How long?* one of the younger men had asked eagerly. Weeks, the man had answered.

Weeks, Keled thinks now. How many – two? Three? Maybe longer? Surely he doesn't need much food himself? It's not as if he works up much of an appetite; it's hard to exercise with only one leg. He used to be able to lean on his crutch and hobble his way around the house, but Francziska took that away from him months ago – it drove her mad, she said, to hear his constant banging about. It got on her last nerve, she said, the way she was always wondering what he would knock over next – maybe the milk jug, or the pie freshly baked and cooling on the window sill?

It's June, now, and Francziska has put him in the chair that looks out over the front porch; if he cranes his neck, he can just about see his crutch, leaning against the steps. He knows that it would be useless to try and reach it. His remaining leg is weak and wasted through lack of use. Even if he got down on his front and dragged himself across the floor, Francziska is bound to hear him thumping before he even gets close. And even if he manages to reach the crutch, what then? She'll just take it away from him again.

In the middle of the night, the pain in Keled's vanished leg wakes him up, and he sits in the darkness listening to his stomach. He hears the clock in the kitchen strike three, but light spills out from under the bedroom door – she's still awake, then. One of Keled's buttocks has gone numb, and he rocks himself back and forth in his chair. She stopped helping him to bed when he stopped eating. She'd never said as much, but the first evening that he'd sat silently over dinner, staring down at the *gulyás* that sat, warm, steaming and untouched in front of him, ten o'clock had come, their normal bed time, then ten thirty, and before he realised what was happening, the door to the bedroom was closed and he was sitting alone in the dark.

Four years is a long time to look after a person, Keled knows, particularly when those four years bring about such changes. On the rare occasions that he catches sight of his reflection, he barely recognises what he sees – the grey, unruly hair, the flabby face, the pot belly – a far cry from the fit, handsome man he'd been in his twenties. In some ways, he could hardly blame Francziska. She's only in her thirties, still attractive – she could aspire to so much more than this. But still . . .

He still doesn't understand why he's so sure of what she's doing. He's known for years that something's been going on in the village, of course. Back when he still had friends to visit him, they would rarely make any outright accusations, but he understood the implications of what was never said, and he knows that it's pride that has resulted in so many deaths; the inability to believe that one's own wife could ever rise up against one.

Keled had never had that illusion, even back before the war – Francziska had always had spirit, always prepared to shout at him or even slap him if she felt herself slighted. Hers had always been a quick temper, though, and even as he watched the funerals go past his window, even as he knew something was going very, very wrong in Falucska, he felt safe. Francziska simply did not have the temperament for that sort of behaviour.

She was a terrible cook, though, mainly because she found it boring and was unable to spend more than fifteen minutes preparing a meal. Keled had never minded this before, and so when she had spent over an hour, five days ago now, preparing an elaborate *gulyás*, that's when he had started to suspect. And when she had sat opposite him at the table, fair head bent, unable to meet his gaze, that's when he had known. Keled doesn't want to die, but he still loves Francziska, despite everything, and so he can't bring himself to rage at her. Instead, he silently puts down his spoon and refuses to eat, and before long Francziska's entreaties die on her lips.

Keled blinks and turns his head away at the sudden light as the bedroom door opens. Francziska stands in the doorway, her cotton nightgown transparent against the lamplight, and Keled feels a wave of tenderness wash over him as he looks at the silhouette of her thickening thighs.

'Are you still awake?' she asks, the first words she has spoken to him in days, and then, in a rush: 'Can I get you something to help you sleep? Some warm milk perhaps?'

Keled nods.

Five minutes later, he holds the mug in his hand. It has been five days since he drank anything other than water, and he can smell the thick, creamy scent – it makes his mouth water. As he lifts the mug to his lips, he catches sight of Franczsiska's face and sees that she is crying, silently, tears slipping down her still face almost unnoticed. He drinks deeply, tastes something bitter on the back of his tongue, gulps it down, drinks again. The mug is drained. For a long moment, neither of them says anything; then Francziska wipes the tears roughly from her cheeks with the flat of her hand.

'Well, then,' she says, her voice thick. 'Shall we go to bed?'

1925

CHAPTER TWENTY-THREE

Lujza knows what they think of her, and sometimes she agrees with them. Even when she was a child she had always felt as if she was a random collection of thoughts and feelings and body parts, strung together with wire, and Péter's death stretched that wire to breaking point. It's not that she's mad, she thinks. She's known mad people; every small village has to have at least one, but Lujza hasn't taken on that role yet. She still knows who she is, and where she is; she still knows how to behave. It's just that things get tangled sometimes.

Things are calmer these days, and she's glad. For the first two years after Péter died, there had been a roaring in her head that she couldn't shut out, and the only way she'd known to cope was to shut herself away, minimising all outside noise until the noise inside her became more bearable. Her family had been kind, if baffled by her behaviour – it's not so unusual to lose a husband, after all, and women for centuries have been shouldering their burdens and carrying on with things. Lujza's always been a little unusual, though.

It wasn't until the village men started coming back from the front that she started seeing Péter. In hindsight, of course, it makes sense that he couldn't come back from the battlefield until the war was over; he'd always been conscientious, and even death was never going to get in the way of him doing his duty. It was late 1918 when she first caught sight of his face outside the window and she moved faster than she had in months, flinging wide the window, staring out into the dusk as if she couldn't open her eyes wide enough to see all that she wanted to see. Of course, no one had been there, but she realised, when she closed the window and drew the curtains, that the roaring in her head had stopped.

After that, Luzja started to see him everywhere, catching sight of his profile out of the corner of her eye; hearing his steps behind her as she walks through the house, but he's always gone when she turns around. She knows he's not real, yet at the same time she knows that he's as real to her as he ever had been, and soon she stops turning around when she feels him at her elbow, closing her eyes instead and breathing in his presence. She talks to him, too. To start with she holds the conversations inside her head, but before long she starts to forget, finding it harder and harder to distinguish between what she says quietly and what she says out loud.

Sari used to visit her almost every day, back when Lujza refused to leave the house, but these days she comes less and less often. There's one reason for that, the same reason that everyone else has for giving Lujza a wide berth: that spending time with a woman who walks the border between fantasy and reality can be unsettling for even the most pragmatic of people. But there's another reason as well. Ever since Péter has come back, Lujza's become more and more aware of things that other people don't notice. When Sari comes to visit, now, it's as if a bell rings in the back of Lujza's head, telling her to be on her guard, and from the way that Sari looks at her, Lujza knows that she's sensed her wariness. Sari has always been different – that had always been what Lujza liked about her – but something has changed; Sari vibrates at a different pitch now, a pitch that sets Lujza's teeth on edge. One morning, when Sari's just left and Luzja is bent over the potatoes she's peeling for dinner, she decides to ask Péter: *do you know?* And the answer comes back: *yes* – with a sudden vivid memory of Ferenc's funeral – *and so do you.*

When Sari stopped visiting so often, Lujza felt mingled sorrow and relief – she misses Sari, but is glad to be rid of the way that Sari's presence raises the hairs on the back of her neck these days. More than Sari, though, she had missed Sari's child, the red-haired daughter who would sit, silent, on the floor of Lujza's house while Sari and Lujza made stilted conversation, the little girl whose wild, wide eyes had reminded Lujza of her own. And then one afternoon when Lujza has been dozing over her embroidery, when she opens her eyes there is Sari's girl, sat at her feet, paper in one hand, pencil in the other, absorbed in her drawing. Lujza barely dares to breathe for fear of disturbing the child, but she can't help herself from stretching out a hand to touch the bright coil of the girl's hair. The child looks up into Lujza's face, and that's when Lujza catches sight of what she is drawing – and it is Péter.

1928

CHAPTER TWENTY-FOUR

'They've just pulled *another* body out of the river.'

'Oh, *honestly*. I keep telling them – don't throw bodies into the river. Especially at this time of year; the river's up so high, and you can never tell where they're going to end up . . .'

'We've already had one wash up as far downriver as the next village; it's just luck that they assumed it was a drowning. But if more and more bodies start piling up down there, it's going to start looking pretty suspicious, isn't it?'

'So who was it this time?'

Sari sits down at the table and starts to haul her boots off.

'Oh, God, that poor Krisztina woman, Orsolya's cousin. I heard they had a disagreement a week or so ago, something about some jewellery of their grandmother's – stupid of her, really; no one in their right mind would mess with Orsolya these days – so it's not too surprising. It's just Orsolya's style, too, to toss the body into the river. She was so smug and proud when her mother-in-law was found downriver and was certified drowned; I think she thinks she's just going to get away with things like this forever.'

Judit shakes her head, snorting dismissively. 'Stupid woman. She really does think she's beyond reproach, doesn't she? Anyway, I suppose we should just give stricter warnings in future. No more bodies in the river – the last thing we need is anyone from outside the village getting caught up in all of this.'

'Quite.' Sari turns to the corner where Rózsa sits, slumped, legs splayed, small, wiry body hunched over a drawing. 'Rózsi, darling, come here and give me a kiss.'

The girl obeys. Nine years old she is, tall and skinny with Sari's translucently pale skin and a whip of shockingly bright red hair – and those unsettling green eyes; well, unsettling eyes seem to run in the family, Sari thinks, but Sari's eyes are unsettling because they seem to be cutting right into the heart of you, while Rózsi's eyes are unsettling because she seems to be looking out at an entirely different world. Sari's never been able to work out whose child she is. In certain lights the shadow cast by her jaw is reminiscent of Ferenc's strong face shape, but at other times the quirk of an eyebrow takes Sari's breath away with memories of Marco. Either way, she's no one's as much as she is Sari's; her father doesn't matter.

Rózsi is nine years old and she's never said a word. She just stares with her wide, wild eyes and stays silent. Sari's used to it now, used to most aspects of her child's strangeness, but it hasn't always been the case. She's mainly stopped blaming herself for it, too, but sometimes it creeps up on her, catching her by the throat in the middle of the night. Is there something wrong with Rózsi's brain, perhaps, brought on by the kick Sari took in the stomach early in Rózsi's pre-birth life, or by the fever Sari suffered during pregnancy, or by the abrupt way that Rózsi slithered into the world, in the middle of the night, when Sari was so confused and panicky with pain that she was struck dumb, unable to even call Judit to help? Oh, Rózsi seems intelligent enough. She can read and write and she follows instructions, so presumably she can hear and understand what people say to her. She's just unable, or unwilling, to speak herself.

Judit adores the child beyond all reason, to the extent that Sari suffers an occasional twinge of jealousy, for surely Judit never doted on Sari to the same extent when she was Rózsi's age? But Judit is a blessing for Sari, really: she's Rózsi's wicked grandmother and father-substitute in one; she takes care of Rózsi's interests and won't tolerate Sari's occasional morbid ramblings on the subject of her child.

'When I was her age . . .' Sari began once, around Rózsi's sixth birthday, the sight of her silent, delicate child bringing back memories of herself at six, outspoken and prickly and fearless.

But Judit wouldn't let her continue. 'No,' she said. 'She is not you. She has her own gifts.'

While Sari has always felt this herself, she has never quite shaken the idea that it stems from misplaced maternal pride, so to have Judit back up her suspicions is comforting.

What can Rózsi do, then? Well, she can cook like an angel, something that makes both Judit and Sari laugh – such a conventionally feminine gift for someone in their household to have! Judit can't cook at all, and Sari's cooking is passable but uninspired. Rózsi, on the other hand, was found in the kitchen early one morning at the age of seven, mixing up ingredients for what turned out to be the most delicious stew the three of them had ever tasted up until that moment.

Where did she pick it up? Who can tell? It's true that she spent the first few years of her life clinging to Sari and Judit's skirts, following them wherever they went, including the market and the kitchen, but neither of them ever dreamt that she was paying attention to what they were doing, watching and learning. She does almost all of the cooking now, without being asked – she will simply trot around the village, buying ingredients where she can, and prepare meals of such delicate, subtle flavours that both Judit and Sari feel that their tongues have not been fully alive until now.

Rózsi is welcome everywhere in the village, a fact that amazes Sari when she remembers the wariness and fear with which she was treated as a child. She's even befriended Lujza Tabori. Sari can barely bring herself to visit Lujza now, since she has become so strange, but Rózsi loves Lujza and visits her unprompted.

She can also draw. Even when she was a baby she would conjure images from whatever was to hand. Her first sketches were wobbly and uncertain, full of skewed perspective and unearthly shapes, but there was something heart-stilling about them. After looking at a drawing of Rózsi's, it's the rest of the world that seems odd, tilted a little on its axis. Rózsi's drawing is improving as she gets older. Both Sari and Judit have piles of her sketches, and the dry wooden walls of Judit's house are papered with them. They can't bear to throw any of them away.

Rózsi's the centre of Sari's life, now; she's a flesh and blood barrier between Sari and what's going on in the rest of the village. Orsolya was only the first. Her husband (a nice, unassuming man, Sari had always thought, but no matter) had expired after a short, painful illness, and once that was over Sari felt mingled relief and dread – relief, because Orsolya had lost whatever incentive she may have had to report Sari's activities to her policeman cousin, and dread because she sensed that it was just the start, the ripple of wind that spreads over the grass to signal that a storm is coming.

And so it proved. Word got out – of course it did – that Sari and Judit were doling out death from that little wooden house, and slowly, slowly women started coming. Some of them Sari could countenance – the village may have been small, but there was no shortage of bad husbands, ill husbands, burdensome husbands – and Sari never blamed the women who were hit or abused or disrespected for wanting to find a way out. After all, it was something she'd done herself, and something she'd helped Anna do. But some of them . . .

The third night that she'd been sick and unable to eat at the thought of some poor blameless man dying, if not by her hand, then with her tacit agreement, Judit had sat her down and had words with her.

'You have a choice, as always,' Judit had said. 'You don't have to be doing this. You could refuse. You could leave.'

'But—'

Refusal meant death, Sari knew. Any woman frustrated by her non-compliance could bring the whole enterprise crashing down on everyone's heads. And leaving was next to impossible. It was barely three months after Rózsi's birth, and fleeing into the dark plain, in the middle of winter, having not yet fully recovered her strength from the birth, with a tiny infant probably meant death, just as much as refusal did.

Judit shrugged. 'They're not good choices, I admit. We're in a tight spot. But you could be the martyr here, you could put these lives above yours, and you choose not to. Accept that about yourself, Sari, and get on with it, or don't. Just don't torture yourself with the results of your choices, because it doesn't do any of us any good.'

And oddly, Judit's harsh words had worked. What's the

difference, Sari asks herself now, between one death, and ten, and a hundred? What's the difference between the death of an abusive husband and a bed-ridden mother-in-law? What's the difference between a motive of survival, and a motive of greed? The world has just come out of a war in which millions of lives were easily forfeited, and fundamentally meaningless. After a year, Sari stops minding (or stops thinking about it – whichever way, it works), and after two, she's able to joke with Judit about the ironic little sideline that's become their main business: one hand giving, and the other taking away. They've always been dealers in death to a certain extent; Judit's never tried to hide her activities as an *angyalcsináló*, an angel maker, an abortionist.

'We're just making rather bigger angels now,' Judit says to Sari, with her twisted grin, and Sari can even allow herself to laugh at that, now. It's only Rózsi who gives her pause. What do you tell your daughter about this way of life, Sari wonders. Do you let her grow up thinking it's normal, thereby avoiding blame for your own part in it, or do you tell her that things aren't the same everywhere, and in doing so, open yourself up for the sort of questions that could carve your heart out? Sari whispers things to Rózsi when she's asleep, ideas and images of Somewhere Else, a Somewhere Else that she can't quite believe in herself. She is occasionally thankful that a child who doesn't speak also means a child who doesn't ask awkward questions.

Sari doesn't like to think of what her father would say about the way his old house is being used. Sari and Rózsi live with Judit most of the time these days, but since they've gone into the murder business, having alternative premises is useful.

Should anyone arrive at Judit's house unexpectedly, no matter how hard they looked, they would not find a thing that did not fit in with the image of Sari and Judit as single, hardworking but honest midwives and nurses. All evidence of their alternative activities is strictly limited to Sari's house, which is far enough from the centre of the village that it's unlikely for anyone to stumble on it unexpectedly. Even if a curious stranger came upon it, peering through the ground floor windows would reveal nothing more interesting than a seemingly abandoned, but well-kept old house.

Upstairs, though – that's a different story. The bed has been pushed to one side to make room for all the bowls dotting the floor, revealing different stages of the process, from sodden messes of soaking flypaper to neat little piles of innocent-looking powder. Sari comes to the house every second day, ostensibly to clean and sweep the leaves off the porch, but in reality to collect some more powder for the endless parade of would-be murderesses. She wonders sometimes why she keeps up the pretence of cleaning the place. Surely everyone in the village knows what's really going on by now, even if they don't admit it? But there's no harm keeping up appearances: unlikely as it would be, you never know when a stranger might wander into the village, and it wouldn't do to look anything less than totally normal.

Sari has always known that they can't go on like this forever. In her more optimistic moments, she hopes that it'll all just tail off of its own accord, that people in the village will run out of people that they want to kill, or that things will quietly implode, with all the poisoners poisoning one another – leaving her and Judit in peace, of course. She's not optimistic very often, though, and when she's not, she realises that things are likely to end with their being discovered. No matter how isolated and insular the village is, no matter how beholden everyone has become to one another, something this virulent and peculiar is bound to seep out sooner or later, like a dangerous gas escaping its canister to leak into the pure air outside. Some day, Sari knows, someone in charge will notice the unusually high death rate in the village, or a body will wash up elsewhere, and an overly curious doctor will cut it open to find its insides riddled with poison. They've been lucky so far, but luck can't last. It never does.

In the end, it doesn't happen the way that Sari would have imagined, but it does happen. A tearful Francziska Imanci turns up at Judit's house one day. It takes them a while to get the full story out of her, but as soon as she starts, haltingly, to speak, Sari's heart lodges itself stubbornly in her throat, as if it's become a tough piece of meat that she's unable to swallow. Francziska murdered her husband six years ago, and it had been an easy job – he'd lost a leg in the war, and had been largely housebound, and therefore disinclined to make any fuss about being poisoned. At the time, Sari had thought that would be the end of it. Francziska had always struck her as a rather pleasant, straight forward type, unlikely to murder more than the bare minimum of family members. But since her husband's death, she'd become rather more closely associated with Orsolya (whose dead family members now number six), and had clearly been persuaded to expand her oeuvre somewhat to incorporate her mother-in-law, largely incapacitated, generally useless, and sitting on top of a not inconsiderable amount of possessions that would otherwise go to Francziska. So Francziska had come back to Judit's a week before, and they had given her what she asked for – with a degree of ill grace, Sari has to admit; she doesn't much like to support women killing women. And now here she is, back again, saying between sniffs and sobs and gulps that she'd started on her mother-in-law, yes, and she'd given her a couple of doses, and then she'd gone round there this morning, to look in on her like she does every morning, and the old bitch was gone.

Sari looks at Judit just in time to see her draw a weary hand over her eyes, but, as always, she recovers quickly, gives Sari a grim, tight smile.

'Well, then,' she says, shrugging. 'Bound to happen eventually, really.'

'So, you think she knew what you were doing?' Sari asks Francziska, who nods.

'I suppose so. I thought I was doing all right, keeping up the pretence, not acting any differently to normal, but I've never been a good actor. I was round there yesterday, making her dinner, and she kept looking at me. Just . . . just *looking*. I could feel her damned eyes on me even when my back was turned.'

'Did she—' Sari frowns. It's so hard to put this delicately. 'Did she know about her son?'

Francziska seems to catch her meaning. 'I don't know. She suspected, probably, but she never said anything. Never said anything about any of it. You know what it's like.'

Sari does know. People have drawn into themselves; it's become a liability to care about anything but one's own immediate well-being. She can't help feeling a sudden surge of contempt for old Mrs Imanci, though. How can you sit silently by when you think something's happening to your child? She shoots an instinctive glance at Rózsi, seemingly oblivious in the corner, head drooping over paper, a pencil curled into her fist. Perhaps it's different when they're older, when you know that they should be able to look after themselves. Perhaps it's different when they're married. Sari can't imagine it, though, simply cannot imagine a time where she wouldn't tear the guts out of anyone harming her child.

'What was her health like when you last saw her?' Judit asks. She's trying to work out how far the woman could have gone, whether it's safe to hope that she might be dead in the long grass just outside the village.

'Not perfect, of course, but all right. I was trying to do it slowly. So that she wouldn't get suspicious.'

Francziska makes a noise somewhere between a sob and a laugh, and sniffs loudly. Absently, Sari passes her a handkerchief – she's so used to doing this sort of thing for Rózsi – and Francziska dabs her face with it.

'She has family in the next village,' she goes on. 'Her cousin. I think she might be trying to go there.'

Sari calculates; she herself could walk it in two hours, and so even allowing for her age and illness, it seems likely that Mrs Imanci would be there by nightfall, depending on what time she left. Whether or not she would alert the authorities when she got there was anyone's guess, but she certainly had nothing to lose by doing so with her son and husband already dead (her husband, at least, from natural causes) and her only relation in Falucska having tried to kill her.

'I'm sorry,' Francziska ventures. Her eyes are red rimmed and swimming, and she seems well aware of what she may have set in motion.

Judit snorts derisively at her apology, but Sari's more sympathetic. *It could have happened to any of us,* she thinks. Francziska's mistake hasn't come from arrogant stupidity, unlike the women who've been trying to fake drownings.

Francziska certainly has no reason to believe that she's invulnerable, and hasn't acted like it, or no more so than any of the rest.

'It's all right,' she says, her voice weary but steady. 'Nothing may come of it. But we have to be very careful, now.' She thinks for a moment. 'Right. I need you to bring some people here. Orsolya, for one. And—' she reels off a short list of five women, all strong personalities, all well connected, all with at least one death to their name. They'll be the best for spreading the word.

They're back within the hour and when Sari looks at the white, hunted faces, she can't help feeling a little vindictive. Although her head is on the proverbial block as much as any of the others, she feels that this lot have had it too easy. *Let them worry for once*, she thinks.

Francziska's obviously given them the gist of what's happened, but Sari recaps it briefly for the sake of clarity, and she's barely finished speaking before Zsofia Gyulai bursts out, 'Well, we must find her, mustn't we? She might not have reached the village by now. If we're quick, we could make sure she never gets there.'

'And then?' Sari asks.

Zsofia reddens. Sari's always found it peculiar, how many of these women will happily feed poison to their nearest and dearest, but heaven forfend that their lips should form the words to describe what they're doing. 'Bring her back?' Zsofia suggests lamely, though that clearly isn't her intention. Sari has a mercifully brief vision of a group of them finishing off the old woman out there on the plain – bashing her head in with a branch, perhaps? No.

'No,' she says. 'To go after her would be idiocy. She's got hours on us. She may well have reached the village by now, and even if she hasn't, a group of six women roaming the plain is bound to get noticed. As it stands, there's always the chance that, even if she does try and tell people what's been happening here, she'll just be discounted as a mad old woman.'

All five – six, Judit included – look sceptical. Sari is sceptical too, but continues: 'It's unlikely, true, but think how much easier it would be for her to be believed if it's obvious that us lot don't want her to get where she's going.'

The women still look doubtful, but reluctantly they nod. Sari tries hard not to feel a twinge of triumph when she notices Orsolya looking at her expectantly, waiting for guidance. This is not the way that she would have chosen to earn Orsolya's respect, but she'd have to be made of stone not to derive a slight shiver of pleasure from it.

'So what do we do?' Matild Nagy asks sulkily. Sari's never been particularly fond of her, one of Orsolya's little acolytes. 'Just wait here to be arrested?'

Sari sighs, slightly ostentatiously. 'They can't arrest us just on Ilona Imanci's word. Nothing might come of it at all, and even if anything does, there'll have to be a proper investigation. We need to expect inspectors to arrive here over the next few weeks. We'll deal with that if and when it happens. Until then, everything stops. This place has to look as much like a normal village as possible. We can't have people ill if they come; we can't have any evidence of what's been happening. Pass the word around to everyone you know who's been involved in this. I don't want anyone coming around here asking for extra privileges or special treatment, because they won't get them. From now on, it's all over.'

CHAPTER TWENTY-FIVE

He's not sure what he expected, but it wasn't *this*. Géza Forgacs has spent almost all of his nineteen years in Budapest, and in the city, you're fed images about the beautiful simplicity of bucolic life. While he'd known that they must be false, that life in the villages could be brutal and harsh, he hadn't expected it to be so immediately evident. The way that the brown wooden houses cluster around the river, as if straining away from or towards something; the suffocating blackness of the nearby woods, and the stark reality of the existence of the village in the middle of the breathless plain – these things combine to make him feel unsettled, ill at ease. He pushes these feelings to the back of his mind, feeling that they are pure superstition.

The older man isn't so sure. Béla is twenty-four, and he grew up in a household with a cook from the plain, from a village, he thinks now, probably very much like this. She'd been a funny mixture of sweet and sour when he'd been a child, slipping him pastry off-cuts one minute, and scaring him to death with fairy stories the next. She'd been young, casually cruel in the way that only girls barely out of their teens can be, and Béla had adored her with all of his childish heart. She'd had a full repertoire of stories about fairies and demons and incubi but the ones that had frightened him the most were the ones that were closest to the truth, the stories about the women in the countryside who would take in unwanted children from rich city women, which the cook had always presented in the manner of cautionary tales.

'They're called the angel makers,' she'd said, and even now, seventeen years later, Béla can still see the way that her knuckles whitened as she kneaded the dough while she was speaking. Seven-year-old Béla knew what angels were, knew that people became angels when they died, but couldn't quite grasp how a person could make an angel, and he'd asked, unable to restrain his curiosity, despite knowing from bitter experience that he wouldn't like the answer.

'Well, the rich women don't want the children,' the cook had said, 'so the poor women in the countryside take their money to look after them, and the mothers can go back to the city, happy that their children are being looked after. But the angel makers, they know that these rich women aren't going to come back and look for their children, so do you think they're going to use that money feeding and clothing a child that's not theirs, that they couldn't care less about? So they kill the children, and keep the money.' She'd turned back to the bread then, a glimmer of triumph on her face at Béla's stricken expression.

'But how?' Béla had asked. He had to know, couldn't bear not to.

The cook had shrugged. 'Whatever's easiest. Depends how old they are, too. If they're small, they'll smother them.' Seeing that Béla didn't understand, she flipped one of the kitchen cloths over his face, holding it there with a gentle pressure. He'd stood as still as death, too frightened to move, and after only a moment she removed it. 'That's smothering,' she said coolly, turning back to the bread. 'Or they'll leave them out in the cold. Or for the older ones, they'll just stop feeding them. And that,' she finishes with a flourish, 'is what happens to children when their parents don't want them any more.'

The implication had been clear, and Béla's dreams had been haunted by the angel makers for years afterwards and, if he's honest with himself, they haunt him still. In his dreams he wakes, but even before he's opened his eyes he knows that he isn't in his warm, comfortable bed in town, that his parents have decided that they don't want him any more, and he's been sent off to the angel makers. The dreams are always painfully vivid. He can feel the coarse, woollen blankets on his skin; the air that he breathes in is cold and icy, and in his head is an image of a grim, gaunt hamlet, shuddering its way out of the plain. And then he hears the footsteps, and he knows that She's coming, coming with a cloth in her hand, coming to finish him off, and he wakes, properly this time, shaking and sweating, unable to believe that the dream hadn't been true, and that he is safe.

He realises now, with a touch of irony and very little surprise, that the village he sees spread out in front of him is similar to the village from his dreams, and although he knows that much of the similarity is due to his subconscious bending the memory of the dreams so that they fit the reality he's now seeing, it doesn't make him feel any happier about where he is. He wishes, not for the first time, that he was safely back in Város and far away from here.

'This is nonsense,' Béla says to himself, forgetting for a moment that Géza is beside him, until, out of the corner of his eye, he sees the boy jerk slightly. For the first time, he's glad that the boy is with him. Béla persists in mentally calling Géza *The Boy*, despite there being scarcely five years between their ages. He'd been reluctant to bring him at first, certain that this was a wild goose chase, and it would be better for Géza to stay behind in Város, where there were lots of things that he could be getting on with.

Certainly, when they'd first heard the stories about the village, they'd all smiled and dismissed them as the rantings of a mad old woman. Yes, perhaps her daughter-in-law had tried to finish her off. It was plausible, but not really worth making a fuss about. Domestic murders haven't exactly been uncommon since the war. It's not that they're not serious, but, in Béla's experience, once the intended victim has been removed from the situation, the murderer or murderess is unlikely to try and turn their hand to anyone else. Besides, Mrs Imanci had hardly been a reliable informant: when she'd been brought into the office by her cousin, she'd rambled on for nearly an hour, a bizarre mixture of accusations of murder, aimed at her daughter-in-law, and witchcraft, aimed at the rest of the village she'd come from, and when she left they'd laughed.

But something had alerted the attention of Béla's superior, that much-vaunted instinct that Béla had been taught was vital for a successful inspector, and which Béla was desperately trying to develop, and the next day Béla had come in to find Emil poring over a sheaf of documents at his desk.

'Look at this,' Emil said, and Béla had looked. It was a list of the deaths in Falucska over the past ten years. It did seem very high, but then . . .

'What about the influenza? Plenty of villages have lost large numbers of people because of that,' he'd suggested.

'Could be,' Emil said thoughtfully, but Béla could tell that he wasn't convinced. He wasn't sure whether he was entirely convinced, either, but he certainly wasn't worried. People in the villages got ill a lot; it was, and always had been, a fact of life.

He said as much to Emil, and Emil had nodded again in that faintly irritating manner of his, as if agreeing purely for the sake of politeness. 'True. But it's a small village. And also, do you notice anything else?'

Béla squinted at the paper. 'Look at the names,' Emil hinted.

'Men,' Béla said suddenly. 'They're almost all men.' He looked at Emil in surprise, and Emil nodded, smiling this time.

'Quite. It's not what you would expect. Usually, if it's an illness or an epidemic it's women who dominate the lists of the dead. Men tend to be stronger, more resilient. And yet—' he waved his hand at the paper again. 'Of course, it might be nothing. But it might not.'

'So . . .?'

'I want you to go out there, have a look around, ask some questions. Particularly of this Imanci woman. And—' he ruffled through the papers again, 'find Sari Arany. She's one of the village midwives, and has been responsible for filing the death certificates. Talk to her, ask her what she thinks about all of this.'

Béla had been quite happy about that, envisioning a few relaxing days in the countryside. In the middle of the town in the middle of the day, he was well able to ignore the gloomy, sinister villages of his dreams. He'd been discomfited, though, when ordered to take Géza with him.

'But surely he'd be better off staying here?'

Emil shook his head. 'I can't send you out there alone. It might be nothing, but it might be something, and if it is, it's best if there's two of you.'

It wasn't that he had anything against Géza, Bela mused, and in a way it was flattering that, young as he was, Emil trusted him enough to put him in a position of responsibility over the younger man. But still, all those questions of Géza's that always need answering! Béla has enough of his own work to concentrate on, and prefers not to have to worry about someone else's on top of it. He's been trying to fight back his resentment all the way to the village, but now, as they walk towards the village from the spot where the farmer was able to drop them off, he finds he's glad of the young man's company.

'Where will we stay when we get there?' Géza asks, breaking the silence. 'Will there be an inn?'

Bela laughs. 'I doubt it very much, not in a place this size. It's not on the way to anywhere; why would anyone want or need to stay there? An inn-keeper wouldn't make any money.'

'So where will we get lodgings?' Géza asks. He's feeling more than a little anxious, sensing both that Béla is uneasy about something, and that Béla doesn't want him there.

Béla has the idea that they should ask the priest, and that's the first surprise that they face when they get into the village. They're on the outskirts when they first encounter a person, and it's a middle-aged woman, her eyes wide with what seems to be fear. *I suppose they're not used to strangers here*, Béla thinks, and puts on his friendliest smile.

'Good evening,' he says, because by then the darkness is closing in. 'We need lodgings in the village for a few days. I don't suppose you could take us to the village priest, who might be able to provide us with beds?'

For a moment, the woman looks so shocked to be addressed by strangers that Béla thinks that she'll flee, or at the very least stay silent, but she pulls herself together after an instant. Her accent is countrified and some of the words that she uses sound archaic to Béla's ears, but he puts that down to the isolation of the village.

'There is no priest,' she says, and Béla raises his eyebrows. 'No priest?' he queries.

'We had one,' the woman goes on. 'Father István. But he left here years ago. He had no family here. No one knows where he went. We kept expecting a new priest to replace him, but none ever came.' She appears to mistake Béla's look of consternation as a criticism of her faith. 'Some of us sometimes go to the next village for church,' she says defensively. 'But it's seven miles away, so it's hard to manage every week . . .'

'No matter,' he says, cutting her short. 'Do you know of anyone else who might be able to provide us with lodgings?'

The woman bites her lip for a moment, then appears to come to a decision. 'I'll take you to Sari,' she says.

'Would that be Sari Arany?' Géza asks, suddenly excited, remembering the name from the conversation they'd had with Emil before leaving Város. He subsides when Béla shoots him a quelling look.

'Do you know her?' the woman asks.

'We know of her,' Béla replies, in a tone that invites no further questions. She nods, and leads them down towards the village, to a wooden house in the centre, by the river. She knocks on the door, which is opened by a young, dark-haired woman, who looks coolly at Béla with her startling blue eyes. And Béla feels his heart stop.

Sari knows who they must be as soon as she opens the door and sees Kornelia Gyulai, looking scared out of her wits, standing in front of two smartly dressed men. She heaves an internal sigh. Things had been quiet for a couple of weeks, and she'd allowed herself to hope that it would all blow over, that they were safe. It's all up to her now; up to all of them, really, but she's learnt from bitter experience that if she wants something done properly, she has to do it herself. They seem very young, which is a comfort – if anyone was taking this seriously, surely they would have sent someone a little more senior?

'These men—' Kornelia blurts. 'They need somewhere to stay, and I thought maybe you . . .'

Sari nods in what she hopes is a gracious manner. 'Of course. Good evening, gentlemen. My name is Sari Arany. Please come in.'

They tramp up the stairs, scraping their boots as they do so, and Kornelia dithers, unsure whether she is included in the invitation.

'Sari – should I—?'

Sari shakes her head. 'It's all right. Leave them with me,' she says, and Kornelia, looking absurdly relieved, vanishes into the gathering darkness. Sari turns back to the men, who are standing politely by the table. The men from the village – the few of them that remain – would be seated by now, feet up on the table; it's been so long since Sari's encountered a man with manners.

'Miss Arany,' the taller one says. 'My name is Béla Illyés, and this is my assistant, Géza Forgacs.' Géza inclines his head in what is intended to be an elegant, manly gesture, and Sari feels her lips twitch slightly. 'We're from the Police Department in Város, and we're here to investigate an accusation that has been made against someone in this village.'

Sari frowns, feigning confusion. 'Someone here? But – I'm sorry, excuse me. It's none of my business.'

'On the contrary, Miss Arany, we were hoping that we would be able to talk to you about this matter. Not right now, of course. We will be staying in the village for a few days, and we were hoping that you could help us find some suitable accommodation.'

'Of course, of course! You must be tired, coming all the way from Város. It's a good thing that Kornelia brought you here. My father's house is on the edge of the village, and it's empty. It's not very large, but it's clean and secure. You can stay there for as long as you need to. Would you like to go straight there now, or can I offer you some food?'

Béla shakes his head, much to Géza's disappointment. 'Thank you, but no. We had a large lunch, and we wouldn't dream of putting you to any trouble.'

'Fine, fine. If you can just wait for a moment—' Sari goes into the kitchen, where Rózsi is preparing the evening meal, with Judit looking on. Judit grimaces as soon as she catches Sari's eye, and Sari grimaces back, saying out loud, 'I'm just going to take these gentlemen over to my father's house. I'll be back before long.' She can't help reaching out and touching Rózsi's hair; despite her composure, her insides are squirming with fear. Rózsi looks up at her and gives her a glowing smile, and as always, it lifts Sari's heart, bolsters her spirits. She sometimes wonders whether she needs her daughter more than her daughter needs her.

When she gets back, twenty minutes later, Francziska is sitting at the kitchen table, visibly trembling, while Judit plies her with *szilva*, patience clearly dwindling.

'I suppose you heard about our visitors,' Sari says dryly.

Francziska nods. 'What are we going to do?'

'Deny everything, that's what. No matter what they say, deny it. I think we might still be all right, you know. They're both young – if they really thought there was something going on here, they would have sent more senior people. We might be all right.'

Francziska's mouth is working, her eyes are panic-stricken, and Sari can see it coming. 'Couldn't we just . . . just finish them?'

Judit puts her head into her hands, and Sari takes a deep breath. 'For God's sake, Francziska. That really is the most ridiculously stupid idea that you could have come out with.'

'But—'

'Think about it. We might be all right as it stands, but what are they going to do, over in Város, if the boys they've sent out here don't come back? They're *all* going to be out here, swarming over the village. We simply couldn't do anything more suspicious. Do you understand me?'

'I – I suppose so.'

Sari sighs. 'This is the problem,' she says, to no one in particular, as Judit already understands, and Francziska never will. 'This is how we've got into this situation. Everyone's started thinking that finishing people off is the best way to deal with problems, and it's not. It might sort things out in the short term, but in the long run, it just gets everyone into a far bigger mess than there was to start with.'

Béla sits at the kitchen table, listening to Géza crashing around upstairs, thankful for some time to himself to think. His reaction to Sari disturbed him, but now that she's gone, he's able to put it into a far more acceptable context. Here he is, practically on his own (Géza barely counts as company) in some peculiar little village in the middle of the plain – a village that doesn't even have a village priest, a fact that upset him more than he would ever admit to himself – and the first person that he'd come across had been decidedly odd. Taking that into consideration, his feelings for Sari had simply been down to relief at finding someone intelligent and collected and – and somehow *refined*, he thinks, despite her countrified dress and the crude way that her hair had been piled on top of her head, in this strange place. Relief and surprise.

But then there's the other thing, the fact that when he closes his eyes he can still see the faint afterimage of *her* eyes, the fact that it took a couple of moments after she left for his heartbeat to still, the fact that it trips and stutters and speeds up a little when he thinks of her returning the next morning. She's not *beautiful*, he tells himself. She's not. She must be ten years older than him at least. She's too thin, almost scrawny, with lines on her face and a few threads of white in her hair. Her eyes are startling, that's all. Béla is a rational man, a sensible man, and he's tired and anxious and everything will look different in the morning. It's bound to.

Sari noticed his reaction to her. He'd hidden it well but she'd noticed the infinitesimal pause when she'd opened the door, the blink of surprise, and she'd certainly noticed that his eyes landed on her whenever he thought she wasn't looking. *Well*, Sari thinks. *That could be useful.* For a moment she wishes that she were more like Lilike or Lujza had been, more like almost *anyone*, really. After all, she's only had two experiences of this sort of thing in her lifetime, both of which seemed to happen by accident, rather than by any design of her own, and neither of which she would count as an unqualified success. She wishes she were more aware of how she could use this to her advantage – to all of their advantages.

He'd seemed a pleasant man, young and polite and she'd found herself, irritatingly enough, wanting to make him and his young companion comfortable, wanting to *please* them. When she'd taken them to her father's house, she left them downstairs while she made the beds upstairs, scanning the rooms for any trace of anything they might find suspicious, although she'd already been over all of these rooms several times since Francziska's mother-in-law disappeared. When she came back downstairs, the younger one – Géza, was it? – was sitting at the table, looking morose, but Béla had been standing by the bookshelf, running his fingers along the rainbow of spines. He turned as she entered.

'Have you read all of these?' he asked. She suppressed a shrug.

'All of them, several times.' She smiled at him. 'It's very hard to get books out here. I could probably recite all of those to you. Backwards.'

He laughed. 'Perhaps when I get back to Város,' he said, haltingly, 'I could send some books to you. To say thank you, for—' He spread his hands, 'for all of this.'

She wishes that she didn't *like* him. It would make things so much easier.

CHAPTER TWENTY-SIX

Béla passes a bad night, but when he comes downstairs the next day, he finds to his surprise that things *do* look better in the morning. The sun shines in through the kitchen windows, there are blessedly normal sounds of village activity coming from outside, and it would be silly to read anything into the bad dreams anyway; they were just down to being in an unfamiliar bed.

Géza is already up, sitting downstairs, poring over notes that he must have read a hundred times already, but Béla notices that his face has relaxed; the menacing village in his mind has obviously resolved itself into the unthreatening village of reality. Béla sits down and smiles at Géza encouragingly. Everything's fine, then. The village is odd, of course, but only because it's so isolated, and because he's looking at it through his citified eyes. They've come here because Emil is thorough, but there's bound to be nothing seriously amiss here. Béla prides himself on being a rational man, and feels a little sympathy for the weary, uneasy man that he was last night, but doesn't spare him much thought. It's time to get on with work.

There's a knock on the door and Sari puts her head around it, smiling.

'Good morning! I brought you some food, for breakfast.

I would have come around earlier, but I didn't want to wake you, as I was sure you must have been tired after your journey.'

She brings light with her into the kitchen; her head is haloed with it. Béla gulps, almost imperceptibly.

'Thank you very much. Would you join us?'

Sari reddens a little. *How could I have thought she was ten years older than me?* Béla asks himself. She looks no more than a teenager now.

'Thank you, but I couldn't possibly,' she responds politely.

Béla nods. Géza watches their exchange with a touch of confusion and consternation, head swivelling back and forth.

'You mentioned yesterday that you wanted to talk to me about . . .' she pauses slightly, '. . . about the reason that you're here. Would you like to do that today?'

'Please. But first, we need to talk to – ah—' He stretches a hand out towards Géza, who passes the documents to him. 'To – ah – Francziska Imanci. Do you know her?'

'Of course. It's a small village. Everyone here knows everyone else. I can take you to her after breakfast, if you like.'

'That would be perfect, thank you.'

'Do you remember where I live? Good. Just come when you're ready and I'll take you to Francziska.' She opens the door. 'I'll see you in a little while, then.'

After she's gone, Géza looks at Béla, frowning. 'She didn't seem very curious about why we're here, did she?'

Béla clicks his tongue disapprovingly. 'She was just being polite, that's all.' Instinctively, he looks over to the patch of floor by the door where Sari had been standing a moment before, then shakes himself mentally, and gets to his feet. 'Come on, Géza. Breakfast.'

When Francziska lets Sari in, she looks terrified.

'Thank God it's only you. I thought—'

'I know what you thought,' Sari cuts her off, 'and they'll be coming in an hour or so, after breakfast. I can't stay long.'

'Oh, God!' Francziska looks as if she's going to vomit, but thankfully doesn't. 'What am I going to do? *What am I going to do?*'

'You're going to calm down, to start with,' Sari instructs firmly. 'And then when they come here, you're going to answer their questions as truthfully as you can, without landing us all in it. Let's see . . .' Sari thinks for a moment. 'How ill was your mother-in-law when she left?'

'She'd had a few headaches and some stomach trouble, but she was no worse that that. She can't have been,' Francziska's face reddens in fury, 'or she wouldn't have been able to make it all the way across the damn plain!'

'True. You're in luck, then. I doubt that she was showing any symptoms that would look like she'd been poisoned. All that counts against you are her accusations, and, of course, any accusations that she might be making about the death of her son.'

'Oh, Jesus,' Francziska moans.

'Would you *stop* that,' Sari demands, irritably. 'All you can do is just deny everything. When they ask about your mother-in-law, tell them that you never got on, that she was going a bit mad in her old age, and that probably made her a bit suspicious of you. If you can muster up a bit of anger, so much the better. Something like: *how dare she accuse me of this, after all the time I've spent looking after her!* Do you think you can manage that?'

Francziska nods with enthusiasm. 'Oh, yes, I certainly think I can manage a bit of anger.'

'Good. And if they ask you about your husband, tell him that he was weakened by the injuries he took in the war, so he died of influenza. Try and squeeze out a couple of tears, if you can.'

Francziska looks doubtful. 'I'm not sure . . .' her voice quavers.

'Either way, it doesn't matter. Anyway. No matter what they ask you, don't deviate from those answers. Whatever you do, *don't* try and make up any sort of clever story. Keep it all as simple as possible.'

Francziska nods. 'All right. But—' She stops, looking awkward.

'But what?'

'What if they ask me about the – the others? You know, it must be pretty obvious that – that more people have died here than is normal . . .'

Sari sighs. There's no easy explanation for it, really, no matter how hard she's tried to think of one. 'Tell them that we've been unlucky. Tell him that a lot of men came back from the war weak, and that we've had a lot of ill-health here.' She grimaces a little. 'It won't hurt to mutter darkly about a curse, something like that.'

'But—'

'Look, they're men from the town, and we're women from the country. They'll happily believe that we believe in things like that.' She adds, wryly, 'In fact, they might even suggest it themselves.'

Géza doesn't know quite what to think. It's not that Francziska wasn't convincing, but more that he doesn't know what convincing is supposed to be for a woman in her state. Is it normal for a woman who's been accused of murder by her mother-in-law to rant and rave, alternating between sobbing with distress and snarling with rage? All in all, it's been one of the hardest hours he's spent in his life, and he's rarely been so glad to leave somewhere. The air tastes fresher than normal, and the sun is brighter. Béla's face is as impassive as ever, and Géza indulges himself in a small spasm of hero-worship. *One day*, he thinks, *one day.*

Meanwhile, Francziska makes herself a cup of coffee, and congratulates herself on a job well done.

Béla knows that he shouldn't be as open as this with Sari, but he's relying on that much-lauded instinct that Emil's always been going on about, and so he knows, knows instinctively rather than factually, that if anything odd has been going on in this village, Sari has nothing to do with it.

'I knew her mother-in-law had disappeared, of course,' Sari is saying, 'Francziska was very worried about her, because she hadn't been well. She mentioned that she hadn't been herself, for a few days before she left.'

They are walking through the village, back towards Sari's house. By coincidence, Béla and Géza bumped into her as they were on their way out of Francziska's house, and she invited them back for lunch.

'If you have to speak to me anyway,' she'd said, with that glinting smile of hers, 'you may as well get fed at the same time.'

Beguiled by her smile – it's her intelligent mind he likes, nothing more, Béla keeps reminding himself – he finds himself telling her all about the conversation they'd had with Francziska, ignoring Géza's disconcerted expression.

Sari reacts with surprise and concern, a concern that Béla is finding hard to interpret. He knows a little about female friendships, mainly from books, but he imagines that Sari is above such things, and not inclined to protect Francziska through some arcane bond of womanhood.

'Welcome,' Sari says, as she pushes open the door to her house. 'Judit? Rózsi?' she calls. A tall, red-haired girl appears, poking her head around the door – her eyes, Béla notices, are just as startling as Sari's, but green rather than blue. 'Béla, Géza, this is my daughter, Rózsa. We call her Rózsi.'

Béla starts. 'I – I'm sorry, I assumed that you were unmarried . . .'

'Oh, I am,' Sari says, smiling a little.

Béla dithers. Should he assume that she is a widow, or could she have . . .

She answers his silent question. 'I've never been married. I'm sorry if that shocks you. I was engaged once, to Rózsi's father, but he died before we could marry.' She shrugs a little. 'I know that it's not the way that things are supposed to be done, but out here, people don't mind so much.'

'Well, then,' Béla says, trying to recover his composure. It's not so unusual, really, for a woman to have a child out of wedlock, he tells himself. Rózsi seems entirely unmoved by this conversation, and as he sits down at the table, he turns to her, tentatively. He's never been quite sure what to do with children. 'Hello, Rózsi!' he says, with false cheerfulness.

'Oh, she doesn't talk,' Sari explains, her hand on Rózsi's head, as Rózsi smiles up at her. 'We don't know why. She understands when people speak to her, but we think that she's got nothing she really wants to say, yet. And this is Judit.'

Standing by the table, Béla jerks in shock at the sight of the angel maker of his imagination, come to life.

Judit grins toothlessly. 'Hello, boys,' she says.

'Judit and I work together,' Sari explains. 'I've lived with her since my father died, when I was fourteen.'

Over lunch – prepared by Rózsi, Béla notices to his surprise – they make small-talk, about the weather and the village and the work that Sari and Judit are doing at the moment. Béla can't take his eyes off Sari, and he still can't work out quite why that is, as he passes much prettier girls on his way to and from work every day. She's just . . . there's something magnetic about her, he thinks, something that Géza doesn't see (evidently, otherwise he'd hardly be sitting there munching so contentedly), something that no one all the way out here in this isolated village *can* see, surely? She seems so out of place here, a fact that is becoming increasingly frustrating to Béla. He finds himself wondering what she would be like elsewhere, what she would do if she were somehow transplanted to Város or Budapest, rather than sat at a rickety table in a muddy village in the middle of nowhere, surrounded by a mute, red-headed child and a hag. He tries to hide his distaste for Judit – distaste, and yes, a certain amount of fear as well. She's harmless, of course; to think otherwise would be rank superstition – and she can't have noticed, can she, the way that his eyes keep tracing the line of Sari's neck, the slippery curve of her waist? But she's been grinning at him in a most unpleasant manner, and he's hugely relieved when she leaves as soon as lunch is over, taking Rózsi with her.

'So,' Sari says. 'What would you like to talk to me about?'

Suddenly, discussing work is the last thing that Béla wants to do with Sari. He'd love to hear her views on the books that she's read, or to probe her about the intricacies of her work. A dry dissection of the papers that he has in his bag is utterly unappealing, and, of course, utterly necessary.

'You know that we came here because of the accusations of Francziska Imanci's mother-in-law?' he asks, and she nods. 'Well, she also made some rather outlandish accusations about things going on in the village in general. Things like . . .' He sputters a little under her steady gaze.

'Like witchcraft?' she asks calmly, and he blushes.

'Yes. I know it sounds ridiculous.'

'Oh, it's hardly a new accusation as far as Judit and I are concerned. I imagine that she was claiming that we've put curses on the village?'

'Something like that, yes. Of course we don't take accusations like that seriously, but then we did look at the death records, and it does seem that a disproportionate number of – of men have died here. And as the person who filed the death certificates, we wanted to find out what you think about . . . about it all,' he finishes lamely.

Sari spreads her hands in an elegant gesture, and seems to consider for a moment before she speaks.

'I'm sure that it must seem strange to you, and it seems

strange to a lot of people here, as well – there's more than one person who's spoken about a curse!' She laughs a little, and Géza looks up from the notes that he's taking.

'Mrs Imanci – Francziska – said that.'

'Well, you can understand why people think it. But the facts are, firstly, we had an unusually high number of men go away to war and of course many of those who came back didn't come back in very good health, which meant that they were susceptible to all the diseases that came through the village. And again, because we're isolated, it's very rare for an ill person here to be able to see a doctor. Judit and I do our best, but—' She shrugs. '– we can't do the job of qualified doctors, no matter how hard we try.'

She smiles a little, the sun catches her hair, and something catches in Béla's throat. What a brave woman she is, he thinks, selflessly nursing people in the village back to health, and what does she get in return but accusations of witchcraft? He's heard about this sort of thing before, healers and midwives in the countryside being thought supernaturally responsible when things go wrong as much as when things go right, but for a moment he feels a violent surge of fury towards old Mrs Imanci with her bizarre, unjust accusations. At his elbow, Géza sits poised, ready to take notes, but really, Béla thinks, it would be cruel and unnecessary to probe her further. Instead he sits back in his chair, and smiles.

'Perhaps you could tell me a little about the work you do? I'd be very interested to learn more about it.'

Sari's exhausted. It's hard work to charm and sparkle all afternoon, especially when you're unused to it, but Béla has proven unexpectedly pleasant. After giving a detailed account of the trials and tribulations of a country midwife, they turned to the subject of books, and Béla even went so far as to write down a couple of titles that he promised to send to her when he goes back to Város. The two of them finally left about fifteen minutes ago, and now Sari is slouched at the table with a cup of coffee, enjoying the silence, when Judit and Rózsi suddenly burst through the door, Judit grinning maliciously.

'Well, then, how did it go? Though I think I can guess.'

'Better than I could have hoped. He asked me a couple of simple, straightforward questions, seemed to believe my answers, and then we talked about herbs and books for the past couple of hours. The young one, Géza, looked absolutely baffled.'

Judit's grin widens. 'You cunning bitch! You've got him wrapped around your finger. How the hell did you do it?'

'Not intentional, I promise. Sometimes these things just happen, don't they?'

'Makes me think that there might be someone looking down on us after all.'

Sari takes a deep breath. 'We might just be all right, you know. We might.'

'This is a lovely place, don't you think?' Béla says offhandedly to Géza on the way back to Sari's father's house. Géza isn't convinced. Certainly, it's a lovely day, but the village is far from his personal definition of lovely. If it weren't a deeply heretical thought to have, Géza would believe that Béla's new-found fondness is less for Falucska than for Sari Arany, but he doesn't dare suggest an idea like that even to himself, let alone to Béla.

'So what do you think about—' Géza jerks his head back towards the house that they've just left.

'What? What Miss Arany was saying? Sounds pretty convincing to me. We can't fall into the trap of seeing crimes where there are none. Doesn't do anyone any good.'

'But—' It's not that Géza disbelieves Sari. It's just that he's long had an idea of what a police investigation is supposed to entail, and it involves rather more rigorous questioning and research than what has just gone on.

'We should go and see Mrs Imanci again, of course,' Béla says thoughtfully, 'but aside from that . . .' He shrugs.

'Don't you think,' Géza ventures after a pause, 'that perhaps we should speak to some of the other people in the village? Perhaps some of the relatives of the people who have died? It's not that I don't believe Miss Arany,' he adds swiftly, noticing Béla's face darkening, 'but she might not be aware of everything that's going on here. Just to make sure.'

Béla considers. On one hand, it seems the gentlemanly thing to do to simply take Sari at her word, and conclude that nothing peculiar has been going on in Falucska whatsoever. On the other hand – well, Emil might ask some awkward questions if it looks like they've returned to Város with the job half done. It wouldn't look good.

'It's probably a good idea if we stay a week or so, then,' Béla declares. 'Talk to a few more people.' He ignores the tiny quiver of excitement he feels at the thought of a week's more exposure to Sari.

CHAPTER TWENTY-SEVEN

Tuesday, and: 'Mrs Gersek,' Géza says decisively, looking up from the papers.

Béla nods. It can't hurt Géza to have a go at running the investigation here, particularly as it's all bound to come to naught in the end, he considers.

'Very well,' Béla says. 'We'll go and see her in the morning.'

'Mrs Gersek,' Béla announces to Sari the next morning when she arrives with food for their breakfast.

'I'll take you there after you've finished eating,' Sari says, and leaves, on the pretext of tending to Rózsi's breakfast.

'They're coming to see you today,' she says to Jakova Gersek, five minutes later.

Another wasted morning, Géza thinks, coming out of Mrs Gersek's house around midday. Mrs Gersek had been intractable, furious from the moment of their arrival, shrieking over and over about how *dare* they accuse her of murdering her husband, how *dare* they? That had been before they'd even had time to say what they were there for.

'Oh, I can guess,' she'd spat, when Béla pointed this out. 'I know you were round at Francziska Imanci's yesterday morning, harassing the poor woman, after all she's had to put up with!'

The rest of the morning had proceeded roughly along those lines, with Mrs Gersek occasionally calming down, only to explode into fury again at the implications of some innocuous-seeming remark on Béla or Géza's part.

'That seemed pretty conclusive,' Béla says to Géza, who frowns.

'Well, yes. But . . . it seemed a bit much, maybe, didn't it? Almost as if – as if she was putting it on for our benefit?'

Béla smiles. 'Perhaps, perhaps. But you have to understand, Géza, that these people are innocent until proven guilty. We can't do anything – and we shouldn't do anything – unless we have concrete proof of some wrong-doing.'

'What sort of thing do you mean?'

'In this case, it would have to be a confession. Or, perhaps, the discovery of a murder weapon. None of which seem forthcoming, do they?'

'But what about the bodies? Couldn't we—'

'Géza, any justification we have for investigating things here is nothing more than suspicion and speculation. To get permission to exhume corpses.' He shakes his head. 'We'd need something significantly more concrete than we have at the moment. Can you imagine the reaction of the people here if we started digging up their churchyard? Anything that Mrs Gersek said to us this morning would be nothing compared to that.'

Géza shrugs. 'I suppose so.' He's not happy about it, though. They've spent nearly three days in the village now, and the absence of male faces has struck him sharply. He's never been anywhere like this before, and he can't quite bring himself to believe that there's a natural explanation for it.

And in little gushes and trickles, he can feel his stored up respect for Béla ebbing away, however hard he tries to tell himself that Béla is right, and that he's doing the right thing. It's difficult. Géza has felt something akin to hero-worship for Béla for the year that they've been working together, and watching one's idol fall is not an enjoyable experience. Anyway, perhaps he *is* doing the right thing, Géza tells himself. But he can't ignore the way that Béla has been looking at Sari Arany. Even now, walking beside him, Géza can feel something like longing coming off Béla in waves.

They round the corner, and Judit's house come into view. The door opens, and Sari comes out onto the step, waving. Géza looks at Béla's face and sighs.

On Wednesday, Béla and Géza visit Mrs Gyulai in the morning, who doesn't rage at them like Mrs Gersek did, but sits weeping quietly through the entire interview, which makes them feel somehow worse. On Wednesday afternoon, Béla and Sari discuss Goethe at the kitchen table while Géza painstakingly writes up his notes of the morning's discussions. He tries to ignore the nagging voice in his head, which keeps telling him, *this is not the way things should work.*

On Thursday, Béla and Géza visit Mrs Kiss in the morning. Not even Béla is won over by this woman, who sits through the interview in preternatural calm, her face occasionally slipping into an unpleasant smirk at seemingly random times. She doesn't express any grief when discussing the death of her husband, or her mother, or even her son, in a string of freak accidents and illnesses.

Géza's fairly bursting with excitement by the time they leave the house, but as ever, Bela shakes his head.

'You can't prosecute someone just for being an unpleasant person, Géza.'

'But—'

'Remember what I said about confessions or evidence? We can't do anything without that.'

Géza subsides sulkily. Béla is right on this, it's true, but he's convinced by this point that Béla simply isn't trying hard enough to elicit a confession or find evidence. This Mrs Kiss, for example. Géza is convinced, as convinced as he could possibly be, that not all of her dead family members died of natural causes, and he's almost positive that he would be just as convinced even if Mrs Kiss hadn't been so smug and unctuous. No normal family has that amount of freak accidents – or, Géza corrects himself, even if they did, no woman would accept it with the bland smile that Mrs Kiss presents to the world. And yet Béla only asked Mrs Kiss the simplest questions, and invariably took her answers at face value, and Géza is certain that she contradicted herself at a couple of points, about the symptoms her son suffered leading up to his death, but Béla didn't even seem to notice, let alone pursue the contradictions.

Women, Géza thinks dismissively, unable to believe the hold that they can get over men. He sneaks a look at Béla out of the corner of his eye, taking in the anticipatory gleam in his eyes, and mentally braces himself for yet another afternoon discussing herbs and literature.

On Friday, Géza suggests that it might be useful to talk to Judit Fekete alone, and, shrugging, Béla agrees, though neither of them much relish the idea of a morning spent in Judit's company. Sari obliges them easily enough, disappearing into the forest with Rózsi on a herb-gathering mission. The two hours that Béla and Géza spend with Judit are practically pleasant compared to their time with Mrs Kiss the day before, but once the conversation is over, Géza feels as if he's learned nothing at all about the deaths in the village. Judit has truly amazing circumlocutory powers. Whenever asked a direct question, she gives the impression of considering it, before leading Géza and Béla down the most confusing series of narrative back alleys, to the extent that, by the time she lapses into silence, the two inspectors have usually forgotten what the question was in the first place.

'She keeps evading our questions,' Géza hisses to Béla when Judit excuses herself to use the privy, but Béla just laughs, irritating Géza beyond belief. It would seem that not only is Sari above reproach and criticism, but so is anybody closely associated with her, even though Judit is clearly a malevolent old hag, Géza thinks viciously.

'Think of how old she is,' Béla whispers back. 'People's minds start to wander at that sort of age. It's not her fault. I'm sure that she's doing the best that she can.' But when Judit comes back into the room, Géza eyes the sly grin on her face, and he finds he can't believe that Judit has any good intentions at all.

The more people they talk to, the more comfortable Béla is becoming, and, the more suspicious Géza is. No one in Falucska seems to behave like a normal person. Francziska was as twitchy as a man just back from the front; then there was Mrs Gersek's pathological raging, Mrs Gyulai weeping like a martyred saint, Mrs Kiss's unbearable air of self-satisfaction. Even Sari Arany is strange; that degree of self-possession and intelligence in a place like this can't be natural. But in the end, of course, it's Béla's view, not Géza's, that matters. Géza finds this an increasingly insupportable idea.

Evening is darkening the sky like a bruise, and Béla thinks that he hasn't felt this way since he was a child at school, who had taken a groundless fancy to the daughter of a neighbour. His heart had sunk when Sari had been unable to eat with them at lunchtime – an illness to tend to, apparently – but she had seemed genuinely sorry, particularly when he said that they would probably be leaving the next day, after a valedictory talk with Francziska Imanci.

Then her face had brightened. 'As it's your last night here,' she suggested, her voice slow and drawn out like honey, 'why don't we eat supper together tonight? Géza, too, of course. Rózsi and Judit will be all right without me for one evening, I'm sure.'

Béla's not quite sure of the propriety of this, but finds that he doesn't care; it's as if his heart is no longer beating, but instead jumping up in great, breathless leaps. He looks at himself in the mirror – not an overwhelmingly handsome man, no, but acceptable, surely? He smoothes down his wavy brown hair one last time, and leans in to the mirror to check that nothing untoward is caught between his teeth. It's nothing more than a dinner, nothing more, but maybe he won't see her again after tonight, and that makes any effort worthwhile.

Sari arrives as the sun is nodding below the trees. She's abrought *gulyás* – 'I made it myself,' she says, smiling shyly.

'Rózsi's is better, but I wanted to make it myself' – and a bottle of red wine. They sit at the weathered wooden table and the flames of the lamps rear up towards the ceiling.

Géza looks bored and says little, but to Béla, the minutes slip by like the tiny silver fish that race through the river outside the cottage. Conversation is awkward, stilted, as Sari tries to draw out the obstinately close-mouthed Géza, and Béla wishes as hard as he can that Géza would leave – surely it can't be pleasant for him sitting here in that glutinous silence? He wills him to go and finally Géza gets to his feet, with a polite bow in Sari's direction.

'Thank you for the meal,' he says, 'I don't wish to be rude, but I have to write up my notes from today's interviews.'

Béla narrows his eyes, knowing perfectly well that the notes were written up in the afternoon, but of course he doesn't argue. Raising an unmistakeably sardonic eyebrow in Béla's direction, Géza leaves the room – for a split second, Béla has time to woefully realise that Géza will be totally unmanageable when they get back to Város, but he's swallowed by Sari's gaze before he has time to muse on it any more.

As soon as Géza is gone, their conversation seems to catch alight; no longer sluggish, it snaps and burns between them. It's dark outside, and with her face half-shrouded in shadow, Sari seems to let go of some of her inhibitions. While their discussions before have been impassioned, they've also been impersonal, whereas now, Béla feels sufficiently emboldened to ask Sari about herself.

She talks a little about her fiancé, Ferenc, the one who died; her words are precise and carefully chosen, but Béla senses a weight of grief behind them. She talks also about her interests, about the books that she wishes that she could read, about her passion for reading plays that she wishes that she could see performed. She says a few words about her father, how he infused a love of learning into her, and what a shock it was when she learnt that a formal education was more or less and impossibility for someone like her.

Béla sips his wine – it's not bad, he's surprised to note, not bad at all – and he finds himself asking what he's been wondering for days. 'Do you ever think about leaving?'

Her eyebrows shoot up. 'Leaving the village? And going where?'

'I – I don't know. Budapest, maybe, or – or one of the towns.' He deliberately doesn't mention Város.

'I thought about it, of course, when I was younger, before Rózsi was born. What was keeping me here? No family, no husband; most of my friends have left, either with their families or alone, and those who are still here . . .'

She doesn't need to elaborate; she's spoken to him of Lujza before, of the broken woman the war made of her. 'And someone like me is always going to be on the outskirts of village life. What did I have to lose by leaving?'

She shrugs. 'I would have needed money, more money than I've ever had access to. I have no family here, it's true, but I have no family anywhere else, either, and no friends in towns or cities who could take me in while I tried to find a job. And what job could I get, anyway? I have no skills that would be useful in a town. I can't sew with any degree of skill. I'm not a great cook. Perhaps I could be a maid, yes, but then would my life in the city, as a maid, be any better than my life here, as a midwife? I wouldn't be able to afford to buy books, or go to the theatre, and I wouldn't have the friends or the respect that I have here.'

She sighs suddenly, with such force that the flame of the

lamp flickers. 'When I was young, I didn't care about that sort of thing so much. If I'd just had enough money to get me to the city in the first place, I would have been prepared to take a chance on the rest of it. Now, with Rózsi, it's imposs-ible. When you have a child, you can't take risks any more.'

He licks his lips, trying to find the words. 'Would it be different if you did have a friend in town, who would help you to find work, and to find somewhere decent to live?'

Sari looks at him sharply. 'Mr Illyés?' Under the intensity of her gaze, he stops caring about finding the right words; any words at all will do.

'I don't want to offend you, or to – to suggest anything improper at all, I can assure you of that. But over these past days that I've spent here, I – I can't claim that I know you well, of course, I've known you for such a short time, but I think that perhaps I know you a little, maybe, and under-stand you a little, and it has occurred to me – forgive me, please – but it has occurred to me that you are out of place here, that you have a – an intelligence that is wasted here, and that would serve you well elsewhere. I earn good money, and I have more money that I inherited from my parents, and I have no family, and so I could quite well afford to – to give you the money to come to Város, and to find you a place for you and Rózsi to live, and to – to support you for as long as it took for you to find work.'

That's it. His voice sputters into silence. She's still looking at him, her expression utterly unreadable. He can't look at her, his eyes sliding relentlessly from her face.

'Mr Illyés – Béla,' she says at last. 'That – that's a very, very kind offer. But . . .'

He holds up a hand. 'Please. Don't decide now. Take some time to think about it. I will give you my address in

Város, and you can let me know of your decision. My offer will always be open.'

She smiles at him. 'All right. I promise you that I will think about it. But you know, Judit is a concern. She'd never get on in the town, but I couldn't just abandon her here, after everything that she's done for me. And when she dies, what would the village do without a midwife?' She checks herself. 'I'm sorry. I really will think about it.'

'For *your* sake, Miss Arany, yours and Rózsi's. Perhaps you should stop thinking about the good of everyone else for a moment.'

They sit in silence for a while, lamps casting wavering shadows on the walls, until a gust of wind rattles the windows, and seems to rouse Sari.

'I should be getting back,' she says, and casts an eye around the disordered kitchen. 'I can come back for the pots in the morning.'

He nods, and gets to his feet. 'Can I walk you home?'

Sari shakes her head. 'No need. Anyway, I'm going to drop in on Éva – the person who was ill this afternoon – see how she is.'

'All right.' She opens the door to leave, and then with a swift, fluid movement, she leans towards him and kisses him on the cheek. In an instant, Béla's nerves are laid bare to her. He feels every atom of her smooth lips as they brush his cheek, and the smell of her hair – herbs and clear water – fills his nostrils, fills his whole head. He's almost thankful when she pulls away. What should he make of that intensity of feeling? He can't speak, but thankfully, she just says, 'Goodnight, Béla,' and is gone without expecting an answer.

Sari crunches home through the first frost of the season, the stars fizzing and crackling above her. It occurs to her that ten years ago, the offer that Béla has just made would have filled her with clear, uncomplicated joy, rather than the muddied, calculated sense of relief that it brings her now – a relief that's not tied to the offer itself, but to its motivation, what it says about his feelings for her, what it means for her safety and her escape. She feels a dislocated breath of sadness, but it leaves as quickly as it arrived. *It's going to be all right*, she thinks, a bubble of certainty that breaks free of her and sails through the sharp night air.

In the dim, warm light of the kitchen, Béla leans with one hand on the closed door, and with the other, unbuttons his trousers, and takes himself in his hand. It only takes a few moments. Afterwards, he doesn't even feel shame, like he normally does. Instead, he feels cleansed, as if his soul's been wiped cleaner than it's ever been in his entire life.

CHAPTER TWENTY-EIGHT

Morning, and Béla can hardly force himself to listen to Francziska's words. The same affirmations and denials that he's heard so many times before wash over him, making about as much impression as the ripples of a puddle on a Budapest pavement. He can see the twitching end of Géza's pencil out of the corner of his eye, and thinks sourly that he hardly needs to listen, in any case, as Géza's doing all the listening for him. Asking the questions, too, something that Béla has presented as a special treat, but which is really a treat for Béla himself, allowing him to drift off and fantasise unmolested.

Their bags are packed and they plan to leave around midday. One of the taciturn old men of the village has, according to Sari, offered to give them a lift in his cart as far as a nearby village, from whence they will be able to pick up the train back to Város, and they should be there by nightfall. After an uneasy night, Sari's smile when she knocked on the door first thing was like balm on a wound, and he realised after hours of troubling uncertainty that she will take him up on his offer. Perhaps not straight away, but he's prepared to wait, especially now that he's certain – because surely she couldn't smile at him with such warmth if she were determined that they would never see each other again.

His head jerks slightly as Francziska says something particularly vehement, but it's of no consequence, and he lets himself slip back into daydreams again, making a mental wager with himself that Sari and Rózsi will be in Város before the end of the year.

Béla's roused by silence, and realises that Géza and Francziska are both looking at him expectantly. Clearly, the interview is over.

'Well,' he says jovially. 'That concludes things, then.'

Francziska eyes him warily as they both get to their feet and move towards the door. Béla mumbles thanks and apologies, trying to make her see that it was nothing personal, they were just doing their job, and that she's certainly managed to put their minds at rest. She nods and smiles and they move towards the door, collecting coats and bags on the way.

And then everything seems to happen at once. Géza picks up his case and as he turns towards the door, the case, gripped lightly in his hand, describes a shallow arc in the air, knocking against the side table that stands by Francziska's door. Béla turns towards the sound of the disturbance, a reprimand for Géza on his lips, and they all watch as a narrow, inelegant vase on the table shudders, pirouettes slowly on its wide base, and falls on its side. From its gaping top something small appears, rolls inexorably across the top of the table, falls, hits the floor, and shatters, leaving glass fragments and white powder patterning the floorboards like an exploded star.

Sari had made her promise to get rid of it, of course, but Francziska hadn't quite been able to make herself do it – you never knew when you might need it, she'd thought – and now she curses herself, silently, with every foul name that she can think of, as Géza kneels on the floor, collecting a few grains on the tip of his finger. They both turn towards her, questions rather than accusations on their faces, and Francziska realises that she could still have got away with it, at exactly the same time as she realises that she's just given herself away by the expression of frozen, abject horror on her face.

'It wasn't just me,' she says.

As soon as Jakova Gersek sees the two of them coming up the path to her house, she knows what they're there for, and something curdles inside her. When they tell her that they've come from Francziska Imanci, she feels nothing but disgust and contempt for Francziska. Jakova has always known that Francziska is a coward, that if discovered, she would want to spread the blame as widely as possible, and she's not surprised that Jakova's name was the one Francziska chose to give up; the stupid bitch, too superstitious to implicate the midwives, as if they have some sort of power to curse anyone who acts against them. Well, Jakova certainly isn't that stupid; it comes of being one of Orsolya Kiss's friends, and as soon as it becomes clear that her flurry of furious denials are falling on deaf ears, the decision to spread the blame still wider isn't a difficult one.

'Sari Arany,' she says.

On the other side of the room, the world crashes down on Béla's head.

Her first mistake, Sari thinks, was ever to assume that she was safe. Her guts twist when she remembers the sense of light-hearted relief with which she woke up that morning. She should have known: it was never going to be over until the two of them were safely out of Falucska; until then, there was always the chance that something could go wrong.

She denies everything. Géza tells her that Francziska Imanci and Jakova Gersek have both confessed, and that the latter has implicated her. It's a battle to stop her rage from showing on her face, but she manages it, swallows it down, showing only confusion. It's not entirely an act; she can't believe how quickly things have fallen apart, can't believe that Francziska and Jakova have collapsed so quickly, surrendered to their own deaths. It's not over, she tells herself. For Rózsi's sake, and for her own, it's not over.

Béla will not meet her eyes.

Béla is certain that if he spends one more second looking at the triumph and pride wreathing Géza's boyish face, he will vomit. He doesn't feel like himself any more; he feels somehow subtracted. He can't believe it, it's not true – the others, maybe, yes, but not Sari. It's yet another example of how an intelligent, courageous, and unconventional woman is punished by a small, closed-minded community. And yet she's been accused, and he cannot fail to act, because Géza will not let him pretend that nothing's happened.

They are standing outside Sari's house, and from the moment that the door shut behind him, Géza has not shut up about the logistics of what they have to do next. Béla's hand itches with the desire to punch him.

'Of course, now that the two of them have confessed, we have to arrest them,' Géza says. 'But there's obviously a need for ongoing investigation in the village, so what should we do? We have to think of a way of securing Mrs Imanci and Mrs Gersek so that they don't try and leave while we're questioning other people.'

'The church,' Béla says dully. He can see it from where they stand – empty, with large double-doors that can be easily blocked from the outside, windows small and high enough to prevent escape.

Géza's face lights up. 'Excellent! We can shut them in there, while we . . . Well, and that's the other question. What are we going to do about Miss Arany? We could arrest her on the strength of Mrs Gersek's accusation, couldn't we? She's far more reliable than old Mrs Imanci was when Francziska Imanci was concerned, surely? Or if we needed more evidence, then we could go back to Francziska Imanci. If she hears that Mrs Gersek has implicated Miss Arany, surely she'd be prepared to back her up?'

He pauses, thinking. 'On the other hand, if Miss Arany really is the one who supplied the poison to the other women, is it worth arresting her straight away? Perhaps we should watch her, see what she does. Perhaps she'll go and warn some of the other women, and we'll be able to take some more of them in . . .?'

It's obvious that Géza is thinking aloud, barely expecting a response from Béla, who simply shrugs. Acid floods his stomach. Of course Sari isn't responsible for this, there's no way that he can reconcile the woman that he knows with the image of a murderess. And yet, there's the question of her dead fiancé. What had she said? That he died ten years ago, around the time of the end of the war, making him the first of the ten-year plague of non-specific illnesses. He curses himself for even daring to think it. She wouldn't, of course she wouldn't. But she would know how, wouldn't she? Of all the people in the village, she and Judit would know how. He bites his lip and tastes blood.

'Let's go and get Mrs Imanci and Mrs Gersek,' he says to Géza, cutting him off mid-flow. 'You're right, it's a good idea not to arrest Miss Arany straight away. We'll see what she does.'

And pray God she does nothing, he thinks, but doesn't say.

'They're back,' Judit announces from her post at the window. She's been stationed there since Géza and Béla left that morning. She was banished to the bedroom while they were talking to Sari, ostensibly looking after Rózsi, but of course she was crouched by the door the entire time, listening to what was going on, and when she'd emerged, Sari hadn't had to explain anything to her. Sari has hardly moved since, poised at the table, but Judit knows that she is thinking, and she knows that giving up hasn't crossed Sari's mind. Judit's given up, because it never mattered much to her in the first place. She's had a very good run, and she always knew that it would end, and she'd said as much to Sari as soon as Béla and Géza left. She'd looked into Sari's white, stricken face, and told her.

'Don't you dare think about me,' she'd said. 'I'm staying here. What will come will come. But you get out of here if you can, and take Rózsi with you.'

Sari hadn't answered, just stared at her quizzically, and Judit had taken it as a challenge. 'Don't be ridiculous, Sari!' she'd snapped. 'I may well be dead before they even get me on the gallows. I couldn't care less. All I care about is that you get yourself out of here.'

And Sari had nodded, and she hasn't said another word since. Judit's been giving her time to think, trying to help as much as she can by keeping her apprised of any developments. She watched Béla and Géza go off towards Francziska's house, bring her back to the church and lock her inside. She watched them do the same with Jakova, and now they've come out of the church and are settling themselves just behind the porch of the Jokai house with only the tops of their heads visible, so that they would probably be overlooked by anyone who hadn't been scrutinising their movements intently for the past half an hour. Judit feels a faint, indulgent contempt.

'They're watching the house,' she tells Sari.

For a moment Sari stays as still as she's been all morning, and then rouses herself, visibly sloughing off her thoughts.

'They want to see what I'll do,' she says.

'Yes,' Judit agrees. She thinks it's probably safe to leave the window now, and comes to sit opposite Sari at the table.

'What do they want me to do?' Sari asks. 'What could I do now that would be any help to them?'

'Francziska led them to Jakova. Jakova led them to you.' Judit shrugs, leading Sari to draw her own conclusions.

'They want me to lead them to other people,' Sari says slowly. She nods. 'Yes, that makes sense. But if I do that, it's as much as admitting what I've done.' She's silent for a moment. 'Jakova has already accused me. Francziska's not going to hold out if she knows that Jakova's already given them my name. They've got me whichever way you look at it, haven't they?'

Judit grimaces. 'Looks that way.'

'So the question is whether I go down alone, or whether I take other people with me.' She grins swiftly at Judit, but no, it's not a grin; it's more of a snarl, and Judit, familiar as she is with horror, feels her blood chill slightly. 'Well, there's no real question there, is there? If I'm going to hang, that bitch Kiss and her damn friends are going to be right beside me.'

Judit recovers quickly. 'That's the spirit. And there's another thing, too.'

Sari thinks fast, and then smiles, a real smile this time. 'There's only the two of them. The more people I lead them to, the less time they can concentrate on me.'

'You don't need long. You know the area around here better than anyone else I've met. All you need is enough time to get back here, collect Rózsi and enough food to last for a little while, and get to the woods. Hide out there for a couple of days, until they've taken the others off to Város, and then go.'

Sari nods. There's no point in asking where she should go. She remembers the conversation she had with Béla, just last night, about needing money to leave. Yes, of course she needs money, money would make this mess a whole lot easier, but if it's a choice between life and death, it's actually no decision at all. She knows enough about how to live off the land to ensure that she and Rózsi won't starve. It's a chance, enough of a chance to be worth taking.

'Rózsi's at Lujza's,' Sari says. 'Go and get her. Pack enough food for a few days. Make sure it's ready for when I come back.'

'All right.'

Sari gets to her feet. 'Right, then,' she says. Impulsively she bends and kisses Judit's withered cheek. 'I love you, Judit.'

Judit shakes her off with feigned irritation. 'I know that, you stupid girl. Now get going.'

Béla sees the door open, and next to him, Géza gasps. 'Here we go!' he says.

'Don't get too excited,' Béla admonishes. 'It might be nothing.'

Dear God, let it be nothing, he says to himself. He watches Sari emerge, look around, and, obviously seeing no one, descend the steps. *Just go to the river,* Béla urges her, *or to the forest. Look for herbs. Don't, please, God, don't do anything more to implicate yourself.* He knows he can't avoid arresting her now that Francziska has tearfully added her voice to Jakova's, but maybe, if nothing else happens, maybe she can avoid being convicted. Maybe.

Sari's at the bottom of the steps now, and she turns, to Béla's dismay, not in the direction of the forest, or the plain, but towards the cluster of houses at the centre of the village. Géza hisses with excitement. She rounds the corner and they ease themselves out from where they've been hiding, and follow her, Béla with utmost reluctance and Géza trying to hold himself back from a run. They catch sight of her again, and she's approaching a house. It's not a house that they've been to before, and Béla feels a brief blossoming of hope; perhaps this is the woman who was sick yesterday, perhaps that's why Sari's visiting her today. It might still be all right. Perhaps.

For five minutes, there's no movement. Béla is acutely conscious of the way the wind feels on his skin, the faint prickling as his body hair stands up in anticipation . . . and then Sari comes out of the house. Five minutes, Béla tells himself; plenty of time for a cursory medical examination. No matter that Sari doesn't have any equipment with her; she could just be checking on the woman's well-being, planning to come back later if further attention's needed.

Géza urges them closer. 'I'll stay outside,' he whispers, 'see where she goes next. You knock on the door.'

Obediently, for he has no energy to challenge the sudden revolution that's left him powerless and Géza in charge, Béla climbs the front steps, and knocks quietly. No answer. Well, that would make sense; an ill woman wouldn't want to open the door to a stranger. He looks back down at Géza, who gives a frustrated signal: *go on!* Béla knocks again. Again, no answer, but a noise comes from inside the house, a confused, fumbling rattle. Béla tries the door handle, and to his surprise, finds it open. He walks into the house, feeling like a cad for infringing on a poor woman's privacy like this. The living room is empty, but has a curious atmosphere of warmth and movement, as if it's been occupied until very recently. Working on a hunch he can't let himself ignore, Béla moves on silent feet to a room at the back of the house, which he knows to be the bedroom, and there he finds Matild Nagy easing her plump, comely body out of the sash window.

It's as good as a confession.

There's no time to take her down to the church. Uncomfortably certain that it's very much against procedure, Béla sits her down on a chair, binding her hands and feet with hastily torn up sheets, to which she submits with unexpected placidity. Perhaps she's in shock; perhaps her abortive escape attempt has shaken all the life out of her. By the time he's able to leave the house, Géza's already crouched like a cat by the porch of a nearby house. As Béla approaches, he raises his eyebrows in a wordless question. Béla nods, feeling sick.

'Sari left here about a minute ago,' Géza whispers, and Béla's insides twist – she may be a murderess, but that doesn't give Géza any right to use her first name. 'She's gone up there – Orsolya Kiss's house. She's still inside. We'll go there next.'

As they mount the stairs, Béla realises that it's the house of Zsofia Gyulai. It's not a surprise, therefore, when they open the door to the sound of agonised sobs.

They tie her up, too. Géza's as discomfited by the idea as Béla is, but can't come up with an alternative solution; 'We'll be back for you in an hour at the most,' he says to Mrs Gyulai, in an attempt at consolation, but she just sobs harder.

Béla has been looking out of the window at intervals, and saw Sari leave the Kiss house a few minutes before, heading back to Judit's. 'Let's go,' he says to Géza. Arresting Orsolya Kiss is going to be one of the only redeeming features of this entire fiasco.

They knock on the door once, for courtesy, and predictably, the house is silent. Predictably again, the living room is empty, and Béla beckons silently to Géza, drawing him towards the bedroom, where he feels certain they'll find Orsolya trying to make a break for freedom through the window. He's surprised, then, to find Orsolya sitting, still, head bowed, on the very edge of the bed. But any hopes that she would come quietly are dashed when she raises her head, giving them an oddly coquettish smile, which distracts them just long enough for her to raise the pistol held loosely in her right hand.

The bullet sails harmlessly past Béla's right ear, but it's enough to scare them both, and within a second Géza has tackled her and brought her heavily to the ground. After the initial resistance, she doesn't struggle, though Béla kneels beside them just in case. When it seems certain that she's subsided, he turns to the dresser on his left, yanking open drawers until he finds her underwear drawer, whereupon he snatches up a couple of handfuls of stockings. Géza heaves her onto her front and starts to bind her hands behind her back, and Béla stands, brushing himself down, and that's when he catches sight of something glinting alluringly in the opened drawer.

'I'll go and pick up Miss Arany,' he says.

From his awkward position on the floor, Géza twists himself around and gives Béla a searching look.

'Why don't you take over here, and I'll go and pick up Miss Arany?'

Béla shakes his head. 'No, no. You're doing an excellent job here.'

'But—'

At that, Béla's last remaining nerve, already painfully frayed, decides to snap.

'Géza! I am ordering you! Stay here. Subdue Mrs Kiss, and take her to the church. Then go and collect Mrs Nagy and Mrs Gyulai and take them to the church. I'll meet you there.'

For a moment, their eyes lock, Béla's wide with feigned innocence, Géza's narrowed with suspicion. Then Orsolya

Kiss gives a final, desperate lurch, like a landed fish, demanding Géza's full attention, and Béla slips away.

He doesn't knock this time, just leaps up the steps three at a time and pushes open the door, and . . .

'Ah,' says Sari. She is holding Rózsi with her right hand, she has a cloth bag in her left, and looks remarkably calm, all things considered. 'Ah,' she says again. 'Well. It was worth a try.'

For a moment he can't summon any words at all, and then only banalities. 'We've arrested Mrs Nagy, Mrs Gyulai, and Mrs Kiss,' he says lamely.

She nods, smiling. 'Well, that's something, at least. They'll probably be able to give you some other names – I doubt they'll need much persuasion, really.'

'Sari,' he says, tasting her first name for the first time. Bittersweet, it stops up his throat and he can't go on. Instead, wordless, he tosses her the small leather pouch he has in his right hand.

'What's this?' she asks, puzzled, and he makes an aggravated gesture with his hands: *open it*. She does. Pearls, gold jewellery, money. She suppresses a gasp, biting her lip swiftly, and then looks up at him through narrowed eyes.

'Orsolya?' she asks, and he nods. She takes a deep breath, once, twice. 'Why?'

Finally, he finds words. 'I could ask you the same thing,' he says, damning his voice for trembling, and then relents. 'You said that you needed money. To get to the city.'

She shuts her eyes for a moment, and Béla wonders whether this is the first genuine emotion he's seen pass over her face. 'Thank you,' she says.

337

'I hate myself for doing this,' he bursts out. It's true; he's not sure whether he hates himself or her more. He used to be proud of his behaviour, particularly with regard to his job. He used to be proud of his ability to read people. Now he questions everything. There's a smile on her face that seems faintly sympathetic, but how can he possibly start to interpret her?

'I'm sorry for that.' She flicks her eyes nervously to the door.

'Don't worry, there's time. Géza is taking the other three down to the church.'

'Very well.' She trains her implacable eyes on his face, anticipating the question before he asks it.

'How did this all happen? Why did you . . . ?' he can't finish the sentence. There's no way he can sum up all he feels, or even if he could, there's no way that he could bring himself to say it to her: *how could a woman like you, a woman I thought I could love, have done all of this?*

She seems to understand though, and raises an eyebrow. 'I chose to put myself first,' she says simply. 'Myself and my child. Just as you've chosen to help me. You probably want to hear that I was treated badly by my fiancé, some nice, neat, explicable reason why I've done the things I've done. It's true. He did treat me badly. But that's not what's important. What's important is what I chose to do about it. I was tired of just letting things *happen to me*, and I imagine that many of the other women here feel the same way.'

She hefts the bag in her left hand. 'And now we've got to go. Judit—'

Béla turns. He hadn't even noticed the old woman sitting there, grinning her manipulative grin, hands neatly folded in her lap.

'Ha!' she crows, seeing his surprise. 'I'm the consolation prize. As a matter of fact, I was the one who gave Sari poison in the first place, so really, I'm more culpable in all of this than she is. Not a bad bargain, me for her, wouldn't you say?'

She turns away before he can offer an answer, fixing Sari with a gimlet stare. 'Get going, both of you,' she says roughly. 'And for the devil's sake, be careful.'

Sari nods once, and Rózsi stretches out a hand to Judit, who grips it fiercely before letting it go. The two of them move towards the back steps, and Sari gives Béla one last glance. 'For what it's worth,' she says, 'I would have found this all a whole lot easier if I didn't genuinely like you.'

You've got to take consolation where you can find it, Béla tells himself. He watches out the window as Sari and Rózsi cross the back garden, as Sari lifts Rózsi over the fence and follows her, as they move swiftly towards the wood, staying carefully in the shadow of the houses. Their silhouettes get smaller and smaller, vulnerable stick-figures against the vastness of the plain. Béla shudders, and jumps when Judit puts her gnarled claw on his shoulder, in a gesture evidently meant to be comforting. He hadn't even noticed her move beside him.

'They'll be all right,' she says. 'Don't you worry about them. They'll be just fine.'

Together, they stand and watch until the tiny shadows of Sari and Rózsi are swallowed up by the large, looming shadow of the woods.

'Right then,' Judit says, her voice bright and brittle. 'Let's go.'

EPILOGUE

I watched from the woods, when they went to get men from the nearby villages to guard over the church, while Géza made more arrests, and Béla went to Város for reinforcements. They looked for me, naturally, combed the forest, but that forest has been my playground since I could walk; I know every leaf and every tree, and evasion was simple. There were twenty-five women in the end, led away from the village in a way that was almost processional, and I heard afterwards that eight were hanged. I never heard which eight. I hope that Judit was right when she guessed that she'd be dead before she stood on the gallows.

Now, we walk. My main aim is to put as many miles between ourselves and Falucska as possible. My secondary aim is not to get caught, which involves detours and decoys and occasional backtracking, but generally we walk west. I know this plain like the back of my hand, the inside of my own eyelids; that's how I'm able to move through it without being seen, and that's why I want to leave it as far behind as possible. I'm sick of the *whisha-whisha* of dry grass in the wind, the ominous smudge of a pine wood at night, the fat, complacent moon. I tell Rózsi that we're ready for somewhere warm and fragrant. Maybe somewhere by the sea. She doesn't answer, but sometimes she smiles. She knows, as well as I do, that we'll be all right.

We walk west, tracing our steps in the deepening snow.

THE ANGEL MAKERS READER'S GUIDE

1. The central characters of *The Angel Makers* are ordinary people who do extraordinary things. Do you sympathize with the decisions that the main characters make? Why or why not?

2. The prologue and epilogue are the only parts in the novel when we directly hear Sari's voice, and throughout the novel we see Sari through the eyes of a number of different characters. But how do you think Sari sees herself? And what sort of person do you think she would be outside of the context of the village?

3. The novel opens with a funeral, foreshadowing the central role of death in *The Angel Makers*. Do you think that there are other examples of foreshadowing in the novel? Are the events that unfold predictable or unexpected?

4. How do you think the setting of the village and the plain affect the mood and the action of the novel?

5. The question of whether Judit and Sari have powers beyond the mundane comes up many times in the novel. Where do you think the line lies beyond reality and the supernatural, in terms of what Judit and Sari do?

6. Although the majority of the main characters are women, there are some very significant male characters in the novel. How would you describe gender relations within the world of *The Angel Makers*? Do you feel it's an accurate portrayal?

7. Much of the book deals with a series of small and gradual changes that bring about a highly unusual situation in the village. Do you feel that there is a turning point in the book, where things could have turned out differently, or are the outcomes inevitable because of what has come before?

8. Following Marco's death, Sari tells herself that their relationship would never have worked beyond the specific context in which started. Do you think that this is true, or is Sari just trying to convince herself? Similarly, do you believe that Marco really loves Sari as he claims?

9. One of the central themes of the book is the idea of personal choice and responsibility. Why do you think Bela chooses to give Orsolya's money to Sari? How do you imagine this choice will affect him in future?

10. Do you find the ending of the novel to be a hopeful one? What sort of future do you envisage for Sari and Rozsi?